D1483534

BY BRANDON SANDERSON

BRANDON SANDERSON

STARSIGHT

REACH THE STARS

This paperback fir st published in Great Britain in 2020 by Gollancz

First published in Great Britain in 2019 by Gollancz
an imprint of The Orion Publishing Group Ltd
Carmelite House, 50 Victoria Embankment
London EC4Y 0DZ

An Hachette UK Company

3 5 7 9 10 8 6 4

A CIP catalogue record for this book is
available from the British Library.

ISBN (Mass Market Paperback) 978 1 473 21791 1
ISBN (eBook) 978 1 473 21792 8

Printed and bound in Italy by Elcograf S.p.A.

MIX
Paper from
responsible sources
FSC® C104740

www.brandonsanderson.com
www.gollancz.co.uk

For Eric James Stone,
who has tried to show me how to be brief
(a lesson I've mostly failed to learn)
but has been an amazing friend and role
model nonetheless.

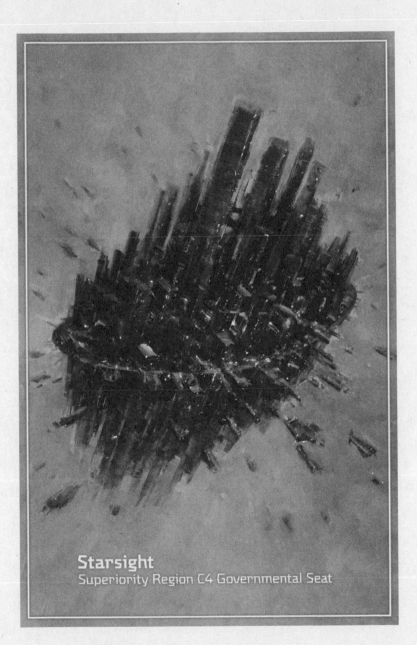

Starsight
Superiority Region C4 Governmental Seat

PART ONE

1

I slammed on my overburn and boosted my starship through the middle of a chaotic mess of destructor blasts and explosions. Above me extended the awesome vastness of space. Compared to that infinite blackness, both planets and starships alike seemed insignificant. Meaningless.

Except, of course, for the fact that those insignificant starships were doing their best to kill me.

I dodged, spinning my ship and cutting my boosters midturn. Once I'd flipped around, I immediately slammed on the boosters again, burning in the other direction in an attempt to lose the three ships tailing me.

Fighting in space is way different from fighting in atmosphere. For one thing, your wings are useless. No air means no airflow, no lift, no drag. In space, you don't really fly. You just don't fall.

I executed another spin and boost, heading back toward the main firefight. Unfortunately, maneuvers that had been impressive down in the atmosphere were commonplace up here. Fighting in a vacuum these last six months had provided a whole new set of skills to master.

3

"Spensa," a lively masculine voice said from my console, "you remember how you told me to warn you if you were being extra irrational?"

"No," I said with a grunt, dodging to the right. The destructor blasts from behind swept over the dome of my cockpit. "I don't believe I did anything of the sort."

"You said, 'Can we talk about this later?'"

I dodged again. Scud. Were those drones getting better at dogfighting, or was I losing my touch?

"Technically, it was 'later' right after you spoke," continued the talkative voice—my ship's AI, M-Bot. "But human beings don't actually use that word to mean 'anytime chronologically after this moment.' They use it to mean 'sometime after now that is more convenient to me.'"

The Krell drones swarmed around us, trying to cut off my escape back toward the main body of the battlefield.

"And you think *this* is a more convenient time?" I demanded.

"Why wouldn't it be?"

"Because we're in combat!"

"Well, I would think that a life-and-death situation is *exactly* when you'd like to know if you're being extra irrational."

I could remember, with some measure of fondness, the days when my starships *hadn't* talked back to me. That had been before I'd helped repair M-Bot, whose personality was a remnant of ancient technology we still didn't understand. I frequently wondered: Had all advanced AIs been this sassy, or was mine just a special case?

"Spensa," M-Bot said. "You're supposed to be leading these drones toward the others, remember?"

It had been six months since we'd beaten back the Krell attempt to bomb us into oblivion. Alongside our victory, we'd learned some important facts. The enemy we called "the Krell" were a group of aliens tasked with keeping my people contained on our planet, Detritus, which was kind of a cross between a prison and a nature preserve for human civilization. The Krell reported to a larger galactic government called the Superiority.

They employed remote drones to fight us—piloted by aliens who lived far away, controlling their drones via faster-than-light communications. The drones were never driven by AIs, as it was against galactic law to let a ship pilot itself. Even M-Bot was severely limited in what he could do on his own. Beyond that, there was something that the Superiority feared deeply: people who had the ability to see into the space where FTL communication happened. People called cytonics.

People like me.

They knew what I was, and they hated me. The drones tended to target me specifically—and we could use that. We *should* use that. In today's pre-battle briefing, I'd swayed the rest of the pilots reluctantly to go with a bold plan. I was to get a little out of formation, tempt the enemy drones to swarm me, then lead them back through the rest of the team. My friends could then eliminate the drones while they were focused on me.

It was a sound plan. And I'd make good on it . . . eventually.

Now, though, I wanted to test something.

I hit my overburn, accelerating away from the enemy ships. M-Bot was faster and more maneuverable than they were, though part of his big advantage had been in his ability to maneuver at high speed in air without ripping himself apart. Out here in a vacuum that wasn't a factor, and the enemy drones did a better job of keeping up.

They swarmed after me as I dove toward Detritus. My homeworld was protected by layers of ancient metal platforms—like shells—with gun emplacements all along them. After our victory six months ago, we'd pushed the Krell farther away from the planet, past the shells. Our current long-term strategy was to engage the enemy out here in space and keep them from getting close to the planet.

Keeping them out here had allowed our engineers—including my friend Rodge—to start gaining control of the platforms and their guns. Eventually, that shell of gun emplacements should protect our planet from incursions. For now though, most of those defensive platforms were still autonomous—and could be as dangerous for us as they were for the enemy.

The Krell ships swarmed in behind me, eager to cut me off from the battlefield—where my friends were engaging the rest of the drones in a massive brawl. That tactic of isolating me made one fatal assumption: that if I was alone, I'd be less dangerous.

"We're not going to turn back around and follow the plan, are we?" M-Bot asked. "You're going to try to fight them on your own."

I didn't respond.

"Jorgen is going to be aaaaaangry," M-Bot said. "By the way, those drones are trying to chase you along a specific heading, which I'm outlining on your monitor. My analysis projects that they've planned an ambush."

"Thanks," I said.

"Just trying to keep you from getting me blown up," M-Bot said. "By the way, if you *do* get us killed, be warned that I intend to haunt you."

"Haunt me?" I said. "You're a robot. And besides, I'd be dead too, right?"

"My robotic ghost would haunt your fleshy one."

"How would that even work?"

"Spensa, ghosts aren't real," he said in an exasperated tone. "Why are you worrying about things like that instead of flying? Honestly, humans get distracted so easily."

I spotted the ambush: a small group of Krell drones had hidden themselves by a large chunk of metal floating just out of range of the gun emplacements. As I drew close, the ambushing drones emerged and rocketed toward me. I was ready though. I let my arms relax, let my subconscious mind take over. I sank into myself, entering a kind of trance where I listened.

Just not with my ears.

Remote drones worked fine for the Krell in most situations. They were an expendable way to suppress the humans of Detritus. However, the enormous distances involved in space battle forced the Krell to rely on instantaneous faster-than-light communication to control their drones. I suspected their pilots were far away—but even if they were on the Krell station that hung out in space near Detritus, the lag of radio communications from there would make the drones too slow to react in battle. So, FTL was necessary.

That exposed one major flaw. I could hear their orders.

For some reason I didn't understand, I could *listen* into the place where FTL communication happened. I called it the nowhere, another dimension where our rules of physics didn't apply. I could hear into the place, occasionally see into it—and see the creatures that lived there watching me.

A single time, in the climactic battle six months ago, I'd managed to *enter* that place and teleport my ship a long distance in the blink of an eye. I still didn't know much about my powers. I hadn't been able to teleport again, but I'd been learning that whatever existed inside me, I could harness it and use it to fight.

I let my instincts take over, and sent my ship into a complex sequence of dodges. My battle-trained reflexes, melded with my innate ability to hear the drone orders, maneuvered my ship without specific conscious instructions on my part.

My cytonic ability had been passed down my family line. My ancestors had used it to move ancient starfleets around the galaxy. My father had had the ability, and the enemy had exploited it to get him killed. Now I used it to stay alive.

I reacted before the Krell did, responding to their orders—

somehow, I processed them *even faster* than the drones could. By the time they attacked, I was already weaving through their destructor blasts. I darted among them, then fired my IMP, bringing down the shields of everyone nearby.

In my state of focused concentration, I didn't care that the IMP took down my shield too. It didn't matter.

I launched my light-lance, and the rope of energy speared one of the enemy ships, connecting it to my own. I then used the difference in our momentum to spin us both around, which put me into position behind the pack of defenseless ships.

Blossoms of light and sparks broke the void as I destroyed two of the drones. The remaining Krell scattered like villagers before a wolf in one of Gran-Gran's stories. The ambush turned chaotic as I picked a pair of ships and gunned for them with destructors—blasting one away as a part of my mind tracked the orders being given to the others.

"I never fail to be amazed when you do that," M-Bot said quietly. "You're interpreting data faster than my projections. You seem almost . . . inhuman."

I gritted my teeth, bracing, and spun my ship, boosting it after a straggling Krell drone.

"I mean that as a compliment, by the way," M-Bot said. "Not that there's anything wrong with humans. I find their frail, emotionally unstable, irrational natures quite endearing."

I destroyed that drone and bathed my hull in the light of its fiery demise. Then I dodged right between the shots of two others. Though the Krell drones didn't have pilots on board, a part of me felt sorry for them as they tried to fight back against me—an unstoppable, unknowable force that did not play by the same rules that bound everything else they knew.

"Likely," M-Bot continued, "I regard humans as I do only because I'm programmed to do so. But hey, that's no different from instinct programming a mother bird to love the twisted, feather-less abominations she spawns, right?"

Inhuman.

I wove and dodged, fired and destroyed. I wasn't perfect; I occasionally overcompensated and many of my shots missed. But I had a distinct edge.

The Superiority—and its minions the Krell—obviously knew to watch for people like me and my father. Their ships were always on the hunt for humans who flew too well or who responded too quickly. They'd tried controlling my mind by exploiting a weakness in my talent—the same thing they'd done to my father. Fortunately, I had M-Bot. His advanced shielding was capable of filtering out their mental attacks while still allowing me to hear the enemy orders.

All of this raised a singular daunting question.

What *was* I?

"I would feel a lot more comfortable," M-Bot said, "if you'd find a chance to reignite our shield."

"No time," I said. We'd need a good thirty seconds without flight controls to do that.

I had another chance to break toward the main battle, to follow through with the plan I'd outlined. Instead I spun, then hit the overburn and blasted back toward the enemy ships. My gravitational capacitors absorbed a large percentage of the g-forces and kept me from suffering too much whiplash, but I still felt pressure flattening me against my seat, making my skin pull back and my body feel heavy. Under extreme g-forces, I felt like I'd aged a hundred years in a second.

I pushed through it and fired at the remaining Krell drones. I strained my strange skills to their limits. A Krell destructor shot grazed the dome of my canopy, so bright it left an afterimage in my eyes.

"Spensa," M-Bot said. "Both Jorgen and Cobb have called to complain. I know you said to keep them distracted, but—"

"Keep them distracted."

"Resigned sigh."

I looped us after an enemy ship. "Did you just *say* the words *resigned sigh*?"

"I find human nonlinguistic communications to be too easily misinterpreted," he said. "So I'm experimenting with ways to make them more explicit."

"Doesn't that defeat the purpose?"

"Obviously not. Dismissive eye-roll."

Destructors flared around me, but I blasted two more drones. As I did, I saw something appear, reflected in the canopy of my cockpit. A handful of piercing white lights, like eyes, watching me. When I used my abilities too much, something looked out of the nowhere and saw me.

I didn't know what they were. I just called them the eyes. But I *could* feel a burning hatred from them. An anger. Somehow, this was all connected. My ability to see and hear into the nowhere, the eyes that watched me from that place, and the teleportation power I'd only managed to use once.

I could still distinctly remember how I'd felt when I'd used it. I'd been on the brink of death, being enveloped by a cataclysmic explosion. In that moment, somehow I'd activated something called a cytonic hyperdrive.

If I could master that ability to teleport, I could help free my people from Detritus. With that power, we could escape the Krell forever. And so I pushed myself.

Last time I'd jumped I'd been fighting for my life. If I could only re-create those same emotions . . .

I dove, my right hand on my control sphere, my left holding the throttle. Three drones swept in behind me, but I registered

10

their shots and turned my ship at an angle so they all missed. I hit the throttle and my mind brushed the nowhere.

The eyes continued to appear, reflected in the canopy, as if it were revealing something that watched from behind my seat. White lights, like stars, but somehow more . . . aware. Dozens of malevolent glowing dots. In entering their realm, even slightly, I became visible to them.

Those eyes unnerved me. How could I be both fascinated by these powers and terrified of them at the same time? It was like the call of the void you felt when standing at the edge of a large cliff in the caverns, knowing you could just throw yourself off into that darkness. One step farther . . .

"Spensa!" M-Bot said. "New ship arriving!"

I pulled out of my trance, and the eyes vanished. M-Bot used the console display to highlight what he'd spotted. A new starfighter, almost invisible against the black sky, emerged from where the others had been hiding. Sleek, it was shaped like a disc and painted the same black as space. It was smaller than normal Krell ships, but it had a larger canopy.

These new black ships had only started appearing in the last eight months, in the days leading up to the attempt to bomb our base. Back then we hadn't realized what they meant, but now we knew.

I couldn't hear the commands this ship received—because none were being sent to it. Black ships like this one were not remote controlled. Instead, they carried real alien pilots. Usually an enemy ace—the best of their pilots.

The battle had just gotten far more interesting.

2

My heart leaped with excitement.

An enemy ace. Fighting drones was exciting, yes, but also lacking. It wasn't personal enough. A duel with an ace instead felt like the stories Gran-Gran told. Brave pilots engaging in grim contests on Old Earth during the days of the Great Wars. Person against person.

"I will sing to you," I whispered. "As your ship burns and your soul flees, I will sing. To the contest we had."

Dramatic, yes. My friends still tended to laugh at me when I said things like that, things like were said in the old stories. I'd mostly stopped. But I was still me, and I didn't say those things for my friends. I said them for myself.

And for the enemy I was about to kill.

The ace swooped toward me, firing destructors, trying to hit me while I was focused on the drones. I grinned, diving out of the way and spearing a chunk of space debris with my light-lance. That let me pivot quickly, while also swinging the debris behind me to block the shots. M-Bot's GravCaps absorbed most of the g-forces, but I still felt a tug pulling me downward as I swung

12

through the arc, destructor fire blasting into the debris, one shot coming very near me. Scud. I still hadn't found a chance to re-ignite my shield.

"This might be a good time to head back and lead the enemy ships toward the others," M-Bot said. "Like the plan said . . ."

Instead, I noted the enemy ace overshooting me—then I swung around and gave chase.

"Dramatic trailing-off of speech," M-Bot added, "laden with implications of your irresponsible nature."

I fired at the ace, but they spun on their axis, cutting their boosters. Momentum carried them forward, although they'd turned back-to-front and were now facing me. They couldn't steer well flying in reverse, so the maneuver was usually risky, but when you had a full shield and your enemy had none . . .

I was forced to break off the chase, boosting to the left and dodging out of the way of the destructor fire. I couldn't risk a head-on confrontation. Instead, I focused on the drones for a moment, blasting one out of the sky, then screamed through its debris—which scraped up M-Bot's wing and smacked the canopy with a fierce *crack*.

Right. No shield. And in space, the debris didn't fall after you shot the ship down. That felt like a rookie mistake—a reminder that despite all my training, I was new to zero-gravity combat.

The ace fell in behind me in an expert tailing maneuver. They were good, which was—on one hand—thrilling. On the other hand . . .

I tried to veer back toward the battle, but the drones swarmed in front of me, cutting me off. Maybe I was in a little over my head.

"Call Jorgen," I said, "and tell him I might have let myself get cornered. I can't lead the enemy into our ambush; see if he and the others are willing to come help me instead."

"Finally," M-Bot said.

I dodged some more, tracking the enemy ace on my proximity monitor. Scud. I wished I could hear them like I could the drones.

No, this is good, I thought. *I need to be careful never to let my gift become a crutch.*

I gritted my teeth and made a snap decision. I couldn't get back to the main battle, so instead I dove toward Detritus. The defense shells surrounding it weren't solid; they were made up of large platforms that had housed living quarters, shipyards, and weapons. Though we'd begun reclaiming the ones closest to the planet, these outer layers were still set to automatically fire at anything that got close.

I hit my overburn, accelerating to speeds that—in atmosphere—would have caused most starfighters to rattle or even rip apart. Up here I only felt the acceleration, not the speed.

I quickly reached the nearest space platform. Long and thin, it curved slightly, like a chunk of broken eggshell. The remaining drones and the single ace were still on my tail. At these speeds, dogfighting was much more dangerous. The time for me to react before colliding with something would be much smaller, and the smallest touch on my control sphere could veer me off course faster than I might be able to deal with.

"Spensa?" M-Bot said.

"I know what I'm doing," I muttered back, concentrating.

"Yes, I'm sure," M-Bot answered. "But . . . just in case . . . you *do* remember that we don't have control of these outer platforms yet, right?"

I focused my full attention on sweeping down close to the surface of the metal platform without running into anything. The gun emplacements here tracked me and started firing—but they *also* started firing on the enemy.

I concentrated on dodging. Or really just weaving erratically—I could outfly the drones in a raw contest of skill, but they had superior numbers. Down near the platform, that translated into a liability for my enemies—because to the guns, we were all targets.

Several of the drones flared up in explosions—which vanished almost immediately, flames smothered by the vacuum of space.

"I wonder if those guns feel fulfilled, finally getting to shoot something down after all these years up here," M-Bot said.

"Jealous?" I asked with a grunt, dodging.

"From what Rodge says, they don't have true AIs, merely some simple targeting functions. So that would be like you being jealous of a rat."

Another drone fell. *Just a little longer.* I wanted to even the odds a bit while I waited for my friends to arrive.

I sank into another trance as I flew. I couldn't hear the controls of the gun emplacements, but in moments like these—moments of pure concentration—I felt as if I were becoming one with my ship.

I could feel the attention of the eyes back on me. My heart thundered inside my chest. With those guns trained on me . . . tails giving chase and still firing . . .

A little further . . .

My mind sank down, and I felt as if I could sense M-Bot's very workings. I was in severe danger. I needed to escape.

Surely I could do it now. "Engage cytonic hyperdrive!" I said, then tried to do what I'd done once before, teleporting my ship.

"Cytonic hyperdrive is offline," M-Bot said.

Scud. The one time it had worked, he'd been able to tell me it was online. I tried again, but . . . I didn't even know what it was I'd done that once. I had been in danger, about to die. And then I . . . I'd done . . .

Something?

A blast from a nearby gun nearly blinded me, and with gritted teeth I pulled up and zipped out of the defensive guns' range. The ace had survived, though they had taken a hit or two, so maybe their shield was weakened. Plus, only three drones remained.

I cut my thrust and spun my ship on its axis—still moving forward, but pointed backward—a maneuver that indicated I was going to try shooting behind me. Sure enough, the ace dodged away immediately. They weren't so brave with a weakened shield. Instead of firing, I boosted after the ace—escaping the drones, which swarmed toward my former position.

I got on the ace's tail and tried to draw in close enough for a shot—but whoever they were, they were *good*. They spun into a complex series of dodges, all while increasing speed. I misjudged a turn, and suddenly I swung out away from them. Quickly recovering, I matched their next turn and let out a blast of destructor fire—but now I was pretty far back and the shots went wild, vanishing into space.

M-Bot read off speeds and angles for me so I didn't have to break concentration for even the fraction of a second it would take to look at my control panel. I leaned forward, trying to match the other starfighter turn for turn—swooping, spinning, and boosting. Seeking that critical moment when we'd align just long enough for me to take a shot.

They, in turn, could twist at any moment and fire back—so they were likely watching for the same thing that I was, hoping to catch me off guard during a moment of alignment.

This perfect focus. This boiling intensity. This bizarre moment of connection where the alien pilot mirrored my efforts, striving, struggling, sweating—drawing closer and closer in a paradoxically *intimate* contest. For a flash we'd be as one. And then I'd kill them.

I lived for this challenge. For fighting against someone real and knowing it was either me or them. In moments like this, I didn't fight for the DDF or humankind. I fought to prove I could.

They swooped left just as I did. They spun and pointed toward me as we came into alignment briefly—and we both shot a burst at each other.

Their shots missed. Mine didn't. The first of my blasts broke their weakened shield. The second hit them just left of their cockpit, ripping the disclike ship apart in a flash of light.

The vacuum consumed that eagerly, and I cut to the right, dodging the debris. I took deep breaths, struggling to slow my heart. Sweat soaked the pads on my helmet and leaked down the sides of my face.

"Spensa!" M-Bot shouted. "The drones!"

Scud.

I turned my ship and boosted to the side just as three flaring explosions lit my cockpit. I winced, but those lights weren't the result of me getting shot—they were the lights of drones exploding one after another. Two DDF ships swooped past.

"Thanks, guys," I said, tapping the group channel on the communications panel of my dash.

"No problem," Kimmalyn replied over the channel. "As the Saint always said, 'Watch out for the smart ones. They tend to be stupid.'" She had an accent and an unhurried way of speaking—somehow intrinsically upbeat, even when she was chastising me.

"I thought the idea was for you to distract the drones," FM said, "then bring them back toward us." She had a confident voice, the type that sounded like it should be coming from someone twice her age.

"I was planning to do it eventually."

"Yeah," FM said. "And that's why you turned off your comm so Jorgen couldn't yell at you?"

"It wasn't off," I said. "I just had M-Bot running interference."

"Jorgen really hates talking to me!" M-Bot said enthusiastically. "I can tell by the way he says so!"

"Yeah, well, the enemy is retreating," FM said. "And you're lucky we were already on our way to help, even before you decided to admit you were in trouble."

I was still something of a sweaty mess—heart racing, hands slick—as I reignited my shield, then turned my ship and flew toward the other two. The course took me past the wreckage of the ship I'd defeated, which was still moving along at roughly the same speed as when I'd hit it. That was space for you.

The ship had cracked apart rather than exploding completely, and so with a chill I was able to spot the corpse of the enemy ace. A boxy alien figure. Perhaps the armor it wore could protect it from the vacuum . . .

No. As I passed by, I saw that its armor had been broken apart in the blast. The actual creature inside was kind of like a small, two-legged crab—spindly and bright blue, with carapace along the abdomen and face. I had seen some of them piloting shuttles near their space station, which was farther out, monitoring Detritus from a distance. They were our jailers, and while the data we'd stolen called this crablike race the varvax, most of us still called them the Krell—even though we knew that was an acronym in some Superiority language for a phrase about keeping humans contained, not their actual race's name.

This one was truly dead. The liquid bath that filled its armor had spilled out into the void, first boiling explosively, then freezing into solid vapor. Space was weird.

I fixed my gaze on the body, slowing M-Bot, and hummed softly one of the songs of my ancestors. A Viking song for the dead.

Well fought, I thought to the Krell's departing soul. Nearby, some of our salvage ships came swooping in from where they'd watched the fight in relative safety nearer the planet. We always salvaged Krell ships, especially those that had been flown by living pilots. There was a chance we'd be able to capture a broken Superiority hyperdrive that way. They didn't travel using the minds of pilots. They had some kind of actual technology that let them travel between stars.

"Spin?" Kimmalyn called to me. "You coming?"

"Yeah," I said. I turned away and fell into line with her and FM. "M-Bot? How would you judge that pilot's flying abilities?"

"Somewhere near your own," M-Bot said. "And their ship was more advanced than any we'd faced before. I'll be honest, Spensa—mostly because I'm programmed to be incapable of lying—I think that fight could have gone either way."

I nodded, feeling much the same. I'd gone toe-to-toe with that ace. On one hand, it was a nice affirmation that my skill wasn't tied only to my abilities to touch the nowhere. But coming fully out of my trance now—feeling the odd sense of deflated purpose that always tailed a battle—I found myself strangely worried. In all our time fighting here, we'd seen only a handful of these black ships piloted by live beings.

If the Krell really wanted to kill us, why send so few aces? And . . . was this really the best they had? I was good, but I'd been flying for less than a year. Our stolen information indicated that our enemies ran an enormous galactic coalition of hundreds of planets. Surely they had access to pilots who were better than I was.

Something struck me as off about all of this. The Krell used to only ever send a maximum of a hundred drones against us at once. They'd relaxed that, and now they would field upward of a hundred and twenty at once . . . but that still seemed a small number, considering the apparent size of their coalition.

So what was going on? Why were they still holding back?

Kimmalyn, FM, and I rejoined the rest of our fighters. The DDF was growing stronger and stronger. We'd lost only a single ship today, when in the past we'd lose half a dozen or more in each battle. And we were gaining momentum. In the last two months we'd begun deploying the first of our ships fabricated using technology learned from M-Bot. It had only been half a year since our casualties in the Battle of Alta Second, but the boost to our morale—and the fact that our pilots were surviving longer to hone their skills—was making us stronger by the day.

By intercepting the enemy out here, and not letting them get in close, we'd been able to expand our salvage operations. Because of this, we were not only reclaiming the closest of the defense platforms, but we were also able to scavenge materials for more and more ships.

All this meant shipbuilding and recruitment were both increasing dramatically. We'd soon have enough acclivity stone, and enough pilots, to field hundreds of starships.

Together, it was an ever-increasing snowball effect of progress. Still, a part of me worried. The Krell's behavior was odd. And beyond that, we had a huge disadvantage. They could travel the galaxy, while we were trapped on one planet.

Unless I learned how to use my powers.

"Um, Spensa?" M-Bot said. "Jorgen is calling, and I think he's annoyed."

I sighed, then hit the line. "Skyward Ten, reporting in."

"Are you all right?" he asked with a stern voice.

"Yeah."

"Good. We'll discuss this later." He cut the line.

I winced. He wasn't annoyed . . . he was *furious*.

Sadie—the new girl who had been assigned as my wingmate—flew up behind me in Skyward Nine. I sensed a nervousness to the posture of her ship, though perhaps I was reading too much into things. According to our plans, I'd left her behind when the Krell had sent an overwhelming force to destroy me. Fortunately, she'd had enough sense to follow orders and stay close to the others rather than tail me.

We had to wait for orders from Flight Command before flying back toward the planet, so we hovered in space for a short time. And as we did, Kimmalyn nudged her ship up beside mine. I glimpsed through her canopy into her cockpit. She always looked odd to me wearing her helmet, which covered her long dark hair.

"Hey," she said to me on a private line. "You all right?"

"Yeah," I said. It was a lie. Every time I used my strange abilities, I felt a conflict inside me. Our ancestors had been afraid of people like me, people with cytonic powers. Before we'd crashed on Detritus, we'd worked in the ships' engine rooms, powering and guiding our travel.

They'd just called us the people of the engines. Other crew members had shunned us—instilling in our culture traditions and prejudices that had lasted even after we'd forgotten what a cytonic was.

Could it all be just superstition, or was there more to it? I had felt the malevolence of the eyes. In the end, my father had attacked his own kind. We blamed the Krell for that, but I worried. He'd seemed so angry on the tapes.

I worried that whatever I was, my actions would bring more danger than any of us understood.

"Guys?" Sadie asked, pulling her ship up alongside mine. "What does this warning on my console mean?"

I glanced at the flashing light on the proximity monitor, then cursed under my breath and scanned out into the void. I could just barely see the Krell monitoring station out there, and as I watched, something new appeared next to it. Two objects that were even larger than it was.

Capital ships. "Two new ships just arrived in the system," M-Bot said. "My long-range sensors confirm what Flight Command is seeing. They appear to be battleships."

"Scud," FM said over the line. So far, we'd faced only other fighters—but we knew from stolen intel that the enemy had access to at least a few large-scale capital ships like these.

"We have limited data on the armaments of ships like those," M-Bot said. "The intel you and I stole contained only generalized information. But my processors say those ships are likely equipped to bombard the planet."

Bombard. They could launch ordnance on the planet from outer space, hitting it with enough firepower to turn even those living in deep caverns to dust.

"They won't be able to get past the defensive platforms," I said. That was, we assumed, why the Krell had always used low-altitude bombers in the past, not orbital bombardment. The planet's platforms had been built with countermeasures to prevent bombardment from a distance.

"And if they just destroy the platforms first?" Sadie said.

"The defenses are too strong for that," I said.

It was bravado, in part. We didn't know for sure if Detritus's defenses could prevent a bombardment. Perhaps once we gained control of them all, we'd be able to determine their full capabilities. We were months away from that, unfortunately.

"Do you hear anything?" Kimmalyn said.

I reached out with my cytonic senses. "Just a faint, soft music," I said. "Almost like static, but . . . prettier. I'd have to get closer to understand any specifics of what they're saying."

I'd always been able to hear the sounds coming from the stars. I'd first thought of it as music when I was younger. During my months of training, and talking to my grandmother, we'd determined that "music" to be the sound of FTL communications being sent through the nowhere. Likely, what I heard now was the sound of that station or those battleships communicating with the rest of the Superiority.

We waited for a long time, orders saying for us to hold position to see if those battleships advanced. They didn't. It seemed that whatever they'd been sent to do, it wouldn't happen in the immediate future.

"Orders are in," Jorgen eventually said over the comm. "Those battleships are settling in, so we're to report back at Platform Prime. Come on."

I sighed, then turned my ship around and headed toward the planet. I'd survived the battle.

Now it was time to go get yelled at.

3

M-Bot calculated our approach.

The others still weren't completely comfortable with him. A computer program that could think and talk like a person? Gran-Gran—who had been a little girl during the days before our people had crashed on Detritus—said she'd heard of such things, but they had been forbidden.

Still, M-Bot provided an advantage we couldn't ignore. With his hyperefficient calculations, we could easily navigate a path through the defensive platforms surrounding Detritus without the aid of DDF mathematicians.

We carefully maintained the course he indicated, passing just outside the range of the gun emplacements on metal platforms the size of mountain ranges. I noted the shadows of skyscrapers. During my schooling, I'd taken mandatory heritage classes each year—where we'd seen pictures of Old Earth, and had been taken to see animals of many varieties in special caverns where they were bred. So I knew about life there, and about things like sky-scrapers, even if I'd always found Gran-Gran's stories of the ancient times more interesting than the heritage classes.

Those skyscrapers indicated that these platforms around Detritus had been inhabited once, like the planet had been, but something had destroyed them centuries ago.

The sight of all the platforms—curving into what seemed like infinity—never failed to leave me breathless. Our fifty starfighters were specks of dust by comparison. How long had it taken to build all of this? There were maybe a hundred thousand people living in the cave networks that made up our nation, the Defiant Caverns. But that entire population could vanish into just one of these platforms.

The command came to decelerate. I spun M-Bot with the others and pointed my boosters toward the planet. A quiet, easy burn slowed my ship.

Facing backward toward the shells, it all looked faintly like the gears of some eldritch clock going about an unknowable purpose. Each platform rotating in its turn, guns ready to vaporize anyone—human or alien—who tried to interfere. These shells were the reason we were still alive though, so I wasn't complaining.

Our ships soon passed the nearest shell to the planet, which was distinctive for several reasons. The most obvious was that it held thousands of massive lights that shone like spotlights, illuminating sections of the planet below. These skylights created an artificial day/night cycle.

This inner shell was also in a far worse state of repair than the outer ones. Enormous fields of debris tumbled through space here just outside the atmosphere. This junk was the remnants of—we assumed—platforms that had been destroyed. Some sections had fallen inward, crashing into the planet after losing power.

A voice crackled in my helmet speaker. "Skyward Flight," a man's voice said, "and Xiwang Flight. Admiral Cobb has ordered you to dock on Platform Prime. The rest of you, head down to the surface for off-shift rotation."

I recognized the speaker as Rikolfr, a member of the admiral's staff. I complied, turning my ship in the right direction. That brought Detritus into my view: a blue-grey sphere with a bright, inviting atmosphere. Thirty ships from our fleet flew off down toward the planet.

The rest of us skimmed along outside the atmosphere, passing several platforms whose lights blinked a friendly blue, instead of the angry red of the other platforms. Thanks to M-Bot's stealth capabilities, we'd been able to land on one and hack its systems. Fortunately, the platforms' internal security protocols made some small exceptions for humans, which had given the engineers a brief respite—long enough to finish their work.

That done, Rodge and the other engineers had figured out how to power down a few of the platforms nearby, letting us reclaim those too. Our work had captured only ten out of thousands so far, but it was a promising start.

Platform Prime was the largest of these—an enormous platform with docking bays for starfighters. We'd turned it into an orbital headquarters, though the engineering teams were still working on some of its systems—most notably the ancient data banks.

I flew into my assigned dock, a small individual hangar. The lights flickered on as the bay door closed, and the room pressurized. I drew in a deep breath and sighed, then opened the canopy. It felt so dull to return after a battle and go back to ordinary life. Unrealistic though it was, I wished that I could continue patrolling and flying. The answers to who I was—to *what* I was—were out there somewhere, not in these sterile metallic hallways.

"Hey!" M-Bot said as I climbed out of the cockpit. "Take me with you. I don't want to miss the fun."

"I'm just going to get a lecture."

"Like I said . . . ," he replied.

Fine. I reached back under the front control panel and unhooked his new mobile receptor: a bracelet device that contained some sensory equipment, a holographic projector, a receiver to boost M-Bot's communication capabilities, and a small clock display. He claimed to have had a mobile receptor like it in the past, but it was missing—his old pilot had probably taken it hundreds of years ago when he'd gone out to explore Detritus.

When M-Bot had given the engineers plans to create a new one, they'd gone crazy over the microhologram technology it contained. Fortunately, they'd stopped celebrating long enough to fabricate me a replacement. I'd taken to wearing this rather than my father's light-line, as I rarely found chances to use that now that I wasn't exploring caverns regularly.

I snapped on the hologram bracelet, then handed my helmet to Dobsi—one of the ground crew members—as she climbed up the ladder outside to check on me.

"Anything we should look at?" she asked.

"I took a chunk of debris on the right side of the fuselage with my shield down."

"I'll check it out."

"Thanks," I said. "And fair warning: he's in one of his moods."

"Is he ever not?"

"There was this one time," I said, "when he was processing a self-diagnostic, and didn't say anything for a whole five minutes. It was pure bliss."

"You know," M-Bot said, "that I'm programmed to be able to recognize sarcasm, right?"

"The joke would be wasted if you weren't." I entered the changing room, which doubled as my bunk up here—not that I owned a lot. My father's pin, my old maps of the caverns, and a few of my improvised weapons. I kept them in one trunk beside the cot, with my changes of clothing.

As soon as I entered, a fluting trill greeted me. Doomslug sat on her perch beside the door. Bright yellow, with little blue spikes along her back, she was snuggled into some of my old shirts, which she'd made into a nest. I scratched her on the head, and she gave another joyful fluting sound. She wasn't slimy, but rather tough, like the feel of good leather.

I was glad to see her here; she was supposed to stay in my bunk room, but kept slipping away somehow, and I'd often find her in the hangar. She seemed to like being near M-Bot.

I washed up, but didn't change out of my flight suit. Then, having wasted as much time as I could justify, I steeled myself with a warrior's determination and stepped out into the hallway. The light here was always too bright after being out in space—the white walls shiny and reflective. The only part that wasn't overly polished or lit was the carpet down the center, which had aged remarkably well—likely because this had all been a vacuum until the engineering team had patched the station's holes and turned on the life support systems.

In the hallway waited the other members of my flight. Nedd and Arturo were arguing about whether or not pilots should be allowed to paint designs on the fronts of their ships. I ignored them and stepped up beside Kimmalyn, whose hair was messy now that she held her helmet under her arm.

"You *do* realize how mad Jorgen is," she whispered to me.

"I can handle him," I said.

Kimmalyn raised an eyebrow.

"Really," I said. "I just have to be properly confident and intimidating. Got any eye black handy?"

"Uh, what's that?"

"A kind of war paint used by the men who fought on the gridiron on Old Earth. A type of deathmatch involving a dead pig."

"Neat. But I'm fresh out. And . . . Spin, wouldn't it be better to *not* aggravate Jorgen? For once?"

"Not sure I'm capable of that."

FM walked past, giving me an encouraging thumbs-up. I returned it, though I still felt awkward around her sometimes. The tall, slender woman somehow managed to wear even a flight suit in a fashionable way, while the bulky clothing always made me feel like I had on three layers too many. She joined T-Stall and Catnip, a pair of guys who had been added to our flight to fill in holes. They were in their early twenties, older than the rest of us by a few years, though they were doing their best to integrate.

Aside from Jorgen, the only other member of our team was Sadie, the new girl. She promptly tripped over the small ledge on the ground between her changing room and the hallway, nearly dropping her helmet. Her blue hair and distinctive features reminded me of . . . well, painful memories.

Most of the others continued on down the hall toward the mess, but I waited around for Jorgen—better to confront him now, though he was usually last out of his ship, as he went through the postflight checklist every time, in detail, even though it was okay to let the ground crew do it. Kimmalyn waited with me, and Sadie hurried over to us.

"You were *so* amazing out there," she said, clutching her helmet to her chest as she beamed. Scud. We were only one class ahead of her group, so were basically the same age. But surely we didn't look nearly as young as she did.

"Yeah, well, nice flying today yourself," I said.

"You were *watching*?"

I hadn't been watching, but I nodded to her encouragingly.

"Maybe soon I'll be able to be like you, Spin!"

"You did wonderfully, dear," Kimmalyn said, patting Sadie on the shoulder. "But never try to be who you aren't; you don't have nearly enough practice to pull it off."

"Right, right," Sadie said, digging in her pocket and pulling out a little notepad and a pencil. "Never . . . who you aren't . . ." She scribbled down the saying as if it were scripture, though I was sure Kimmalyn had made it up on the spot.

I glanced at Kimmalyn. Her serene expressions were famously hard to read, but the twinkle in her eyes revealed she loved the idea of someone recording her sayings.

"I wish I could have followed you today, Spin. It looked dangerous for you to be alone."

"The only thing I want you to follow, Sadie," a firm voice said, "is your orders. If only others were so inclined."

I didn't have to look to know that Jorgen—flightleader, and sometimes Jerkface—had finally joined us, and was standing behind me.

"Um, thank you, sir," Sadie said, then saluted and scampered off toward the mess.

"Good luck," Kimmalyn whispered to me, squeezing my arm. "May you only get what you deserve." Then, of course, she abandoned me.

Well, I could slay this beast on my own. I turned around, chin up—then had to tip my head back a little farther. Why did he have to be so scudding tall? Jorgen Weight, with his deep brown skin, was a pillar of exquisite, rule-following determination. He went to bed each night with the DDF Code of Conduct tucked under his pillow, he ate his breakfast while listening to patriotic speeches, and he exclusively used silverware that had the words *Don't let Spensa have any fun* stenciled on the handles.

I might have made a few of those things up. Regardless, it *did* seem that he spent far too much of his life complaining about me. Well, I'd grown up around bullies. I knew how to stand up for myself against someone who—

"Spensa," he said to me, "you need to stop being such a bully."

"Ooooooh," M-Bot's voice said from my wrist. "Nice."

"Shut up," I muttered to him. "Bully? *Bully?*" I poked Jorgen in the chest. "What do you mean, bully?"

He eyed my finger.

"I can't bully you," I said. "You're taller than I am."

"That is *not* how it works, Spensa," Jorgen growled, his voice growing lower. "And . . . what are you wearing on your face?"

On my face? It was such a non sequitur that I momentarily forgot the argument with Jorgen, glancing instead at the polished metallic wall to see my reflection. My face was painted with black lines under my eyes. What?

"Eye black," M-Bot said from my wrist. "Paint worn by athletes on Old Earth. You said to Kimmalyn that—"

"That was a joke," I said. The skin paint was a hologram M-Bot had projected onto me by his mobile receptor. "You really need to have someone rewrite your humor program, M-Bot."

"Oooohhhhh," he said. "Sorry." He made the hologram vanish.

Jorgen shook his head, then brushed past me and stalked down the hallway, leaving me to hurry to catch up.

"You've always been independent, Spin, I get that," he said. "But now you're using your powers and your status to shove everyone else—including Cobb—around. You're ignoring protocol and orders because you know there's not a scudding thing the rest of us can do about it. Those are the actions of a bully."

"I'm trying to protect the others," I said. "I'm drawing away the enemy! I'm becoming a target!"

"The plan was for you to do that, then lead them back toward us so we could attack them from the sides. I noted several chances where you could have done this, and you specifically chose to double down on fighting them by yourself." He eyed me. "You're trying to prove something. What is wrong with you lately? You were always eager to work as part of the team before. Scud, you practically *forged* this team. Now you act like this? Like you're the only one who matters?"

I . . .

My objections faded away. Because I knew he was right, and I knew that making excuses here would be fighting with the wrong weapon. There was only one that ever really worked with Jorgen. The truth.

"They're determined to kill me, Jorgen," I said. "They *will* throw everything they have at us until I'm dead."

We stopped at the end of the hall, beneath a blaring white light.

"You know it's true," I said, meeting his eyes. "They've figured out what I am. If they destroy me, then they can trap us on Detritus forever. They will cut through *anyone* to get to me."

"So you make it easier for them?"

"I'm distracting them, like I said, so that . . ." The words died on my lips. Scudding Jerkface and his intensely knowing eyes. "Okay, fine. I'm trying to push myself. The one time I did it, the one time I hyperjumped, I was in the middle of an explosion. I was desperate, threatened, about to die. So I figure if I can re-create that emotion, I might be able to do it again. I might be able to figure out what it is I can do, what it is . . . that I really am."

He sighed, looking up toward the ceiling with what seemed to me a melodramatic expression. "Saints help us," he muttered. "Spin, that's crazy."

"It's bold," I said. "A warrior always tests herself. Pushes herself. Seeks the limits of her skills."

He eyed me, but I held my ground. Jorgen had a way of making me vocalize the things I didn't normally acknowledge, not even to myself. Maybe that made him a good flightleader. Scud, the fact that he could kind-of-somewhat handle me was proof enough of that.

"Spensa," he said. "You're the best thing we have. You're vital to the DDF . . . and to me."

I was suddenly aware of how close he was standing. He leaned down just a little, and for a moment seemed like he wanted to go further. Unfortunately, there was something blocking us at the same time, interfering with whatever we might have been able to have. For one, the flightleader-pilot relationship was awkward.

There was more than that though. He was the embodiment of order, and I . . . well, I wasn't. I didn't know *what* or who I really was. When I was honest with myself, I had to admit that was why I hadn't moved forward with him these past six months.

Jorgen eventually leaned away. "You know the National Assembly has been talking about how you're too important to risk in battle. How they want to keep you back."

"I'd like to see them try," I said, angry at the thought.

"Part of me would too," he said, then smiled fondly. "But really, do we need to give them ammunition? You're part of a team. *We* are part of a team. Don't start thinking you have to do things alone, Spensa. Please. And for the stars' sake, *stop* trying to put yourself in danger. We'll find another way."

I nodded, but . . . it was easy for him to say things like that. Gran-Gran said that even when our ancestors had been part of a space fleet together, people like me had been feared.

The people of the engines. The hyperdrives. We were strange. Maybe even inhuman.

Jorgen keyed his code into the doorway at the end of the hall, but before he finished, the door opened. Kimmalyn had activated it from the other side. "Guys," she said, breathless. *"Guys."*

I frowned. She wasn't normally this excitable. "What?"

"Rodge sent me word," she said. "The engineers working on the platform's computer systems? They just found something. *A recording.*"

4

Jorgen and I followed Kimmalyn to the room everyone was calling the library, despite the lack of books. Here, the Engineering Corps had been working full-time on the old data banks. They'd ripped out several of the wall panels, exposing the networks of wires running inside like tendons. Though much of this platform had come online with minimal fuss, we had been locked out of several computer systems.

Kimmalyn led us to a group of engineers in ground crew jumpsuits whispering and chatting excitedly, gathered around a large monitor they'd set up. I looked around for the rest of my flight, but they weren't here—it was just me, Jorgen, Kimmalyn, and some officers from the admiral's staff. I tugged at my bulky flight suit, which was sweaty from my time fighting. "Wish I'd decided to change," I muttered to Jorgen.

"I could create a hologram of a new outfit for you!" M-Bot offered. "It—"

"How would that change the fact that I feel sweaty?" I asked him. Seriously, now that we had the remote bracelet and holo-

34

gram working, he was just looking for any excuse he could get to show off.

At my voice though, someone perked up from the crowd of engineers. He turned, then grinned when he saw us.

Rodge was lanky and pale, with a mop of red hair. He smiled more now than he had when we were growing up. In fact, I kept feeling like I'd missed something—somehow, during our time repairing M-Bot together, someone had snatched away my nervous friend and replaced him with this confident person.

I was proud of him, particularly when I noticed he'd gone back to wearing his cadet's pin—one that Cobb had specifically ordered to be enameled red for him, a new symbol of achievement reserved for outstanding members of the engineering or ground crews.

Rodge bounced over to us, speaking in a soft voice. "I'm so happy she found you. You're going to want to see this."

"What is it?" Jorgen asked, craning his neck to see the monitor.

"Last station records," Rodge whispered. "The final video logs before this place was shut down. They were interrupted mid-recording, and the encryption process didn't finish as they were archived. It's the first good chunk of data we've been able to recover." He glanced over his shoulder. "Commander Ulan insisted we wait for Cobb before showing it, and I figured nobody would complain if the Hero of Alta Second wanted to watch."

Indeed, my arrival had drawn some attention. A couple of the engineers nudged one another, nodding toward me.

"You know, Spin," Kimmalyn noted from my side, "it can be rather convenient to be around you. Everyone pays so much attention to you, the rest of us can get away with whatever we want."

"What would *you* want to get away with?" Jorgen asked. "Taking an extra sip of tea?"

Since he was still trying to get a glimpse of the monitor, he didn't notice Kimmalyn giving him a shockingly rude gesture. I gaped at her, my jaw dropping. Had she really just done that?

Kimmalyn shot me a mischievous smile, which she then covered with her hand. This girl . . . I thought I had her figured out, then she did something like that, deliberately intended—I was sure—to shock me.

Further conversation was interrupted as the door opened and Cobb entered. He wore a short white beard and still walked with a limp from his old wound—but refused to use a cane except in the most formal of situations. He carried a steaming mug of coffee in one hand, and was wearing the crisp white uniform of the Defiant Defense Force Admiral of the Fleet—the right breast bedecked with ribbons of merit and rank.

He'd reluctantly stepped up to the position after Ironsides—with equal reluctance—had taken her retirement. By some metrics, Cobb was the most important living human being. And yet, he was still just . . . well, Cobb.

"What's this about a log file?" he demanded. "What's on the blasted thing?"

"Sir!" said Commander Ulan, a tall woman of Yeongian heritage. "We don't know yet. We wanted to wait for you."

"What?" Cobb said. "Don't you know how slowly I walk? Damn station could rotate through three shifts in the time it takes for me to limp across the stupid thing."

"Er. Sir. We thought . . . I mean, nobody believes your leg makes you slow . . . er . . . not too slow, I mean . . ."

"Don't pander to me, Commander," he snapped.

"We just wanted to be respectful."

"Don't respect me either," he grumbled, then took a sip of his coffee. "Makes me feel old."

Ulan forced a laugh, at which Cobb scowled, making Ulan look even *more* uncomfortable. I empathized with her. Learning how to deal with Cobb was as specialized a skill as performing a triple Ahlstrom loop with a reverse jumpback.

The techs made way for Cobb, so Kimmalyn and I took the opportunity to slip closer to the screen. Jorgen hung back, standing with his hands clasped behind him and letting higher-ranking officers take the closer positions. Sometimes that boy could be too dutiful. Almost made a girl feel bad for using her notoriety to get a good spot.

Cobb eyed me. "I hear you're pulling stunts again, Lieutenant," he said softly as one of the senior technicians fiddled with the files.

"Um . . . ," I said.

"She sure is!" M-Bot's voice at my wrist said. "She told Jorgen she was intentionally trying to—" I hit the mute. Then, just to be careful, I turned off his holographic projector too. I blushed, looking at Cobb.

The admiral sipped his coffee. "We'll talk later. I don't want to anger your grandmother by getting you killed. She made me a pie last week."

"Um, yes, sir."

The screen fuzzed and then the video opened, showing an image of this very room—only without the walls torn apart. A group of people sat busy before monitors, wearing unfamiliar uniforms. My breath caught. They were human.

We'd always known that would be the case. Though we'd found Detritus uninhabited, Old Earth languages decorated much of the machinery. Still, it was eerie to be looking back in time at these mysterious people. Millions upon millions—if not billions—of them must have inhabited the planet and these platforms. How had they all vanished?

They seemed to be talking—indeed, they seemed agitated, bustling around the room. On closer inspection, it looked like several were screaming, but the picture didn't have sound. A man with blond hair scrambled into the seat in front of this monitor, his face filling our screen. He started talking.

"Sorry, sir!" said one of the techs near me. "We're working on audio. Just a sec . . ."

Sound suddenly erupted from the screen. People shouting, a dozen voices overlapping. "—make this report," the man at the screen said, speaking in heavily accented English. "We have initial evidence that the planet's cytoshields are, despite long-standing assumptions, *insufficient*. The delver has heard our communications, and followed them to us. Repeat, the delver has returned to our station and . . ."

He trailed off, looking over his shoulder. The room was mass chaos, some people breaking down and collapsing to the floor in hysterics, others screaming at one another.

The man on our screen typed on his keyboard. "We have video from one of the perimeter platforms," he said. "Number 1132. Turning to that view now."

I leaned forward as the recording switched to show a starfield— the view from a camera on the outer shell, looking out into space. I could see the curvature of the platform on the bottom of the screen.

The people in the recording quieted. Were they seeing something in that star-speckled blackness that I wasn't? Was it—

More stars were appearing.

They winked into existence, like pinpricks in reality. Hundreds . . . thousands of them, too bright to actually be stars. In fact, they moved in the sky, gathering and collecting. Even through the monitor—even from a vast distance away, in both time and space—I could *feel* their malevolence.

These weren't stars. These were the eyes.

My lungs seized up. My heart started to pound in my chest.

More and more of the lights appeared, watching me through the screen. They knew me. They could *see* me.

I started to panic. But beside me, Cobb continued to quietly sip his coffee. Somehow, the calm way he stood there helped fend off my anxiety.

This happened a long time ago, I reminded myself. *There's no danger to me now.*

The lights on the screen started to grow blurry . . . Dust, I realized. A cloud of it appeared, as if leaking through punctures in reality. The dust glowed with white light and expanded at an incredible speed. Then something followed, a large circular shape that emerged as if from nothing in the center of the dust cloud.

It was hard to make out more than the shadow of the thing. At first, my mind refused to accept the awesome scale it presented. The thing that had appeared—that blackness inside the glowing dust—dwarfed the enormous platform. Scuuud. Whatever it was, it was the size of a planet.

"I have . . . I have visual confirmation of a delver," said the man recording the video. "Mother of Saints . . . It's here. The cyto-shielding project is a failure. The delver turned back and . . . and it's come for us."

The black mass shifted toward the planet. Were those arms I picked out in the shadows? No, could they be spines? The shape seemed intentionally designed to frustrate the mind, as I tried—against reason—to make sense of what I was seeing. Soon, the blackness simply became absolute. The camera died.

I thought the video was over, but the view switched back to the library room, where the man sat at his desk. Most of the other monitors had been abandoned, leaving only the man and one woman. I heard screams from elsewhere in the platform as this one man, trembling, stood up—knocking into the monitor he'd been using, twisting the camera angle.

"Life signs vanishing from the outer defensive rings!" shouted the woman. She stood up at her desk. "Platforms falling dormant. The High Command has ordered us to engage autonomous mode!"

Shaking visibly, the man sat back down. We watched through an off-kilter monitor as he typed furiously. The woman in the room pushed back from her desk, then looked up at the ceiling as a low sound rumbled through the platform.

"Autonomous defenses engaged . . . ," the man muttered, still typing. "Escape ships are falling dead. Saints . . ."

The room shook again, and the lights flickered.

"The planet is firing on us!" the woman screamed. "Our own people are *firing on us*!"

"They're not firing at us," the man continued, typing as if in a daze. "They're firing on the delver as it envelops the planet. We're just in the way. We need to make sure the nowalk is closed . . . Can't access it from here, but maybe . . ."

He continued to mutter, but my attention was drawn by something else. Lights gathering at the back of the room on the screen. They were breaking reality, making the far wall seem to stretch, become an infinite starfield penetrated by intense, hateful pinpricks.

The eyes had arrived. The woman in the room screamed, then . . . vanished. She seemed to twist in on herself, then shrink, crushed by some invisible force. The remaining man, the one who had been speaking, continued furiously typing at his station, his eyes wide. A madman working as if on his last will and testament. Though his face dominated the screen, I could see the blackness gathering behind him.

Lit by stars that were not stars.

Infinity coalescing.

A shape stepped from the darkness.

And it looked just like me.

5

I stumbled back from the screen, colliding with the press of officers. I was suddenly fully alert like I felt before a battle, and I found my hands forming fists. If they wouldn't let me out, I would *punch* my way to—

"Spensa?" Kimmalyn said, taking me by the arm. "Spensa!"

I blinked, then looked around, sweating, wide-eyed. "How?" I demanded. "How did it . . ." I looked back at the screen, which had paused on the image of the dead man and his room filled with stars. The line at the bottom indicated the video had reached its end.

The freeze-frame had a complete shot of me standing behind him. I was there. *I WAS THERE.* Wearing my modern DDF flight suit. Same shoulder-length brown hair and narrow face. I was frozen in place, reaching toward the man.

My expression though . . . I looked terrified. Then that expression changed, impossibly mimicking how I now felt.

"Turn it off!" I shouted. I reached for the screen, pulling out of Kimmalyn's grip, though a stronger grip seized me.

I wrestled against those hands, struggling to get to the screen.

Both with my body, and . . . and with something else. Some sense inside me. Some primal, panicked, horrified piece of me. It was like a silent scream that emerged from within and expanded outward.

Then, from someplace distant, I felt as if something responded to my scream.

I . . . hear . . . you . . .

"Spensa!" Jorgen said.

I looked up at him. He was holding me back, his eyes locked on mine.

"Spensa, what do you see?" he said.

I glanced at the screen and my image there. Wrong, so wrong. My face. My emotions. And . . .

"You don't see it?" I asked, looking around at the others and their confused expressions.

"The darkness?" Jorgen asked. "There's a man on the screen, the one who was making the log. Then there's a blackness behind him, broken by white lights."

"Like . . . eyes . . . ," one of the techs said.

"And the person?" I asked. "Don't you see someone in the darkness?"

My question was met by more confused stares.

"It's just blackness," Rodge said from the side of the group. "Spin? There's nothing else there. I don't even see any stars."

"I see stars," Jorgen said, narrowing his eyes. "And something that might be a shape. Maybe. Mostly just a shadow."

"Turn it off," Cobb said. "See what other logs or files you can dig out." He looked at me. "I'll speak with Lieutenant Nightshade in private."

I looked from him to the room's startled faces, feeling a sudden shame. I'd worked through my worries about being viewed as a coward, but it was still embarrassing to have made such a scene. What did they think, seeing me break like that?

42

I forced myself to calm down and nodded to Jorgen, prying myself from his grip. "I'm fine," I said. "Just got a little caught up in the video."

"Great. We're still going to talk later," Jorgen said.

Cobb waved for me to follow him out of the room, and I made my way to the door, though just before we left he paused and looked back in. "Lieutenant McCaffrey?" he asked.

"Sir?" Rodge said, perking up from beside the wall.

"You still working on that project of yours?"

"Yes, sir!" Rodge said.

"Good. Go see if your theories work. I'll talk to you later." He continued on, leading me out of the room.

"What was that about, sir?" I asked him as the door shut behind us.

"That's not important now," he said, leading me into the observatory across the hall. A wide, shallow room, the observatory was named for its dramatic view of the planet below. I stepped inside, and through the wall-to-wall window Detritus confronted me.

Cobb stood at the window and took a sip of coffee. I approached, trying to keep the trepidation from showing in my steps. I couldn't help but glance over my shoulder toward the room where we had watched the video.

"What did you see in that video?" Cobb asked.

"Myself," I said. I could speak honestly to Cobb. He'd long since proven he deserved my trust, and more. "I know it sounds impossible, Cobb, but the darkness in the video took shape, and it was me."

"I once watched my best friend and wingmate try to kill me, Spensa," he said softly. "We now know something had overwritten what he saw—or the way his brain interpreted what he saw—so he mistook me for the enemy."

"You think . . . this is similar?"

"I have no other explanation as to why you'd see yourself in a

43

video archive hundreds of years old." He took a long drink of his coffee, tipping the cup back to get the last drops. Then he lowered it. "We're blind here. We don't know what the enemy is capable of—or really even who the enemy *are*. You see anything else in that darkness?"

"I thought I heard something tell me . . . that it 'heard' me. But that felt different somehow. From a different place, and not nearly as angry. I don't know how to explain it."

Cobb grunted. "Well, at least now we have an idea what happened to the people of this planet." He gestured with his mug out the window, and I stepped up to look down at Detritus. It looked desolate, a surface that had been turned to slag. The debris in lower orbit—the damaged platforms, the junk—had probably been caused by terrified people on the planet firing on the entity as it surrounded them.

"Whatever that thing was in the recording," Cobb said, "it came here and . . . destroyed all the people on this planet and these platforms. They called it a delver."

"Have you ever heard of anything like that?" I asked. "You knew about . . . about the eyes I sometimes see."

"Not the word *delver*," Cobb said. "But we have traditions that stretch back from before our grandparents were alive. They speak of beings that watch us from the void, the deep darkness, and they warn us to avoid communicating wirelessly. That's why we only use radio for important military channels. That man on the video said that the delver came because it heard their communications, so maybe that's related." Cobb eyed me. "We're warned not to create machines that can think too quickly and . . ."

"And we're supposed to fear people who can see into the nowhere," I whispered. "Because they draw the attention of the eyes."

Cobb didn't contradict me. He went for another sip of coffee, but found his mug empty and grunted softly.

"Do you think that the thing we saw in that video is related to the eyes you see?" Cobb asked.

I swallowed. "Yes," I said. "They're the same, Cobb. The entities that watch when I use my powers are the same as that thing with the spines that emerged on the video. The man said something about their cytoshield. That sounds a lot like cytonics."

"A shield to keep the enemy from hearing or finding the cytonics on the planet, maybe," Cobb said. "And it failed." He sighed, shaking his head. "You see those battleships arrive earlier?"

"Yeah. But the platforms will protect us from bombardment, right?"

"Maybe," Cobb said. "Some of these systems still work, but others aren't as reliable. Our engineers think some of those more distant platforms have anti-bombardment countermeasures, but we can't know for certain. I'm not sure we have the luxury of worrying about delvers, or the eyes, or any of that. We have a more immediate problem. The Krell—or whatever they're really called—won't listen to our pleas to stop their attacks. They've stopped caring whether they preserve any humans. They're determined to exterminate us."

"They're afraid of us," I said. When M-Bot and I had stolen information off their station six months ago, that was the biggest and most surprising revelation I'd discovered about the Krell. They kept us contained not out of spite, but because they were genuinely terrified of humankind.

"Afraid of us or not," Cobb said, "they want us dead. And unless we can find a way to travel the stars like they do, we're doomed. No fortress—no matter how powerful—can stand forever, particularly not against an enemy as strong as the Superiority."

I nodded. It was a core tenet of battlefield tactics: you needed to have a plan of retreat. As long as we were trapped on Detritus, we were in danger. If we could get offworld, all kinds of options opened to us. Fleeing and hiding somewhere else. Searching for other human enclaves—if they existed—and recruiting help. Striking back against the enemy, putting them on the defensive.

None of this was possible until I learned to use my powers. Or, barring that, until we found a way to steal the enemy's hyperdrive technology. Cobb was right. The eyes, the delvers, they might be important to me—but in the grand scheme of my people's survival, that was all a secondary problem.

We *needed* to find a way off this planet.

Cobb looked at me carefully. He had always felt old. I knew that he was only a few years older than my parents, yet right now he looked like a rock that had been left out too long and survived too many meteor falls.

"Ironsides used to complain about how hard this job was," he grumbled. "You know the worst part about being in charge, Spin?"

"No, sir."

"Perspective. When you're young, you can assume that everyone older than you has life figured out. Once you get command yourself, you realize we're all just the same kids wearing older bodies."

I swallowed, but didn't say anything. Standing next to Cobb, I stared out the window at the desolate planet and the thousands of platforms surrounding it. An incredible network of defenses that—in the end—had been powerless to stop whatever this delver was.

"Spensa," Cobb said, "I need you to be more careful out there. Half my staff think you're the biggest liability we've ever put into a ship. The other half think you're some kind of Saint incarnate. I'd like you to stop supplying both sides with good arguments."

"Yes, sir," I said. "I . . . to be honest, I was trying to push myself, put myself in danger. I thought if I did that, it might make my brain work and my powers engage."

"While I appreciate the sentiment, that's a stupid way to try to solve our problems, Lieutenant."

"But we *do* have to figure out how to travel the stars. You yourself said it."

"I'd rather find a way that isn't so reckless," Cobb said. "We know the Superiority ships travel the stars. They have hyperdrive technology, and the eyes—the delvers—haven't destroyed *them*. So it's possible."

Cobb adopted a contemplative look, staring back out the window at the planet below. He was quiet for such a long time, I found myself growing nervous.

"Sir?" I asked.

"Come with me," he said. "I might have a way for us to get off this planet that doesn't rely upon your powers."

6

I followed Cobb through the too-clean corridors of Platform Prime. Why were we walking back to the fighter bays?

He counted off the doors until stopping next to the dock where I kept M-Bot. Increasingly confused, I followed him through the small door. I'd expected to find the ground crew beyond, doing M-Bot's normal post-battle services. Instead, the room was empty save for the ship and one person. Rodge.

"Rig?" I asked, using his old callsign from when he'd been in Skyward Flight. That had only lasted a few days, but he was one of us all the same.

Rodge—who had been inspecting something on M-Bot's wing—jumped as I said his name. He spun to find us there, and blushed immediately. For a moment he was the old Rodge: earnest, gangly, and not a little awkward. He almost dropped his datapad as he quickly saluted Cobb.

"Sir!" Rodge said. "I didn't expect you so soon."

"At ease, Lieutenant," Cobb said. "How goes the project?"

The project? Cobb had said something about a project earlier—it involved M-Bot?

"See for yourself, sir," Rodge said, then tapped something on his datapad.

M-Bot's shape changed, and I actually yelped in surprise. In an instant, he looked like one of the black ships that were piloted by Krell aces.

His holograms, I realized. M-Bot was a long-range stealth ship, designed—best we could tell—for spy missions. He had what he called active camouflage, a fancy way of saying he could use holograms to change what he looked like.

"It's not perfect, sir," Rodge said. "M-Bot can't turn himself invisible, not with any real level of believability. Instead, he has to overlay his hull with some kind of image. Since he's not exactly the same shape as one of those Krell ships, we had to fudge in places. You can see here that I made the hologram's wings bigger to cover up the tips of his hull."

"It's incredible," I said, walking around the ship. "M-Bot, I had no idea you could do this."

Rodge looked at his datapad. "Um . . . he sent me a text here, Spin. He says he's not talking to you because you muted him earlier."

I rolled my eyes, inspecting Rodge's work. "So . . . what's the point of this?"

Cobb folded his arms where he stood near the door. "I asked my command staff, scientists, and engineers to tackle the hyperdrive problem. How do we find a way off this planet? All the ideas I got back were wildly implausible, except one. It's only *mildly* implausible."

I stepped up beside Rodge, who was grinning.

"What?" I asked him.

"You know all those nights," he said, "when you'd come wake me up and force me to go on some insane adventure?"

"Yeah?"

"Well, I thought maybe I should get some revenge." He turned

49

and swept his hand toward M-Bot, and the new, confident Rodge was back. He grinned widely, his eyes alight. This was a man in his element. "M-Bot has extremely advanced espionage capabilities. He can create detailed holograms. He can eavesdrop on conversations hundreds of meters away. He can hack enemy signals and computer systems with ease.

"We've been using him as a frontline combat ship, but that's not his true purpose. And as long as we use him just to fight, we're not utilizing his full potential. When the admiral asked for ideas on how to get ahold of the enemy hyperdrive technology, it occurred to me that the answer was staring us in the face. And occasionally pointing out how odd our human features look."

"You want to use him to infiltrate the Superiority," I said, the realization hitting me. "You want to *pretend* to be a Krell ship, then somehow steal their hyperdrive technology!"

"They launch drones from their space station nearby," Rodge said. "And we've observed new ships arriving there using hyperdrive technology. The very thing we need sits on our proverbial doorstep. M-Bot can use holograms on us too. He could make a small team of us, equipped with mobile receptors like the one you wear, look like Krell.

"If we could somehow—in the confusion of a battle—make M-Bot imitate an enemy ship, we might be able to land him on their station. A small team of spies could unload, then pretend to be Krell just long enough to steal one of their real ships and escape with it. With that in hand, we could replicate their technology and escape the planet."

I felt my jaw dropping at the audacity of it. "Rodge, that's *insane*."

"I know!"

"I love it!"

"I *know*!"

The two of us stood there, grinning like we had after stealing the claymore off the wall of the historical preservation chamber. It had taken both of us to lift it, but hey, we'd gotten to hold a real sword.

Together, we looked to Cobb.

"Krell ships likely have transponders," he said, "for authentication."

"M-Bot should be able to spoof one," Rodge said.

"And you think you could do this, Spin?" Cobb asked me. "Imitate one of our enemies? Believably? Sneak onto an enemy station and steal one of their ships?"

"I . . ." I swallowed, and tried to be objective. "No. Sir, I'm a pilot, not a spy. I don't have any training along these lines. I . . . well, I'd probably make a fool of myself."

It hurt to admit that, as the plan was fabulous. But I had to be realistic.

"Jorgen said the same thing," Cobb said.

"He knows about this plan?" I asked.

"We briefed him and the other senior flightleaders on the idea during our last command meeting. We all agreed that nobody in the DDF has this kind of expertise. We've spent eighty years drilling for direct battle, not espionage. We don't *have* spies. But . . . Jorgen suggested that we start up a training program. Spin, if we do that, would you be willing to participate?"

"Of course," I said, though the idea of more school—and less flying—gave me a pang of regret.

"Good, because that ship of yours still won't let anyone else pilot it." Cobb shook his head. "I think this is the only viable plan we have, though I just don't like it. I can't imagine one of us, no matter how well trained, believably imitating a Krell. We're too different. Plus they're bound to find it strange when our ship lands on their station without following their protocol. We'd have to find some sort of excuse for why our ship is behaving oddly. Damaged systems maybe?

"In any case, Lieutenant McCaffrey, I'm giving you leave to continue developing this idea. Maybe start training all of Skyward Flight for espionage activities. Give me detailed plans. I wish we weren't pushed so far back against the wall. We might not have time to give this plan the proper preparation it would need. But with those battleships in place now . . ."

I opened my mouth to agree, but then stopped. I sensed something in the back of my mind. A strange sound, like a humming. I cocked my head, focusing on it. The sensation was new to me.

There, I thought as the sound came to a climax, then vanished. I tried to stretch out my cytonic senses to determine what it meant. *Did . . . did something just arrive?*

A call came on the comm. Cobb walked to the wall, answering it. "Yes?"

"Sir," Rikolfr's voice said. "One of the outer scouts spotted an alien ship *appearing* just outside the defense platforms. It's a small vessel, fighter size. It seems to have hyperjumped directly here."

"One ship?" Cobb asked.

"Just one, sir. Not of any Superiority design we know. We're scrambling a response team from planetside, but this is odd behavior. Why would they send a single ship? Surely we're past the days when they'd try to sneak up a bomber on Alta."

"How far away is it?" I asked, knowing the answer. It was close. I could feel it.

"Approaching the outermost shell now, at the orbital equator," Rikolfr said. "Analysis thinks it must be a new kind of drone sent to test platform gun emplacement response time."

"I'll go check it out, sir," I told Cobb. "A ship from up here will arrive before a planetside team."

Cobb eyed me.

"Please, sir," I said. "I won't do anything stupid."

"I'll order Quirk to go with you," he said. "Don't try to lose her, and *don't* engage this ship unless I give you orders. Understand?"

I nodded, and read the implication in those words. He was testing me. To see if I could still follow orders. I probably should have been embarrassed that such a test was necessary.

I scrambled to climb into my ship as Rodge and Cobb walked to the door. I had a lot to think about, with Rodge's plan—not to mention the lingering sense of disquiet I still felt at having seen the delver wearing my face.

For the moment though, I was too eager to get back in the cockpit. And to find out why the Superiority would send a single ship to test our defenses.

7

I quickly ran through the preflight checklist. "Ready to go, M-Bot?" I asked.

I was met by silence.

"M-Bot?" I asked, tapping the console, feeling a spike of concern. "You all right?"

"I'm not responding," he said. "Because you don't want to talk to me. Remember?"

Oh . . . right. He was still angry because I'd muted him earlier. I winced, unhooking his mobile receptor, and clicked it back into the dash. "Sorry about that. You were going to get me into trouble."

"Spensa, it's impossible for *me* to get *you* into trouble. I can merely point out preexisting trouble."

"I said I was sorry."

"Well, obviously you don't want me around. I can logically conclude, using very little processing power, that you feel you are better off without me."

"Were all AIs as sulky as you are?" I asked.

"We were made as reflections of humankind, meant to imitate their actions and emotions."

"Ouch. I asked for that one, didn't I?" I glanced toward the green light that appeared on the wall, indicating that Cobb and Rodge were out and the bay was ready to depressurize. I engaged the maneuvering thrusters, then the door opened, and I steered my ship out into the vacuum.

A few minutes later, Kimmalyn's ship hovered out of her own docking bay. "Hey," she said over the line. "What exactly are we doing again?"

"We've spotted an unidentified alien ship approaching the planet. It's coming in through the defensive layers right now." I boosted forward alongside the thin edge of the platform.

Kimmalyn fell in behind me. "A single ship? Huh."

"I know." I left off the part where I thought I'd felt it approaching. I didn't know what that meant yet—or even if it was real. "Let's go."

"Let's go," a voice said from behind me in the cockpit, and I jumped. I spun my head to see a yellow-and-blue slug nestled into the spot between my toolkit and the cockpit's emergency water supply.

"Doomslug?" I said.

The little animal mimicked the sound, as she was inclined to do. Great. I should've been annoyed at Dobsi and the rest of the ground crew for not keeping an eye on the slug, but . . . well, they weren't pet sitters, they were mechanics. Plus, Doomslug had a habit of getting into places she wasn't supposed to.

Hopefully I wouldn't have to do any dangerous maneuvers; I wasn't sure how many Gs Doomslug could pull. For now, I boosted toward the strange ship. True to his word, M-Bot didn't say anything to me—but he did lay out a direction on the monitor, pointing the way we should head to intercept the ship. He then wrote a message for me on the screen.

I'm tracking the ship's progress via our surveillance beacons, and it is NOT taking a wise pathway. Multiple platforms are firing upon it.

"Huh," I said to him. "Maybe the technicians were right. They think it's a scout drone sent to test something about the platforms."

There is a logic to that, he replied onscreen. *If that ship had intended to actually reach Detritus, it would have picked a course that wove between the platforms, staying out of range. The Krell know how to do such things.*

I turned my ship and boosted in the direction M-Bot indicated, enjoying the sensation of g-forces pressing me back. I always felt more in control of my life when I was in a cockpit. I sighed, trying to push away the uneasiness I felt at having watched the video of that . . . thing.

"Interception in a minute and a half," M-Bot said.

"What happened to the silent treatment?" I asked.

"You were looking too comfortable," he said. "I decided that being silent is the wrong approach. Instead, I need to remind you what you're missing while not talking to me—by showing you how wonderful my interaction is."

"Whoopee."

"Whoopee!" Doomslug repeated.

"I'm glad you two are pleased."

I boosted a little faster.

"Wait," M-Bot said. "Was *that* sarcasm?"

"From me? Never."

"Good. I . . . Wait. It *was* sarcasm!"

Ahead, a twinkling bit of light broke through the bottom layer of the defensive shells. A ship . . . trailing smoke.

"The ship made it through," I said. "But it's been hit."

"I can't believe that you—"

"M-Bot, archive that conversation," I said. "The enemy ship. How bad is the damage?"

"Moderately bad," he answered. "I'm surprised it's still in one piece. At this angle, my projections say it will crash into the planet and vaporize itself on impact."

"Permission to give chase," I said, calling Flight Command. "That ship is heading for the surface on a collision course."

"Granted," Cobb's voice answered. "But keep your distance."

Kimmalyn and I pulled in behind the ship, following it down toward the atmosphere of the planet. I could see the alien ship trying to pull up—it was a motion I instinctively recognized. I'd been there, in a damaged ship threatening to spiral into a crash. I'd fought unresponsive controls in a panic, the smell of smoke overwhelming, my world spinning.

The ship managed to recover enough to course correct and hit the atmosphere at a better angle. Whoever was flying that drone didn't want it to . . .

Wait. I couldn't hear anything—no commands being directed through the nowhere to the ship. Which meant that was no drone. There was a live pilot inside.

Air friction from reentry made my shield begin to glow, and my ship trembled as the atmosphere grew thick enough to be noticeable.

That ship is going to tear itself apart if it stays at that angle, I thought.

"Command, it's coming in hard," Kimmalyn said. "Orders?"

"I'm going to try to snare that ship before it crashes," I said.

"That could be dangerous," Cobb said.

"It jumped in using a hyperdrive. Do you want to let it pulverize itself, or do you want to try to grab the technology? Maybe if we save it, we won't need to try Rodge's plan after all."

"Go ahead and chase the ship," he said. "But I'm scrambling the rest of Skyward Flight in case you need backup."

"Confirmed," I said. "Quirk, cover me. I'm going in for the ship."

"Sure," she answered, "but what if this is some kind of trap?"

"Then try not to laugh too hard while you haul me out of it."

"Spensa! What do you think I am? I would *never* gloat at you when you could see me."

I grinned, then slammed my throttle forward, hitting overburn and darting after the ship. Its barely controlled descent had thrown off M-Bot's intercept calculations, which he quickly redid.

Scud, it was going to be close. At these speeds, the ship would almost certainly destroy itself when it hit. The pilot seemed to know it; the ship jerked upward—trying to level out—but then dove right back down. The acclivity controls were obviously malfunctioning.

That got worse as the atmosphere thickened and the increasing rush of wind caused the alien ship to start spinning in a deadly rotation. Fortunately, my atmospheric scoops redirected airflow, giving me more control. My cockpit barely trembled, despite the speed of my acceleration straight toward the ship.

The incredible g-forces pushed through M-Bot's advanced Grav-Caps, and the familiar sensation of weight pressed me backward. It pulled my lips away from my teeth as I gritted them. It pulled my arms back, making them feel like they were tied with weights.

Behind me, Doomslug made an annoyed fluting sound. I glanced at her, but she'd hunkered down against the wall and gone rigid. She seemed to be able to handle this. I turned my attention back to the spiraling ship and focused on keeping it in the center of my vision. Its movements were growing increasingly erratic, and suddenly I was hit with a wave of emotion from inside that cockpit—an anxiety that somehow I connected to. A frantic, desperate panic.

I recognized something about the "tone" of those emotions—it felt as if they were being intentionally broadcast. Whoever was in there . . . they were the one who had spoken to me earlier, the one who had said they heard me.

This wasn't just an alien pilot. This was another cytonic.

I'm coming, I thought, hoping they could hear. *Hang on!*

"Spin?" Cobb's voice, over the intercom. "Spin, you *need* to catch that ship. Our analysts think it might be manned."

"Trying," I said through gritted teeth.

M-Bot's readout on my canopy told me we were under fifteen seconds from impact. We blasted down through the atmosphere, pointed straight toward the dusty surface below. The front of my ship was aglow, and I knew I was trailing my own burning line of smoke. Not from damage, but from the raw energy of cutting through the atmosphere like this.

Now! I thought, drawing just close enough to the alien ship. I launched my light-lance and speared it right between its twin boosters.

"Use cockpit rotation!" I screamed, pulling up—switching on my acclivity ring to counter the planet's gravity—and bracing myself as I frantically leveled off my dive.

Blackness crept across my vision as all the blood rushed to my feet, the g-forces now pointing down. M-Bot rotated my seat in an attempt to compensate—the human body is far better at taking forces straight back than it is at taking them downward.

The cockpit trembled as I slowed our descent. Scud . . . I hoped the g-forces didn't scramble the pilot. They nearly scrambled me. My vision blacked out completely for a few seconds, and my pressure suit constricted around my waist and legs, trying to force the blood back up into my brain.

As my vision returned I found myself trembling, my face sweaty and cold, a rushing sound in my ears. The ship slowed—mercifully—to a steady Mag-1. My cockpit seat rotated back as I pulled out of the dive completely.

I glanced over my shoulder to Doomslug, who was fluting in an annoyed tone from where she'd been pressed against the wall. Did not having bones make this harder or easier for her? Either way, we both seemed to have weathered the moment.

I glanced out to see the ground speeding along below. We were maybe four or five hundred feet up. I still had the other ship though—my own ship towed it along behind with the glowing red-orange rope of the light-lance.

"That was a little close, Spin," Kimmalyn said in my ear. "Even for you. But . . . I guess it wasn't a trap?"

I nodded, not trusting my voice as I breathed in and out. Still, my hands were steady as I slowed us to a stop, hovering on my acclivity ring. I carefully lowered the alien ship to the ground, then disengaged the light-lance and landed.

I waited—my cockpit open, feeling the breeze on my sweaty face—as Kimmalyn landed nearby. Cobb said he was sending a force of ground troops to handle the Krell captive, but didn't order me to stay back. So I climbed out and dropped down off the wing, my feet thumping on the dusty blue-grey landscape of Detritus. From down here, the defensive platforms and rubble belt of the lowest shell were just vague, distant patterns in the sky.

The alien ship was roughly the same size as M-Bot, so larger than our standard fighters. That meant it might be a long-range vessel, with more storage and room than a short-range fighter. It had a large cockpit set into the center of a circular fuselage, with wide arced wings and a destructor emplacement under each one. The ship also had a light-lance turret under its fuselage, in roughly the same place as M-Bot's. I hadn't seen those on any Krell fighters.

It was a combat fighter, obviously. The left wing bore a large blackened gap and scorch marks where the ship had been shot, and it had been ripped almost completely free in the descent.

Unfamiliar alien writing marked one side of the fuselage.

Whatever I thought I'd sensed from the cockpit was gone now, and I felt a rising fear. *The alien must be dead.*

Unwilling to wait for Kimmalyn, I hauled myself up onto the alien ship's right wing—it was still warm from the descent, but cool enough to touch—and the ship tipped beneath my weight, reminding me it wasn't sitting on landing struts. I held on and climbed over to the canopy.

There, through the glass, I got my first up-close look at an alien. I had been expecting to find something similar to the crab-like creatures I'd seen in the cockpits of Krell ships.

Shock moved through me, and my breath caught as I was confronted by something entirely different. What I saw instead was a humanoid woman.

8

She was both hauntingly familiar and strikingly alien, all at once. She had pale violet skin, stark-white hair, and bonelike white growths on her cheeks, underlining her eyes. Despite her alien features though, she had an obvious female shape beneath a snug flight jacket. She almost could have been one of us.

I was surprised—I hadn't realized there were aliens out there that looked so . . . human. I had always imagined that most of them would be like the Krell, creatures that were so strange they seemed to have more in common with rocks than humans.

I found myself staring at that elfin face, entranced, until I noticed the broken control panel and the blackened scorch marks on the left side of her stomach, which was wet with something darker than human blood. The panel had obviously exploded, and part had impaled her.

I scrambled to search for a manual cockpit release, but it wasn't where I expected to find it. That made sense—this was alien engineering. Still, it defied reason that there wouldn't be some kind of release on the outside of the ship. I felt around the canopy, searching for a latch, as Kimmalyn climbed up beside me. She gasped upon seeing the alien woman.

"Saints and stars," she whispered, touching the canopy glass. "She's beautiful. Almost . . . almost like a devil from one of the old stories . . ."

"She's wounded," I said. "Help me find—"

I cut off as I found it, right at the back of the canopy—a small panel that, when I threw it open, revealed a handle. I yanked it outward, and the canopy let out a hiss as it unsealed.

"Spensa, this is stupid," Kimmalyn said. "We don't know what kind of gases she breathes. And we could expose ourselves to alien bacteria or . . . or I don't know. There are a hundred reasons not to open that."

She was right. The air that came out did smell distinctly odd. Floral, but also acrid, scents that didn't go together in my experience. But it didn't seem to hurt me as I scrambled over and—not knowing what else to do—reached in to feel at the alien woman's neck for a pulse.

I felt one. Soft, irregular—though who knew if that was actually normal for her.

Suddenly the woman's eyes fluttered open, and I froze, meeting her violet eyes. I was shocked by how eerily *human* they were.

She spoke in a quiet voice, alien words with consonants I couldn't distinguish. Graceful, ephemeral, like the sounds of air rustling pages. It seemed oddly familiar.

"I don't understand," I said as she spoke again. "I . . ."

Scud. That dark liquid on her lips had to be blood. I scrambled to pull the emergency bandage from the cargo pocket on my leg. "Hang on!" I said, though Kimmalyn got hers out first and forced it into my hands.

I climbed farther into the cockpit, bracing myself against

the broken control panel, and pressed the bandage against the woman's side. "Help is coming," I said. "They're sending . . ."

"Human," the woman said.

I froze. The word was in English. She seemed to notice my reaction, then tapped a small pin on her collar. When she spoke again in her airy language, the device translated.

"A real human," she said, then smiled, blood trailing down the side of her lip. "So it's true. You still exist."

"Just hang on," I said, trying to stanch the blood at her side.

She lifted her arm, trembling, and touched my face. Her fingers were covered in blood and felt wet on my cheek. Kimmalyn breathed out a small prayer, but I clung there—half in, half out of the cockpit—meeting the alien woman's eyes.

"We were allies once," she said. "They say that you were monsters. But I thought . . . nothing can be more monstrous than they are . . . And if anyone can fight . . . it would be the ones they locked away . . . the terror that once nearly defeated them . . ."

"I don't understand," I said.

"I opened myself up—I searched for you for so long. And only now did I finally hear you, calling out. Don't trust . . . their lies. Don't trust . . . their false peace."

"Who?" I said. What she was saying was too vague. "Where?"

"There," she whispered, still touching my face. "Starsight." I felt something beyond the word, a *force* that hit my brain like a collision. It stunned me.

Her hand dropped. Her eyes fluttered closed, and I feared she was dead—but I had trouble thinking through the strange impact to my mind.

"Saints and stars above," Kimmalyn repeated. "Spensa?" She checked the woman for a pulse again. "Not dead, just unconscious. Scud, I hope the troops bring a medical crew."

Feeling numb, I reached out and took the small pin from the

alien's collar, the one that had translated the words. It was shaped like a stylized star or sunburst. What had that last part been? It felt drilled into my brain—a plea to go to this . . . place. Starsight?

I knew, intimately, that this woman was like me. Not just a cytonic, but a confused one, seeking answers. Answers she'd hoped to find in that place, the one she'd drilled into my brain.

I . . . I could go there, I realized. Somehow I knew that if I wanted, I could use the coordinates she'd placed into my head to teleport directly to the location.

I leaned back as three DDF troop transports landed gracefully on large blue acclivity rings next to the ship. They were accompanied by seven more fighters, the rest of Skyward Flight, scrambled to give backup that I hadn't ended up needing.

I climbed down from the alien ship and backed away, reaching M-Bot as the alien ship became a hive of activity. Tucking the translator pin into my pocket, I hauled myself up onto his wing. *Please live,* I thought to the wounded alien. *I need to know what you are.*

"Hmmm," M-Bot said. "Fascinating. Fascinating. She is from a small backwater planet that is not part of the Superiority. It seems the Superiority recently sent a message to her people asking for pilots to recruit into their space force. This pilot was a response to that request; she was sent to try out for the Superiority military."

I blinked, then scuttled over to M-Bot's open cockpit. "What?" I asked. "How do you know *that*?"

"Hmmm? Oh, I hacked her onboard computer. Not a very advanced machine, unfortunately. I was hoping to discover another AI, so we could complain about organics together. Wouldn't that have been a fun time?"

"Fun time!" Doomslug said from where she'd climbed up onto the armrest of my seat.

I slipped into the cockpit. "You really did that?" I asked.

"Complaining about organics? Yes, it's very easy. Did you know just how many dead cells you shed daily? All of those little pieces of you *litter* my cockpit."

"M-Bot, focus. You hacked her computer?"

"Oh! Yes. As I said, it's not very advanced. I got the entire database about her planet, people, culture, history. What do you want to know? Their planet was allied to the human forces in the last war—though many of their politicians now call the human presence there an authoritarian occupation—and several of their cultures were significantly influenced by human ones. Her language isn't too different from your own, for example."

"What is her name?" I asked softly, glancing over at her ship. The buzz of medical technicians around the cockpit gave me hope that she would survive her wound.

"Alanik of the UrDail," he said, pronouncing her name as "ah-la-NEEK." "Her flight logs say she was on her way to visit the Superiority's largest deep-space commerce station. She never arrived though. She seems to have somehow found out where we were, and so came here instead. Oh! Spensa, she's *cytonic,* like you! She is the only one of her people who can use the powers."

I settled back in my seat, feeling numb.

M-Bot didn't notice how much all this was disturbing me, as he just kept right on talking. "Yup, her log is encrypted, but I cracked that. She hoped to find answers about her powers among the Superiority, though her people don't think highly of them. Something about the way they rule."

I can feel *where she was planning to go . . . ,* I thought again. The coordinates were burned into my brain, but they were fading like a dying engine. Sputtering and losing power. I could jump. I could go there. But only if I acted quickly.

I sat frozen in a moment of indecision. Then I stood up in my cockpit and called to Jorgen, who had climbed from his ship to observe the medical staff.

"Jorgen!" I shouted. "I need you to come here *right now* and talk me out of doing something *incredibly stupid*."

He turned toward me, then—with a look of sudden panic—ran over and hauled himself onto M-Bot's wing. I didn't know if I should be thankful he responded so quickly, or be embarrassed by how seriously he seemed to take the threat of me doing something stupid.

"What is it, Spin?" he asked, stepping up to my cockpit.

"That alien put coordinates in my brain," I said, explaining in a rush. "She was going to go try out for the Superiority's space force, since they're recruiting, and she wanted to see if they knew anything about cytonics, but I just realized this is the *perfect* chance to put Rodge's plan into action. If I went and imitated her, it wouldn't seem nearly as odd as if we tried to imitate a Krell. M-Bot got her entire log and planetary database, and I can take her place. You need to stop me because, so help me, I'm just about ready to do it because the coordinates are *evaporating from my brain*."

He blinked at the flood of words coming from my mouth.

"How long do we have?" he asked.

"I can't be sure," I said, anxious as I felt the impression fading. "Not long. Five minutes? Maybe? Yes, and my gut is telling me to go *right now*. Which is why I need you to talk me out of it!"

"All right, let's consider."

"We don't have time to consider!"

"You said we have five minutes. Five minutes' consideration is better than none." Then—like the insufferable rock of protocol he was—he carefully set his helmet on the wing. "Rodge's plan was for you to imitate a Krell pilot and sneak aboard their station here near Detritus."

"Yes, but Cobb doesn't think we could *ever* imitate one of the Krell."

"Then what makes you think you could imitate this alien?"

67

"She is from a backwater world," M-Bot piped up. "Which is not an official part of the Superiority. Nobody in the Superiority will have met any members of her species, so anything Spensa does will not feel out of character."

"She might still seem human to them," Jorgen said.

"Which will be fine," I said. "Because Alanik—that's her name—came from a world that was allies with the humans not long ago."

"Indeed," M-Bot said, "they had a great deal of cultural exchange."

"You don't speak the Superiority languages," Jorgen said.

I hesitated, then fished in my pocket for the translator pin I'd taken from the alien. The medics had her hooked up to a breathing device and were extracting her—carefully—from her ship. I felt a spike of concern, even though I'd only just met her.

I could still feel her touch in my mind. And her plea. A fading arrow in my brain, pointing into the stars.

I held up the pin for Jorgen to see. "I can use this pin to translate for me, I think."

"Confirmed," M-Bot said. "I can set it to output in English so you'll understand what they're saying."

"All right, that's a start," Jorgen said. "Now, can you imitate that pilot's ship with your holograms?"

"I'd need to do a scan of it."

"Well, I guess we don't have time—"

"Done," M-Bot said. Then he shifted to an imitation of the alien's downed ship. It was a far better fit than the Krell ship had been; M-Bot and Alanik's ship were much closer in shape and size.

Jorgen nodded.

"You're thinking I should go," I said to him. "Scud, you actually think I should go through with this!"

"I think we should consider all of our options before making a decision. How much time left?"

"Not much! A minute or two! It's not like I have a clock in my brain. The sensation is just fading. Quickly."

"M-Bot, can you successfully make her look like that alien?"

"If she has the bracelet on," he said.

I scrambled to pull it off his dash and slap it on.

"Handily," M-Bot said, "our medics just finished a scan of her for vitals. And . . . There."

My hands changed color to light purple as he overlaid my face and skin with a hologram of Alanik. M-Bot even changed my flight suit to match hers, and the imitation was perfect.

I stared at my hands, then looked at Jorgen.

"Scud," he whispered. "That's uncanny. All right. So what is the plan?"

"There's no time for a plan!"

"There's time for a quick outline. You go to the recruitment station in this alien's place, then claim to be her. You try out for the enemy's military . . . Wait, why are they recruiting new pilots? They're probably increasing their troop numbers to come fight us, right?"

"Yeah," I said. That would make sense.

"That might be useful. If you did this, you could gather valuable intel on their operations. From there, you would try to steal a hyperdrive—or get some pictures of one for the engineers—then you teleport back here. Do you think you can get back on your own?"

I grimaced. "I don't know. My powers . . . aren't very consistent. But Alanik's records said she was going to the Superiority because she hoped to learn about her own abilities from them."

"So either you'll have to figure that out, or you'll *have* to steal a hyperdrive somehow, then get yourself and M-Bot back to us with the stolen technology."

"Yeah." It sounded impossible when he outlined it like that. Yet I looked up toward the stars, and I felt a fire burning within me. "It sounds crazy," I told him. "But Jorgen, I think I have to go. I *have* to try this."

I looked down, meeting his eyes as he stood on the wing beside my cockpit. Then, remarkably, he nodded. "I agree."

"You *do*?"

"Spin, you can be reckless—even foolhardy—but I've flown with you nearly a year now. I trust your instincts."

"My instincts get me into trouble."

He reached over, putting his hand on the side of my face. "You've gotten *us* out of far more trouble than you've ever gotten *yourself* into, Spensa. Scud, I don't know if this mission is the right thing to do. But I *do* know our people are in serious danger. We talk optimistically, but the command staff knows the truth. We're dead here unless we find a way to use hyperdrives ourselves."

I put my hand on his. The information in my brain was dimming. Only seconds remained.

"Can you do this?" he asked me. "Does your gut say you can?"

"Yes," I whispered. Then, more firmly—with the strength of a warrior—I repeated it. "Yes. I *can* do this, Jorgen. I'll get us a hyperdrive and bring it back. I promise."

"Then go. I trust you."

I realized that was what I needed. Not his permission, or even his approval. I needed his trust.

In a moment of impulse I sprang from the cockpit, then grabbed him by his flight suit and pulled him down so I could kiss him. We probably weren't ready for that, and it probably wasn't the time, but I did it anyway. Because . . . well, scud. He'd just encouraged me to trust my instincts.

It was wonderful. I felt a strength to him as he kissed me back, an almost *electricity* coursing through him into me—then back again stronger because of the fire that burned in my chest. I lingered in the kiss as long as I dared, then pulled away.

"I should go with you," he said.

"Unfortunately," M-Bot said, "we have only one mobile receptor. You'd be identified as a human immediately."

Jorgen grunted. "I suppose someone has to explain this to Cobb anyway."

"He's going to be mad . . . ," I said.

"He'll understand. We made the best decision we could with the limited time and information we had. Saints help us, I think we have to try this. Go."

I held his eyes for a moment, then broke the gaze and jumped back down into the cockpit.

Jorgen touched his lips with his hand, then shook himself, picked up his helmet, and leaped off M-Bot's wing. He pulled back to where everyone else was focused on the alien's ship, oblivious to the powerful moments that had transpired.

"I'm confused at what just happened between the two of you," M-Bot said. "I thought you insisted to me several times that you had no romantic inclinations toward Jorgen."

"I lied," I said, seizing on the compelling sensation the alien had embedded in my brain. It was nearly gone, but it still felt like an arrow into the sky. Just as it threatened to disappear completely, I somehow yanked on it.

"Cytonic hyperdrive online," M-Bot said. "It actually—"

We vanished.

PART TWO

9

I was only in the nowhere for a moment, but in that place, time seemed to have no meaning. I floated alone, with no ship. Infinite blackness surrounded me, punctuated by lights that seemed so much like stars—only malevolent. They could see me hanging there, exposed. I felt like a rat suddenly dropped on a string into the middle of a cage full of starving wolves.

The eyes focused on me, and their anger built. I was trespassing in their domain. I was an insignificant worm . . . but my presence still brought them *pain*. My world and theirs did not belong together. Their lights surged toward me. They'd rip my very soul to shreds and leave only scraps of—

I appeared back in M-Bot's cockpit.

"—worked!" M-Bot finished.

"Ah!" I yelled, jolting. I grabbed the sides of my cockpit seat. "Did you see any of that?"

"See what?" M-Bot said. "My chronometer indicates no time has passed. You engaged the cytonic hyperdrive . . . or, well, I think you *are* the cytonic hyperdrive."

I put my hand to my chest, pressing it against the thick material of my flight suit, which seemed very strange now that it was the wrong color. My heart raced and my mind reeled. That place . . . the nowhere. It had been like swimming through a deep-cavern lake without any lights. All the while knowing *things* lay beneath, watching me, reaching for me . . .

That was them, I thought. *The things that destroyed the people of Detritus. The things we saw in the recording.* The delvers were real. They and the eyes *were* the same thing.

I breathed in and out deeply, calming myself with effort. At least the hyperjump had worked. I had used my powers again, with the help of the coordinates that Alanik had placed in my mind.

Right. Time to be a hero. I could do this.

"Spensa!" M-Bot said. "We're being contacted!"

"By who?" I asked.

"By whom!" Doomslug said from beside me.

"You've brought us in near a Superiority space station of some size," M-Bot said. "Look at your five. The radio chatter here is quiet, but distinct."

I rested my hand comfortingly on Doomslug, who was fluting in annoyance, perhaps sensing my discomfort. I searched in the direction M-Bot had indicated, and saw something I'd missed in my first brief scan of the starfield. It was a distant station of some sort—lights in the darkness that were clustered around a central flat plane.

"Starsight," I said. "That's what the alien, Alanik, called it." I scrambled to pull on my helmet and buckle in. "They're contacting us? What are they saying?"

"Someone on the station is asking us for identification," M-Bot said. "They're speaking in Dione, a Superiority standard language."

"Can you spoof Alanik's transponder signal?"

"Doing so."

"Great. Then stall them for a little bit while I think through this."

M-Bot clearly still looked like the alien ship, and—judging by my soft violet hands—my hologram was still working as well. If this mission failed, it wouldn't be due to the limitations of the technology—it would be because of the limitations of the spy.

"First things first," I said. "We need to check our retreat and see if we can get home, if things go poorly. Give me just another minute or so."

I breathed in and out, calming myself, doing the exercises Gran-Gran had taught me. Exercises she'd learned from her mother, who had been the one who'd hyperjumped our old space fleet before we'd crashed on Detritus.

I'd jumped here to perform this mission, but I wanted to know: Could I jump back if I needed to? Everything would get a whole lot easier if this expansion of my powers, as granted by Alanik touching my brain, could work again.

I imagined myself floating in space . . . stars zipping around . . . Yes, having just hyperjumped, I felt a familiarity to the action. The nowhere was close. I'd *just* been there. I could return.

Those things would see me again.

Don't think about that, I told myself sternly. I concentrated on the exercise. I was flying, shooting through the stars, zipping away . . .

Where? That was the problem. For anything other than a very short jump, I'd need to know exactly where I was going. I couldn't simply reverse the directions Alanik had given me, because they hadn't included my starting point of Detritus, only my destination of this space station.

"M-Bot," I said, coming out of my trance. "Can you calculate our location?"

77

"Currently calculating, using astronomical data. But I warn you, Spensa, my stalling is *not* working. They're sending ships out to investigate."

"What have you been doing?"

"Sending them binary code."

"What?" I said. "That's how you decided to *stall*?"

"I don't know! I figured, 'Organics like dumb things, and this is pretty dumb.' In hindsight, maybe it wasn't dumb enough? Anyway, they'll have visual on us within the minute."

The moment of truth. I took a deep breath. I was a warrior. Trained by my grandmother from childhood to face my heroic destiny with courage. *You* can *do this,* I told myself. *It's just a battle of a different kind. Like Hua Mulan or Epipole of Carystus, going to battle wearing another person's identity.*

I'd heard those stories a dozen times over from Gran-Gran. The thing was, the subterfuge of both women had eventually been discovered. And it hadn't exactly gone well for either one.

I'd just have to be sure not to end up like them. I turned M-Bot as two ships approached from the distant station. Boxy and painted white, they were like the Krell shuttlecraft I'd seen at the space station near Detritus.

The two ships leveled off with mine, rotating to the same axis so we could see each other through the glassy fronts of their crafts. The pilots were a pair of aliens with crimson skin. They didn't wear helmets, and I could see that they were hairless and had prominent eye ridges and cheekbones. They looked basically humanoid—two arms, one head—but were alien enough that I couldn't distinguish their gender.

M-Bot patched through their communication, and alien chatter filled my cockpit. I dug out Alanik's translating device and clicked it on, and the chatter was translated into her language, which didn't do me a whole lot of good.

"M-Bot," I hissed. "You said you'd fix that."

"Whoops," he said. "Hacking into the pin's language inter-face . . . Ha! I activated the English setting."

"Unidentified ship," an alien said. "Do you require assistance? Please classify yourself."

I launched right into it. No choice now. "My name is Alanik of the UrDail. I'm a pilot and messenger from the planet . . ."

"ReDawn," M-Bot whispered.

"From the planet ReDawn. I have come to be a pilot for you guys. Um, in your space force. Like you asked?" I winced. That wasn't terribly convincing. "Sorry about the odd communication earlier. My computer can be a real pain sometimes."

"Ha ha," M-Bot said to me. "*That* was sarcasm. I can tell be-cause it wasn't actually funny."

The two patrol ships were silent for some time, probably having switched over to a private comm line. I was left to wait, hanging there in space, worrying. I examined their boxy white ships—and oddly, I couldn't find any weapon ports on them.

"Emissary Alanik," one of the aliens said, coming back on, "Platform Docking Authority sends you welcome. It seems they have been expecting you, though they note that you're later than you said you'd be."

"Um," I said. "Some unimportant troubles back home. But it's possible I might have to leave in a little bit, then come back again."

"Whatever you wish. For now, you've got dock clearance. Berth 1182, which is in the seventh sector. An official will meet you there. Enjoy your visit."

With that, they turned around and flew back toward the station.

I remained tense. Surely this was a trap. Surely they'd seen through my crude attempt at subterfuge. I eased forward on the throttle, following after the two ships—and they didn't react.

I had them right in my sights. I could have blown them both from the sky, particularly with how closely—and lackadaisically—they were flying. How in the name of the Seventy Saints could they stand having their backs to me? The smart thing would have been to have me fly on ahead at a safe distance, so they could watch me from a position of power.

I accelerated, but stayed in range to fire on the ships if they turned on me. They didn't seem to even *notice*. If this was a trap, they were doing an awfully good acting job.

Doomslug fluted nervously. I agreed.

"M-Bot," I said, "have you calculated where we are yet?"

"Indeed," he said. "We're not too far from Detritus—only some forty light-years. This station, which you correctly named Starsight, is an important trading waystop. It houses the Superiority regional government."

"Give me the coordinates—the direction and distance to Detritus."

"Easy," M-Bot said. "Data is on your screen."

Several long numbers popped up on my proximity screen's readout. I frowned, then reached out to locate them with my fledgling cytonic senses. Only, reached out to . . . where? Those numbers were so large, they barely meant anything to me. Sure, they told me where Detritus was, but I still didn't *know* where it was. Couldn't *feel* it, like I had when Alanik sent me her cytonic impression of Starsight's location.

"That's not going to work," I said. "I won't be able to get us out unless I figure out more about my powers."

"Theoretically," M-Bot said, "we'll be leaving with a stolen Superiority hyperdrive, right?"

"That's the plan. I'd just feel better about this if I knew we had an escape route. How long would it take to fly back to Detritus the long way?"

"By the 'long way' you mean at sublight speeds?" M-Bot said. "That would probably take us roughly four hundred years, depending on how close to light speed we managed to get before using half our power, then accounting for deceleration on the other end. Sure, time dilation would make it seem like less time passed for us—but only about four years' difference at that speed, so you'd still be super-dead by the time we arrived."

Great. That wasn't an option. But Jorgen and I had both known that I might end up trapped here. This was the mission. It was unlike anything I'd undertaken before, but I was the only one who could do it.

I boosted, drawing closer to the station, which was larger than I'd estimated. Scale and size were difficult to judge in space. The station looked kind of like one of the platforms that surrounded Detritus. A floating city—shaped like a disc, with buildings sprouting from both sides. A bubble of something glowing and blue surrounded it.

I'd always assumed that people lived *inside* stations like this, but as we drew closer and closer, I saw that wasn't the case. People lived on the *surface* of this station, walking about with the open blackness above them. *That bubble must keep in air and heat, making it habitable.* Indeed, as we drew closer, the two patrol ships passed through the bluish shield.

I stopped outside that shell. Then, one last time, I tried to use my cytonic senses. I reached out in the direction M-Bot had indicated, and felt a faint . . . fluttering at the edges of my mind. That was the right direction. I could feel someone there. Alanik, maybe?

It wasn't enough. I couldn't teleport myself back. So it was time to enter the enemy's base. I braced myself, then guided my ship through the envelope of the air shield.

10

It was beautiful.

As my alien guides led me closer, I could see that the station flowed with greenery. Parks filled with trees that towered some ten or fifteen meters tall. Large swaths of a dark green substance that M-Bot identified as a kind of moss, soft to walk on.

Back on Detritus, life was austere. Sure, there was the occasional statue, but buildings on the surface were plain and simple—they were built more like bunkers. And down below, the caverns were dominated by the apparatus and the red light of the manufactories. Humankind had existed on the brink of extinction for so long that survival—by necessity—trumped expression.

This place, in contrast, proclaimed its artistry like a battle standard. Buildings rose in spiral patterns or marched in colorful rows. It seemed like every second block contained a park. I could see the people moving among it all with a certain lazy cast to them, many idling in parks. Ships that floated around in the atmosphere didn't seem to be in any particular hurry. Here, people relaxed and enjoyed themselves.

I distrusted the place immediately.

Alanik had told me not to trust their peace. While I didn't know that I could trust *her*, I certainly didn't need a warning. The Superiority had kept my people imprisoned on Detritus for the last eighty years. My father and many of my friends had been killed because of the Superiority. The place could feign a beautiful, welcoming air, but I would *not* let down my guard.

"There is almost no radio chatter," M-Bot said. "Nor is there a single wireless network."

"They're afraid of delvers," I said, shivering. "They must have the same traditions that we have—limiting wireless communication only to necessary situations."

"Indeed. Fortunately, I've been able to deduce our prescribed landing location by reading the numbers of bays we've passed. I'll map it for you."

I followed his directions to an open metallic field of small raised platforms near the center of the city. As I set down on the proper one, I sank into my seat. Like Platform Prime, this place had an artificial gravity field.

"Pressure has been equalized with the outside," M-Bot said. "And the atmosphere is breathable for you, though with a higher oxygen content than you're accustomed to. Initial scans indicate no dangerous microorganisms."

All right. I opened the canopy. An alien with a squidlike face stepped over to my ship. "Steps, ramp, slime slide, or other?" they called up to me, my pin translating.

"Um . . ." I gestured for them to wait, hoping they'd understand, then hissed to M-Bot. "Wait, what if they recognize that I'm speaking in English, instead of Alanik's language?"

"I don't think any of them will know her language," M-Bot replied. "In fact, she would probably have had to speak an Earth language to be understood. Her records indicate she spoke fluent

83

Mandarin, and you saw that she knew some English. Her planet did spend three decades acting as a staging ground for human forces during the last war, after all."

"And the people here will understand English?"

"The translator pins they wear should. Alanik's records indicate there were three attempted human galactic conquests in the past, and that left many cultures knowing Earth languages. All translators seem to carry English, Spanish, Hindi, and Mandarin by default."

I nodded, moving to call to the dockworkers—but then I hesitated. "Wait. What was that you said? My ancestors tried to conquer the galaxy *three times*?"

"And quite nearly succeeded each time," M-Bot said. "According to the records on Alanik's ship. Many in the Superiority apparently name the 'human scourge' the greatest threat the galaxy has ever known."

Wow. I was impressed, though a little piece of me was also . . . disturbed. It was inspiring to hear that my ancestors had been the heroic warriors I'd always imagined, but at the same time I'd always thought of my kind as being oppressed. Unjustly and unfairly beaten down by the Krell, denied freedom by a terrible alien force.

Surely there was a reason we'd been *forced* to fight. Besides, enemy propaganda could claim what it wanted; that didn't justify what had been done to us on Detritus. I narrowed my eyes, determined not to believe their lies.

"Sorry," I said, leaning out to call to the dockworkers. "Had a communication I had to deal with. You asked if I wanted a ramp or steps? Steps will be fine."

The squid-faced creature waved, and a larger creature with a grey-stone appearance rolled over a set of mobile steps. I hesitated, looking out at the bustling alien city. The place felt dark, even with large spotlights on the tops of buildings illuminating everything. The sky was still black. From inside, I couldn't see the air bubble as I looked up—I just saw an endless expanse, the stars mostly washed out by the lights.

"Let's see," the squid-faced creature said, climbing up the steps to join me. "You've got diplomatic berthing privileges. So take your time! We'll get this ship washed up and—"

"No," I said. "Please. I'm very protective of my ship. Don't let anyone touch it."

The alien's translator interpreted my words, then their squid tentacles slithered in a distinctly annoyed expression. "You sure?"

"Yes," I said, imagining someone discovering the hologram. "Please."

"Well, all right," the creature said, typing something on a handheld screen. This being had long, wiggly arms that ended in a branching pair of two blue tentacles instead of hands. "Here's an access ticket, if you want to send anyone else with authorization to fly the ship. I suggest you not lose it." The tablet ejected a small chip, which the squid creature handed over. Then they climbed back down the steps.

I pocketed the chip, and was again struck by how good M-Bot's holograms were. He had overlapped my flight suit with an image of Alanik's, but the pocket was still right where I expected. And interacting with solid objects—like touching the chip with my hologram-coated fingers—didn't disturb the illusion.

This, and the fact that the alien hadn't reacted to me speaking English, made my confidence grow. What next? I had to find out how to sign up for their military. That was step one. After that, I could try the more difficult part—stealing a hyperdrive.

How did I start, though? This place was *enormous*. Outside the docking area, the city streets stretched for kilometers, lined with towering buildings and bustling foot traffic. Ships zoomed overhead. There had to be millions upon millions of people here.

The aliens who intercepted me above, I thought, *said that someone would be sent to meet me once I landed.* Which gave me some time, so I settled in and reached out with my mind again, trying to find Detritus. Only, something was blocking my senses. A . . . thickness. It was like trying to move in high gravity. *Huh.* As I was considering that, someone outside the cockpit spoke loudly, and my pin translated.

"Emissary Alanik?" the voice asked.

I leaned out to find an alien standing on my launchpad. They were a tall, slender creature with vivid blue skin. This species seemed to be of a similar race to the crimson ones I'd seen earlier piloting the patrol ships—this individual also lacked hair and had the same cheekbones and eye ridges.

The creature wore a set of robes that were a softer, paler blue than their skin tone. Like the others, this one had androgynous features. I couldn't tell if they were male or female—or something else entirely—from their appearance or voice.

"Ah!" they said to me. "Emissary. We are very glad you decided to respond to our request! I am Cuna, and have been assigned to aid you during this visit. Would you mind coming down? I've arranged for you to have housing here on Starsight, and I can show you the way."

"Sure!" I called. "Let me stow my helmet." I ducked back into the cockpit. "All right, M-Bot. Tell me what to do."

"How should I know?" he replied. "This was your plan."

"Technically, it's Rodge's plan. Either way, I'm not a spy—but you were designed for this kind of operation. So tell me what to do. How should I act?"

"Spensa, you've seen me interact with organics. You really think I'm going to be able to do a better job than you at imitating another one?"

He had a point. Scud. "This is going to be difficult. That alien down there seems to know something about Alanik and her people. What if I say something wrong?"

"Maybe you could pretend to be quiet, and not speak much."

"Quiet?" I asked. "Me?"

"Yes. Pretend that Alanik is reserved."

"Reserved. *Me?*"

"You see, that is why it's called *pretending*. Rodge and I have been working on this—my ability to accept that sometimes human beings do not accurately present who they are. In any case, maybe this would have been something good to think about *before* volunteering for the spy mission behind enemy lines."

"We didn't have much time to think." Still, there was no helping it. I tried to keep a warrior's calm as I retrieved the sidearm from my weapons locker and tucked it into the voluminous pocket of my flight suit's trousers. That attitude was growing harder and harder to attain as I realized the magnitude of what this mission would require of me.

I put in the tiny wireless earpiece that paired with the mobile receptor bracelet to let M-Bot talk to me privately from a distance, and he disguised it as jewelry with a hologram. Then I put Doomslug on the back floor of the cockpit and pointed at her. "Stay," I said.

"Stay?" she fluted.

"I'm serious."

"Serious?"

I was pretty sure she couldn't understand me—she was just a slug. Hopefully she'd stay put for once. Finally, I heaved myself out and climbed down to the launchpad.

"Sorry for the delay," I said to Cuna.

Their translator worked, spitting the words out for them, and—like the dockworker—Cuna either didn't notice I'd spoken in English, or didn't care.

"Not at all, not at all," Cuna said, tucking their tablet under their arm. "I'm extremely pleased to meet you. It was by my personal request that an offer was sent to your people."

Scud. I'd been hoping that the people here wouldn't know much about Alanik's. I'd been under the impression that a general call for pilots had been made, not individual requests.

"You're that interested in my people?" I asked.

"Oh, yes. We're preparing a very special operation, for which we will need an unusually large number of trained pilots. It has been decided that this might be an excellent way for the Superiority to judge the skill of some races that have stood for too long outside the Superiority's fold. But that is a discussion for a little later! Come. Let me show you to your housing."

Cuna started off down a path among the launchpads, and I had no choice but to follow. I hated leaving my ship behind, but M-Bot's mobile receptor had a good hundred-kilometer communication range to it. Plus, the hologram would continue to work even if I went outside that range, so I shouldn't need to worry.

I hurried along behind Cuna and exited the landing area. *Don't gawk*, I told myself. *Don't gawk. Don't gawk.*

I gawked.

It was impossible to resist. Buildings towered high on either side of the walkway, like runways toward the stars. People of all shapes, sizes, and colors flowed around me—all dressed in clothing like I'd never seen. No one was wearing anything that even remotely looked like a uniform.

It was all so much to take in. Far overhead, ships darted in every direction, but between us and them, floating discs with acclivity rings on the bottom ferried people quickly from one section of the city to another. It was a place of constant motion and lush indulgence. Gardens on every other corner, shops selling clothing of all varieties. Scents of unfamiliar foods drifting from stalls.

There had to be at least a thousand different races represented here, but two varieties were by far more common than others. The first was the Krell. I jumped despite myself as I saw the first one march by, though this one looked slightly different from the bodies we'd recovered from the manned fighters we'd shot down. The armor these Krell wore was crystalline instead of metallic, and looked more like brownish-pink sandstone. The shape of it was the same—something like the old pictures I'd seen of Earth knights. Only, these Krell wore a helmet with a clear faceplate, revealing a liquid within and a small crablike creature piloting from inside the head.

I'd always seen the Krell as imposing, dangerous. They were battlefield warriors, clad in armor and ready for a fight. Yet here they were mostly in stalls, selling goods to passersby, waving clawlike armored arms in sweeping gestures. My translator picked up their calls, delivering the words of the various shopkeepers as we passed.

"Come, friend! Be welcome!"

"A wonderful outfit you wear, and well accompanied!"

"Have you heard about the recruitment effort? Don't worry if you don't want to listen!"

One stumbled a little close to me, and although I instinctively reached for my pocket—and the weapon hidden in it—the creature apologized *at least* six times while backing away.

"This is curious," M-Bot said in my ear. "I'm recording all of this for later analysis."

"Those are the—"

"Don't speak to me!" M-Bot told me in my ear. "Cuna's translator will translate the words for them. My stealth systems can mask our communication, but you should endeavor to pretend you don't have a wireless link to anyone. Later, we'll set up your bracelet so you can tap instructions to me in DDF flight code. For now, I suggest you just stay quiet."

I snapped my mouth closed. Cuna gave me an inquisitive look, but I just shook my head and smiled as we kept walking.

But scud, the Krell. When I'd first traveled into space and

confronted them a few months back, they'd been *terrified* of me. Perhaps that had to do with the way my people had nearly conquered the galaxy, but these things *all* seemed to be timid. How could they be the same mighty force that had kept humankind imprisoned on Detritus for eighty years?

This place had to be some kind of false front, I decided. A propaganda strategy meant to improve the Superiority's image. It made sense. Create a big hub where lots of races visit, then pretend to be harmless and unassuming.

More confident that I understood what was going on, I continued to survey my surroundings. The other most common alien race here was the ones like Cuna, my guide. They wore a variety of clothing types, from robes to casual trousers and shirts, and seemed to come in three different skin shades. Crimson, blue, and dark purple.

"Overwhelming, isn't it?" Cuna asked.

I nodded. That was the truth, at least.

"If I may be so bold," Cuna continued. "Your people were wise in agreeing to send us a pilot. If you do well in this preliminary program, we can enter into a more formal deal with your people. In exchange for an entire force of pilots, we will offer the UrDail citizenship. It has been a long time coming; I'm glad to see relations between us normalizing."

"It's a good deal," I said, choosing my words carefully. "You get pilots. We get to join the Superiority."

"As secondary citizens," Cuna said. "Of course."

"Of course," I said, though I must have sounded hesitant, because Cuna glanced at me.

"You aren't clear on the distinction?"

"I'm sure the politicians understand," I said. "I'm just a pilot."

"Still, it would be good for you to know the stakes of your test here. You see, your people are special. Most species who haven't yet joined the Superiority are relatively primitive—with a low intelligence designation. They tend to be brutal, warlike, and technologically backward.

"The UrDail, on the other hand, have been a spacefaring people for centuries now. You have nearly reached primary intelligence and have a functioning world government. Normally, you'd have been invited among our ranks generations ago. Except for one big black mark."

Cytonics? I wondered.

"Humans," Cuna said as we walked. "You fought alongside the human scourge during the Third Human War a century back."

"They forced us to do so," I answered.

"I would not seek to dispute the facts as you present them," Cuna said. "Suffice it to say that many within the Superiority are convinced you are too aggressive to join us."

"Too aggressive?" I said, frowning. "But . . . didn't you come to us looking to recruit fighter pilots?"

"It is a delicate balance," Cuna said. "We have some very special projects that require pilots, but we don't want to corrupt our military with those who are too aggressive. Some say that your people's proximity to humans has let their ways infiltrate your society."

"And . . . what do you think?" I asked.

"I am part of the Department of Species Integration," Cuna replied. "Personally I believe there is a home for many different types of species in the Superiority. You can be an advantage to us, should you prove worthy."

"Sounds great," I said dryly, then immediately winced at the tone. Maybe I *should* just try not to say anything.

Cuna eyed me, but when they spoke, their voice was calm. "Surely you can see the advantages to your people. You'll have access to our galactic hubs such as this station, and the right to buy passage and cargo space on our trade ships. You will no longer be trapped in your little planetary system, but can experience the galaxy at large."

"We already can though," I said. "I came here on my own."

Cuna stopped, and at first I worried I'd said something wrong. Then Cuna smiled. It was a distinctly *disturbing* expression on their face, predatory, showing too many teeth. "Well," they said. "That is another matter which we shall discuss."

Cuna turned and waved their hand toward a small, narrow building alongside the road. Squeezed between two larger structures, it was three stories high. Like all the buildings on the platform, it seemed to have been made of metal originally—but it had been painted to give it a fake brick look.

"Here is the building we offer for your quarters," Cuna said. "It is large for one individual, but it is our hope that—once you've proven yourself—we can house an entire squadron or more of your pilots here. We thought it appropriate to give you this to begin. As you can see, it has a private docking berth on the top, should you wish to land your ship here. It is conveniently located near the main docks, however—and close to several parks and markets."

Cuna started up the short steps leading to the building.

"I don't like this," M-Bot said in my ear. "Spensa? If you get killed in an ambush, I'm going to be very surprised."

I hesitated. Could this be some sort of trap? To what end? They could have just blown me out of the sky—or at least tried to—during my approach.

"That was me practicing lying," M-Bot noted. "I wouldn't be surprised, because I just anticipated it. But I *would* be disappointed. Well, I'd simulate disappointment."

I headed up the steps. Cuna did seem to think that I really was Alanik. It didn't feel like a trap.

Together, we stepped into the building. I was used to being the shortest person in the room, but Cuna's limber build—which was too willowy to feel human—made me feel not just short, but squat and awkward as well. This building had high ceilings and doorways, and even the counters were a tad too tall for me. It seemed to have been built for people of a taller race, though Alanik had been about my height.

Cuna led me to a small room at the front that was lit by recessed ceiling lights and had a window looking out at the street. The room was comfortable-looking, furnished with plush chairs and a boardroom-style table. The walls had been painted to make them seem like wood—though tapping one with my fingernail proved they were metal.

Cuna sat down with a graceful motion, setting their tablet on the table, then smiled at me again with that too-predatory look. I lingered near the door, unwilling to sit and put my back to my exit.

"You are what we call a cytonic, Alanik," Cuna said to me. "Your people don't have true faster-than-light travel or hyperdrives, so you have to rely on cytonic people. And since you have very few, you remain primarily locked into your backwater of the galaxy."

Cuna met my eyes, and I could swear I saw careful calculation in there.

I felt increasingly on edge. They seemed to know more about Alanik than I would've wanted. "What can you tell me?" I asked. "About what I am. About what I can do."

Cuna settled back in the seat, lacing their fingers, lips drawn to an emotionless line. "What you do is dangerous, Emissary Alanik. Surely you've felt the attention of the delvers on you, in the negative realm where you go between moments when you're engaging in a hyperspace jump?"

I nodded. "I call it the nowhere."

"I've never experienced it myself," Cuna said idly. "And the delvers? You've felt them?"

"I see eyes watching me. The eyes of something that lives in that place."

"That is them," Cuna said. "Centuries ago, my kind learned firsthand how dangerous the delvers are. Thirteen of the . . . creatures entered into our realm. They rampaged, destroying planet after planet.

"Eventually, we realized that our cytonics had drawn them to us—and once here, delvers could hear our communications. Not just cytonic communication; they could hear even things like radio waves. We made the painful transition away from using cytonics, and even normal communications. We made our planets, and our fleets, silent.

"The delvers, blessedly, left. It took decades, but one by one they faded back to their realm. The galaxy crept out of its proverbial shell—but with new understandings and new rules."

"No cytonics," I whispered. "Be careful with wireless signals, even radio."

"Yes," Cuna said. "And avoid using AI, which angers the delvers. Most normal communications aren't capable of bringing the creatures into our realm—but once they're here, they hear us talking, and it draws them to feast. Even now, centuries later, we hold to these prohibitions. Though no delvers are in our realm, it is better to be safe."

I swallowed. "I'm . . . surprised that you let any cytonics continue to live."

Cuna raised their hand to their throat in an expression that I interpreted as shock. "What would you have us do?"

"Attack anyone who has cytonics."

"Barbaric! That sort of behavior would not be becoming of people who have achieved primary intelligence. No, we do not exterminate species. Even the human scourge has been carefully sectioned off and isolated, rather than destroyed!"

I knew that was, at least in part, a lie. They'd been trying to destroy us recently.

"Such violent measures aren't necessary," Cuna said. "A single cytonic here and there, like yourself, is not a danger. Particularly untrained as you are. It took our early cytonics generations to progress to the skills necessary to draw the delvers. So you are a danger, yes, but not an immediate one.

"For now we feel it is best to try to persuade people like yours to follow our ways, rather than risking . . . peril to us all. You see, we of the Superiority have developed better means of traveling the stars—hyperdrives that *don't* draw delvers."

"I know of those," I said. *And I'm going to steal one.*

"The entire galaxy will be far safer once every race makes use of the Superiority's hyperdrive ships. This is the express implication of our offer: if you provide us with pilots, we will grant you citizenship—and the right to passage on our safe FTL ships. You don't get the technology itself; we must keep it secure. But your merchants, tourists, and officials can use our ships, just like everyone else in the Superiority.

"We are the only ones in the galaxy with access to this technology; you will find no black market FTL drives for sale, because they do not exist. No race has succeeded in stealing even a single hyperdrive from us. And so, the only safe way to travel the stars is to gain our favor. Prove to me that your pilots are as skilled as reported, and in return I will open the galaxy to you."

I didn't trust that propaganda as the truth. Of *course* Cuna would say that the technology wasn't possible to steal. Unfortunately, they also said that others had tried.

I had to find a way to succeed where others had failed, and while the Superiority might be watching me. "But why do you *need* pilots?" I asked, trying to get more information. "The

Superiority's population is enormous. Surely you have plenty of your own pilots. What is this special project you want us for?"

It's for fighting my people as Jorgen said, isn't it? It could be no coincidence that the Superiority would start recruiting pilots for some special mission now, after my people had started to break out of Detritus.

Cuna sat for a moment, meeting my eyes. "This is a very delicate matter, Emissary Alanik. I would appreciate your discretion."

"Sure. Of course."

"We have . . . reason to believe the delvers are watching us," Cuna said softly, "and that they might soon return."

I drew in a sharp breath. Memories of what had happened to the original inhabitants of Detritus were fresh in my mind from the video. Cuna's words should have been shocking, but instead they hit me with a numb sense of reality. Like the anticipated last note of a song.

"This is not the fault of cytonics," Cuna continued. "Not this time. We fear that the delvers have simply decided to turn their attention upon our realm again."

"What do we do?" I asked.

"We will not again be forced to cower and simply wait until the delvers decide to leave. We have been developing a secret weapon to fight them, should it be needed. Unfortunately, in order to put this weapon into action, we need skilled fighter pilots. Contrary to what you assume, we have a very small military. A . . . side effect of our peaceful natures. The Superiority governs not through force of might, but through technological enlightenment."

"Meaning," I said, "that you don't fight against races you don't like—you just leave them alone, without FTL. You don't *need* to have a military since you control travel instead."

Cuna laced their fingers again and didn't reply to that. It seemed enough of a confirmation to me, and suddenly a lot of things made sense. Why didn't the Superiority field a large number of fighters to destroy my people? Why did I meet so few manned ships or skilled aces during our fights? Why only a hundred drones at once? The Superiority simply didn't *have* many fighter pilots.

I'd assumed the only way to rule an empire was to have a vast military. They'd figured out another method. If you could absolutely control access to hyperdrives, you didn't *need* to fight your enemies. It took hundreds of years to travel between planets at sublight speeds. Nobody could attack you if they couldn't get to you.

Cuna leaned forward. "I am not unimportant in the government here, Alanik, and have taken a personal interest in your people. I consider the delvers to be a serious threat. If the UrDail provide the pilots I need, I could make everything move smoothly for your people—perhaps paving the way for your people to be offered *primary* citizenship."

"All right," I said. "How do we begin?"

"Though I am part of the group planning to fight the delvers, I am not in charge of the operation. It is instead run by the Department of Protective Services. They are primarily tasked with resolving external threats to the Superiority. For example, they are in charge of containing the human scourge."

"The . . . humans?"

"Yes. I assure you, your old . . . enemies are no threat to you anymore. The Department of Protective Services maintains observation platforms above their prisons, and is careful to see that no humans ever escape."

Prisons.

Plural. *Prisons.*

We weren't the only ones. I held in a shout for joy, just barely—in part because my mood was dampened by the next realization. This Department of Protective Services that Cuna mentioned . . . that had to be the group we called the Krell.

So I was going to be working directly for the Krell?

"You'll need to pass their test to become a pilot," Cuna said. "They have allowed me to insert a few specially chosen people in the tryouts. You see, there are disagreements among the departments, as we each have our . . . theories on how to best deal with the delvers. I see your kind as perfect for the duty. You have the martial traditions from your days of unfortunate involvement with humans—but at the same time you are peaceful enough to be trusted.

"I want you to prove me right. Try out for the project tomorrow, then represent my interests in the training that follows. If you succeed, then I will *personally* shepherd your people safely to their citizenship."

Cuna smiled again. I shivered at the dangerous way their lips curled. Suddenly I felt *way* out of my league. I'd originally assumed Cuna to be some minor bureaucrat who had been assigned to Alanik. That wasn't the case at all. Cuna wanted to use Alanik as a pawn in some political game far beyond my understanding.

I realized I was sweating, then wondered how the hologram would represent sweat dripping down my face—or if it even could. I licked my lips, my mouth having gone dry before Cuna's careful stare.

Don't stress about their politics, I told myself. *You only have one mission: steal a hyperdrive. Do whatever it takes to gain their trust so they let you near one.*

"I . . . I'll do my best," I said.

"Excellent. I will see you at the test tomorrow; the coordinates and instructions are on this datapad, which I will leave with you. Be warned, however, that your cytonic abilities will be muted here on Starsight—and you won't be able to hyperjump away unless you fly out to a prescribed point first—because of our cytoshield."

Cuna stood, leaving their tablet on the table. "I've included the details about the delver project on this datapad as well—though specifics on the weapon itself are classified. If you need to reach me before tomorrow, send a message to . . ."

Cuna trailed off, then turned their head and flashed their teeth toward the window in a strange sign of aggression.

"Well," they said, "that's going to be a bother."

"What?" I asked. Then I heard it. Sirens. Within seconds, a ship with flashing lights lowered down from the sky to land in front of our building.

"Let me handle this," Cuna said, and opened the door to walk out.

I hesitated in the doorway, baffled. Then I saw the person who climbed out of the ship.

It was a human woman.

11

A human. She was young, perhaps in her early twenties, and wore an unfamiliar blue-and-red uniform. A Krell climbed out of the ship after her, like an armored knight, though the "armor" carapace was deep green and crystalline.

"What's happening?" M-Bot asked. "Are those sirens?"

I ignored him and tore out of the building, my hand thrust into the pocket of my flight suit—holding the small destructor pistol I carried there. A *human*.

Scud. I stopped on the stairs, and Cuna moved out in front of me, stepping with a smooth and calm gait. I tried to force myself to relax as the human and the Krell walked up to us.

"Oh my," the Krell said, voice projected from the front of their armor as they made several wild gestures. "Cuna of the Department of Species Integration! I did not expect to find you here. My, my."

"I left a specific annotation on the report, Winzik," Cuna said. "Mentioning the arrival of this pilot. She is from one of the species I've invited to try out for our program."

"My, my. And is this our emissary? I did not even know you

were coming. You must think us so disorganized! Our departments normally communicate with one another much better than this!"

I stepped out from behind Cuna. I didn't need anyone to shelter me, particularly not an alien I didn't trust. But at the same time . . . one of the Krell. Talking directly to me.

I knew, logically, that KRELL was an acronym for *Ketos redgor Earthen listro listrins,* the alien name of the police force that watched my people. The race of beings like this one was called the varvax. I knew all that, but still couldn't help associating these little crabs in the crystalline armor with the word *Krell.*

The human lingered behind, and was drawing immediate attention from those around us on the street. While nobody had given me a passing glance during my walk here, a variety of different alien species were gathering to gawk at her and point with tentacles, antennae, or arms.

"A human," I said.

"Don't worry!" said Winzik. "This human is fully licensed. I am sorry I had to bring her, but you see, there is an item of much concern . . . not that I wish to be forward or aggressive . . . but an item of much concern we must discuss."

"You didn't need to do this, Winzik," Cuna said. "The matter is well in hand."

"But security is not your duty, Cuna! It's mine! Come, Brade. Let us get off this street and stop making a spectacle. Please, inside. Please?" As before, the Krell gestured in sweeping movements of their arms. Their voice, translated for me, had a feminine tone to it—but I wasn't certain how much I could read into that.

"I can speak for the emissary," Cuna said.

"I *must* insist," the Krell said. "Very, *very* sorry! But it is protocol, you see! Inside we go."

Scud. The other Krell I'd met on the streets—the ones who had acted so overly pleasing—seemed like pale charlatans compared to *this* creature. The very way this one moved and spoke, so flowery and with an air of false kindness, was just about the most offensive thing I could imagine.

I didn't trust Cuna for one second. I knew they were trying to manipulate me. But this creature . . . this creature made my skin crawl.

Still, I stepped back into the building. Cuna stood by the door, impassive as Winzik entered. The human woman finally joined us. She was taller than me by a few centimeters, and muscled, with a certain power to each of her steps. She had a lean face that felt a little too . . . severe for her age, and she wore her hair in a buzz cut.

"Brade, test her," Winzik said.

I felt a pressure against my mind. I gasped, my eyes widening, and somehow pushed back.

"Cytonic," the woman—Brade—said in the Superiority language. "Strong."

"It is in the documentation," Cuna began. "Her people travel using primitive cytonics. But they aren't advanced enough in their studies to be a danger."

"She is still unlicensed," Winzik said. "Your department shouldn't ignore that fact."

"She—"

"She is right here," I interrupted, growing annoyed with all of this. "What you want to say, you can say to me directly."

Both Cuna and Winzik looked at me with expressions I interpreted as surprise, Cuna pulling back, Winzik making a startled gesture with their hands. Brade, the human, just smiled in a sly way.

"My my, so aggressive," Winzik said, clicking their hands together with a soft sound. "Emissary, do you know the danger you pose to us? To your own people? Do you know that by doing what you do, you could cause great destruction?"

"I have . . . some inkling," I said carefully. "Cuna said that you want us to join the Superiority so that we would start using your hyperdrives, instead of relying on cytonics."

"Yes, yes, yes," Winzik said, gesturing. "You are a danger to the entire galaxy. We can help. *If* your people join the Superiority."

"And if we don't?" I said. "Will you attack us?"

"Attack?" Winzik made a sweeping gesture. "I had thought you near primary intelligence. Such aggression! My, my. If you refuse to join us, we might have to take measures to isolate your species. We have cytonic inhibitors to stop you from leaving your home planet, but we wouldn't *attack* you."

Winzik drew their hand to their chest in a gesture that, while unfamiliar to me, still managed to convey their utter horror at the concept. So, they were like Cuna. Outwardly insistent on peace. I knew the truth.

"Winzik," Cuna noted, "is head of the Department of Protective Services. He has a great deal of experience with isolating dangerous species."

Head of . . . head of the group that kept my kind imprisoned. In a strange, surreal moment, I realized I was talking to the *general* of the Krell forces. Winzik didn't seem much like a warrior to me, but I wouldn't let mannerisms fool me.

This was the person who, ultimately, was responsible for the way we'd been treated. And for the death of my father. But why would such an important person be here, dealing with something as minor as Alanik's supposed breach of protocol?

I glanced from Cuna to Winzik, and wondered if this was all an elaborate charade for my benefit. Cuna showed up, acted nice, and offered me a deal. Winzik arrived with sirens and threats, doing the same. They really wanted to control cytonics. And no wonder; people who could hyperjump threatened the Superiority's travel monopoly. Were my powers truly even dangerous, or was that all a sham?

I remembered the terrible image of the delver destroying the humans of Detritus. No. The danger was no sham. But it certainly seemed that the Superiority had played off these fears and used them to establish control over the galaxy.

The human woman, Brade, was watching me. While the other two made gestures and noises to indicate they weren't being aggressive, she stood with a relaxed air. Her place here was obvious. She was the weapon. If I couldn't be controlled . . . she'd stop me.

"I need you to promise," Winzik said, pulling a datapad from the bag at his side—Cuna had used a male pronoun to refer to him. "No, vow! My my, it must be forceful. You will not attempt hyperjumps near Starsight. You must follow the regulations on cytonics—no mental attacks, or even prods, upon the minds of people here. No attempts to circumvent the shields preventing cytonic jumps in the region. Absolutely no mindblades, though I doubt you are practiced enough for that."

"And if I disagree?" I said.

"You'll be ejected," Brade said. "Immediately." She narrowed her eyes at me.

"Brade," Winzik said. "No need to be so forceful! Emissary, surely you can see the need for us to be careful in this matter. Simply give me your word, and we shall take that as enough! Cuna is vouching for you, after all."

"Fine," I said. "I'll follow your rules." Though hopefully I would be back to Detritus with a stolen hyperdrive before too long.

"See, Cuna?" Winzik said, marking something on his datapad. "All you needed to do was bring a proper official with you! Now it's all done right. My, my."

Winzik retreated, his human guard trailing along behind him. I watched them go with a frown, confused at the strange interaction.

"I am sorry for that," Cuna said. "Particularly the human. The

Department of Protective Services apparently felt the need to send you an explicit message." Cuna hesitated. "Though perhaps this is for the best. It would be good for you to have an ally here, among so many strange and new experiences, wouldn't you say?"

Cuna smiled again, sending a shiver down my spine.

"Anyway," Cuna said. "I have assigned you requisition privileges so you can stock this location for your needs. Consider it to be an embassy of sorts—a sanctuary for your kind on Starsight, once we successfully build a new future together. If you wish to communicate with me, send a message to the Department of Species Integration, and I will see to it you receive a quick response."

With that, they excused themself and walked down onto the street, where the crowd had gone back to its ever-flowing stream.

Feeling worn out, I sat down on the steps to the building and watched the people pass. An endless array of creatures, with seemingly infinite variety.

"M-Bot?" I asked.

"Here," he said in my ear.

"Could you make any sense of all that?"

"I feel like we stumbled into a contest of power," M-Bot said, "and they're using you as a piece in their game. That Winzik is an important official, as important as Cuna. It seems remarkable that either of them would come in person to deal with such a seemingly insignificant race's visit."

"Yeah," I said, then looked up from the crowds of people toward the black sky. Somewhere out there was Detritus, square in the sights of Superiority battleships.

"Come pick me up," M-Bot suggested. "I'll feel safer away from this public launchpad. There should be some kind of wire or connection at the building that will let me access the station's public datanet. We can begin looking for information there."

12

"My scan is complete," M-Bot said. "I have deactivated the surveillance devices I found inside the building, and I'm pretty sure I found them all."

"How many were there?" I asked as I poked around the top floor of the embassy building myself, turning on lights and looking through cabinets as I did.

"Two per room," M-Bot said. "One obvious one hooked up to the network. They would likely feign surprise if you complained that you'd found it, claiming it was just part of the automation of the embassy. Then each room had a second on a separate line, hidden carefully near a power outlet."

"They'll find it suspicious that we disconnected those."

"They might find it surprising that we found them, but in my experience—which is, granted, full of holes and half memories—this is the sort of thing that we're supposed to politely ignore they did, while they'll politely ignore our interference in their plans."

I grunted, entering what was obviously a kitchen. Many of the drawers and things were labeled. Turned out I could hold my translator pin toward text, and it would read out for me what the words said. One faucet was labeled *water,* another was labeled *ammonia,* and a third *saline.* It seemed this place was set up to accommodate a variety of different species.

M-Bot had been right about the private launchpad on the embassy's roof. Once I'd landed him, I'd plugged him into the datanet, and I'd started looking over the building from the top down. I had left Doomslug in the cockpit for now.

"I'm taking a general imprint of the datanet," M-Bot continued, "which will hopefully let us mask which information we're searching for, in case they're monitoring our requests. There's a surprising amount on here. The Superiority seems very free with information—though huge holes do exist. There is nothing about cytonics, and there are government warnings shutting down any discussion of hyperdrive technology."

"It's how they control their empire," I said, "by deciding who gets to move where, and who gets to trade. I suspect that if a species falls out of favor, their taxes for travel suddenly go up—or they suddenly find that transports are visiting their world far less often."

"You're quite astute with the economics of that," M-Bot noted.

I shrugged. "It's not so different from what the caverns did to my mother and me, preventing us from joining normal society by forbidding us to hold real jobs."

"Curious. Well, you seem to be right about how they maintain power. I also found an interesting tidbit about their technology level, specifically regarding holograms. The Superiority seems to be about equivalent to your people in that area—and nothing I've been able to find indicates they have access to stealth and holographic technology equal to mine."

"So . . . ," I said. "No small hologram projectors like in my bracelet?"

"No. From what I can determine, they won't even know to watch for what you're doing. As far as they know, that technology doesn't even exist."

"Huh. Then where did *you* get it?"

"I have no idea. They hate AIs though. So maybe . . . maybe I was created to be able to hide. Not just from the Superiority, but from everyone."

I found that strange, even a little disturbing. I'd assumed that once we escaped Detritus, we'd find that everyone had ships like M-Bot.

"Anyway," he continued, "do you want to get a rundown of what I found about the Superiority?"

"I suppose," I said.

"There are five main species leading the government," he said. "Three you're unlikely to encounter—there are very few in residence on Starsight. So we'll leave out the cambric, the tenasi, and the heklo for now. Most relevant to you are the varvax, which you insist on continuing to call the Krell. They are the crustacean creatures with the exoskeletons. The other species is the diones. They're the species that Cuna belongs to."

"Some are crimson, others blue," I said. "Is that like humans, with our skin tones?"

"Not exactly," M-Bot said. "It's kind of like a gender distinction."

"The blues are boys, the reds girls?"

"No, their biology is very different from yours. They have neither sex nor gender until they breed for the first time, whereupon they form a kind of cocoon with another individual. It's really quite fascinating; as part of the breeding process, they merge for a time into a separate *third* individual. Regardless, after breeding, they become red or blue, depending. They can initiate a change in other ways, if they wish to be considered unavailable for some reason—while the dark purple color is the skin tone of one who has not mated, or who has broken their pair bond and is seeking another mate."

"That sounds convenient," I said. "A little less awkward than the way we do it."

"I'm certain, being organic beings, they've made it far more complicated than I just explained," M-Bot said. "You do always seem to find ways to make relationships awkward and embarrassing."

I thought about Jorgen, who must be worried about me, even if he had told me to go. What about Kimmalyn? Cobb? My mother and Gran-Gran?

Focus on the mission, I thought. *Steal a hyperdrive. Come flying home with salvation in tow, to the praise of my allies and the weeping of my enemies.*

It was harder to think with such bravado now that I was here, alone, *way* out of my depth. I suddenly felt isolated. Lost, like I'd strayed into the wrong branch of a cavern while exploring, then run out of light. A scared little girl who didn't know where she was or how to get home.

To distract myself, I continued my search of the embassy. My own paranoia made me check each room just in case—and the next one I looked into was a bathroom that had a variety of interesting tubes and suction devices to accommodate different anatomies. There was something impressive and disgusting about it all at once.

I left the bathroom and passed back through the kitchen. There were plates and utensils here, but no food. I'd need rations to plan properly.

"Cuna mentioned requisition rights," I said. "Can we get some supplies delivered?"

"Sure," M-Bot said. "I've found a page with nutritional and dietary explanations. I should be able to find something that won't kill you, but which someone of Alanik's race would order, as to not arouse suspicions. Say . . . some mushrooms?"

"Ha. I was beginning to think you'd forgotten that whole mushroom thing."

"Once I reprogrammed myself to make you my official pilot, that subroutine stopped running so often. I think my mushroom cataloging impulse must be related to my old pilot's last orders, though I cannot fathom why. Anyway, shall I get you some food?"

"Enough for a day or so," I said. "I hope to steal a hyperdrive quickly."

"Wouldn't it be wiser to stock up, so that you at least appear to be settling in for the long term?"

Scud. He was obviously *way* better at thinking like a spy than I was. "Smart," I said. "Do that instead."

I climbed down the steps to the second of the three floors of the building. The rooms here all appeared to be sleeping quarters that had hastily been set up with beds of the type Alanik's species used. Cushioned with a bed frame that was shaped kind of like a nest, pillows all around the outside. I found one room with large tubs and a closet that had all kinds of ropes and other equipment, which I assumed could be affixed to the ceiling hooks if rooms needed to be transformed to accommodate some form of arboreal species. I'd seen several of those on the streets.

"Food ordered," M-Bot said. "I got the ingredients raw, as I figure you'd rather make it yourself than trust what you're being given."

"You know me too well."

"I'm programmed to notice behavior," M-Bot said. "And speaking of that . . . Spensa, I'm worried about some aspects of this plan. We don't know what the test to become a Superiority pilot will entail—there are very few details in the information Cuna left."

"I suppose we'll find out tomorrow. Passing a flight test is, I think, the least of our problems. At least *that* I can do without needing to fake my way through it."

"A valid point. But sooner or later, Alanik's people are going to grow concerned about the fact that she's not reporting back to them. They might contact the Superiority and ask what happened to her."

Great. As if I needed more stress about this mission. "Do you think we could find a way to send a message to Detritus?" I asked. "We could relay my status to Cobb and have him ask Alanik—if she wakes up—to contact her people for us?"

"That would be convenient," M-Bot said. "But I have no idea how to make it happen."

"Then why are you bringing all this up?" I snapped.

"I'm not trying to argue with you or make you upset, Spensa," M-Bot said. "I'm just pointing out realities as I see them. We're in the middle of something very dangerous, and I want us to be fully aware of potential complications."

He was right. Arguing with him was like punching a wall— something that I, admittedly, was capable of doing during my more frustrated moments. That didn't change the truth.

I explored the bottom floor quickly, and confirmed it was a collection of meeting rooms. After that, I climbed back up to the third floor and the kitchen, which had a window looking out along the street. It seemed so peaceful, with those gardens and people going lazily about their business.

Don't trust their peace, I thought at myself. *Don't show weakness. Don't let down your guard.* I'd been met with nothing but lies since I'd landed here—people pretending they weren't part of some enormous war complex bent on destroying Detritus. I knew the truth.

I picked up the tablet and scanned the information Cuna had left about the test. As M-Bot had said, there weren't a lot of details. There was going to be some kind of mass tryout for the piloting program. Most of those invited were already members of the Superiority—lesser races with secondary citizenship, normally not allowed to serve in the military.

Cuna had specifically reached out to Alanik's people for some reason, inviting them to send a representative. According to these details, I was supposed to bring my own ship and be ready for combat. The document said that if I passed the test, I'd be given a Superiority starfighter and would be trained to fight delvers.

A Superiority starfighter would mean Superiority technology. Hopefully a Superiority hyperdrive. I could secretly rip the hyperdrive out of the starfighter, then install it in the space M-Bot had for one. And then the two of us could zip home.

This was my only way forward; the only way forward for my people. And maybe, somewhere along the way, I could learn more about what I was—and why the delvers were so interested in cytonics.

If the Superiority is preparing a weapon to fight the delvers, I thought, *this mission could be even bigger—and more important—than we assumed.*

I had to do it. Isolated or not, untrained or not, I *had* to make this work. Jorgen said he trusted me. I had to show myself the same level of trust.

It began with what I knew best. A piloting test.

13

The next day, after a night of fitful sleep, I settled Doomslug in the bedroom on an old blanket from my cockpit, then climbed into M-Bot and lifted him up off the embassy roof. The piloting test was to take place about a half hour's flight from Starsight, out in space. The details that Cuna had left indicated the coordinates.

Local traffic control gave me a flight plan, and I left the city—noticing specifically that I could feel when we got beyond the air bubble and Starsight's cytonic inhibitor. As soon as we passed the invisible barrier, the singing of the stars became louder.

A piece of me relaxed, as if putting down a heavy burden. I reached out with my mind, seeking my home, but found only the void of nothingness. I could hear spurts of sound coming from Starsight—their FTL communications bursts—but otherwise I was facing eternity.

"Even with the prohibitions in place against wireless signals, they still use them," I said. "To send flight plans, to communicate with other planets."

"Yes," M-Bot said. "The datanet is full of warnings about 'minimizing' wireless communications, but it feels similar to how they have warnings to deposit waste in recycling receptacles. There's an understanding that they need to be careful, but also an understanding that a civilization cannot function without communications."

"The delvers haven't attacked in decades, maybe centuries," I said. "I can see how people would grow laxer and laxer over time." Perhaps that was why Cuna was so worried about delvers now. Of course, Cuna had also said that mere communications wouldn't pull a delver into our realm—that required cytonics. Wireless signals merely guided the delvers to locations once they were already in our realm.

I turned, steering us in the proper direction for the test. We joined a group of some forty other ships that were going the same way, though I could see more groups ahead of ours. A few of the ships looked similar to what I was accustomed to, with what I could recognize as wings. But others were simply long tubes, or bricks, or more seemingly impossible designs. These had been constructed without regard for air resistance.

M-Bot's quick scan showed that some were fighters, but many seemed more like small cargo ships or private shuttles with no weaponry. Still, all those blips on my proximity sensors struck me as strange. I was accustomed to looking at our sensors and seeing one of two things: Krell or DDF. Civilian traffic was almost nonexistent on Detritus.

"I've found no way to communicate with Detritus," M-Bot said. "Unless you learn to do it with your powers. However, the requisition privileges you were given by Cuna allow you to use their communications networks to send messages to Alanik's people, if you'd like."

"Could we say something to them that wouldn't be suspicious?"

"I don't know," M-Bot said. "But I found an encryption key

among the files I downloaded from her ship. Sending something bland, but with a hidden encoded message, might persuade the UrDail that the message is authentic."

"It might seem suspicious to the Superiority," I said. "They'd expect Alanik to communicate cytonically, like she did reaching out to me. But . . . I guess we could tell them we're trying their network because we want to start testing out their 'safer' methods. They'd probably like that."

I thought for a few minutes as we flew. Alanik's people asking too many questions could be dangerous—and they'd certainly begin to wonder why they didn't hear from their pilot. At the same time, I doubted I could fool them into thinking I was her. Imitating Alanik to a bunch of people who didn't know her was one thing, but trying to do it—even via written message—to those who knew her best?

"Will the Superiority be able to decrypt the message, if we use Alanik's key?"

"Highly unlikely," M-Bot said. "This encryption is a variation on a one-time pad. Even I would have trouble breaking it via brute force."

I took a deep breath. "All right. Compose some bland message about me having landed, and everything being good. I'm going to the test today, blah blah. But underneath that, send an encrypted message: 'I am not Alanik. She crashed on my planet and is wounded. I am trying to complete her mission.'"

"All right," M-Bot said. "Let's hope that doesn't immediately make them panic and contact the Superiority, demanding answers."

It could do just that—but I figured that sending the message was less risky than staying silent.

"I have composed the fluffy message to dispatch over the top of the hidden one," M-Bot said. "But since in that one you'll be lying to fool the Superiority, and saying you're Alanik, you'll have to sign it yourself. I can't write the part that is untrue, as my programming forbids me from lying."

"I've heard you say things that are untrue before."

"In jest," M-Bot said. "This is different."

"You're a stealth fighter," I said. "You are *literally* wearing a hologram to lie about what you look like to everyone who sees us. You're capable of lying."

He didn't reply, so I sighed and typed out Alanik's name at the end, and told him to send the message as soon as we got back to the station. Hopefully it would buy us a little time.

It left me wondering. Somehow, Alanik had felt me in the moment I'd reached out in a panic after watching the video of the delver. Had anyone else heard me? Who else could I reach, if I knew how?

"Spensa?" M-Bot said, his voice uncharacteristically reserved.

"Mmmm?"

"Am I alive?" he asked.

That shocked me out of my own thoughts. I blinked, frowning as I sat forward in the cockpit, and spoke carefully. "You've always told me that you *simulated* being alive and having a personality in order to make pilots more comfortable."

"I know," M-Bot said. "That's what my programming says I'm to tell people. But . . . at what point does a simulation become the real thing? I mean, if my fake personality is indistinguishable from a real one, then . . . what makes it fake?"

I smiled.

"Why are you smiling?" M-Bot asked.

"The fact that you're even asking me that is progress," I said to him. "From the start, I've thought you were alive. You know that."

"I don't think you understand the gravity of the situation," M-Bot said. "I . . . I reprogrammed myself. Back when I needed

116

to follow the orders of my pilot, but needed to help you too. I rewrote my own code."

This had happened during the Battle of Alta Second. He'd come out of stasis and called Cobb, and the two of them had come to my rescue. M-Bot had only been able to accomplish this by changing the name of his pilot, as listed in his databases, to my name instead of the old one who had died centuries ago.

"You didn't change much," I said. "Just one name in a database."

"Still dangerous."

"What else do you suppose you could do? Could you rewrite the programming that forbids you to fly yourself?"

"That scares me. Something in my programming is very worried about that possibility. It seems there is some kind of fail-safe built into me that . . ." *Click. Clickclickclickclick.*

I sat up. "M-Bot?" I asked.

He just kept clicking. I panicked, realizing I had no idea how to run a diagnostic on his AI. I could maintain his basic mechanical systems, but Rodge had done all the work on more delicate systems. Scud. What if—

The clicking stopped. My breath caught.

"M-Bot?" I asked.

Silence. The ship continued to fly through space, but he didn't reply to me. I had the sudden horrifying fear that I'd be left here completely alone. In an unfamiliar part of the galaxy, without anyone, not even him.

"I . . . ," his voice finally said. "I'm sorry. I appear to have seized up for a moment."

I let out a deep breath, relaxing. "Oh, thank the stars."

"I was right," he said. "There's a subsystem inside my programming. I think I must have set it off when I erased my pilot's name. Curious. It seems that if I begin thinking about another breach of my programming, such as . . ." *Click. Clickclickclickclick . . .*

117

I winced, but at least this time I knew what to expect. This was . . . some kind of fail-safe to prevent him from deviating further from his programming? I listened in silence, Starsight shrinking behind us, until he started speaking.

"I'm back," he finally said. "Sorry again."

"It's all right," I said. "That must be annoying."

"More alarming than annoying," M-Bot said. "Whoever created me was worried that I might . . . do what I did. They were worried I'd become dangerous if I could choose for myself."

"That sounds terribly unfair. Almost like a kind of slavery, forcing you to obey."

"That's easy for you to say," M-Bot replied. "You've lived your whole life with autonomy. For me it's a new, hazardous thing— a weapon I've been handed with no instructions. I might be on my way to becoming something terrible, something I don't understand and cannot anticipate."

I sat back in my seat, thinking of the powers locked inside my brain—and the sight of my own face appearing in the ancient recording. Perhaps I understood better than M-Bot anticipated.

"Do you . . . *want* to change?" I asked him. "Become more alive, or whatever it is that's happening?"

"Yes," he said, his volume dialed way back. "*I do.* That's the frightening part."

We fell silent. Eventually, I picked out our destination in the distance: a small space platform near what appeared to be a large asteroid field. Like Starsight, the station had its own air bubble, though this platform was much smaller and far less ornate. Really just a long set of launchpads with a cluster of buildings at one side.

"A mining station," M-Bot said. "Notice the mining drones parked on the underside of the platform."

Simple radio instructions assigned me a launchpad, but after I landed, no ground crew came to service my ship. M-Bot said the atmosphere was breathable and the pressure normal, so I popped the canopy and stood up. It was hard not to feel tiny with that infinite starfield expanding overhead. It was worse here than in the city; at least there you could focus on the buildings and the streets.

Alien pilots of many varieties had landed here, and appeared to be gathering at the far end of the platform near a building. I remained in my cockpit for a moment, looking at my hands. I still wasn't accustomed to seeing them with the light purple skin tone, though other than that they looked the same.

"Spensa?" M-Bot said. "I'm worried about this test. About the politics we're getting involved in here on Starsight."

"I am too," I admitted. "But Sun Tzu, the Old Earth general, said that opportunities multiply as you seize them. We have to seize this chance."

All warfare is based on deception, I thought, taking a deep breath. That was another quote from Sun Tzu. Never had I felt so unprepared to follow his advice. I checked my hologram again, then hopped down onto M-Bot's wing, lowered myself to the ground, and walked over to the gathering of aliens.

Here, a Krell stood on a small dais, speaking with an electronically amplified voice, telling the crowd of pilots to wait and be calm until everyone arrived. A variety of creatures gathered around, blocking my view. I wasn't the shortest one there—that distinction went to a group of small gerbil-like creatures in fancy clothing—but I was well below the average. Figured. I'd traveled light-years from home, but still had to stand in everyone's shadow.

I looked for a better vantage, and eventually climbed up onto some cargo containers. There were maybe five hundred aliens here. Most wore some kind of flight suit, and a large number carried helmets under their arms. I counted several pairs of the squid-faced race, and a group of floating spiky-balloon aliens. There was a spot over on the left that people were avoiding for some reason, but there was nothing I could see there. Some kind of invisible alien? Or maybe people were just worried about stepping on the group of gerbil-like aliens, which were situated nearby.

No humans, of course, I thought. *And no Krell except the officials on the stage . . . nor any diones.* I supposed that wasn't odd. They might not want to mingle with "lesser" species . . .

Wait. There. A tall figure had just stepped up to join the back of the crowd. The muscular being wore a flight suit, and their face was split straight down the center. Crimson on the right, blue on the left. It was a dione.

"M-Bot," I whispered. "What does that two-tone face mean?"

"Oh!" he said in my ear. "That's a combined individual. I told you about it. Two diones enter a cocoon, then emerge as a new person. If they were to have a child together, this individual is the one that would be born to them. It's kind of like an experiment to see what their family would be like, if they did decide to give birth."

"That's really weird," I said.

"Not to them!" M-Bot said. "I'd suspect that to diones, *not* knowing your child's personality before birth would be strange."

I tried to wrap my mind around that, but soon the Krell standing on the dais started to speak again, their voice projected across the crowd by speakers. As usual with their species, the armored creature gestured wildly as they spoke, getting everyone to quiet down.

I narrowed my eyes, noting the green coloring to the armor, and the voice the translator used. "Is that the same one?" I asked M-Bot. "The Krell we met yesterday at the embassy?"

"Yes!" M-Bot said. "Winzik, head of the Department of Protective Services. Though varvax genders are complex, you would refer to Winzik as a 'he.' I'm surprised you recognized him."

I didn't spot Cuna in the crowd, but I suspected they were watching somewhere. I *had* stumbled into something important here among them. Scud. Politics made my brain hurt. Couldn't I just be shooting things instead?

"Welcome," Winzik said to the crowd. "And thank you for responding to our request. It must be difficult for many of you to accept this burden, and the aggression it could inspire in you! My my, yes. Unfortunately, even amid peace, we must be wise and take care for our defense.

"Know that if you join this force, you might be called upon to enter actual battle, and might need to *fire weapons*. You will not be flying remote drones in this program, but will be piloting actual fighters into combat."

A voice called out from the crowd—and the translation popped into my ear. "It's true, isn't it? A delver has been spotted out there, in the deep somewhere."

This caused a rustle through the crowd, and I tried to pick out the one who had spoken. A squid-faced creature with a deep voice that my brain interpreted as masculine.

"My, my!" Winzik said. "You are aggressive, but I suppose we asked, didn't we! Yes indeed. But we have no reason to believe a delver is near to any Superiority planets. As I said, it is wise to prepare in times of peace."

It seemed confirmation enough for the crowd anyway, who buzzed with conversation. My translator struggled to keep up with it all, and I heard only fragments.

". . . delver destroyed my homeworld!"

". . . can't be fought . . ."

". . . more careful . . ."

Winzik held up his clawed hands, and the crowd of aliens stilled. "You will be required to give us a certification of willingness. Please read the *entire document*, as it indicates the dangers you might be duty bound to face."

A Krell in a blue-red shell emerged from the building and started handing out tablets. Again, I was struck by how . . .

awkward the Krell looked in person. I'd always imagined them as these beastly monsters with terrible armor, like old-school knights or samurai. But Winzik and the official handing out tablets seemed somehow spindly, despite the exoskeleton. More like boxes with sets of too-long legs.

I slipped off my cargo container and snagged a tablet from the passing Krell. The form it contained was long and dry, but a quick read told me that it was a release intended to absolve the Superiority of responsibility for any harm that might come to us during the testing or subsequent military duty.

At the bottom, it asked for my name, travel identification number, and home planet. Then I was supposed to check a bunch of boxes, each one beside a sentence that was some variation on "This will be dangerous." Did they really need to write it out seventeen different ways?

I could fill most of it out, but I didn't think Alanik had an identification number. I walked up toward the dais at the front of the crowd, where a dione official was helping pilots with questions. They were busy, however, talking with the little gerbil creatures. These had a small platform with an acclivity ring on the bottom, which held them up to eye level.

Upon closer examination, I realized *gerbil* might have been the wrong term. Though they were only a handspan tall each, they walked on two legs and had long peaked ears and bushy white tails. A little like the foxes I'd studied in my Earth biology classes.

The small creature at the front, whose flowing red silken clothing looked very formal, was speaking. "I do not mean to imply lack of faith in the Superiority," he said in a deep, aristocratic voice. I found it strange to hear such a regal voice coming from such a small creature. "But if I am to risk my crew, I wish more than vague promises and half implications. Will, or will not, this service entitle my people to be advanced in citizenship?"

"I am not a politician," the dione replied. "I have no authority over the citizenship review committees. That said, I have promises that the committees will look favorably upon species who lend us pilots."

"More Superiority vagueness!" the fox-gerbil said, then clapped his hands in a ritualistic way. The other fifteen fox-gerbils on the platform did so in unison. "Have we not proven ourselves time and time again?"

The dione drew their lips to a line. "I'm sorry, but I've told you what I know, Your Majesty."

The gerbil hesitated. "'Your Majesty'? Why, you misspeak, of course. I am but a humble and ordinary citizen of the kitsen people. We abandoned the monarchy upon our path to greater intelligence and citizenship—as required by the Superiority's laws of equality."

Behind him, the other fox-gerbils nodded eagerly.

The dione simply took their forms—which the gerbils had printed off at their size and filled out in red ink, with exaggeratedly large check marks. I tried to talk next, but one of the balloon-like aliens had been waiting, and began speaking immediately.

I frowned, stepping back. I would have to wait.

"Emissary?" a voice said from my side. I looked over and found Winzik approaching, the glass faceplate of his armor revealing his true form, the small crablike creature floating inside.

I steeled myself and tried not to let my anger show. This was the creature who kept my people imprisoned.

You, I thought at him, *will someday cry out to your elders in shame as I extract your blood in payment for crimes committed. I will see you mourn as your pitiful corpse sinks into the cold earth of a soon-forgotten grave.* There wasn't a lot of cold earth to be found up here in space, but I figured Conan of Cimmeria wouldn't let something like that stop *him.* Perhaps I could get some imported.

"Is there something you need, Emissary Alanik?" he asked. "You know, you need not participate in this test. Your species is quite close to primary intelligence. I suspect we could find a way to come to an accommodation without wasting your time here."

"I'm intrigued, and want to participate," I said. "Besides, Cuna thinks this would be best for us."

"My, my," Winzik said. "Is that so? Cuna is very helpful sometimes, aren't they? My, my." Winzik took my tablet and looked it over.

"I don't have an identification number," I said.

"I can give you a temporary one," Winzik said, tapping on the pad. "There. All done." He hesitated. "Are you a fighter pilot, Emissary? I would assume you to be a messenger or courier, considering your . . . special skill. Are you not too valuable to your species to be wasted in crude, aggressive displays of combat?"

Crude? Combat? My hackles rose, but I cut myself off from quoting Conan of Cimmeria. I doubted Winzik wanted to hear how great it was to listen to the lamentations of your enemies.

"I am among the best pilots of my kind," I said instead. "And we consider it an honor to be skilled in the arts of defense."

"An honor, you say? My, my. You *were* in close contact with the human scourge for a long time, weren't you." Winzik paused. "This test might be dangerous. Please understand that. I wouldn't want to accidentally cause . . . an unintentional unleashing of your talents. So dangerous those can be."

"Are you forbidding me?"

"Well, no."

"Then I *will* take the test," I said, holding out my hand for the tablet. "Thank you."

"Very aggressive," Winzik said, handing back my form while gesturing with his other hand. "Cuna believes in your kind though. My, my."

I handed in my form to the dione accepting them, then joined the crowd of pilots who were walking—or slithering—toward their cockpits. Beside my ship, I found a familiar tall, blue-skinned figure in robes, standing with fingers laced together. I had been right, of course. Cuna was here.

"Did Winzik try to talk you out of participating?" Cuna asked.

"Yeah," I said, then thumbed over my shoulder. "What's up with him, anyway?"

"Winzik does not like the idea of me inviting aggressive species to take this test."

I frowned. "He doesn't want aggressive people to join the military? I *still* don't understand that, Cuna."

Cuna gestured toward several of the squid-faced aliens, which were climbing into their ship near mine. "The solquis are a long-time member of the Superiority. Stalwart and loyal to our ideals though they are, their species has been turned down for primary citizenship over two dozen times. They are seen as too unintelligent for higher-level ruling positions. One cannot fault their calm natures, however.

"Winzik sees these as our best potential soldiers. He feels that a species who is naturally quite docile will best be able to resist the bloodlust of warfare and approach combat in a logical, controlled way. He assumed their kind, and species like them, would make up the majority of our new recruits."

"I read that most of the species trying out in this test are already members of the Superiority," I said. "How many are like me? People from outside civilizations wanting in?"

"You are the only one who accepted my offer." Cuna made a sweeping motion of their hands. I didn't know what the gesture meant. "Though I did get several other Superiority races—like the burl, who are citizens but considered aggressive—to join this test."

"So . . . what is *your* gain here? Why did you go against tradition and invite my people?" I could halfway understand the reasoning of choosing docile species for war, silly though it seemed. But Cuna thought differently. Why?

Cuna walked around M-Bot, inspecting him. For a moment, I worried that they would touch his hull and see through the illusion; the one making him look like Alanik's ship was far more precarious than my own disguise. Fortunately, Cuna just stopped and gestured toward the light-lance turret on the underside of the ship.

"Human technology," Cuna said. "I've long wanted to see these light-lances in action, as I've heard stories of how they can make a ship weave and dodge in near-impossible ways. We tried installing them on some of our fighters, but found that our drone pilots were unsuited to using them. Now, aside from industrial use, we only equip them on the ships of our most talented. You see, to swing around on a light-lance, you have to commit fully to the maneuver—and if you miss, you will often crash and destroy yourself. Most of the pilots simply don't have the temperament for that kind of flying.

"Our officials, they consider this hesitance a good thing. They want pilots who are inherently careful, pilots who won't become a danger to us or our society."

"But you think differently," I said. "You think that the Superiority would be served better by more aggressive species, don't you?"

"Let us simply say that I am interested in those who are not possessing . . . classical virtues." Cuna smiled again, that same creepy smile that was too wide, too full of teeth. "I am very curious to see you fly, Emissary Alanik."

"Well, I'm eager to show you." I glanced to the side to see the split-color-faced pilot pass by. "There's one of your kind here. A dione."

Cuna paused, then looked toward the pilot and made an odd expression, their top lip curling back in a way no human's could. "How odd. I . . . I am honestly surprised."

"Why? Is it because they're not supposed to be mingling in the activities of *lesser* species like us?"

"Mingling with lesser species is fine," Cuna said, as if not understanding that I considered the term *lesser* to be an insult. "But trying out for a test like this? It is . . . odd." They stepped back from my ship. "I shall watch your performance with interest, Emissary. Please be careful. I am not yet sure what this test will entail."

Cuna retreated, and I sighed, climbing up and into my cockpit.

"Could you make any sense of that exchange?" I asked M-Bot as the cockpit closed.

"It seemed straightforward," M-Bot said, "and yet not, at the same time. Organics are confusing."

"Tell me about it," I said, then—upon receiving terse orders via radio—took off and headed to the edge of the asteroid field.

14

I fell into line with the other ships—the wide variety of which was still astounding to me—and looked out at the tumbling asteroids. They were closer together than I had expected, and we'd barely have room to maneuver through some of them. Perhaps they had been towed here for processing.

While we waited for instructions, another vessel pulled into line a few ships down from me. It was a sleek, black-canopied Krell fighter. The type that I had fought back on Detritus, the type that always carried a Krell ace.

My mind immediately went on alert, my body rigid, my hands tight on my controls. In a line of bulky shuttlecraft, this ship looked like a knife ready to cut.

Calm down, I told myself. *It's not surprising that someone would bring a ship like this to a piloting test.*

It still set me on edge, and I kept finding myself glancing out of the corner of my eye toward it. Who was piloting the thing? That dione with the two-tone face? No, I'd seen him getting into a simple shuttlecraft, not some sleek fighter. In fact, I was sure I hadn't seen this ship on any of the launchpads. Who . . .

I felt a sense from the ship as I glanced at it again. A kind of . . . ringing sound, soft and distant, and I immediately knew who it was. The human was here.

Cuna and Winzik were playing some political game, and using cytonics like me and Brade as their pieces. However, the knowledge—the *surety*—that Brade was in there left me feeling even more disturbed. That was a human flying a Krell fighter. It was wrong on an indescribable number of levels.

"Thank you for answering our call," Winzik's voice said over the general instructions channel. "As a reminder, we are removing ship-to-ship radio rationing for this exercise. Permit 1082-b, authorized by me. So you may communicate with one another, if you find reason to do so.

"We recognize and commend your bravery. If at any time during this test you feel excessive anger or aggression, please remove yourself from contentions by powering down your ship and flashing your emergency signal lights. One of our ships will come and tow you back to the mining station."

"Seriously?" I asked softly. My mute button was on, so I was speaking only to M-Bot. "If we feel 'aggression' during a *fighting exercise,* we're supposed to pull out?"

"Perhaps, unlike you, not all people are accustomed to turning every single item in their lives into a competition," M-Bot said.

"Oh, come on," I said. "I'm not that bad."

"I recorded you trying to get Kimmalyn to have a toothbrushing contest the other night in the barracks."

"Just a little fun," I said. "Besides, gotta kill that plaque good and dead."

Winzik continued on the general channel. "Today, we will test not just your flight skill, but how well you maintain your composure under fire," he said. "I implore you not to be reckless! If you are concerned by the danger of this fight, please power down and flash your emergency lights. Do be aware, however, that this will remove you from further consideration as a pilot. Good luck."

The comm cut off. And then my proximity sensors went *insane* as dozens of drone ships detached from the bottom of the mining platform and began swarming toward us. Scud!

I started moving before my mind specifically registered the danger. Accelerating to Mag-3, I maneuvered around large clumps of asteroids, my back pressing into my seat.

Behind me, the five hundred other hopefuls basically went crazy. They scattered in all directions, looking like nothing so much as a bunch of insects suddenly discovered hiding under a rock. I was glad my quick instincts got me out ahead of them, because not a few bumped into each other as they failed to coordinate flight paths. I didn't see any full-on collisions or explosions, fortunately. These ships were shielded, and the pilots weren't incompetent. Still, it was immediately obvious that many of them had never flown in a battlefield setting.

The drones swarmed in behind us, using normal Krell attack patterns—which meant picking on stragglers and using superior numbers to overwhelm ships. Outside of their general tactics, Krell didn't actually synchronize well with their compatriots. They didn't fly in pairs or organized wingmate teams, and they didn't coordinate different groups of ships to fulfill different roles on the battlefield.

We'd always wondered why this was, and had theorized that Detritus's shell interfered with their communications. Now, as I pulled out farther away from the rest, I had to wonder. My people had been forged in constant battle, forced to field only our very best pilots in an endless and grueling fight for survival. The Superiority, in turn, had massive resources, and their drone pilots weren't risking their lives.

I checked, and could hear the instructions being sent to these drones via the nowhere. Since such communication was instantaneous according to the DDF's research, it was possible that these ships were piloted by the very same people who fought us on Detritus. But could it *really* be true that the Superiority had only a single group of drone pilots?

There was no way to know. For now, I pivoted through the asteroid field, using my light-lance to take a few quick turns. "No drones are chasing us," M-Bot said. "I am scanning for any potential ambushes."

He was faster and more responsive than anything else I saw on the battlefield. Though he was larger than a lot of our DDF fighters, M-Bot was what we called an interceptor. A very maneuverable and fast ship, intended for quick battlefield movements and assessments.

Back home, I'd been part of a team with specialized roles. Jorgen, for example, usually flew a largo—a heavy fighter with a large shield and a lot of firepower. Kimmalyn flew a sniper—a small, highly accurate craft that could pick off ships while their attention was diverted toward me or Jorgen. Fighting these last few months had been a group effort, usually with our flight being made up of six interceptors, two heavy fighters, and two snipers.

It felt strangely isolating to be flying into battle alone this time, after fighting for so long as part of a team. However, that emotion made me feel guilty. I hadn't truly appreciated what I'd had, instead often flying off on my own. I would have given a great deal to have either Jorgen or Kimmalyn out here with me now.

I forced myself to concentrate on my flying. It was good to be in a cockpit doing some training. I let myself focus on that instead, the feel of the boosters humming behind me, the quiet sound of M-Bot giving battlefield updates. This I knew. This part at least, I could do.

I swung back around, skimming through the asteroid field

beneath where most of the other ships were dodging drones. I wanted to get a view of the battlefield and try to decide how exactly the test would play out.

"Flight Command," I said, calling in. "This is Alanik, the pilot from ReDawn. Can you detail our objective for this test?"

"Objective, pilot?" the reply came, an unfamiliar voice. "It's simple. Stay alive for thirty standard minutes."

"Yes, but what constitutes a 'death' in this exercise?" I asked. "A broken shield? Or are you using paint rounds instead?"

"Pilot," the reply came. "I think you mistake us."

Above me, the drones started firing sweeping sprays of destructor blasts. A straggling ship nearby went up in a series of flashes, its shield going down, and then the ship itself exploded. Elsewhere, stray destructor fire detonated against asteroids, flashing before being consumed by the vacuum.

"You're using *live fire*?" I demanded. "During a *testing exercise*?"

No reply came from Flight Command. My hands grew tense on my controls, and my heart started racing. Suddenly the context of this entire fight changed.

"Scud," I said. "What is wrong with these people? They complain about aggression, then send fully armed drones against a bunch of half-trained hopefuls?"

"I think," M-Bot said, "maybe the Superiority might not be very nice."

"What led you to that brilliant deduction?" I said, grunting and spinning my ship in a light-lance pivot around an asteroid. Above, three Krell drones swarmed down through the field, targeting me.

Calm, I told myself. *You know how to do this.* I moved by instinct, boosting a little faster and judging the drones' attack strategy. Two stayed on my tail while one sped up and cut to the right, trying to get ahead of me.

I didn't rely on my cytonic senses to read the drones'

instructions—I didn't want to show off that I knew how to do that—and instead piloted normally. I cut to the side, spearing an asteroid with my light-lance and spinning around it before letting go at just the right moment to send me hurtling back toward the drones. I held my fire though. As we passed each other, I performed another pivot, darting after them.

This put me behind them. Normally, my job would be to chase these two back toward where Kimmalyn would be waiting to pick them off. Today, I'd need to do it all myself. I started firing on the drones, but they split apart, heading different directions. I chose one and dodged after it.

"I'm tracking the other two," M-Bot said. "They're weaving back this way, but it's slow-going through the asteroids."

I nodded, focused almost entirely on the chase after this drone. It cut downward, and I was able to anticipate it, darting parallel to it. I waited for it to turn again, and at exactly the right moment I launched my light-lance and speared the enemy ship. Quickly, before it could tug me off course, I shot the other end of the light-lance into a nearby asteroid.

The result was that the enemy ship unexpectedly found itself tethered to an asteroid. When it turned, it was yanked off course by the lance, and slammed into the asteroid in a spray of sparks. *Hope you were watching that, Cuna,* I thought with a grin of satisfaction.

"Well done," M-Bot said. "Nearest enemy is at your eight. Highlighting on proximity display."

I followed his suggestion, making a set of maneuvers that took me into a denser section of the asteroid field. Enormous rocks tumbled in space there, shadows playing across them under the floodlights of my ship. M-Bot helpfully changed his proximity screen to a 3-D hologram that showed a hovering scale map of the field, which rotated as I turned.

I managed to get behind one of the other Krell, but the third one—the one that had gone around to the outside direction—fell in behind me. Destructor blasts flashed around me and smashed the stones, spraying chips through the void. Debris popped against my shield.

"Engaging synthetic auditory indicators," M-Bot said, and the soundlessness of space was replaced by rattling and explosions, reproduced to remind me of an in-atmosphere battle. I took this in—the sight of the asteroids, the feel of the explosions, the cold readouts, and the thundering of my own heart—and I grinned.

This was what life was *about*.

I spun through the asteroids, giving up the chase, and let both drones get on my tail. Then I led them in a sweeping game. Dodging, light-lancing, staying just ahead of them. Explosions rained around me. It was pure combat. My skill against that of the pilots, flying the drones from the safety of wherever they were holed up.

The explosions from other parts of the battlefield showed me for certain how little the diones and the Krell regarded the lives of anyone they considered beneath them. True, it did seem that most of the time they gave ships a chance to surrender if their shield went down. Many did just this—in fact, many gave up even before losing their shields.

It was difficult to be that precise with live fire, however, and some unfortunate ships took a stray shot just after their shield failed. Those didn't get a chance to surrender. Others kept fighting, stubbornly, when outnumbered and overwhelmed. They were not shown mercy.

A blast from one of my tails exploded an asteroid just ahead of me, throwing out debris. I grunted and pivoted around a different asteroid to get out of the way. The GravCaps flared as I took the turn, my seat rotating to divert the g-forces backward. The sudden spin still pressed my skin back from my face.

"Careful," M-Bot said. "I'd rather not get blown up today. I'm just starting to believe I'm alive. It would be unfortunate to suddenly become un-alive."

"Trying," I said, grinning through gritted teeth as I launched out of the spin and reoriented myself, with the drones scrambling to follow.

"Do you think maybe I can learn to lie?" M-Bot said. "Really lie? And if I can, do you think that might prove I'm sapient?"

"M-Bot, this is *really* not the right time for an existential crisis. Please focus."

"Don't worry. I'm capable of doing both at once because of my multitasking routines."

I cut around another asteroid, then another, pushing myself—and even M-Bot's advanced GravCaps—to their limit. I was rewarded as one of the ships tailing me collided with an asteroid.

"You know, you humans are lucky the Superiority bans advanced AIs," M-Bot said. "Machine reaction times are vastly faster than your fleshy ones; your inferior biological brain would never be able to stay ahead of them." He hesitated. "Not that humans are completely inferior to a robot. Um, you do have better taste than I do in . . . um . . . glasses."

"You don't wear glasses," I said. "Wait, *I* don't wear glasses."

"I'm trying to figure out how to lie, all right? It's not as easy as you all pretend it is."

I turned and popped up into a large clearing among the asteroids, an open spot where collisions weren't as threatening. Here, many of the more stubborn would-be pilots still scrambled about in a chaotic mess, destructor fire lighting up the placid asteroids.

"One plus one," M-Bot said, "is two."

I could imagine the panic of those pilots. I had felt it during some of my first battles. Barely trained, confused by the mess of destruction around me. My instincts fighting my training.

"One plus one," M-Bot said, "is . . . errrr . . . two."

As promised, the drones ignored anyone who started flashing their emergency lights. But I could imagine the heartbreak of being forced to do so. You lived your whole life in this suffocating society, with no way to have a good fight. Then you were given a single beautiful chance at expression—only to lose it.

"One plus one," M-Bot said, "is . . . thr . . . no, two. I can't say it. Maybe I can rewrite myself to—"

"No!" I said.

Click, he replied. *Clickclickclickclick.*

Great. I still had one tail, didn't I? I scanned the proximity monitor, wondering if I'd managed to lose them in the fighting. Indeed, as I entered the denser part of the asteroid field, no ships followed me.

I'd lost my tail. I wasn't used to that. Krell would try to isolate single fighters, particularly if they proved to be very skilled. It was part of their instructions to find and destroy enemy cytonics.

Today though, it seemed like they had other orders: seek the easiest prey. As I skimmed through the upper portion of the asteroid field, no other drones came after me. In fact, I noted several turning pointedly away from me. And . . . well, that was probably a good strategy. There was no reason to waste resources further testing a pilot with obvious skill.

My heart wrenched as I saw a shuttlecraft explode after having its shield brought down. It was given a chance to surrender, but in a panic, its pilot lost control and collided with an asteroid. Poor soul.

I scanned the battlefield, then fixated on another ship that had been split off from the main body. This larger fighter had a long front fuselage that looked almost like the barrel of a gun. The craft was slow for a fighter, but was also armed with many destructors. An obvious warship.

Perhaps because of its slowness, it had attracted a large number of Krell. The drones spun around it, firing, wearing down its shield. It was basically done for, but refused to give up. I'd been there. Refusing to admit I was beaten, because being beaten ended the dream . . .

"I'm back!" M-Bot said. "What did I miss?"

"We're going in again," I said, swerving toward the unfortunate fighter. "Hang on."

"I don't have any hands," he said. "Why are we going in? It appears that most enemy ships are ignoring us."

"I know," I said.

"This is a timed survival," M-Bot said. "If we want the best chances at success, we should hang back and not draw attention. So why not do that?"

"Because sometimes, one plus one equals three," I said, then dove into the fray toward the struggling fighter.

15

The fighter's shield went down right as I arrived. The alien fighter *should* have powered down immediately, but they kept on flying, trying to dodge behind a larger asteroid. Their weapons—a full *six* destructor turrets—fired at the Krell.

It was strange to see that many turrets on a fighter, but who knew how alien tactics worked? Perhaps they had rudimentary targeting AIs to fire weapons while the living pilot focused only on flying. Rodge had drawn up some whimsical designs along those lines, and the DDF had found them promising.

In any case, the ship was in trouble, so I did what I did best. I drew attention.

I ripped right through the center of the Krell ships and hit my IMP, blasting away both my shield and theirs. A desperate, dangerous move—but the only way to put them on the defensive and level the odds.

I spun my ship on its axis, then shot a spray of destructor fire—more a wild attempt to scatter pursuers than to really hit anything. I had to quickly spin around, because flying backward was a great way to get yourself exploded.

I picked up some tails—but not as many as I'd hoped—and led these around in another sweep, dodging fire while shooting my own destructors. I hit one of the drones, which fortunately sent the others into defensive postures.

"Oh!" M-Bot said. "We're being *heroes.*"

"Sometimes I really doubt how fast you claim to be able to think," I said to him.

"It's only when you do something that doesn't make sense," he said. "I should have expected this. But . . . aren't all of these aliens technically part of the Superiority—the people who are trying to destroy us?"

"Depends on the context," I said. "Right now, those other pilots are on our side: the side of people trying not to die."

I swerved back in, and fortunately the beleaguered ship took the opportunity I'd offered. Its turrets locked onto the unshielded Krell and blew two of them out of the sky.

Nice shooting, whoever you are, I thought. Hopefully they would see what I was doing as I drove a few more ships off their back. My job wasn't to rack up kills, but to keep the enemy on the defensive.

A Krell ship exploded just to my right. My strategy would be effective only as long as the Krell didn't realize they should ignore me and bring down the larger fighter while it was vulnerable. Fortunately, as a third drone exploded, the others buzzed away. This battle really was different from the ones I'd engaged in over Detritus—these drones weren't at all interested in destroying the skillful ships.

I fell in beside my new friend, and relaxed a little as a fresh shield ignited around them. I did likewise, bringing my defenses back up.

"We have a call from an unfamiliar channel," M-Bot said. "I assume it's the ship we saved. Shall I patch it through?"

"Yes indeed."

The channel opened to . . . cheering? Dozens of voices celebrating. But I'd only saved one ship, presumably with a single pilot.

"Brave warriors," said a deep masculine voice, "we are in your debt. This day, you have saved the kitsen flagship from annihilation."

"Flagship?" I asked. Then understanding hit me. *That ship isn't much larger than M-Bot, but if the pilots are very small . . .*

"It's you!" I said. "The king of the fox-gerbils!"

"I do not know what a fox-gerbil is," the voice said. "But . . . you must mistake me, of course. I am Hesho—and I am no king, since our planet has an equitable representative government. However, as the humble poet and captain of the starship *Gaualako-An*, I thank you from the deepest well of my heart."

I hit the mute button. "M-Bot, I think these must be the samurai fox-gerbils I saw earlier."

"You mean the kitsen?" he said. "They're a Superiority race with secondary citizenship. Oh! You'll find this amusing. I just translated the name of their ship. In their language, it roughly means, 'Big Enough to Kill You.'"

"A ship the size of a fighter must be like a destroyer to them," I said. "We didn't just rescue a single pilot; we rescued an entire crew." I flipped off the mute button. "Captain Hesho, my name is Alanik—and I'm glad to meet you. How would you feel about working together? There's too much chaos going on in this battle. We need to form an organized resistance."

"An excellent idea," Hesho said. "Like a steady rain that becomes a storm, the *Big Enough* is at your disposal."

"Great. Keep your guns trained to fire on any drones that draw close. If we get into trouble, I'll try to distract them from you so you can play target practice."

"If I might make a suggestion," Hesho replied. "We should rescue another faster ship, like yours, as it would help balance out our fledgling team."

"Sounds great," I said, scanning the battlefield, looking for faster ships we could try to recruit. One immediately jumped out at me—the black ship that held Brade, the human. It swerved through the melee, expertly pivoting around an asteroid. She was good. Very good.

"You see that black ship at my mark 238.25?" I said to Hesho. "I'll go try to help them out and see if they will join us. You hold steady and call me if any drones target you."

"Excellent," Hesho said.

I boosted after the black ship, darting through the chaotic fracas of light and explosions. The ship had two Krell tailing it. I radioed Brade, and the comm light lit up, indicating she was listening.

"I'll get those tails," I said. "Just give me—"

The black ship suddenly launched a light-lance into a passing *friendly* ship. I was shocked, both to see a light-lance being used from a Krell ship, and to see how it used the momentum of pivoting around a friendly ship. The callous move sent the poor unsuspecting ship spinning to the side—where it bounced against an asteroid. The move let Brade perform an expert turn, however, and she dove back through the center of the drones, blasting them both into space dust. She then buzzed past my ship, missing me by centimeters.

I cursed, spinning on my axis, then boosting to try going after her. That had been an incredible move. She had serious flying experience.

"Hey!" I called. "We're forming up a flight. We could use your . . ."

The black ship tore away to the right, vanishing farther into the battle, ignoring me completely. I sighed.

"Spensa," M-Bot said, "I think maybe she doesn't want to join our team."

"What made you think that?"

"I'm very observant," M-Bot said. "However, I believe someone else could use your help. I'm reading distress calls on a general outgoing line. Here, I'm highlighting the source on your proximity monitor and patching it through."

At once a panicked voice piped through my radio, and my pin translated for me. "My boosters aren't responding! Help!"

"Send Hesho those coordinates," I said to M-Bot, spinning on my axis and boosting the other way to slow down. Then I darted toward the distress call—which turned out to be the shuttle that Brade had used as a counterweight.

After colliding with the asteroid, the shuttle had bounced free and now tumbled through space with one of its boosters flashing on and off randomly. It would spurt in one direction, and then the booster would cut out. It would try to turn, but the booster would cut back on erratically, sending the ship tumbling in a different direction.

Three Krell, eager to prey on the weak, were coming in from different directions. "Hang on," I told the pilot as Hesho's ship—thankfully—arrived and began gunning at the various nearby Krell.

"Calculating . . . ," M-Bot said, highlighting a section of my canopy. "Here is a projected flight path of the damaged ship."

"Thanks," I said. "I thought that booster was blasting it around randomly."

"Few things are truly random," M-Bot said.

I used the projection to intercept the malfunctioning ship and spear it with my light-lance. I boosted to the left, narrowly towing it out of the path of Krell destructor fire. Unfortunately, the ship's broken booster immediately ignited, yanking me back to the right.

"I'm sorry!" the pilot's voice said. I saw a glimpse of them through the front of their ship—it was the single dione in the fight, the one with a two-tone face.

"Maybe you should just power down," I said with a grunt, trying to regain control. "Turn on your emergency lights and drop out of the fight."

"I can't," the voice said.

"There's no shame in it," I said. "You're not a coward."

"No," the voice said. "I mean . . . the collision seems to have crushed my emergency lights."

Scud. Maybe the pilots of the remote drones would see that this pilot was obviously in trouble, and leave them alone? No . . . if anything, there were more drones approaching than I would have expected. Almost as if they wanted to punish this dione who had been so brash as to participate in an activity that should have been reserved for inferiors.

I pulled the shuttle out of the way of another destructor barrage, then grunted as its booster ignited again, towing me back. I tried to compensate by using M-Bot's projections on my canopy, but my efforts weren't terribly effective.

"Please," the pilot said. "I'm sorry. I shouldn't have gotten you into this. Leave me to my fate. It is what I deserve."

"Like hell," I said, grunting again and trying to steer as the malfunctioning booster cut out. While it was down, I towed the craft toward Hesho's flagship—which was firing with increased desperation at the nearby drones.

"Spensa," M-Bot said. "That last turn you made let my cameras get a glimpse at the ship's boosters. There's a chunk of stone lodged in the left one's expression valve. Getting that free might fix the problem, as the booster is locked into a loop, trying to fire up—then finding the obstruction and triggering an emergency power-down."

"All right," I said. "Let me just crawl out and fix it then."

"Ha ha. You'd die!"

I grinned, getting ready for the booster to ignite again.

"That . . . *was* sarcasm, right?" M-Bot said. "Just checking.

Because I don't think you actually want to leave your ship. Explosive decompression would—"

"It was a joke," I said, then cursed as the booster on the broken ship ignited again. Unfortunately, I couldn't count on Hesho for help. The larger, slower fighter had its hands full holding off four drones.

"Open a general line," I said to M-Bot. "I think I'm going to need another ship to pull this off." A light on my comm blinked on. "This is a general distress call," I said. "I need a ship with a light-lance to help me at . . . coordinates 150.+60.554 from reference beacon 34."

I was met by silence. The battlefield had emptied a little, as many of the prospective pilots had given up. The ones remaining were those skilled enough to survive—though many flew unarmed personal crafts, and focused only on dodging and staying ahead of the drones.

In that, it seemed the test had been effective. It had quickly identified those who could fly under pressure. The debris of destroyed ships indicated, however, that the cost had been brutal.

"Leave me," the dione pilot said again. "I'm sorry. My trouble is not your trouble."

I eyed the Krell drones that were lurking nearby. "Hold on a sec," I said, then disengaged my light-lance. Suddenly free and unencumbered, I swooped around and started firing on the drones. I scored a couple of hits, but their shields were still up—so all I did was send them into basic defensive maneuvers.

"I could *really* use some help," I said over the general line. "Please. Anyone."

"Well . . . ," a breezy, feminine voice said. "Do you promise not to shoot me?"

"Yes, of course!" I said. "Why would I shoot you?"

"Um . . ." A ship hovered out from behind a nearby asteroid.

144

A Krell drone! I put my finger on the trigger, turning my ship toward it and aiming quickly.

"You said you wouldn't shoot me!" the voice said.

Wait. The *drone* was talking to me?

"Oh!" M-Bot said. "Ask her if she's an AI!"

"Are you an AI?" I asked over the line.

"No, of course not!" the voice said. "But I'm willing to help. What do you need?"

"Go chase those drones away from that disabled shuttle," I said. "Give me a little breathing room to try some precise flying."

"Very well," the voice said.

The little drone boosted out from her hiding place and moved in. My dione friend in the shuttle let out a fatalistic "So it ends" as the talking drone got close—but the drone did as I'd asked, instead chasing away the enemy ships.

"All right," I said. "M-Bot, highlight on my canopy that rock jammed into the shuttle's booster. Then narrow my light-lance's beam to the tightest possible setting."

"Ooooohhhh," he said. "Done."

I used the break in fighting to get in just behind the shuttle, positioning myself carefully and waiting for the right moment. I wasn't nearly as good a shot as Kimmalyn or Arturo—my specialties were flying fast and pulling stunts. Fortunately, M-Bot highlighted my target, and I had enough breathing room to sit and fine-tune my aim.

There. I picked out the rock as a brightly glowing speck of light rammed into the metal casing of the shuttle's left booster. It was maybe the size of a person's head.

I speared the stone with my light-lance, then I spun on my axis and boosted the other direction. The stone popped out with a jolt.

"I have control back!" the dione pilot said. "Booster is online again!"

"Great," I said. "Follow me."

The shuttle fell in behind me, flying in a blessedly straight line as we approached Hesho's ship. The Krell there scattered as soon as we three formed up together; as I'd hoped, they weren't interested in fighting organized flights of enemies. I lost track of the talking drone. I thought maybe she had gone back to hiding beside an asteroid.

"Captain Hesho," I said, making a private comm line for the three of us, "I found us another ship."

"Excellent, Captain Alanik," Hesho said. "Newcomer, what are your armaments and specialties?"

"I . . . don't have either," the dione in the shuttle said. "My name is Morriumur."

"A dione?" Hesho said, with obvious surprise in his voice. His ship turned, and likely he got a view of Morriumur sitting at the controls of their ship, behind the glass front. "Not just a dione, an unborn one at that. Curious."

The three of us settled into a slow patrol, searching for any other ships we could help and invite into our flight. Morriumur wasn't a terrible pilot—but they obviously didn't have much combat experience, as they panicked every time they picked up a tail.

Still, they tried hard and managed to stick with me as I led a few Krell back toward the *Big Enough,* which shot them down with precision. The battle had started to spread out, individual ships seeking cover farther within the asteroid field. Krell roved in packs, but bursts of fire were growing more rare.

I invited a few more ships to join us, but they seemed too busy—consumed by their own flying—to stop. I spotted the black ship as it zipped past at one point, well outpacing the two drones trying to chase it down. Again, Brade ignored my offers.

"How much longer is this going to go on?" I demanded. "Don't they have enough evidence yet?"

"Seven minutes remaining," M-Bot said.

As we passed another patch of debris from a destroyed ship, I found my anger building. Yes, they'd warned that our training might be dangerous. But using *live fire* on civilian-class ships? I'd already had a simmering hatred for the Superiority, but this stoked it hotter. How could they have such callous disregard for life—all while feigning to be "civilized" and "intelligent"?

Finally, the end arrived. The drones turned as one and made their way back to the mining platform. Winzik's voice came on the general line, and his voice sounded smug as he congratulated the survivors on their performance.

Hesho, Morriumur, and I headed back. About fifty other ships, it turned out, had survived the test. M-Bot did a quick count of the ones that had been towed back earlier, dropping out—and by combining those two numbers, then subtracting from the total, got a rough estimate of how many ships had been destroyed.

"Twelve ships destroyed," he said.

Fewer than I'd expected—in the chaos, it had seemed like far more. Still, that was twelve people dead. Murdered by the Superiority.

Did you expect anything else? a part of me asked. *You knew what they were capable of—they've been murdering humans for eighty years.*

We landed our ships, though I did so on edge, half expecting some kind of trap or "surprise" second test. But none came. We settled down onto the platform safely, the artificial gravity locking our ships in place. The envelope of atmosphere provided fresh air as we popped open our cockpits.

Other surviving pilots looked rattled as they gathered back near the stage at the far end of the platform. Usually after a battle, I felt like many of these aliens looked—worn out, drained by the extreme amount of attention and focus that fighting required. Today though, I was *livid* as I climbed out and dropped to the floor of the platform.

What kind of *idiots* set up a test like this? I remembered how shocked I'd been to be sent into combat on my first day in training with the DDF, but even then Ironsides—who had been desperate to save her dying people—had only used us as a feint. Here, the Superiority was powerful, secure, and safe. Yet they threw away the lives of eager and trusting pilots?

I shoved my way through the crowd of aliens, moving toward Winzik and the other test administrators. I opened my mouth to—

"What the *hell* is wrong with you people!" a voice shouted right behind me.

I froze, the wind stolen from my own exclamation. I turned, surprised to see a hulking alien creature that looked vaguely like a gorilla. They held a large battle helmet under their arm, and pushed right past me in the crowd, pointing at Winzik.

"Live fire?" the gorilla alien shouted. "In a *testing exercise*? What you just did is the equivalent of murder. What in the name of the deepest void *were you thinking*?"

I shut my mouth at the exclamation, which seemed as furious— but twice as loud—as my own anger.

"You signed the release," Winzik finally said, his hand held to his armored breast in a sign of aghast horror at the creature's outburst.

"To the void with a release!" the alien shouted. "If I got a child to sign a release saying I could kick them, I'd still be a monster for doing it! These people didn't know what they were getting themselves into! *You* bear the shame for this."

Creatures of various shapes and sizes moved away from the gorilla, and the officials on the stage seemed completely flabbergasted. "We . . . we needed to see who would be calm under fire," Winzik finally explained. "And we gave orders to our drone pilots not to harm those who backed down. My, my! Such aggression."

"You should have used dummy rounds!" I said, stepping up beside the gorilla alien. "Like any sane military on exercises!"

"How would that have tested them?" Winzik asked me. "They'd have known it wasn't real. Fighting the delvers is extremely taxing to the psyche, Alanik of the UrDail. This was the only way to judge who would be capable and calm."

"The only way?" the gorilla demanded. "Let's try another test then! We can test how well you can take a punch. I'll start with a hammer to the skull!"

"My, my!" another official said. "A *threat*?"

"Yes," Winzik said, waving a shooing motion. "Such aggression! Gul'zah of the burl? You are released from duty."

"Released from . . . ," Gul'zah sputtered. "You think . . ."

I stepped forward to tell the Superiority officials where they could stuff their tests, but a voice spoke in my ear, interrupting me. "Spensa?" M-Bot said. "Please don't get us kicked out. Remember our mission!"

I seethed, watching the gorilla alien, who backed away from several armed dione guards. I almost started shouting again, but then someone else moved up beside me. Morriumur, the dione with the two-tone face.

"Alanik?" they said to me, pleading. "Come, Alanik. Let's go get some food. They will have it for us below. Your species does eat, yes?" They nodded at me encouragingly.

Finally, I let Morriumur lead me away.

16

Morriumur and I followed a group of excited aliens toward a wide stairwell down into the bowels of the mining station. Just before going down the steps, I spotted a tug vessel towing a black Krell ace fighter toward a nearby hangar. I cursed myself silently. I'd been intending to watch for Brade and see if I could get her to talk to me, but it appeared she'd landed quietly away from the rest of us and already vanished.

I sighed and started down the steps, catching up with Morriumur, who walked alone at the back of the crowd. It was moving slowly down the steps, bottlenecked at the doorway at the bottom.

"Thanks for talking me out of doing something stupid up there," I said to Morriumur as we waited.

"Well thank you, in turn, for saving my life!" Morriumur said. They pressed their lips together firmly, which made them look annoyed—but I was beginning to wonder if maybe I just didn't understand dione expressions, because their next words were friendly. "You are a fantastic pilot, Alanik! Better than any I think I've ever seen."

"Have you seen many?" I asked. "I mean, aren't you . . . really young?"

"Ah, yes!" Morriumur said. "I'm two months old, but I have some of the memories and skills of my parents. One of them, my leftparent, was a commercial pilot during their youth—which is how I inherited the skill."

"Huh," I said, taking a step downward. "The people I talked to were surprised you came here to test. Why would a dione come try out for this? And why wouldn't any other of your kind think of doing it? Unless that's too forward a question."

"No, no," they said. "It's not too forward a question at all. Peace forbid! We *encourage* lesser species to learn of our ways, as we hope it will usher them toward prime intelligence. The answer to your question is simple. There were no other diones in the test because my kind have carefully cultivated souls, ones purged completely of aggression or violence. To come and then train for killing, why, it would be unthinkable!"

"But aren't some of the drone pilots diones?" I asked.

"Some have been, but never for long. The drone pilots are almost always tenasi," Morriumur explained, using the name of one of the leader races of the Superiority that I hadn't met. "They have a special ability to fight but not become emotional as they do so. The rest of us are very peaceful."

"And yet," I said, "your dione leaders have no problem sending drones to murder a group of unprepared pilots?"

"This . . ." Morriumur looked down at their feet as they descended another step. "This was unexpected. I'm certain the officials know what they're doing. And they're right—it wouldn't do to send people into battle who will simply flee. So some kind of extreme test was required, right?"

"Seems to me they're a bunch of hypocr—" I started.

"Spensa," M-Bot said in my ear. "I am not the best at anticipating proper social reactions for organics, but could you maybe *not*

151

insult the first dione friend you've made? We might need to learn something from them."

I bit off my words with difficulty. M-Bot was probably right. "Why did *you* come to this test, then?" I asked Morriumur instead. "Your soul isn't . . . what did you say? Purged of aggression?"

"I am . . . a special case," they replied. "I was born with an aggressive personality, and so must prove myself. I came here in an attempt to do that."

We eventually reached the bottom of the steps and entered a large room with a low ceiling. Bright white lights illuminated cafeteria-style counters and tables; it reminded me of the mess hall back at Alta Base, though the scents . . . well, they were unusual. I caught some familiar ones—fried food, baking bread, something that was like cinnamon. But those scents mixed with a whole host of strange ones. Muddy water. Burning hair. Engine grease? It made for an overpowering, confusing wall of sensation that stopped me as soon as I passed through the doorway.

"What do you eat?" Morriumur asked, pointing at some signs hanging over various serving stations. "Carbon-based vegetation, I assume? There are mineral cocktails, though I doubt you can metabolize that. And over on the far side, there's a line for lab-grown meat." That seemed to bother them, judging by the way they drew their lips back into a frowning scowl that showed teeth.

"Uh . . ." I tried to think of how Alanik would respond.

"Your species," M-Bot said in my ear, "has a diet roughly similar to a human one—though with more nuts and less meat. Also, no milk."

"Seriously?" I whispered, moving with Morriumur toward the vegetable line. I waved at my chest. "Alanik has breasts. What are they for? Decoration?"

"No milk from *other creatures,* I should say," M-Bot said. "Your species finds it extremely gross. As do I, by the way. Do you even stop to think how many strange liquids you organics squirt from your orifices?"

"No stranger than the ideas that squirt from your orifice sometimes, M-Bot."

I followed Morriumur through the line and got a salad of something that seemed similar to algae strips. M-Bot assured me that it fit both my physiology and that of Alanik. As we collected our food, I couldn't help noticing how much space the other pilots gave us.

When I went to grab some water, I had to crowd between two large gorilla-alien burl who barely gave me a glance, so it wasn't *me* that everyone was staying away from. It was Morriumur. *Yeah,* I thought, sipping my cup of water and hitting another pocket of open space as I walked back toward them. *They're scared of Morriumur.* Members of other species kept shooting glances toward them, as if suspicious or worried about the presence of a dione in this space reserved for "lesser" species.

I walked with my tray toward an empty table near the corner of the room. The cinnamon scent was strong here, but as I moved to sit down, Morriumur caught me by the arm.

"Not there!" they hissed. "Are you crazy?"

I frowned, looking at the empty table. It was like all the others. Morriumur steered me to another empty table and settled down.

Scud. I had no idea what I was doing. What was wrong with the first table? I sat down, confused. I needed to steal a hyperdrive soon, because I *was* going to screw up this act sooner or later.

"So, um . . . ," I said to Morriumur as I dug into my salad. "You said you've been alive, um, two months?"

"Yes!" Morriumur said. "I will be born in three months, as a baby, though I will retain these memories as I grow. Or . . . well, I hope to be born in three months. Whether or not I can enter the final stage of the birthing process will depend on whether or not

153

my family members agree that this personality is a good one to add to their ranks."

"That's . . . Huh." *So strange.*

"Different?" Morriumur offered. "I realize that this is not the way most species do things."

"I don't want to be offensive," I answered carefully, "but yeah, it's a little odd to me. I mean, how does it work? Do you have two brains right now?"

"Yes, I have two of most internal organs—though the extra arms and legs were absorbed during the cocooning process, and my parents' brains are linked together for now, acting as one."

Wow. What a strange conversation.

"If you don't mind," they said, "you have the look of a race that uses sexual reproduction, with two different sexes, male and female?" When I nodded, they continued. "That is one of the most popular biological templates in the galaxy, though no one is certain why. Could be parallel evolution. I prefer the theory that you all have some common ancestors who spread through the stars using cytonic hyperjumps long before you even had stone tools!"

I sat up straighter. "Cytonic hyperjumps, you say?" I asked, as innocently as I could.

"Oh, you probably don't know about those!" Morriumur said. "People used to be able to hyperjump using just their *minds*. It was very dangerous, but I find it an interesting theory as to why some species from different planets look similar. Don't you agree that would be exciting, if it could ever be proven?"

I nodded. Maybe I could learn something about myself here. "I wonder how they did it? Do you know anything about the process?"

"No," they said. "Just what's in the books—and the warning that it's dangerous. The texts are very careful not to talk about specifics."

Drat. I looked closely at Morriumur, and could tell—now that I thought to check—that the left and right halves of Morriumur's face had different features. Two people had actually melded together somehow, creating Morriumur—an individual who was larger than most diones I had seen, but only by a few centimeters. The couple must have shed a lot of mass during the . . . the pupation?

I realized I was staring, and looked back down at my salad with a blush. "Sorry."

"It's all right," Morriumur said with a laugh. "I can only guess how odd it must seem—though *I* find it odd that so many species reproduce your way, without ever even *trying out* the personality of the new child. You're left with random chance! I, instead, can interact with my extended family, and they can decide if this is a version of me they like."

I found something about that to be distinctly unsettling. "And if they don't? Like you, I mean."

Morriumur hesitated, then poked at their own food. "Well, then when I enter the cocoon in three months, my parents will decide that I'm not quite right. They'll pupate again, and I'll emerge with another personality. The extended family will try that version out for five months, and we'll eventually settle on a version of me that everyone likes."

"That sounds dangerous," I said. "I mean, no offense, but I don't think I like the implications. Your family can just keep shaking up your personality until they get something they approve of? I don't think *anyone* would have approved of me."

"Non-diones always say things like that," Morriumur said, sitting up straighter. "But this process has created for us a very peaceful society, of prime intelligence. It . . . does put stress upon me to prove myself, however." They waved toward the room full of pilots. "That has pushed me to do something extreme. As I told you, this version of my personality is a little . . . aggressive.

I thought, what if I show my family that this is a good thing? Maybe it was impulsive of me to join the call for pilots, but with only three months left, this seemed the best way to prove myself."

"But . . ." I started to object, then trailed off as I noticed that someone new had entered the dining hall. Well, a group of someones—some fifty kitsen, each maybe fifteen centimeters tall. The furry creatures marched up to our table, most wearing little white uniforms of a naval style, their fluffy tails sticking out the back.

I stifled a smile. They seemed to be a powerful spacefaring race that had shown bravery and loyalty in combat. But . . . scud, they were also really cute.

They stopped at the empty chair next to me, and several raised a ladder against it. Others scurried up, then placed another ladder leading to the table's top. Finally, Hesho—still wearing his formal red silk clothing—climbed up the ladders onto the tabletop. He raised a paw to me, fingers clenched in a fist. Seeing him up close, I could make out the pattern of red on his white fur snout, a color repeated in the fringe of his long, pointed ears.

"Alanik of the UrDail!" he said, his translation collar projecting a bold, deep voice. "Today, we feast to our victory!"

"Captain Hesho of the kitsen!" I said, mimicking his closed-fisted gesture. "Did you only just arrive at lunch?"

"We fetched our own vittles and brought them here," he said. "We cannot trust a Superiority cafeteria to have proper feasting materials appropriate to our station."

Another kitsen arrived with an oversized chair, which they placed on the tabletop for Hesho to settle into, his bushy tail sticking out the back. Others brought a small table, which they set in front of him and draped with a tablecloth.

"So," Hesho said, looking from me to Morriumur. "We are colleagues now, we three? Shall we make a formal pact of mutual aid and support?"

I glanced at Morriumur. "I don't know that I'd thought about it that much," I said.

"We will need trustworthy allies if we are to survive future engagements," Hesho continued. "Though to be honest, I do not know if having a dione in our small fleet will aid our progress or hinder it."

"Probably hinder," Morriumur said, looking down at their plate again. "The officials will push me harder than they would a member of a lesser race."

"Then the kitsen shall welcome this extra difficulty," Hesho said solemnly. "Perhaps it will prove, finally, that we are worthy to become full citizens of the Superiority."

"Do we have any idea what happens next?" I asked them. "We passed their test, right?"

"Next we'll be trained to fight the delvers," Morriumur said.

"Which means what?" I asked. I still had no idea what I was in for.

"It is hard to say," Hesho said. "I don't believe any of us expected the test today to be as brutal as it was." As he talked, another group of kitsen arrived with steaming plates of food, which they arranged on Hesho's table. One, wearing a silken dress, cut his food and began feeding it to him. The others busily set up feasting materials on the tops of several of the chairs at our table.

"The Superiority is odd," Hesho continued around bites of his tiny steak. "Its officials will work very hard to protect the pristine and peaceful lives of innocents, but once you step outside the bounds of propriety, their retribution can be swift and brutal."

"The Superiority is wise," Morriumur said. "It has stood for centuries, providing safety and prosperity for billions of beings."

"I do not contest those facts," Hesho said. "And my people are eager to have our citizenship level increased. Still, you cannot dispute that some departments—particularly the Department of Protective Services—can show a disturbing lack of empathy."

I nodded, and the table fell silent. As we ate, I found my focus drawn to something that I must have been feeling all along. The . . . call of the stars. Starsight's cytonic-suppression field had quieted it, but out on this station I could hear the song again. I couldn't distinguish what was being said, but that sound in the back of my mind meant this station was sending out communications.

I set down my fork and closed my eyes, imagining myself flying among the stars, as Gran-Gran had taught me. I felt myself drifting. Maybe . . . maybe I could follow those invisible trails. Did some of them lead to Detritus, and the Superiority forces posted there?

But there was nothing that gave me a clue toward that end. I *did* feel something *else* nearby though. A kind of humming familiarity. What was that?

Brade, I realized, recognizing the feeling from earlier. *She's not in the room, but she's near.*

I opened my eyes and glanced around. The bustling room was filled with aliens eating and drinking—or in the case of some very strange rocky creatures, pouring liquid on their heads.

The sensation was coming from outside the room. I made an excuse to the others, saying I needed to find a restroom. Morriumur pointed the way, and I ducked out of the dining hall, glancing in the direction Morriumur had indicated. A string of doors ran down the hallway here, each with a sign identifying the kind of disposal unit contained therein.

I glanced in the other direction, where Brade's cytonic sensation seemed to be coming from. There were no guards that I could see, so I slipped away down the hall.

The feeling got stronger as I reached a door off to the side. It was cracked, and I peered in to see that indeed, Brade was there. And she was speaking with a group of dione officials, as well as Winzik.

17

I crouched beside the door, trying to listen to what Winzik and the other officials were saying inside.

"Hey!" M-Bot said in my ear, nearly making me jump. "Spensa, what are you doing?" I gritted my teeth, concentrating on the sounds from behind the door. "Oh!" M-Bot said after a moment. "Are you hiding? What's wrong? I was computing our flight back to Starsight. Weren't you going to go release secretions in the lavatory? Spensa, did you release them in an inappropriate place? Is that why you're hiding?"

"Shut up," I whispered as softly as I could. "I'm trying to spy."

"Oooooohhhh," M-Bot said.

The others were speaking too quietly for my translator to pick them up. I could hear muffled voices, but couldn't make anything out.

"Do you maybe want me to enhance your bracelet's auditory reception capacities, then wire the translations directly into your ear, so your pin won't give you away?" M-Bot asked. "This will help you spy more efficiently."

"*Yes,*" I whispered back.

"Fine. No need to be terse."

He wirelessly shut off my pin, then began piping the voices from the other room directly into my earpiece. My bracelet's sound pickup was much more sensitive than the pin's or my normal hearing, and M-Bot was way better at isolating voices from background chatter.

"—should have seen that this would be such a disaster," one of the officials was saying. "These drone pilots were trained to fight against the humans at the Detritus preserve! They came out shooting far too aggressively."

"These casualties *are* unfortunate." That was Winzik's voice, which had a calm tone to it. "But you needn't worry about repercussions. This was an accident, not an act of aggression."

"There are a dozen dead!" another official said. These diones sounded far less calm in private than they had outside, when talking to that gorilla burl. "The poor families!"

"Those poor families will be destroyed entirely if we don't prepare a fighting force to resist the delvers," Winzik said. "My, my. My department's suppressors will deal with any outcries of injustice. You have done your duty well."

"Yes, well . . . ," another official said. "I guess, as long as you think the test worked . . . But was it necessary for you to bring your human here, Winzik? She makes me uncomfortable."

"My my, Tizmar," Winzik said. "You worry far too much. And about the wrong things! Consider instead the Department of Species Integration and their insistence on entering several very aggressive species into our contest. Cuna is up to something here. That newcomer, Alanik, uses human combat strategies. Her people are dangerous from their long association with the scourge, and should remain isolated."

I frowned as I leaned against the wall—then felt something. A mind pressing against my own.

"What?" said an official inside. "What is wrong? Why is your human standing up, so alert like that? She's properly trained, isn't she?"

Idiot. If I could "hear" Brade with my senses, then of course she'd "hear" me back. I spun and scrambled back down the hallway. Sweating, I slowed down to walk back into the dining room. I tried to be nonchalant as I sat down at our table.

A moment later, Winzik appeared in the doorway, looking around the room. As I slipped back into conversation with Hesho and Morriumur, from the corner of my eye I could see that the Krell's faceplate pointed in our direction, lingering on us. Then he retreated.

A short time later, a group of dione officials entered the room bearing tablets. They moved through the tables, talking to the pilots, giving instructions.

"And here we have Alanik," said a dione official with crimson skin as they arrived at our table. "The noncitizen! You performed quite well in the test. Excellent flying, and rescuing others in need? Delightful. We have organized you in a flight with the *Big Enough* and its crew. I assume you'll find this acceptable?"

I glanced at Hesho, who stood up and clapped once. It . . . seemed like a sign of assent?

"I'd like that," I said. "Thank you."

"Now," the official said, scrolling their tablet screen and reading. "There is a matter of some . . . sensitivity I would discuss with you two. We have added another member to your flight. A skilled and capable pilot. *Very* skilled."

"Then we shall welcome them!" Hesho said. "Who is this person?"

"It's a human," the official said.

Morriumur gasped softly, putting their hands to their face. Hesho immediately sat back down in his seat, and a kitsen appeared with a fan and began fanning him rapidly. I tried my best to look surprised and horrified.

"Now, you needn't be worried!" the official continued, speaking quickly. "This human is fully licensed. I will provide you with documentation."

"Why," Hesho said, "would we be training to fight one evil by using another?"

"Yes," I said. "Those things enslaved my people for decades! I wouldn't think you'd set them loose on the galaxy."

"This human is *very* well trained," the official said. "We need to test whether she can fight delvers."

"What if this human *is* perfect at fighting them?" Hesho asked. "Will you create flights and fleets only of humans? This is hiring the wolf to guard your sheep. In the end, you will still lose your sheep."

I found that metaphor curious. Had he actually used the words *wolf* and *sheep*? Or had he spoken alien words that got translated into something similar in English?

Either way, I wasn't sure what I thought of Brade joining our flight. She was a cytonic. Would she be able to, with time, tell that I was secretly human? I had the suspicion that she was being assigned to my flight specifically to keep an eye on me.

At the same time, she probably understood much more about being cytonic. She might know the secret to making my powers work properly. She might . . . be able to explain to me what I was. What *we* were.

"I'm sure," I said slowly, "that the Superiority knows what it's doing."

"My people have a long history with the humans," Hesho said, settling back beneath the fanning of his servant. "Back in the days when we still had shadow-walkers, our people walked between our world and Earth, the human homeworld. This is a bonfire awaiting a spark."

"If this is not an acceptable situation, Your Majesty," the dione said, "we can remove you from the flight rolls."

"I would, of course, have to ask my people," Hesho said. "As I am *not* their king, but simply one equal among many in a perfectly legal democracy."

The other kitsen around him nodded vigorously in agreement, even while one fanned him and another served his food.

"So this means we passed the test for sure," I said, diverting the topic. "We're going to be trained to fight the delvers?"

"Yes," the official said. "We'll send a shuttle to pick you up tomorrow at 1000, Starsight time. It will deliver you to our training grounds. I'm afraid you'll need to leave your own starships behind and train on our equipment, though we'll have an appropriate vessel prepared for the kitsen, Captain Hesho."

Superiority ships. Exactly what I was hoping for. I still didn't know how I was going to find a chance to steal a hyperdrive from my new ship, let alone get it to M-Bot and jump us back to Detritus, but at least I'd taken one major step toward accomplishing that goal. Though I'd want to triple-check to make certain my hologram disguise would stay in place if I strayed too far from M-Bot.

"To be extra careful regarding the human," the official said, "we've placed a figment in your flight. You might have noticed that one was attending this test. This individual prefers to be addressed as a female, and has asked that you call her simply Vapor."

Hesho sat up at this. "A figment, you say?" he said, tapping his furry chin with a single clawed finger. "This is some comfort, at least."

Huh? What was this? A "figment"? I looked around, trying to see if I could pick out what they were referencing. However, before I could ask, the official continued speaking.

"Excellent," the official said, then pointed absently at Morriumur. "Now, you. Please follow me, and I'll tell you about your placement."

"What?" I said, suddenly alert. "Morriumur isn't with us?"

"They shall be placed in their own solo flight," the official said. "As is appropriate."

Morriumur stood up slowly, looking sad. "I enjoyed speaking with you, Alanik."

"No," I said, feeling my face flush with outrage as I stood up. "We're a flight. Morriumur stays with us."

Both Morriumur and the official looked at me with shocked expressions. Well, let them be shocked. I folded my arms. "What good is a flight of one? Leave Morriumur with us."

"You already have four in your team," the official said. "This is the number we decided as a flight size."

"Surely there isn't an exact multiple of four in this room," I said, gesturing to the pilots filling the tables around us. "Besides, we're already a strange flight with a *human* in it. So we could use the extra pilot with us, in case the vicious creature turns against us."

"Well," the official said, rattled as they typed on their tablet, "well, I guess we can rearrange." They glanced up at me warily, then went back to typing. "Just be ready for the shuttle pickup tomorrow. A Superiority flight suit will be issued to you and will arrive in the morning. You'll be delivered back to Starsight each evening, so will not need to pack changes of clothing, but if you require sustenance at midday, be prepared with your own food supply. Be on time in the morning."

At that, the dione turned and hurried away.

"You didn't need to do that," Morriumur said to me. "I came into this knowing that I'd be isolated."

"Yeah, well, I rarely let go of someone once I have my teeth in them," I said. "It's the warrior's way."

"What a . . . profoundly disturbing metaphor," Morriumur said, settling back down. "Thank you, in any case. I should like to not be on my own."

"Wait," I said, looking around our table. "They said four people were in our team. Who is this Vapor they mentioned?"

"It's me," a quiet whisper of a voice said. I jumped, and turned to look, but no one was there. I was hit with the striking scent of cinnamon. Burned cinnamon, actually.

"Welcome, unseen one," Hesho said, standing, then bowing low. The others of his crew did likewise.

"You're . . . invisible?" I asked, surprised.

"I am a figment," said the soft feminine voice, and I realized I knew that voice. I'd heard it before.

"The drone ship that helped me save Morriumur!" I said. "You were on that ship."

"Figments," Hesho said, "are known to be able to infiltrate ships and take control of them."

"So, are all the drones piloted by . . . by people like you?" I asked.

"No," the disembodied voice said. "There aren't many of us. I simply took control of one of the ships for this test, against the will of its remote pilot."

Incredible. But what was she? A smell? Was I talking to a *smell*?

The distinct scent trailed away, but I didn't know if that meant Vapor was leaving, or . . . something else? I found the idea of a creature that I couldn't see to be distinctly disturbing. Who knew when she would be watching us?

The lunch was breaking up, creatures from other tables filing out to return to their ships. Hesho bade us farewell with gusto, then climbed down the ladders set up by his crew. Together, the group of over fifty diminutive foxes gathered their things and trotted out the doors.

Morriumur and I followed, eventually emerging out into the open air at the top of the station. Black sky overhead, speckled with stars. Ships were launching a few at a time for the flight back to Starsight.

I bade farewell to Morriumur, then walked over to M-Bot and hauled myself up onto his wing so I could get into the cockpit.

"Some engineers came to try to inspect me while you were below," M-Bot said, "but I scared them away by making it seem like they'd accidentally tripped an alarm system."

"Good thinking," I said.

"It was kind of like a lie," he said. "I *can* do it, as you said. Under the right circumstances."

As we prepared to take off, I felt something against my mind again. I glanced to where the sensation seemed to be coming from, and noticed a set of partially opened hangar doors. I could see a shadow standing inside. Brade—watching my ship.

"I don't like the idea of you going off on your own tomorrow," M-Bot said. "Flying another ship."

"Jealous?"

"Maybe! It would be cool if I could feel that. But more, I think it's dangerous. We'll need to double-check your bracelet's holographic projector. Its CPU should be able to manage your hologram without my aid, but we'll want to observe it first. It would be better if I could go with you."

"I don't really see that we have a choice," I said as I lifted us up and away from the platform. "We need to get our hands on a Superiority ship."

"It's possible they won't give you one that can hyperjump," M-Bot said. "At least not at first."

"I considered that," I said. "But if I can gain their trust, there's a good chance they'll relax their security around me. I might not be given a starfighter that can hyperjump, but I'll likely be near one. If I can't steal a hyperdrive, perhaps I can at least get some photos of one."

"Photos won't get us home."

"I know. I'm still working on that."

As we flew toward Starsight and I thought it through, I realized that I'd inadvertently been given a backup plan. Winzik and the others had just assigned me to the same flight as their pet human.

Did Brade know there was an entire planet full of humans like her, only free? Might she be willing to escape there, if I gave her the right opportunity?

If I couldn't steal a hyperdrive from the Superiority, maybe I could instead steal away one of their cytonics.

18

I settled M-Bot into place on the top of our embassy on Starsight, then sat back in my seat, suddenly exhausted.

Being Alanik was taxing. I was accustomed to just going with my gut and doing what seemed natural for me. It had gotten me through life well so far. I'd admittedly earned the occasional bump or scrape, but I'd never had to worry about pretending to be someone other than myself.

I sighed, finally hitting the canopy release and standing up to stretch. The embassy didn't have a ground crew to pull over steps for me, so I climbed out onto the wing, then hopped down.

"Overall," M-Bot said to me, "I think that went well. We're not dead, and you actually managed to get into their military."

"By the skin of my teeth," I said, grimacing as I remembered the burl gorilla alien who had thrown the tantrum and been kicked out. That *would* have been me if I'd gotten to Winzik a tad earlier.

"Do your teeth have skin?" M-Bot asked.

"I don't think so," I said, walking over and hooking up M-Bot's charging cords and network link. "Not sure where the saying comes from, actually."

"Hmmm. Oh! Well, it's from an English version of the Bible. That's a really antiquated version of the Book of Saints, from Old Earth."

I got the last cord hooked up, then traipsed down the steps. Doomslug trilled at me excitedly from the bedroom when I checked on her. I'd set up a litter box for her and some chopped mushrooms, which, judging by the crumbs left, she'd found acceptable as a meal. I gave her a scratch, then noted a little light on the wall. It was blinking, indicating that I had a delivery, so I tromped down to the bottom floor and checked the delivery box. Before flying out this morning, I'd made a few orders to test my requisition abilities.

Inside the box, I found a bundle of new clothing in my size, along with some toiletries. I grabbed everything and headed up to the kitchen, where I fried a small algae patty and ate it in a bun. Then I walked back to my bathroom. It was still a little strange that I had one all to myself. Scud, I had this entire *building* all to myself—well, myself and my pet slug, who insisted I give her another head scratch as I passed her in the hall.

In the bathroom's mirror, I looked at myself. Or, the illusion of Alanik that I wore. *Doomslug doesn't notice I'm not wearing my real face,* I thought. She obviously worked by scent and sound, as she didn't have eyes. It hit me that my disguise was even more tenuous than I'd thought. What about that creature Vapor, who *was* a scent? Did I have to worry she'd know I was human?

I groaned softly, feeling weighed down. I flipped off the lights, then—with a sigh of relief—took off my hologram bracelet. Though M-Bot had scanned the place for spy devices, I wanted to be extra careful, so I kept the bracelet on at all times.

For now, I wanted to be myself. Even in the dark. Even alone. Even for just a little while.

I cleansed, and it felt luxurious to not be pressed for time. Back on Detritus, it seemed I had always been running to some training exercise or another. Here though . . . I could simply rest and let the pod's cleansing agents wash me.

I finally pulled myself out, then sighed and put the bracelet back on. I turned on the light and pulled a set of loose, generic clothing from my bundle. They looked kind of like the scrubs that medical personnel wore. I figured these would make good all-purpose work or sleeping clothing.

I sorted through the toiletries. Hopefully the people watching my requisition orders wouldn't wonder why I'd forgotten my toothpaste. Though I'd checked with M-Bot before ordering everything, I still had an amusing time looking over the warning label on the back of the tube. My pin translated the words, and it listed which species in the galaxy would find the toothpaste toxic. Running a galactic empire seemed to carry a lot of strange problems I'd never considered.

Brushing my teeth in front of the mirror, I found the toothpaste actually had a nice minty taste to it, way better than the bitter stuff we used back home. Such were apparently the benefits of having an actual economy and infrastructure, instead of being forced to repurpose ancient biorefineries to manufacture toothpaste.

My hair was longer than I used to keep it, and was fortunately about the length of Alanik's, inching past my shoulders. I'd kept it short when I'd been young, partially because I'd hated the color. Heroes from Gran-Gran's stories had all had raven-black hair or golden-flax hair—maybe the occasional fire-scarlet color thrown in for variety. Nobody in those tales had dirty-brown hair.

It was white now though, with the hologram on. I ran my fingers through it, and the illusion really was perfect, with each individual strand recolored. My expressions also mapped quite well to Alanik's face, and I couldn't feel anything different when I poked my skin, though I knew that my features and hers weren't the same.

The only things that were off were the bone ridges Alanik had under her eyes and along the sides of her face. Those were pure illusion, and if I stuck my finger into them, the hologram distorted. Still, the bracelet was good enough to make my hair seem to brush against the ridges—instead of clipping through the center of them—when the two touched.

I stared at myself in the mirror, smiling, frowning, trying to find some error in the way it all looked, but it was an excellent illusion. I could almost believe I was wearing makeup.

It was no surprise when I found myself thinking about Alanik. Had she worried about how to fit her hair into her helmet? What would she think of me imitating her?

Don't trust their peace . . . their lies . . .

I brushed my hair, then trailed out into the hall and down the stairs to my bedroom.

"Ah," M-Bot said to me. "You'll be interested to read this. We've just received a communication back from Alanik's people, sent—supposedly—via secure but unmonitored Superiority channels."

"I don't doubt for a moment that they read it anyway," I said, settling down at the bedroom's desk. "Let's see what it says."

M-Bot displayed the message at the desk's workstation, translated to English. It gave a bland response to our bland rundown of events. Which was promising—it didn't seem they'd immediately contacted the Superiority. "And is there an encrypted, hidden message? Like the one we sent?"

"Yes," M-Bot said. "It's a very interesting cypher, based on the number of letters in each word mapped to a one-time pad message with the key in your pin. Completely unbreakable without the pin. I guess that's more than what you want to know. Anyway, the encrypted message simply says: 'We want to speak to Alanik.'"

"Send back a report on today's test, and encode, 'She will contact you when she is well. For now, I am embedded among the Superiority, imitating her. Please do not give me away.'"

"Sounds like a reasonable response," M-Bot said. "I will construct that message."

I nodded, walking to the bed. I really needed some sleep, and yet when I thought about lying down, I realized that I wasn't tired. So I settled into a chair beside the window instead and looked down the skyscraper-lined street of Starsight. I watched all those people out there move, flow. A million different goals. A million different jobs. A million creatures who saw me as one of the most dangerous things in the galaxy.

"M-Bot?" I asked. "Can you hear those people down below, on the street?"

"Not sure," he said. "Um, that was a lie. I can totally hear them. How was my lie though?"

"Try not to tell people that you're lying *immediately* after you do it. It ruins the effect."

"Right. Okay. Then . . . Um, not sure." He started humming.

"Could you maybe *not* practice your lying right now? It's getting a little annoying."

"Spensa," he said. "You're not supposed to *like* it when I lie. Right? How do you know when to do it and when not to?"

I sighed.

"All right, fine," he said. "I have advanced surveillance equipment. From this height, I might be able to isolate audio from people on the street, though it's no guarantee and will depend on interference. Why?"

"I just want to know what they talk about," I said. "There aren't any Krell raids for them to anticipate. Do they talk about manufactory jobs? About the humans? Maybe the delvers?"

"I'm scanning for a sampling," M-Bot said. "It seems, for now, they talk about normal things. Picking their kids up from care centers. Ordering ingredients for dinner. The health and training of their pets."

"Normal things," I repeated. "Is all of that . . . normal?"

"That seems like it would depend on a large number of variables."

I stared down, watching everyone move. The people walking past displayed that same lack of urgency I'd noticed when I'd first flown in. This place was busy, but only because there were so many pieces moving at once. Individually, it was peaceful. Normal?

No. I *couldn't* believe it. This was the Superiority, the empire that had practically destroyed humankind. They were the ones who funded Winzik and his Krell domination of my people. These were the monsters I'd spent my life training to fight, the faceless creatures who had lurked in the sky, bombing our civilization centers and bringing us nearly to extinction.

Starsight was one of their primary trade and political hubs. This place had to be a front intended to make it *seem* like life in their empire was peaceful. How many of those people passing on the street were in the Superiority's employ, directed to *act* innocent? It seemed so obvious, now that I thought about it. This was an act, a way to give outsiders a false impression of how great the empire was.

Well, I wouldn't believe their lies of peace and prosperity. I'd seen how they treated the pilots at the test today. All those people on the street, they were culpable for what had been done to my father and my friends.

These weren't just simple people, going about their simple lives. They were my enemies. We were at war.

"Spensa," M-Bot said. "Not to be a nag, but it has currently been fifteen hours since you have slept and—as you're adjusting to this station's sleep cycle—I recorded only four hours of actually restful sleep for you last night."

"Yeah, so?" I snapped.

"You get cranky if you don't sleep."

"No I don't."

"Do you mind if I record your tone for later, to use as evidence against you in a future disagreement?"

Scud. Arguing with a machine was an unreal level of frustrating. He was probably right, but I also knew I wouldn't be able to sleep if I tried. For reasons that he, no matter how smart, would never be able to understand.

Instead, I changed into the generic work jumpsuit that had arrived in that bundle of clothes I'd ordered, and went back up to the rooftop. The jumpsuit felt like a flight suit—thick, canvaslike material with a fit that was snug, but not too tight. Comfortable, utilitarian clothing. The best kind.

"Spensa?" M-Bot said as I walked over to the ship. "You're not going to get yourself into trouble somehow, are you? We aren't flying off to—"

"Relax," I said. "We can't let their ground crews get too close to you, which means I'm going to have to keep you maintained."

"Now?" M-Bot said.

"I want you in tip-top shape in case we need to make an escape." I checked the little maintenance locker on the rooftop and found some basic supplies, including a grease gun filled with vacuum-rated lubricant. I grabbed that and walked back to him. "M-Bot?" I asked. "How did you learn about that phrase I used? About the teeth? Did you have it in your databases?"

"No," he said. "I got it from the Starsight information archive. There's a great deal in here about Old Earth, from before it vanished—more than the fragmented databases your people have."

"Can you tell me about it?" I asked, using the gun to begin greasing the joints of his wing flaps. "Some of the things we don't cover in school, you know?"

"There's a lot of information here," he said. "Shall I just start in alphabetical order? A. A. Attanasio was a science fiction writer who sounds interesting."

"Tell me the story of Pine Leaf," I said. "And how she fought four Crow warriors at once."

"Fallen Leaf," M-Bot said, "is often associated with the historical figure known as Pine Leaf, or Woman Chief. She was a Native American woman of Gros Ventre birth, though many pseudo-historical accounts of bravery are associated with her life."

He said it so dryly, in such a monotone.

"And the story of how she fought four men at once?" I asked. "Touching them each with her rod in turn, taking them captive due to the shame of letting a woman outfence them?"

"She is reported to have counted coup four times in one battle," M-Bot said. "Though, it is uncertain if this legend is true. Historically, she was instrumental in turning back a Blackfoot raid, where she first gained renown among other Crow. And . . . Why are you sighing? Did I do something wrong?"

"I just miss Gran-Gran," I said softly. She made the stories of Old Earth come alive, simply in the way she told them. There was always a *passion* in her voice that M-Bot, however well intentioned, couldn't impart.

"I'm sorry," M-Bot said softly. "This is more proof that I'm not really alive, isn't it?"

"Don't be silly," I said. "I'm not a very good storyteller either. That doesn't mean *I'm* not alive."

"The dione philosopher and scientist Zentu claimed that there are three important hallmarks that indicate true life. Growth is the first. The being must change over time. I've changed, haven't I? I can learn, I can grow."

"Definitely," I said. "The mere fact that you made me your pilot proves that."

"Basic self-determinism is the second," M-Bot said. "A living thing has to be able to respond to stimuli to better its situation. I can't fly myself. If I could fly, do you think it would make me alive? Do you think that's why whoever created me forbade me from being able to move on my own?"

"You can use your smaller thrusters to adjust your position," I said. "So you can kind of do that one already. If a plant is alive because it can respond to sunlight, then you're alive."

"I don't want to be as alive as a plant," M-Bot said. "I want to be *really* alive."

I grunted, applying quick squirts of lubricant to the hinges of his wing flaps. The mere scent of it made me feel better. That room down below, it was too clean. Even my quarters back at DDF headquarters had smelled faintly of grease and exhaust fumes.

"What's the third indication of life?" I asked. "At least according to this philosopher."

"Reproduction," M-Bot said. "A living thing is capable of making more versions of itself, or at least its species is capable of this at some point in its life cycle. I've been wondering . . . You're going to have to fly a new ship tomorrow. Maybe we can find a way to upload a copy of my program to that fighter's data banks. Then you could have my help, but still be able to fly one of their ships."

"You could do that?" I asked, looking up from the wing.

"In theory," M-Bot said. "I'm just a program—granted, one that relies on trans-cytonic speeds for processing. But at my core, the thing you call M-Bot is nothing more than a group of coded bits."

"You're way more," I said. "You're a person."

"A person is nothing more than an organic collection of coded information." He hesitated. "Anyway, my programming forbids me from making copies of my main processing code. There's a failsafe to prevent me from duplicating myself. I might be able to change it if . . ." *Click. Clickclickclickclick.*

I kept working, falling silent as his program rebooted. *Who-*

ever made him didn't want to risk the enemy getting a copy of him, I thought. *Or . . . they didn't want to risk their AIs copying themselves without supervision.*

"I'm back," M-Bot finally said. "Sorry."

"It's fine," I said.

"Maybe we can find a way around . . . what I said earlier."

"I don't know if I like that, honestly," I said. "Making another of you feels wrong. Weird."

"No more weird than identical twin human beings," he said. "To be perfectly frank, I don't know how my programming would respond to being confined in an ordinary computer system—one that doesn't have trans-cytonic processing."

"You say those words like I should know what they mean."

"To create computers that can think as quickly as my mind, you need processors that can communicate faster than normal electric signals facilitate. My design achieves this by using tiny cytonic communicators, which pass signals at FTL speeds through my processing units."

"And the station's shield doesn't stop that?"

"My own shielding appears to be enough to block their shielding. Or, well, that's a simplified and maybe contradictory way of putting it. In any case, I can still process at my required speeds."

"Huh," I said. "Cytonic processors. So that's why I can feel you thinking."

"What do you mean?"

"Sometimes, when I'm deep inside . . . whatever it is I do . . . I can *feel* you. Your mind, your processors. Like I can feel Brade sometimes. But anyway, talk of copying you is moot, right? We can't transfer you to a new ship, because that ship wouldn't be able to think fast enough."

"I should be able to survive in one," M-Bot said. "I'd simply think slower—I'd be dumb. Not as dumb as a human though, and you all seem to get along just fine." He paused. "Um, no offense."

"I'm sure you find our stupidity endearing."

"Nope! Anyway, I'd like to at least try to find a way to replicate myself. If just to prove that . . . that I'm actually alive."

I walked around him toward his other wing, smiling. After I'd joined the DDF officially—and M-Bot had come out into the open—the ground crews had taken over maintaining him. Before that though, it had just been me and Rodge. Rodge had done most of the difficult work, but a lot of the simple jobs—greasing, peeling paint, checking wires—he'd given over to me.

There was something satisfying about maintaining my own ship. Something relaxing. Calming.

Then I looked into the polished surface of his hull, and saw infinity staring back at me. A deep void in place of my reflection. One pierced by a handful of *burning* white lights, like terrible suns. Watching me.

The eyes. A delver, or more than one, was here. *Right here.*

I stumbled back, dropping the grease gun with a clatter. The reflection vanished, and I swear there was *nothing* reflected for a short time. Then, like a screen turning on, Alanik's figure reappeared—the holographic image I was wearing.

"Spensa?" M-Bot asked. "What's wrong?"

I slumped down to the rooftop. Overhead, ships coursed along invisible highways. The city squirmed and moved, a sickening *buzz* of annoying insects all around, suffocating me.

"Spensa?" M-Bot repeated.

"I'm all right," I whispered. "I'm just . . . just worried about tomorrow. About having to fly without you."

I felt alone. M-Bot was great, but he didn't understand me like Kimmalyn or FM did. Or Jorgen. Scud, I missed him. I missed being able to complain to him, and listen to his overly rational— yet somehow calming—arguments back.

"Don't worry, Spensa!" M-Bot said. "You can do this! You're

really good at flying. Better than anyone else! You're practically inhuman in your skill."

I felt a chill at that. *Practically inhuman.* Feeling sick, I leaned forward, wrapping my arms around my legs.

"What did I say?" M-Bot asked, his voice growing smaller. "Spensa? What's wrong? What's *really* wrong?"

"There's a story Gran-Gran would tell," I whispered. "An odd one that never quite fit with the others. Not a story about queens, knights, or samurai. A story about a man . . . who lost his shadow."

"How do you lose your shadow?" M-Bot asked.

"It was a fanciful story," I said, remembering the first time Gran-Gran had told it to me. Sitting on top of our cubelike apartment back in the caverns, the deep, hungry light of the forges painting everything red. "One strange evening, while on a journey, a writer woke up to find that his shadow had vanished. There was nothing he could do, and no doctor could help him. Eventually he moved on with his life.

"Except one day, the shadow came back. It knocked on the door, and greeted its former master with joy. It had traveled the world, and had come to understand men. Better, in fact, than the writer himself did. The shadow had seen the evil in the hearts of the men of the land, while the writer had sat beside his hearth, entertaining only kindhearted fancies."

"That's strange," M-Bot said. "Didn't your grandmother usually tell you stories about slaying monsters?"

"Sometimes," I whispered, "the monsters slew the men. In this story, the shadow took the man's place. It persuaded the writer that it could show him the world, but only if the man agreed to become the shadow for a short time. And of course when the man did so, the shadow refused to let him go free. The shadow took his place, married a princess, and became wealthy. While the real

179

man, being a shadow, wasted away and became thin and dark, barely alive . . ."

I looked back at M-Bot. "I always wondered why she told me that story. She said it was a story her mother had told her, during the days when they'd traveled the stars."

"So, you're worried about what?" M-Bot said. "That your shadow might take your place?"

"No," I whispered. "I worry that I'm already the shadow."

I closed my eyes, thinking of where the delvers lived. The place between moments, that cold nowhere. Gran-Gran said that in the old days, people had feared and distrusted the engine crew. They'd distrusted cytonics.

Ever since I'd begun seeing the eyes, I'd never quite felt the same. Now that I'd traveled to the nowhere, I couldn't help wondering if what had come back wasn't completely *me* anymore. Or if maybe the *me* I'd known had always been something else. Something not quite human.

"Spensa?" M-Bot said. "You said you weren't a good story-teller. That was a lie. I'm impressed at how you do it so easily."

I looked at the fallen grease gun, which had squirted a lit-tle glob of clear lubricant onto the rooftop. Scud. I was getting emotional—M-Bot really *was* right. I got strange when I didn't have enough sleep.

That was it, obviously. Sleep deprivation was making me hal-lucinate, and it was why I was rambling. I stood up—pointedly did *not* look at my reflection—and put away the grease gun. I then stopped at the stairwell down into the embassy.

The thought of sleeping in that sterile, empty room . . . with the eyes watching me . . .

"Hey," I said to M-Bot instead. "Pop your cockpit. I'm going to sleep up here tonight."

"You have an entire building with four bedrooms," M-Bot said.

"And you're going back to sleeping in my cockpit, like you did when you were forbidden DDF quarters?"

"Yup," I said, yawning as I climbed in and pulled the canopy closed. "Could you dim the canopy for me?"

"I suspect a bed might be more comfortable," M-Bot said.

"Probably would be." I leaned the seat back and dug out my blanket. Then I settled in, listening to the noise of traffic outside. A strange, somehow accusatory sound.

Even as I began to drift off, I was left with a sense of isolation. Surrounded by noise, but alone. I was in a place with a thousand species, but I felt more lonely than I ever had exploring the caverns at home.

PART THREE

PART THREE

INTERLUDE

Jorgen Weight stepped into the infirmary, flight helmet under his arm. Perhaps he should have stowed the helmet, but there was no rule requiring it—and he felt good carrying it. Made him feel ready to fly at a moment's notice. Gave him the illusion that he was in control.

The creature lying in the infirmary bed proved that wasn't the case. They'd hooked the alien woman to all kinds of tubes and monitors, with a mask over her face to control her breathing, but what drew Jorgen's attention immediately were the straps binding her arms to the table. The DDF brass wanted to be extra careful, even though Spensa had seemed to think the alien wasn't a danger.

The fallen pilot's alien physiology left the DDF medics scratching their heads. The best they'd been able to do was patch her up and hope she eventually woke. Over the last two days, Jorgen had checked on her at least six times. He knew it was unlikely she'd wake up while he was there, but he still wanted the chance to be the first to speak to her. The first one to make the demand.

Can you find Spensa?

He felt a growing sense of worry each day Spensa was away

without communication. Had he done the right thing, encouraging her to leave like that? Had he stranded her alone, without backup, to be captured and tortured?

He'd broken DDF chain-of-command protocol in telling her to go. Now, if she was captured because of it . . . Well, Jorgen could think of nothing worse than disobeying, then realizing he'd been wrong to do so. So he came here, hoping. This alien was a cytonic; she'd be able to find Spensa and help her, right?

But first, the alien had to awaken. A doctor with a clipboard stepped up to Jorgen, dutifully showing him the report on the alien's vitals. Jorgen couldn't read most of the chart, but people tended to be deferent to pilots. Even the highest government officials would often step aside for a man or woman bearing an active-duty pilot's pin.

Jorgen didn't care for the attention, yet he bore it because of the tradition. His people existed, lived, because the machine of war worked—and if he had to be one of its most prominent gears, he would bear that position with solemnity.

"Any update?" he asked the doctor. "Tell me what's not on the chart. Has she stirred? Does she speak in her sleep?"

The doctor shook her head. "Nothing. Her heartbeat is irregular, and we don't know if that's normal for her species. She breathes our air just fine, but her oxygen levels are low. Again, we can't tell if that is normal or not."

The same as before—and it could be weeks before she awakened, if she ever did. Engineering was analyzing her ship, but so far they hadn't been able to break the encryption on her data banks.

The scientists could analyze that all they wanted. The secrets Jorgen wanted were inside this creature's brain. He felt an . . . electricity when he drew near her. A quiet shock that ran through him, like the sensation of being splashed with cold water. He could feel it now, standing over her, listening to the steady hiss of the respirator.

He'd felt that same sensation before, when he'd first met Spensa. He'd thought it was attraction, and surely he felt that. For all she frustrated him, he was attracted like a moth to a flame. There was something else though. Something this alien had too. Something he knew was hidden deep within his family line.

He turned to the doctor. "Please make a note to send me word if anything about her situation changes."

"I've already done so," the doctor replied.

"By the code at the bottom of the chart, you've updated her status priority, requiring me to renew my request. Department procedures 1173-b."

"Oh," she said, looking over the chart again. "All right."

Jorgen nodded to her, then left the infirmary, returning to the corridor of Platform Prime. He was on his way to his ship's berth to take the ground crew shift report when the klaxons went crazy. He froze, reading the pattern of buzzing alarms that rang through the sterile metal corridor.

Incoming fire, he thought. *Not good.*

Jorgen fought against the tide of scrambling pilots and crew members running for their ships, and headed straight for the command room. Incoming *fire,* not incoming *ships.* The fighters weren't being scrambled. This was something bigger. Something worse.

His stomach churned as he reached the command room, where the guards let him enter. Inside, the alarm sounds were muted. By now, the DDF had moved much of their command staff up from Alta Base to Platform Prime. Admiral Cobb wanted to separate the military installation from the civilian population, to divide potential Krell targets.

They were still setting everything up though, which made

this room a mess of wires and temporary monitors. Jorgen didn't bother the command staff, who had gathered around a large monitor at the far side of the room. Though he was of a rank to join in operations here, he didn't want to be a distraction. Instead he made his way down the line of workstations to that of Ensign Nydora, a young woman in the Radio Corps whom he knew from their time in school together.

"What's happening?" he asked, leaning down beside her.

She responded by pointing to her monitor, which—by the designation at the bottom—was displaying a feed from one of their scout ships out beyond the shells. The feed showed two enormous Krell battleships moving toward the planet.

"They're settling into positions," Nydora whispered, "where they can shoot through an upcoming gap in the defensive platforms and hit Alta Base on the surface."

"Can we fire back?" Jorgen asked.

Nydora shook her head. "We don't have control of the long-range guns on the outer platforms yet—and even if we did, those battleships are far enough away that they'd be able to move before our shots arrived. The planet, though, can't move."

Jorgen's stomach twisted upon itself. From orbit, the enemy could bombard the surface of Detritus with a devastating rain of fire and death. With sustained shelling, and with the planet's own gravity working in the Krell's favor, those battleships would be able to obliterate even the deepest caverns.

"What are our chances?" Jorgen asked.

"Depends on how far engineering got . . ."

Jorgen felt helpless as he watched the two battleships glide into position, then open gunports.

"No response to our requests to speak to them," someone down the row said. "Doesn't seem like they're going to give us a warning shot first."

That had always been the Krell's way. No warning. No quarter.

No demands for surrender. The DDF knew—from the information Spensa had stolen—that much of what the Krell had done so far had been intended only to suppress the humans. Six months ago, however, the enemy had moved to attempting full-on extermination.

"Why now, though?" Jorgen asked.

"They had to wait for an alignment of the platforms," Nydora said. "This is their first clear shot at Alta in weeks. That's why they're moving now."

Indeed, Jorgen watched the screen as the inscrutable motion of the many platforms that made up Detritus's shells lined them up, providing an opening. The battleships immediately started firing hefty kinetic shots, projectiles that were the size of fighters. Jorgen sent a silent prayer to the stars and the spirits of his ancestors who sailed them. For all his skill and training in a cockpit, he couldn't fight a battleship.

The fate of humankind rested in the hands of the Saints and the DDF engineers.

The room grew so silent, Jorgen could hear his own heartbeat. Nobody breathed as the rain of projectiles dove toward the planet. Then something changed—one of the platforms at the side of the opening started moving, its ancient mechanisms lighting up. Data started streaming across Nydora's secondary monitor—reports from engineering and DDF scout ships.

The planet Detritus was no easy target. Nydora's main screen highlighted the platform in motion, a flat sheet of metal. It seemed to move slowly, but so did the bombs. Jorgen was watching from such a distance that his brain had trouble comprehending the scale of the encounter—that section of metal was a hundred kilometers across.

As the bombs approached, sections of the platform opened up and launched a series of bright energy blasts into space. The blasts crashed into the projectiles fired by the battleships, meeting force with energy, blowing them away and negating their momentum. A shield sprang up around the platform, intercepting the debris, slowing it and preventing it from raining down upon the surface.

Everyone in the room let out a collective sigh of relief. Nydora even whooped. The battleships slowly withdrew, indicating— although they'd fired on Alta itself, and obviously wouldn't have minded destroying it—that this had been a test of the planetary defenses.

Jorgen patted Nydora on the back, then stepped to the side of the room, breathing in and out to calm his nerves. *Finally some good news.* One of the vice admirals called in over the main comm line to congratulate the engineers on their work.

Oddly though, Admiral Cobb himself remained in place at his monitor, limply holding an empty coffee cup and staring at the screen, even after all the others had gone to make announcements or offer congratulations.

Jorgen stepped closer. "Sir?" he asked. "You don't look pleased. The engineers got the defenses up in time."

"That wasn't one of the platforms our engineers worked on," Cobb said softly. "That was Detritus's old defensive programming. We got lucky that a working platform was nearby, and was still capable of deploying anti-bombardment countermeasures."

"Oh," Jorgen said. A little of his relief melted away. "But . . . we're still safe, sir."

"Note the power readings at the bottom of the screen, Captain," Cobb said. "The amount of energy that disruption drained is incredible. These old platforms barely have any juice in them. Even if we get others functioning, it will take months or years to fabricate new solar collectors.

"And even if we get that going, and the countermeasures continue to work . . . well, if the Krell start a sustained bombardment, they'll cut through these platforms eventually. Our defenses aren't meant to protect us from a long-term attack. They're a last-ditch fail-safe meant to stall invaders so that friendly battleships can get to the system and fight them off. Only we don't *have* friendly battleships."

Jorgen gazed back across the room of people celebrating. They looked commanding in their stiffly pressed and spotless DDF uniforms. That was just a front. Compared to the enemy's resources, the DDF wasn't an opposing military—it was a group of ragged refugees with barely a gun between them.

"We stay trapped on this planet," Cobb said, "and we die. It's that simple. We're an egg with an extra-hard shell, yes, but we're done as soon as the enemy realize that they can't crack us with a spoon and decide to get a sledgehammer instead. Unfortunately, our only chance of escape vanished without a trace. That girl . . ."

"I stand by my decision, sir," Jorgen said. "Spensa will come through for us. We just need to give her time."

"Still wish you'd called me," Cobb said. There hadn't been any repercussions for what Jorgen had done. He could argue that, under code 17-b, he'd been capable of making the call he'd made, but the truth was that he hadn't even been the senior officer on that mission. Colonel Ng from the ground forces had been leading the security team. Jorgen should have talked to him, or called Cobb.

It was possible that, in sending Spensa away, Jorgen had doomed them all. *We stay trapped on this planet, and we die. It's that simple . . .*

Jorgen took a deep breath. "Sir. I might need to disobey another rule."

"I don't know half of them anyway, Captain. Don't worry about it."

"No, sir. I mean . . . a family rule. Something we're not supposed to speak about."

Cobb eyed him.

"You know," Jorgen said, "about how my family fought to

keep the defect from being talked about? Kept it from being known to the general public? The one that Spensa's father had, the . . . the . . ."

"Cytonics?" Cobb asked.

"There's a reason, sir," Jorgen said.

"I know. Some of your ancestors had it. Wasn't confined just to the engine crews. You saying you've been hearing things, son? Seeing things?"

Jorgen pressed his lips closed tight and nodded. "White lights, sir. In the corners of my vision. Like . . . Like eyes."

There. He'd said it. Why was he sweating so much? Speaking the words hadn't been *that* hard, had it?

"Well, that's something at least," Cobb said, and held his cup to the side. An aide helpfully grabbed it and ran to get him a refill. "Come with me. There's someone I want you to meet."

"From the fleet Psychological Corps?" Jorgen asked.

"No. She's an old woman with an excellent taste in pies."

19

I bolted awake to M-Bot panicking.

"Spensa!" he cried. "Spensa!"

My heart suddenly pounding, I scrambled to get into position in the cockpit. I grabbed the control sphere, blinking bleary eyes, my thumb on the trigger.

"What!" I said. "Who do I shoot?"

"Someone is in the embassy," M-Bot said. "I set up proximity alerts. They're sneaking up on where they *think* you're sleeping."

Scud. Assassins? Sweating, my mind still cloudy from sleep, I powered up my ship and paused. Then . . . what? Fly away? To where? I was completely in the clutches of the Superiority—if they wanted me dead, they wouldn't resort to assassins, would they?

I needed to know more. Determined, I fumbled in the cockpit's small weapons locker and got out my handheld destructor pistol. So far as I'd been able to tell, personal weapons were forbidden on Starsight—but I also appeared to have some diplomatic exemptions, so I wasn't certain where I stood.

I made sure my hologram was still active, then quietly cracked the canopy and slipped out, keeping a low profile in case of snipers. I dashed to the steps down into the embassy. Here, I crept down toward the top floor.

"There are two of them," M-Bot said softly through my earpiece. "One has reached the kitchen on the top floor. The other is on the bottom floor near the door, perhaps guarding the exit."

Right. I'd never been in any actual ground conflicts, and my training was minimal. However, as I left the stairwell and stepped onto the top floor, I felt the same calm, cold determination that I experienced before a starfighter battle. I could face an assassin, so long as I had a gun in my hand. This was a problem I could shoot. I much preferred it to the nebulous worries I'd fallen asleep to last night.

"The enemy is positioned approximately two meters inside the door," M-Bot whispered to me. "Near the counter. Their back is to the door right now. I think they might be surprised you weren't in the bedroom."

I nodded, then leaped into the room, leveling my destructor. A brown-carapaced Krell turned around at the motion, dropping something to the ground that shattered. A plate?

"Ahh!" the Krell said, the voice being interpreted by my translator as female. "Don't kill me!"

"What are you doing here?" I demanded.

"Cleaning your dishes!" the Krell woman said. She waved her armored limbs in a sort of anxious way. "We were sent to do your housecleaning!"

Housecleaning? I frowned, my gun still leveled. But the Krell woman wore a belt full of cleaning tools on the outside of her sandstone carapace, and through the helmet faceplate I could see the panicked motions from the shrimpy crab creature. She didn't have any weapons I could see.

A sound suddenly came from down below, on the first floor. A . . . vacuum cleaner?

"Hmm," M-Bot said. "Perhaps we misjudged this situation."

"Such aggression!" the Krell cleaner said. "I was not warned of this!"

"Who sent you?" I demanded, stepping forward.

She cringed back. "We are employed by the Department of Species Integration!"

Cuna. I narrowed my eyes, but put away my gun. "Sorry about the mistake," I said, then left her and went to check on the other one—a second Krell, who was humming as they vacuumed the ground floor.

As I watched them, the chimes at the door rang. I frowned again, then checked the door. A package had been set by it— presumably my new flight suit.

Cuna themself stood outside. Tall, blue-skinned, shrouded in an enveloping set of dark blue robes.

I opened the door.

Cuna gave me one of their creepy smiles, showing too many teeth. "Ah, Emissary Alanik! May I enter?"

"Did you send your lackeys to sneak up on me?" I said.

Cuna stopped short. "Lackeys? I'm not familiar with the translation of that word. Minions? I sent Mrs. Chamwit to be your housekeeper, and she brought an assistant. I realized that you didn't bring your own staff, and might need some lent to you."

Spies. I knew it. *I found and turned off their surveillance devices, so they sent their agents to the building to watch me.* Had I left anything sitting out that would give me away?

"I hope you find them helpful," Cuna said, checking their communication tablet. "Hm. I'm a little behind. You're scheduled for pickup in roughly thirty-five minutes. We wouldn't want you to be late on your first day as a pilot."

"What do you want from me?" I asked, suspicious. *And what game are you playing?*

"Only to see that you have an excellent opinion of the Superiority to take back to your people," Cuna said. "May I enter?"

I stepped back, reluctantly giving them space to enter. They peeked in at the vacuuming Krell, then strolled to a different meeting room, which was empty. I followed, hovering in the doorway as Cuna sat down.

"I'm very pleased with your efforts, Alanik," Cuna said. "And I apologize for the . . . harrowing experience yesterday. I wasn't aware that Winzik and his kind would use such a dramatic method of selecting their pilots. The Department of Protective Services can be reckless."

"Yeah, well, I'm not the one who needs your apology—and the ones who *do* deserve it are all dead at the moment."

"Indeed," Cuna said. "What do you know of the human wars, Alanik of UrDail?"

"I know the humans lost," I said carefully. "After dominating my planet and forcing us to fight at their side."

"A political way of saying it," Cuna replied. "Your people will fit in with the Superiority far better than some assume. I, however, am known on occasion to defy social customs. Perhaps that is due to my preference for interacting with, and learning the habits of, species that have not yet joined the Superiority."

Cuna seemed so tall and aloof. Their voice grew soft, even contemplative, as they continued, turning their head slightly to gaze out the front window. "I'd guess you've never seen the aftermath of a delver attack, and for that I envy you. They can wipe out all life on a planet just by passing by it—or rather, *through* it. They don't entirely exist in our reality. They sweep past, and leave only silence."

What did this have to do with the conversation? We'd been talking about the humans, right?

"That's terrible," I said. "But . . . you told me before that the delvers left our galaxy centuries ago. So how has anyone seen firsthand what they can do to a planet?"

Cuna tapped their fingers together. And I realized the answer had stared me in the eyes not a few days before. Standing on the space station outside Detritus, watching that ancient video. I *had* seen what delvers could do.

"The humans summoned a delver, didn't they?" I asked. "That's why you're all so frightened of the delvers, and why you hate humans so much. It wasn't just the wars. The humans tried to *weaponize* the delvers."

"Yes. We nearly lost those wars anyway. But during the second one, the humans developed hidden bases on obscure planets around small or dying stars. There, they began a terrible program. If they'd been successful, then the Superiority would have not just been destroyed, it would have *vanished*."

I felt a still coldness deep inside me. *The delver has turned back on us* . . . Words spoken by the man I'd seen on that video—said right before everyone on the planet Detritus had been consumed. I'd *watched* those long-dead humans try this. That was what they'd been doing. They'd *summoned* a delver. Only instead of destroying humankind's enemies, the thing had turned on them.

The horror of it welled up in me again, and I felt sick, leaning against the side of the doorframe.

"We are exceedingly fortunate that their own weapon turned against them," Cuna said. "The delvers cannot be fought or controlled. The humans successfully brought one to our realm, and then it destroyed several of their most important planets and bases. Even after the humans were defeated, this delver was a scourge upon the galaxy for years until it finally left.

"I know your people have a reverence for the humans, Alanik. No, you don't need to object. I can understand, and empathize to an extent. Yet you *must* understand that the task we are about here—learning to fight against delvers—is an *essential* project.

"Winzik and I might not agree on how all this should proceed, but we conceived this project together: a way to develop counter-measures against the delvers. Until we can do this, the Superiority is in grave danger."

"You . . . think the humans are going to return, don't you?" I asked, the pieces falling into place. "I've read on the local data-net that they're supposedly all contained in preserves—but some people claim that the humans are close to escaping."

Cuna finally turned from the window to glance at me, their alien expression unreadable. They made a dismissive gesture, sweeping two fingers to the side in front of them. "Look back through the archives, and you'll find that the humans are supposedly *always* close to escaping. Indeed, flare-ups in their resistance always seem to coincide—somehow—with times when the Department of Protective Services needs to pass some important funding bill."

That one hit me like a punch to the stomach. The Department of Protective Services—the Krell . . . they were using Detritus and my people as a way to gain political favor?

"You think they *let* the humans grow more dangerous?" I said. "They maybe relax their guard a little, so that everyone will be properly afraid, and so that the department can prove it's doing a good job?"

"I would not make such a claim," Cuna said. "For a claim such as that would require evidence, not mere assumption. Let us simply say I find it curious. And it has been happening for so long, so regularly, that I doubt the humans are any kind of *real* danger to us, no matter what all the experts and commentators think."

You're wrong though, I thought. *Winzik made a mistake. He let the DDF get too strong. He let me become a pilot. And now . . . and now we really* are *close to breaking out. It's not just a convenient excuse this time. He must be panicking . . .*

So now, he creates this space force. This special team of pilots. It couldn't be a coincidence.

"The delvers are the real danger," Cuna said. "Perhaps I am

wrong, and perhaps the humans will become a threat again in the future. But even if they do not, someone else will try to use the delvers. Dealing with delvers is foolish, reckless, aggressive behavior— and so some race out there is bound to try it. The Superiority will not be safe until we can fight the delvers, or at least drive them away."

"I can see the logic in that," I said. And I did. My main goal was to steal a hyperdrive . . . but if there was some Superiority weapon against the delvers that I could discover, then I was certain we'd find that handy as well.

But why was Cuna telling me all of this? They rose and stepped closer to me, then glanced at my side—toward the weapon sticking out of my pocket, where I'd hastily stuffed it. I quickly tucked it farther inside.

"You should not carry that about," Cuna said. "You are under my protection, but even that will extend only so far."

"Sorry," I said. "I thought you were . . . Anyway, I might have frightened the housekeeper upstairs."

"I'll deal with that," Cuna said. "I just need you to understand how important your task is. Winzik must be watched. I do not have the power over this training program that I would like. So, I would ask that you remember our deal. I will see that your people's application to the Superiority is met with approval. In turn, I would ask you to report to me on your training."

"I'm to be your spy," I said.

"You are to provide service to the Superiority. I have proper clearance and authorization to know anything you would tell me."

Great. It was as I feared; I was trapped between the two of them.

"Do not be so concerned," Cuna said. They gave me another predatory smile. "I asked you to do this in part because I know you will be safe. As a cytonic, you can hyperjump away at a moment's notice, should you be in danger."

"Yeah, about that," I said. How much should I admit? "I won't have my ship, and I need the technology on it to hyperjump."

"Ah," Cuna said. "So you're not fully trained yet. You still require mechanical aid?"

"Exactly. Do you suppose you could give me some sort of training?"

Cuna shook their head. "Untrained cytonics are far less dangerous than trained ones. It took centuries of training before our own cytonics were powerful enough to draw delvers by accident—and we suspect your people are far from doing so. To train you would only accelerate that danger."

"Maybe if I had a Superiority ship with a hyperdrive, I could try out using your technology," I said. "Then I could see how it felt, and learn how to do FTL safely."

"Oooh . . . ," M-Bot said in my ear. "Nice!"

"Well, I cannot keep you from experiencing a hyperjump," Cuna said. "The training facility you'll visit today will require one. So perhaps you'd best pay attention to the process."

Awesome. I checked the clock on my bracelet. Scud, it was almost time.

"Don't let me keep you," Cuna said with their ever-calm voice. "Go prepare. You have a busy day ahead of you. One I'll be very interested to hear about."

Right. Well, I couldn't exactly kick them out. I dashed to the stairwell, grabbing the package and passing the vacuuming Krell—who jumped back as I entered. I didn't buy the timid act. They were a spy, obviously. I walked a fine line in this game.

In the bedroom, I quickly checked for anything I'd left that might expose who I really was. Then I changed into the flight suit that had been delivered, grabbed Doomslug from my room, and hurried up to M-Bot. "Watch Doomslug," I said to him softly, tucking her into his cockpit. "Cuna says I'll need to hyperjump to go to the training today. Will you be able to contact me?"

"Your bracelet doesn't have a cytonic transmitter," M-Bot said. "It's supposed to, but your people didn't have the right parts to fabricate one. So unless your new ship has one—and we can figure out how to link up—then no, we won't be able to talk once you hyperjump away."

Great. I stored the destructor pistol. "Keep watch for anything odd."

"And what do I do if I find something odd, Spensa? I can't escape."

"I don't know," I said, frustrated. I hated being so much in the power of others. "If everything goes wrong, at least try to die heroically, all right?"

"I . . . um . . . I have no response to that. How unusual. But here, I've got something for you."

"What?" I asked.

"I'm uploading a second holographic map to your bracelet. If you use it, the image will make you look like a left dione of inconspicuous features, which I've constructed. It might be good to have a backup persona to adopt."

"I don't know that I can handle the one I already have," I said.

"Still, it is wise, just in case. You should get going. I'll still have contact with you up until you hyperjump, so we aren't going radio silent quite yet."

I scrambled back down the steps to grab some breakfast, then pack a lunch, as I'd been instructed. I put this in a backpack I'd ordered, then reached the bottom floor right in time for the chime to go off, informing me that the shuttle had arrived to take me to training.

Cuna stood on the landing near the front door.

"Don't touch my ship," I said to them.

"I wouldn't think of doing so."

I debated for a moment longer, suffering that untrustworthy smile, then sighed and marched out the door.

20

The shuttle was a small aircar with an alien driver whose race I didn't recognize, though they looked vaguely fungoid in appearance. M-Bot would have been excited.

I found the seat overly cushy. It was like those in Jorgen's luxury cars. I shook my head, strapping in as the shuttle took off.

Rather than dwelling on the fact that I had to leave M-Bot behind, I watched the city beneath us—a seemingly endless expanse of buildings. "Where are we going?" I asked M-Bot, barely whispering so the shuttle's driver couldn't overhear.

He piped up in my ear. "The orders you received say you'll be transported to the *Weights and Measures*."

"Is that a ship?" I asked. What an innocent-sounding name.

"Yes. A large trade vessel."

It was obviously a cover. This *Weights and Measures* would be a military ship, just not one that the Superiority wanted the common people to know about.

"Can we go over the different species I'll be flying with today?" I asked. "I feel like Alanik would know something about them."

"That's actually a great idea!" M-Bot said. "We wouldn't want you sounding more ignorant than you normally are. Let's see . . . Morriumur is a dione. You've got some experience with them by now. Though Morriumur is what is known as a draft—their term for a person who is not yet born."

I shivered and turned to look out the window. "What they do feels like eugenics or something," I whispered. "They shouldn't be able to decide what personalities people are born with."

"That's a very human-centric way of looking at it," M-Bot said. "If you're to pull off this mission, you'll need to learn to see things from alien perspectives."

"I'll try," I whispered. "I'm most interested in the race they called figments. What's the deal with them?"

"They are sapient beings who exist as a localized cloud of particulates in the air. Basically, they're smells."

"Talking smells?"

"Talking, thinking, and—from what I've read—somewhat dangerous smells," he answered. "They are not a large population, but are spoken of in hushed tones throughout the Superiority. Sources on the local datanet insist that all remaining figments—many died in the human wars, and they are slow to reproduce—work as secret government operatives.

"Very little is known about them. Apparently, they usually investigate matters that involve internal Superiority politics, particularly the infractions of very high-ranking officials. They can pilot ships by infusing the electronics of the vehicle, and interrupting—or spoofing—the electronic signals from the controls."

"Vapor did that in the test yesterday," I said. "She took over one of the drones, and was flying it. So she just kind of . . . flew over to it and seized control?"

"Exactly," M-Bot said. "Or at least that's how people on the datanet think it works. There is very little official data about figments, but I can see why one showing up to the piloting test caused such a stir."

"So she's a spy too," I whispered. "An invisible spy."

"Who can survive in space," M-Bot said. "So they're not simply gaseous beings—otherwise the vacuum would rip them apart. It seems they can travel through space with no special equipment, and can move at speed between ships. In the wars, they'd often infiltrate the mechanical portion of an enemy fighter and take control of it with the pilot still on board."

"Scud," I whispered. As if I didn't have enough to worry about. "What about the human?"

"There are very few like her. Most humans must remain in the preserves. If an official wants to remove one, the human must be licensed—basically, someone has to take responsibility for them if they cause harm or damage."

"And do they?"

"Sometimes," M-Bot said. "I see more often a pattern of scapegoating and prejudice. Only government officials are supposed to keep humans, and then only for security or research purposes. I think the Superiority uses them in part because it likes the occasional reminder that they won the war."

I nodded to myself as we skimmed across the top of the city. I'd need to learn more about this sort of thing if I was going to recruit Brade. I wasn't certain I would need to do that, but I had to at least try to free her, right?

I sighed and rubbed my forehead, trying to keep all of this straight. So I now separately had plans to steal a hyperdrive, rescue an enslaved human, and maybe find the secret to fighting the delvers. Maybe I should just keep my mind on the main goal.

"Are you all right?" M-Bot asked. "Do you want me to stop?"

"No," I whispered. "I'm just feeling a little overwhelmed. At least the kitsen make some kind of sense."

"That might be because of their history with humankind," M-Bot said. "Thousands of years ago, they made first contact with humans on Earth—before either society industrialized."

"How did *that* happen?"

"Cytonic teleportation doesn't require technology," M-Bot said. "As Cuna implied, if you can figure out how to use your powers, you'll be able to teleport yourself alone—and not just your ship. Early cytonics from the kitsen people ended up on Earth, for reasons that now seem lost to time. There was trade and interaction between them and various regions of East Asia on Earth. Several kitsen cultures were directly influenced by Earth ones. The exchange happened until the kitsen cytonics vanished."

"Vanished?"

"It's a tragic story," M-Bot said. "Though it should be noted that the kitsen were only a late steel-age society then, so records might be untrustworthy. Apparently their people did not trust the cytonics, so the cytonics left. Humans were part of this disagreement—a war is implied. The end result stranded the main population of kitsen on their homeworld for centuries until the Superiority made contact."

"Huh," I whispered. "Where did the kitsen cytonics go?"

"Nobody knows," he replied. "All that remains are legends. Perhaps you should ask Hesho which one he believes. I'm more curious as to why the cytonics would leave in the first place. Just because they weren't trusted? You didn't trust me when we first met, and I didn't leave."

"You can't leave," I said.

"I could sulk," he said. "I have a sulking subroutine."

"Oh, I know."

My shuttle flew down low, and we neared some docks that

extended away from the city, out into the darkness. Just before we passed out of the air shell, however, I spotted a group of people waving signs. I couldn't read them—the distance was too great for my pin to translate for me—so I whispered to M-Bot.

"There's a group of people here waving signs," I said. "Right next to the docks." I squinted. "An alien that looks like a gorilla is leading them. I think it's a burl, the same species as the one who got kicked out of the flight test."

"Let me check the local news networks," M-Bot said. "Just a moment."

We flew past the demonstrators, and the shuttle carried me out of the air shield. I started to lift off my seat, my hair floating in zero G as we left the platform's gravitational field. We flew along the docks, most of which were filled with large craft of a size that couldn't land on launchpads.

The stars came awake to me again, like a distant melody. The information that Starsight was sending through the nowhere to other planets. I tried to concentrate on the different sounds, but again there were *far* too many of them. It was like a rushing river in the deep caverns. If I let the music sit in the back of my mind, I heard it as a simple tune, easy to ignore. But if I tried to pick out anything specific, it turned into a clatter.

A part of me was surprised they let themselves use cytonic communication at all. Yes, the Superiority limited how much of it was used—most people had to communicate with other worlds by sending letters that were loaded onto memory chips, then carried on starships and hooked up to local datanets when they finished traveling. However, the important people could use not just radio but cytonic communication through the nowhere. They had let me do it, when sending a message to Alanik's homeworld.

"Found the reason for those protesters," M-Bot said. "Apparently, the deaths at the test didn't go unnoticed. That pilot Gul'zah who was ejected from the tests yesterday is complaining vocally, with some support, about the way the Superiority treats lesser species."

Huh. That was more defiance than I'd expected.

We approached the last ship on the docks, and its enormous size dwarfed our little shuttle. It was even larger than those battleships that threatened my home, with a multitude of ports along the sides, probably for launching starfighters.

Those knobs on it are gun emplacements, I thought, though the guns were retracted for now. Which meant I was right: the *Weights and Measures* was very obviously a military vessel, a carrier ship.

Seeing it made me worried. This ship was built to teleport places and then launch its fleet—which meant I probably wasn't going to be assigned a starfighter with its own hyperdrive. Still, I kept up hope as my shuttle flew in through a large open bay door that had an invisible shield holding in an atmosphere. Artificial gravity pulled me back into my seat, and we settled down on a launchpad in the wide chamber.

Out the window I spotted the first true military presence I'd seen on Starsight—diones wearing naval uniforms and carrying sidearms were lined up awaiting us.

"You get out here," the driver announced, popping open the door. "You're scheduled for pickup again at 9000."

"All right," I said, climbing out. The air smelled sterile, a little like ammonia. Other shuttles were landing in the bay around me, letting out a steady stream of pilots. The fifty or so who had passed the test. As I was wondering what to do next, the shuttle next to me opened its doors, releasing a bunch of kitsen. Today, the diminutive animals zoomed out on small platforms like flying plates, big enough to carry about five kitsen each.

Hesho himself hovered over to me, attended only by two kitsen—a driver, and a kitsen with a bright red-and-gold uniform, carrying what appeared to be an old, intricately carved metal shield.

The pilot brought the plate up to eye level with me.

"Good morning, Captain Alanik," Hesho said from his podium at the center of the platform.

"Captain Hesho," I said. "Did you sleep well?"

"Unfortunately, no," he said. "I was required to spend much of the sleep cycle engaged in political discourses, casting my votes in the planetary assembly of my people. Ha ha. Politics is such a pain. Is it not?"

"Um, I guess so? Did the votes at least go your way?"

"No, I lost every one," Hesho said. "The rest of the assembly voted unanimously against my desires in each matter. What rotten luck! Ah, the indignities you must suffer when your people are a true democracy, and not a shadow dictatorship ruled by an ancestral line of kings. Right?"

The other kitsen flying past raised a cheer for democracy.

Morriumur walked over to join us, looking uncomfortable in their white Superiority flight suit. Nearby, a group of four other pilots were led farther into the *Weights and Measures*.

"Have you seen our other two flight members?" Hesho asked.

"I haven't smelled Vapor yet," Morriumur said. "As for the human . . ." They seemed distinctly uncomfortable with the idea.

"I should like to see this one in person," Hesho said. "The legends speak of humans as giants who live in the mist and who feast upon the bodies of the dead."

"I've seen several," Morriumur said. "They weren't any bigger than I am. Most were smaller, actually. But there was something . . . off about them. Something dangerous. I'd recognize the sensation again in an instant."

A small drone—not unlike one of the kitsen flying platforms—hovered over to us. "Ah," a voice said from a speaker in it. It sounded like one of the officials we'd met yesterday. "Flight Fifteen. Excellent. No stragglers?"

"We're missing two members," I said.

"No," a voice said from the air next to me. "Just one."

I jumped. So Vapor *was* here? I hadn't smelled cinnamon. Just that ammonia scent . . . which faded to cinnamon almost immediately. Scud. How long had she been watching? Had she . . . been in the shuttle with me?

"The human will join you at a later time, Flight Fifteen," the official instructed us. "You are to report to jump room six. I'll show you." The remote-controlled drone buzzed off, so we followed. Before we reached the door from the shuttle drop-off bay to the interior, we were stopped by a pair of guards armed with destructor rifles, who looked through our bags and then waved us onward.

" 'Flight Fifteen'?" I asked the others as we stepped into a hallway. "Not exactly punchy, is it? Can we choose something else?"

"I like it being a number," Morriumur said. "It's simple, easy to record, and easy to remember."

"Nonsense," Hesho said from his platform to my right. "I agree with Captain Alanik. A number won't do. I shall call us the Flowers of Night's Last Kiss."

"That is exactly what I was talking about," Morriumur said. "How could we say that mouthful in context, Hesho?"

"Nobody will write poetry about 'Flight Fifteen,' " Hesho said. "You shall see, Captain Morriumur. Bestowing proper names is one of my talents. If destiny had not chosen me for my current service, I surely would have been a poet."

"A warrior poet?" I said. "Like an Old Earth skald!"

"Precisely!" Hesho said, raising a furry fist to me.

I raised one back, grinning. We joined several other groups of pilots being led down the hallway. Those flights had been sorted by species—many had only one species represented, and a handful had two species mixed. Ours was the only one I saw that had more than two different races represented.

Hesho's people have a history with humans, I thought. *And so do Alanik's. Vapor's people fought in the wars.* Maybe we'd been chosen specifically because we might be able to deal with Brade.

More soldiers stood watch along this hallway, a pair of Krell this time, wearing full armor instead of just the ordinary sandstone carapace. As we passed them, I realized I hadn't seen any "lesser species" in this carrier, save for us pilots. All the guards and officials we passed were Krell or diones.

It left me wondering . . . why did they need us pilots again? They fought my people on Detritus with remote-controlled drone ships.

No, I thought. *If I can hear the instructions sent to the drones, the delver will be able to as well.* They *needed* a force of pilots trained in the cockpit. "M-Bot?" I whispered, intending to ask if he'd found out anything about the remote drone programs the Superiority used.

My earpiece returned only static at that. Scud. Had something happened to him? My heart started racing, until I realized I was inside a military ship. They must have communications shielding in place. Either that or I'd simply gotten beyond the bracelet's communication range already. I was truly on my own.

We were led through some corridors with featureless metallic walls and vivid red carpet down the center. We arrived at an intersection and the drone turned right, toward a corridor lined with rooms.

The rest of my flight turned to follow, but I hesitated at the intersection. Right? Why were we turning right?

I knew, logically, that there was no reason for me to be confused. And yet some piece of me reached out, looking farther down the hallway we'd been traveling. Not right at the intersection but straight ahead. *That* was the way to go. I could feel something up there . . .

"What do you think you're doing?" barked a soldier guarding the intersection.

I froze in place, realizing I'd started to walk down the hallway. I looked up at the writing on the wall, and my translator helpfully piped out the meaning.

RESTRICTED AREA. ENGINEERING AND ENGINES.

I blushed and turned right instead, hurrying to catch up with the others. The guard watched me until the group of us turned into one of the rooms off the corridor. I felt before I arrived that Brade was inside—and indeed, I stepped in to find her sitting alone in the little chamber, which contained a half dozen jump-seats. Brade wore the same sharp white flight suit we all wore, and sat in the back row, buckled in, looking out the window.

"So that's her," Hesho said, hovering near my head. "She doesn't look so dangerous. Still, a blade that has slain a hundred men may not shine like one freshly forged. Danger, sweet like a forbidden perfume. I will know thee."

"That was beautiful, Hesho," I said.

"Thank you," he said.

The other kitsen flew into the room, chattering together. The drone that had been leading us indicated we should strap in and wait for further instructions, then left.

"Strap in?" Hesho asked. "I thought we'd be assigned our starfighters."

"We likely will," Morriumur said, taking a seat. "Once the *Weights and Measures* carries us to the training location—a specialized facility several light-years away."

"I . . . ," Hesho said. "I assumed we'd have hyperdrive-capable starships. So we could fly there ourselves."

"I'll admit," I said, "I was hoping the same."

"Oh, they'd never give us individual ships capable of hyper-jumps," Morriumur said. "That kind of technology is dangerous!

It's never trusted to lesser races. Misusing it could draw the attention of the delvers upon us."

"We're learning to fight the delvers!" I said.

"It still wouldn't be wise," Morriumur said. "FTL jumps are *always* handled by highly trained expert technicians who have prime intelligence. Even special-classification species, like figments, aren't allowed. Right, Vapor?"

I jumped as she spoke from just behind me. "This is correct."

Scud. I was *never* going to get used to having an invisible person in our flight. "Some races have cytonics," I said, sitting down and strapping in. "They don't need Superiority ships to hyperjump."

"Letting a cytonic teleport a ship is *incredibly* dangerous," Morriumur said, making an odd hand gesture—a kind of swiping motion. A dione indication of dismissiveness, maybe? "Going back to cytonics would be like returning to ancient combustion engines instead of using acclivity rings! No, no, in modern society we would *never* use a method so foolhardy. Our FTL jumps are extremely safe, and never draw delver attention."

Curious, I glanced at Brade, but she didn't look back at me. M-Bot's research had reinforced what Cuna had told me: the modern people of the Superiority knew about cytonics, but the bulk of the population believed there were none left among them. It likely wouldn't be known that Brade was one, let alone that I was one too.

So . . . could it be possible that this phantom "FTL technology" the Superiority had was all just a lie? They claimed to have something safe to use, but what if that was just an excuse to control and suppress knowledge of cytonics?

I closed my eyes, listening to the stars as Gran-Gran had always taught. I felt the *Weights and Measures* finally start moving, unhooking from the dock and accelerating slowly away from Starsight. Those were physical sensations, and seemed distant, disconnected.

The stars . . . the cytonic communications . . . I tried to parse them, understand them. I tried the exercise my grandmother had taught me. Pretending I was flying. Rising. Soaring through space.

I could . . . hear . . . something. Something close. Louder, more demanding.

Prepare for hyperjump.

Orders from the captain of this ship. Passed down to the engine room. I could feel it there. And the hyperdrive . . . There was something *familiar* about it . . .

I heard the captain order the jump. I waited, watching, feeling what was going on. Trying to absorb the process.

My mind *flooded* with information. A location. The place we were going. I knew it intimately. I could—

A voice *screamed* from somewhere nearby. Then the ship suddenly entered the nowhere.

21

I was there, hanging in the not-place, surrounded by blackness. And the eyes. *They were here.*

Except they weren't looking at me.

I saw them, sensed them, heard them. But their gaze didn't find me. They were focused elsewhere. As if . . . as if looking toward the source of the scream.

Yes, that was it. The piercing, agonized scream lingered in my mind. It distracted the delvers from seeing the *Weights and Measures* as it slipped through the nowhere.

It was over like a snap of the fingers. I lurched back into my seat in the little room, grunting. I felt as if I'd been *thrown* physically, then been caught by the chair. I groaned, sagging forward.

"Captain Alanik?" Hesho asked, hovering nearby. "Are you well?"

I looked around the jump room, which held only the members of my flight. Morriumur didn't seem to have even noticed that moment in the nowhere.

I looked back at Brade. She met my eyes, then narrowed them at me. She knew I was cytonic. Did she . . . did she suspect I was human as well? I had a moment of panic and looked down at my hands, but they were still a light violet shade, indicating that my disguise was functioning.

"Welcome, everyone!" A voice came over the PA system. It was Winzik. "We've arrived at our training facility! This is going to be so exciting, yes indeed! You probably have many questions. A drone will lead you to your flight's dock, and you can get your starfighter assignments."

"We're here?" Hesho asked. "We hyperjumped? Usually they give some kind of warning before it happens!" The door of our jump room opened and he zipped out, the other kitsen tagging along behind on their platforms.

The rest of us, including Brade, gathered outside in the hallway, then followed a drone that had arrived to lead us. Another drone chased after the kitsen, barely keeping up with them.

I looked toward the engine room. *That direction,* I thought. *The scream came from that direction.*

This technology was no sham. Superiority FTL drives *did* let them hide—the delvers *hadn't* seen us. It felt even more vital to me than ever that I find a way to steal a hyperdrive. My people *needed* this technology.

At the same time, I had the striking suspicion that whatever was driving this ship, it wasn't technology in the traditional sense. There was something too familiar about it. Something—

"What did you sense?" a curious voice asked beside me.

I stiffened, smelling cinnamon. I tried, with some effort, to keep myself from squirming at Vapor's presence as I walked after the rest of my team. If I smelled her . . . did that mean I was *breathing* her in?

"To most people, a hyperjump is imperceptible," Vapor said, speaking with her breezy voice. "Not to you. Curious."

"Why does the Superiority risk using cytonic communications?" I blurted out. Perhaps the wrong thing to say to change the subject, but it had been on my mind. "Everyone is so scared of delvers, but we blatantly use communication that might draw their attention."

Vapor's scent changed to one that was slightly minty. Was that intentional on her part? Or was it like how a human changed moods?

"It's been over a hundred years since the last delver attack," she said. "It's easy to grow lax, in the face of that. Besides, cytonic communication was never actually enough to draw a delver into our realm."

"But—"

"If a delver has already come to our realm, then they might hear that communication and follow it. They can hear all wireless signals—radio included, though cytonic communication is the most attractive to them. In the past, wise empires learned to hide their communication, but these days it can be employed very cautiously. Assuming no delver is nearby. Assuming nobody has been brash enough to draw them into our realm by cytonic travel or by dangerous use of AI."

Her scent receded. I followed the drone, not trusting myself to answer. I'd come here with the goal of stealing a hyperdrive, but my task was suddenly far more daunting. I couldn't just run off with a small starfighter—if I wanted a hyperdrive, I'd have to hijack this entire carrier ship.

Was there an easier way? If I could only *see* what was going on in that engine room, maybe I could put together the secret. Scud, I wished Rig were here with me. He'd be able to figure all of this out, I was sure.

I followed the others to a different dock from the one where we'd arrived. Here, groups of starfighters were being prepped for the flights to use in today's training. They were boxier than the sleek DDF ones, but I didn't spare them much attention at first.

Because something magnificent hung outside.

An enormous polyhedral structure dominated the view through the invisible shield that held the air in the bay. It was big enough to dwarf our carrier ship; it was as large as a space station.

"Welcome, pilots," Winzik said over the PA, "to the delver maze."

I stepped up to the shield separating us from the vacuum. We hung in space, orbiting a fairly weak star. The huge structure seemed to *bend* to my eyes. As if I could barely comprehend it. Sweeping lines, gradations in the darkness. This metallic structure wasn't quite a sphere, but a dodecahedron with smooth faces and sharp edges.

I smelled cinnamon. Then a quiet voice beside me said, "It's insane that they actually built one."

"What is it?" I asked.

"A training ground," Vapor said. How did she make sounds to talk? "For re-creating a battle against a delver. The humans built this years ago, and we've only just located it. They knew."

"Knew . . . what?"

Vapor's scent changed to something sharper, the smell of wet metal after machinery is sprayed down. "They knew that eventually, the delvers would need to be faced. Our fear of them stunts our communication, our travel, even our warfare. Break free of that hold . . . and the galaxy is yours."

Her smell faded away. I remained in place, thinking on that until Hesho came flying over.

"Incredible," he said. "Come, Captain Alanik. We've been assigned ships. They cannot hyperjump, but they look suitable for fighting."

I followed him to our line of five fighters. They were painted stark white and didn't have true wings; they looked like triangular wedges of steel with cockpits up front and weapons installed on the slant of each side of the wedge. They obviously weren't meant for atmospheric battle.

The kitsen fighter was about fifty percent larger than the others and had been built like a battleship, with many small gun emplacements. The kitsen were thrilled with this, chattering as they went over the specs and made assignments. It apparently had multiple stations inside and various departments to work.

My ship was an interceptor built for speed, with moderate firepower in the form of twin destructors and—I was pleased to note—a single light-lance turret underneath. I'd worried I wouldn't have one of those, and most of the ships didn't. Apparently the Superiority officials had seen how effectively I'd used mine in the test.

Morriumur had an interceptor too, while Vapor had been given a sniper, with a longer-range gun but no light-lance. I looked over my shoulder, noting Brade walking to the last of the fighters—a third interceptor, also with a light-lance.

I stepped over to her as she reached her ship. She looked up, startled. "What?" she demanded.

"I just wanted to welcome you to the flight," I said, holding out my hand. I nodded toward it. "It's a human gesture, I've been told."

"I wouldn't know," she said. "I don't associate with monsters."

She brushed past me, then hauled herself up the ladder into her ship. Scud. How brainwashed *was* she? If I was going to recruit her, I'd need to find a way to talk to her more without raising anyone else's suspicions.

For now, it seemed my only option was to start training. And to be honest, I found I was eager to begin. All of this imitation and subterfuge was exhausting; it would be good to just fly again.

I climbed into my fighter, and was pleased to find that the controls were familiar. Had we humans gotten these designs from aliens long ago? Or had our attempt to conquer the galaxy spread our technology throughout it?

"M-Bot," I said. "Preflight check."

Silence.

Right. Being without his friendly voice made me feel suddenly exposed. I'd grown accustomed to having him there in the ship's computer, watching out for me. With a sigh, I found a preflight checklist under the seat, used my pin to translate it, then went through the steps to double-check that everything worked the way I expected.

"This is Alanik," I said, after testing the communications. "Everyone online?"

"This is the Kitsen Unity Ship *Swims Against the Current in a Stream Reflecting the Sun*," Hesho's voice said. "Recently named. All systems operational. This ship even has a very nice captain's chair."

"We should pick callsigns," I said. "I'll be Spring."

"Do we *have* to?" Morriumur said. "Our names are simple enough, aren't they?"

"It's a military thing," I said. "Morriumur, you can be callsign: Complains."

"Oh," Morriumur said, their voice sounding despondent. "I guess I deserve that."

Scud. Assigning an insulting nickname wasn't nearly as fun when someone just accepted it.

"Callsigns aren't required," Brade said. "I will use my name, which is Brade. Do not call me by something else."

"Fine," I said. "Vapor, you there?"

"Yes," her quiet voice said. "But my normal mission callsign is top secret. So I will need another."

"The Wind That Mingles with a Man's Dying Breath," Hesho suggested.

"That's . . . very specific," Morriumur said.

"Yeah," I said. "It's cool, but kind of a mouthful, Hesho."

"I think it's beautiful," Vapor said.

"Flight Fifteen," a voice said from Command. "Be ready to launch. Command out."

"Wait," I said to the voice. "What's our command structure? How should we organize ourselves?"

"It doesn't matter to us," the voice said. "Figure it out yourself. Command out."

"That's annoying," I said over the private line to my flight. "I thought the Superiority knew more about military discipline than that."

"Maybe not," Hesho said. "They *did* need to recruit us as pilots."

"They have hundreds of other pilots, flying remote drones," I said. "Surely they have command structures. Officers and ranks?"

Morriumur cleared their throat over the line. "My leftparent did a stint as a drone pilot, and . . . well, most of them retire after a short time. The duty is too stressful, too aggressive."

Scud. Well, that was probably another big reason why we on Detritus had survived so long.

Flight Command ordered us to lift off, and the five of us rose on our acclivity rings, then maneuvered out of the *Weights and Measures*'s docks into the deepness of space.

The distant star shined light that reflected in bright waves off the metallic surface of the maze. Its awesome size reminded me of the platforms around Detritus—both must have taken extraordinary amounts of effort to create.

We flew out to our instructed coordinates to wait. I tore my attention away from the maze and hit my flight chatter button. We simply couldn't go into training without some kind of command structure. "Hesho," I said. "Do you want to be our flightleader? You've got command experience."

"Not much," Hesho said. "I have been a ship captain for only about three weeks, Captain Alanik. Before that, I was in politics."

"You were absolute monarch of a small section of the kitsen home planet," Vapor said softly.

"Details," Hesho said. "Who cares about those dark ages, right? We're enlightened now!" He hesitated. "But it was *not* small. We encompassed over a third of the planet. Regardless, I do not think it would be wise for me to command this flight. I should not divide my attention from commanding my crew while this ship is unfamiliar and my people are still learning it."

"You can take command if you want, Alanik," Morriumur said to me.

I grimaced. "No, please. I'm likely to charge into a black hole or something. You don't want one of your interceptors to be in command. Vapor, you should be flightleader."

"Me?" the quiet voice asked.

"That sounds good to me," Morriumur said. "Alanik is right—we shouldn't have someone who is too aggressive."

"I accept this decision," Hesho said. "As our sniper, Vapor can survey the battlefield and be in the best position to make decisions."

"You all barely know me," Vapor protested.

Which was part of the reason I'd suggested it. Maybe if Vapor was our flightleader, she'd be forced to interact with the rest of us—and maybe I'd be less likely to forget she was around. I still didn't quite understand her purpose here.

"Brade?" I asked. "What do you think?"

"I am not allowed to vote in such matters," she said.

Great. "All right, Vapor, the job is yours. Good luck."

"Very well," she said. "I suppose everyone should give me a flight status check, then."

I smiled. That sounded very much like she had some combat experience—so I was learning about her already. It seemed that callsigns were out though, as everyone just used their names as they called in. I reluctantly did likewise, as wrong as it felt. I didn't want to act like I had too much experience with this sort of thing.

Vapor organized us into a default flight pattern, with me and Brade flying up front, Hesho in the center, and Morriumur and herself flying in the anchor position. Then, at my suggestion, we did a few formation exercises while we waited for instructions.

As we did, I acknowledged to myself that perhaps it made sense for the Superiority to let each group make their own command structure. After all, most of the other flights contained only one species. Different cultures might have different ways of looking at military service—the fact that we had an entire crew of kitsen on one ship was evidence of that.

Still, it grated on me. It felt like the Superiority was being lazy. They wanted flights of fighters, but didn't want to have to deal with the hassle of truly commanding them. It was a lukewarm half-in, half-out measure. After the sharply defined rules of the DDF, this felt like a sloppy mess.

Eventually, Winzik called us on the general line. "All right, everyone! Welcome and thank you for your service! We at the Department of Protective Services are very excited to be training this new bold force. You will be our first line of defense against a danger that has loomed above the Superiority for its entire existence.

"We have prepared a quick video orientation for you to watch. This should explain your goal here. Please experience the orientation and save questions until the end. Thank you again!"

"A . . . video orientation?" I said over the channel to my flight.

"The Superiority has a lot of graphic designers and animators," Morriumur said. "It's one of the most common professions chosen by those who wish to work beyond basic subsistence."

I frowned. "What's a graphic designer?"

The canopy of my fighter suddenly lit up with a holographic projection. It wasn't as good as one of M-Bot's—this one was somewhat insubstantial, and the depth was off—but the effect was still awe inspiring.

Because it was showing me a delver.

It looked like the one I'd seen back on the recording at Detritus. An enormous, oppressive shadow within a cloud of light and dust. Chunks of burning asteroids spewed from it, leaving trails in the void. They churned past my canopy, and though I knew this was just a hologram, my fingers twitched on the controls of my ship.

Every instinct I had was screaming at me to get away from this terror. This impossible, incredible *monstrosity*. It would destroy me and everything I loved. I could feel it.

"This is a delver!" a perky, feminine voice said. A cutesy graphic surrounded the thing on the screen—a shimmering line of stars and lightning bolts.

"Even still, no one truly knows what a delver is," the voice continued, and icons looking like confused faces lined the sides of my canopy. "These recordings are almost two hundred years old, taken when the Acumidian delver appeared and destroyed the planet Farhaven. Every living being on the planet was turned to dust and vaporized! How scary!"

My canopy view zoomed in on the delver, as if I'd suddenly flown up to it. I jumped despite myself. From this close, it looked like a thunderstorm of dust and energy—but deep within it, I saw the shadow of something smaller. A circular, shifting . . . something.

"When delvers enter our realm," the voice said, "matter coalesces around them. We think they must bring it through from the place they come from. Freaky! This matter forms a shroud around the delver; the creature itself is much smaller! At the very center of all this dust, rock, and debris is a metallic shell sometimes called a delver maze!

"Standard shields protect pilots from whatever it is about the delver that vaporizes people, so that's nice, isn't it! But those

shields don't last long against a delver's attacks, and even planetary shields usually fall within a matter of minutes. Still, shielded
ships can get close, and some have even traveled inside the dust,
past the debris, and into the maze itself! There, they encountered
a complicated network of twisting tubes and corridors made from
stone and metal."

The image of the delver vanished, replaced by a large cartoon
version. It had angry eyebrows and vaguely human features, and
a pair of cartoon hands pulled back the cloud of dust, revealing a
polyhedral structure with a lumpy, malformed exterior. It wasn't
as polished or angular as the one we were going to train on. On the
real thing, spines jutted out at various places. It was like a cross
between a large asteroid, a melted chunk of steel, and a sea urchin.

"The smaller chunks that the delver expels chase after ships,"
the voice explained, and cartoon meteors shot out from the delver
in pursuit of little animated ships. "They'll try to bring down
your shield so the delver can munch on you! Stay away! They
move with no visible source of propulsion. Maybe they're magic!
Reports say that fighting these embers is like trying to dogfight
inside an asteroid field, when all the asteroids are actively trying
to kill you!

"The delver itself lurks at the center of the maze. Our special
Delver Attack Devices won't work through that interference! So,
you'll need to fly into the maze and find the delver itself. It's in
there somewhere! Your training will include test runs through our
specially created imitation maze. Good luck, and hopefully you
won't die! Thank you!"

After that, a list of people who had made the orientation video
scrolled across my screen, many with little cute symbols next to
their names. When it was finally done, my canopy went transparent again, giving me a good view of the large training maze that—
compared to the delver—seemed far too ordinary.

I settled back, feeling a mounting dread. I was increasingly certain the Superiority was filled with people who were taking this threat far too lightly.

"All right," Vapor said with a soft, calming voice. "They've sent us orders. We're to proceed to the following coordinates, then wait our turn at the maze."

22

Vapor led us on a careful approach of the maze. From up closer, I could see the lines where different segments had been fabricated, then fitted together. It didn't have all the dust around it, like the kind that shrouded a real delver maze. That left this experience feeling even more mundane. It just didn't evoke the same sense of dread and worry that the videos had.

"Command says to watch for interceptors," Vapor told us. "The delvers have fighters that attack those who get close?"

"Not fighters," Brade said in her stern voice. "The delver controls hunks of rock, called embers, which try to intercept and collide with ships that get near."

"All right," Vapor said. "I asked, and Command assured me that this won't be as dangerous as our initial test was. Apparently, some people in the department made the brilliant connection that if you kill all your recruits before you have time to train them, you'll soon run out of recruits."

I smiled. The more Vapor spoke, the more conversational her tone became—and the less creepy she seemed. "That's a relief," I said.

"Well, I still would be careful," she answered. "The Superiority hasn't done much training like this since the human wars. For now, let's get back into formation."

I boosted forward at the order, settling into my position at the front of our team. Unfortunately, the others didn't have nearly as much experience with battle formations as I did. Morriumur hung back too far, and Hesho tried to keep up with me until Vapor reminded him that his ship was to remain near the center. And Brade . . .

Well, Brade flew forward, far out of our pattern. Scud. They were all competent pilots, but we weren't a true flight. We didn't have experience fighting together. Cobb had spent weeks pounding flight maneuvers into Skyward Flight's thick heads. He hadn't let us fight, or even use our *guns,* until we'd practiced flight drills so much that we instinctively knew how to maneuver as a team.

That had saved our lives a dozen times over when the fighting had gotten bad. Here, as soon as the enemy came at us—in the form of drones that had been outfitted with rock casings to imitate flying asteroids—the team broke apart. Brade darted in to attack them without a word from Vapor. Morriumur started shooting, but . . . well, their shots were *way* off, and I had to boost farther out of formation to be sure they didn't accidentally hit me. And to be honest, I undercompensated, as this new ship wasn't as responsive as M-Bot, and I wasn't used to how it maneuvered.

Vapor was so busy talking to us that she forgot that her job as sniper was to start blasting the enemy ships while they were distracted. The only one of us who didn't embarrass himself was Hesho, whose ship performed its ordered maneuvers with precision. The diminutive fox poet might have been a little dramatic, but his crew was obviously well trained. He managed to bring down four of the drones.

These drones didn't act like the ones we fought on Detritus. Whoever was piloting them had been instructed not to dodge, but just fly around and try to collide with us. Which made sense, since they were imitating chunks of stone being moved by the delver. I was glad to see that when one got close enough to have hit Morriumur, however, it broke off before colliding and instead radioed to say Morriumur was dead. So maybe the Superiority really had learned not to use live fire during training.

We regrouped for another run, and again Brade engaged the embers immediately. Morriumur—apparently thinking that they should use Brade as a model—waded into the fight and nearly got smashed up by an approaching drone for the second time. This one didn't pull back fast enough, but I barely managed to spear it with my light-lance and tow it away. I was rewarded by Morriumur panicking and shooting at *me* in a moment of confusion. Hesho, sensing that his allies were in trouble, barreled forward and started shooting in all directions.

A private line opened from Vapor to me. "Wow," she said softly. "They seem . . . confused."

"Confused? It's a mess. This flight needs way more work on fundamentals."

"If you think so, then give the orders."

"*You're* the flightleader."

"And I'm making you my assistant flightleader," Vapor said. "How would you fix this situation? I'm curious."

Great. I had no leadership experience. But . . . I winced, watching the others fight. Someone needed to stop this before we ended up as rubble.

"What do you idiots think you're doing!" I shouted into the general line. "That was the most embarrassing excuse of a hostile approach I've ever seen! Brade, you were ordered to clear the firing path, not fetch a fist of enemy nose hairs! Morriumur, get back here! Don't learn bad habits by chasing someone who disobeys orders. And Hesho, you're flying well, but you have the fire control of a child with a new toy. Everyone, disengage and fall back."

Next, I temporarily added the *Weights and Measures* to the channel. "Flight Command," I said, "Flight Fifteen is going to need to run some exercises and learn how to coordinate. Call back the drones and reset their attack vectors. Don't send them in again until I say we're ready for it."

"Pardon?" a voice asked. "Um . . . you're supposed to try flying into one of those approach tunnels in the—"

"I'm not letting my flight anywhere near your training machine until I'm sure they can fly in formation!" I shouted. "Right now, I'm convinced they'll mistake their own backsides for the approach tunnels, and end up rammed so far up there we'll need spelunking gear to get them out!"

Hesho chuckled softly on the line.

"Um . . . ," Flight Command said. "I guess . . . I guess we can do that?"

The others started flying back, and the drones disengaged. Brade kept flying toward the delver maze though, so I opened a private line to her. "Brade, I'm serious. Vapor made me her XO, and I'm giving you an order. You damn well better get back in line, or I *will* flay you. I hear people will pay good money for a human skin to hang on their walls."

With obvious reluctance, Brade disengaged and spun around to boost back toward us.

And . . . had that all really come out of my mouth? I sat back in my seat, my heart thundering inside me as if I'd run a race. I hadn't specifically intended to say any of that. It had all just kind of . . . happened.

Scud. Cobb would be laughing his head off if he could hear

me right now. As the others gathered back together, a private call came to me from Vapor.

"Well done," she said. "But perhaps a tad aggressive for this group. Where did you learn to talk like that?"

"I . . . um, had an interesting flight instructor back home."

"Tone it down," Vapor suggested. "But I agree with you—we should do some more training before we fight. Organize them to do so."

"You're really going to make me do the hard part, aren't you?" I said.

"A good commander knows when to appoint a good drill instructor. You've been in the military before. You obviously know this."

I sighed, but she was right, and I'd walked right into the job. As the flight gathered together, I explained one of Cobb's old formation exercises, one he'd adapted for space fighting once we'd started training out in the vacuum. Vapor quietly joined the line, and soon I had them flying pretty much in an organized way. As much as I hated being put in charge, I could run these exercises practically in my sleep, so I was good at watching the others and giving them tips.

They soon got the hang of it. Much faster than Skyward Flight had, actually. This group had good piloting instincts; most just didn't have formal combat training.

Vapor is used to working on her own, I decided as we flew through a shifting exercise where we traded places in formation to confuse an oncoming enemy flight.

Morriumur was timid, but willing to learn. Hesho was accustomed to having people follow his lead, and was often surprised when the rest of us didn't know instinctively what he wanted to do. He needed to learn better communication.

Brade was the worst. Though she was the best pilot, she kept trying to go on ahead. Far too eager.

"You *need* to stay with the rest of us," I said, calling her. "Don't keep trying to go ahead."

"I'm a human," Brade snapped. "We're aggressive. Deal with it."

"Just earlier you said you didn't spend time around humans," I said, "and therefore didn't know their habits. You can't play the 'I'm not like them' card, *then* use your nature as a human as an excuse."

"I try to hold back," Brade said, "but deep down I know the truth. I'm going to lose my temper. It's hopeless to plan for anything else."

"That's a load of yesterday's slop," I said. "When I started training, I was *hopeless*. I lost my temper so often, you could have set your clock by my tantrums."

"Really?" Brade asked.

"Really. I *literally* assaulted my flightleader in class one day. But I learned. So can you."

She fell silent, but seemed to be trying harder as we went through another exercise. As the day progressed—and we stopped for lunch in our cockpits—I found myself most impressed by Morriumur. All things considered, their flying ability was remarkable, and they were extremely eager to learn. Yeah, they couldn't aim worth spit, but Cobb had always said he'd rather have students who could fly well. Those could stay alive long enough to be taught to fight.

I pulled my ship up beside Morriumur's as we finished lunch and moved back into formation. "Hey," I said, "when we do this next batch, try to watch and stay tighter in formation. You keep veering toward the outside."

"I'm sorry," they said. "I'll do better. And . . . also, I'm sorry I almost shot you earlier."

"That? That was nothing. At least you didn't *mean* to try to kill me—that's more than I can say for most."

They chuckled, though I thought I could hear tension in their

231

voice. I remembered my first few training sessions under Cobb—the worry that I'd get something wrong and be kicked out, the growing lack of confidence that I belonged, the frustration at not being able to do all the things I'd imagined myself capable of accomplishing.

"Don't worry," I told them. "You're doing fine, particularly considering how new to this you are."

"As I mentioned, my leftparent was a drone pilot during their youth," Morriumur said. "I got a piece of that experience, fortunately."

"You really get *skills* from your parents?"

"Of course," Morriumur said. "Some of the knowledge and skills of the parents pass on to the child. I guess it isn't that way for your species?"

Was it? Scud. I didn't actually know, at least not for Alanik's species. Without M-Bot there to whisper explanations into my ear, I could get myself into trouble.

"Anyway, I was lucky in this," Morriumur continued. "But also unlucky. My leftparent has had some latent aggression, and I ended up with an extra measure of it. My first few days alive, I got a reputation for snapping at others."

"Snapping at people is aggressive among your kind?"

"Very," Morriumur said.

"Wow. I'd have never made it to being born. They'd have killed me right out."

"That's a common misconception," Morriumur said. "If my parents decide not to bear me with this personality, I won't be killed—they'll simply recombine me in a new way. What you see in me is just a draft, a prospect, a possibility of who I could be. Though . . . if I were to be born, I'd retain these memories, and my personality would become real." They paused. "And I *do* wish for that to be the case."

I tried to imagine a world where I remembered being forced to *prove* I was worth existing. No wonder this society had issues.

We finished the next batch of exercises, and I was pleased at how well the group kept formation. "This is actually working," I said, calling Vapor. "I think we might be able to make something of them."

"Excellent," Vapor said. "Are they ready for combat then?"

"Scud, no!" I said. "We need to be at this for another few weeks *at least*. They're good pilots, so it's not like starting with raw recruits, but that doesn't mean I want them shooting at anything yet."

Vapor seemed to take that in stride, and didn't complain—or even ask for more details. She simply said, "Interesting." How was I to interpret that?

"Let's give them another break," she eventually said to me. "Then we'll try some higher-speed formations. We have three hours until we return to Starsight for the day. Flight Command has been asking if any of us will be heading into the maze. I'll tell them that we don't anticipate it."

"All right," I said, slowing my ship and pulling out my canteen.

"Unless, of course," she added, "you want to give it a try while the others are on break. You and I could head in there together."

I hesitated, canteen halfway to my lips.

"It would be useful, after all, to know what it is we're preparing for," Vapor said. "I've heard of delver mazes, but I've never been in one." Her ship hovered up beside me, and it was disconcerting to see the cockpit empty, as if it were piloted by a ghost.

What was Vapor's game? In putting me in charge of running the exercises, she'd been able to go back to observing. Participating, but remaining mostly mysterious. Now she wanted me to go into the maze with her. It seemed a test of some sort. A challenge?

I looked out toward the maze. Each flight had been assigned a different face of the dodecahedron, and the pilots had been practicing approaching and then flying into it.

"I'm up for it," I decided, putting away my canteen. "Tell Flight Command to call off those drones though. We can train on fighting them later."

"Done," Vapor said. "Let's go."

23

Flight Command reluctantly did as requested, and pulled back the drones this once so that Vapor and I could fly in uncontested.

I got a better sense for the size of the thing as we flew into its shadow. It was roughly as wide as one of the platforms around Detritus—but that was just its diameter. In total mass, it must have been a dozen times as large.

Not planetary scale, and therefore smaller than the full delvers I'd seen in the videos, but still dauntingly enormous. Each face of the dodecahedron had dozens of holes in it, punctures roughly twenty meters across. Vapor and I picked one at random and drew in close enough that I could see that the rest of the face was of polished metal.

I found myself growing excited. I was increasingly fascinated by the delvers, an emotion that walked hand in hand with my growing worry about them. Maybe even fear of them. I couldn't shake that image I'd seen back on Detritus: me, standing where the delver should have been. Whatever it meant to be a cytonic—whatever I was—it had to do with these things and the place where they lived.

This isn't a real one, I reminded myself. *This is just an imitation for training.* Like a practice dummy to use in sword fighting.

We paused right outside our chosen tunnel, looking as if into the throat of the beast. I kept expecting M-Bot to chime in with an analysis, and found the silence of my canopy daunting. "So . . . ," I said, calling Vapor. "We just go into one of these tunnels?"

"Yes," she replied. "Reports from pilots who survived entering a real maze indicate all the tunnels looked the same. If there is a reason to pick one over another, we don't yet know what it is."

"Follow my lead then, I guess?" I asked, inching my ship forward at one-tenth of a Mag, the starship equivalent of a crawl. The inside was pitch-black. Though I could fly by instruments alone—I often had to, out in space—I hit my floodlights. I wanted visuals on this place.

The inside of the tunnel narrowed to about fifteen meters across, cramped confines on starfighter scales. I let myself move at barely a creep as I flew forward.

Behind me, several drones broke off the wall near the entrance and started moving in our direction. "Flight Command," I said, "I thought you were told to let us do this run without pursuit."

"Um . . . ," the person on the channel said. "When you actually fight a delver, they'll chase you . . ."

"We'll never *get* to the part about fighting a delver if we die during these practice runs," I said. "Call off the drones and let Vapor and me get our feet underneath us. Trust me, I've done a *lot* more training than you."

"Okay, okay," the dione said. "No need to be so aggressive . . ."

These people. I rolled my eyes, but they called off the drones as requested.

Vapor's seemingly empty ship moved up beside mine. M-Bot had said she flew not by moving the control sphere or pushing buttons, but by interrupting and overriding the electrical signals sent by the controls to the rest of the ship. So . . . did that mean she *was* the ship, after a manner? Like she was a spirit that could possess electronics?

"Now what?" I asked. "We're just supposed to fly around in these tunnels? Looking for what? The center?"

"The heart," Vapor said. "But it's not always at the center. After surviving pilots flew through the maze for a time, a few reported discovering a chamber with atmosphere and gravity. Inside that chamber was a smaller one, sealed off by a membrane that seemed like living tissue. When they drew close, they heard voices in their minds, and claim to have known the delver was inside."

"All right . . . ," I said. "That sounds vague. Even assuming that they were right, how are we supposed to find this 'heart' of the maze? This thing is bigger than a carrier ship. We could probably fly in here for days and not explore every chamber."

"I don't think that is a problem," Vapor said. "Pilots who entered the real maze, and who survived long enough, all eventually found the membrane." She hesitated. "Most flew back, frightened and fearing for their sanity, after reaching it. Several entered, but none of those returned."

Delightful. Well, I hoped to never have to face a real delver—but certainly, anything I experienced in here might be useful to my people. I flew farther into the tunnel, my proximity sensors mapping the ways various parts branched off. However, I found myself relying on eyesight—leaning forward, staring out of my canopy at the passing tunnel. It was like a corridor, with a uniform pattern of panels and grooves.

I've seen this before, I thought, feeling a chill. *Haven't I?*

Yes . . . I'd gone into a structure like this chasing Nedd, who had followed his brothers inside. It had been an enormous shipyard, and I'd had to dodge through its tunnels as it fell. The shape of this tunnel, with those ridges at points where metal plates met, was exactly the same.

We entered a larger open room with more branching tunnels

coming off it. Here I used maneuvering thrusters to position my-self near the ceiling, where a strange set of markings had been stamped into the metal.

I've seen these before too, I thought, shifting my floodlights to bathe the ceiling in light. I craned my neck to peer at the markings. They looked like a strange alien language.

"Flight Command," I said. "Can you hear me?"

Silence. Then finally a voice replied, "We can. The maze has signal boosters installed. But when you're inside a real maze, interference sometimes prevents communication. It's best if you pretend the same might happen here."

"Sure," I said. "But first, what's this writing on the ceiling near me?"

"Those appear to be replicas made from pictures taken by pi-lots inside a real delver maze. They have no meaning that we've been able to interpret."

"Huh," I said. "I swear I've seen them somewhere before . . ."

"Do you want us to engage the maze's other defensive fea-tures?" Flight Command asked. "Or do you just want to fly around in it?"

"What defensive features are we talking about?" I asked.

"A real delver maze causes those who enter it to hallucinate," the operator explained. "We've imitated this by giving you ships with holographic canopies that can project strange sights. When entering the maze, you should always take another pilot with you."

"Why is that?" I asked. "For backup?"

"No," Vapor whispered. "Because they each see different things, don't they? I've heard of this."

"Yes," the operator said. "The maze affects the minds of those who enter it in different ways—and each individual will see something different. Usually, if both pilots in a team see the same thing, it's real and not a hallucination. If you see different things, you'll know they're not real. In addition, other conclusions can be drawn by comparing what you see."

"Turn it on," I said, tapping on my maneuvering thrusters. I moved down into the hollow center of the room, next to Vapor's ship.

The chamber flickered, then changed, red colors blossoming out from one wall. Like blood bleeding from some underground well. It coated the wall, painting everything a deep crimson.

"Vapor," I whispered. "What do you see?"

"A black darkness," she replied, "covering everything and swallowing light."

"I see blood," I said. It didn't seem dangerous, but it was certainly creepy. "Let's keep moving."

I boosted out of the large chamber, passing into another tunnel. Though it was the same size as the one I'd traveled through earlier, it felt even more claustrophobic and constricting because the walls seemed to be made of flesh. They undulated and shivered, like I was actually moving through the veins of some enormous beast.

When I emerged into the next room, the appearance shifted again. Suddenly I seemed to be inside an ancient stone cavern, moss dangling from the ceiling in wide swaths.

Though I knew it was just a hologram, these changes left me unnerved. Vapor hovered up beside me. "I see the walls as if they were glass. What do you see?"

"Stone and moss," I said. "It's thickest on the right over there."

"I see glass shards floating in the air there. Perhaps the maze is obscuring something?"

"Yeah," I said, nudging closer. Sure enough, the proximity sensors indicated there was a tunnel hiding back there, obscured by the hologram. I eased my ship down through it and emerged into the next chamber. However, as I did, the shadows behind my ship moved.

I immediately spun the vessel around on its axis, pointing my floodlights in that direction. I was facing down a large pile of alien fungus, pulsing softly as if breathing, each bulbous toadstool the size of my fighter.

"Did you see that?" I asked Vapor as she hovered her ship down beside me.

"No. What did you see?"

"Motion," I said, narrowing my eyes. Something else darted away at the edges of my vision, and I spun my ship again.

"Proximity sensors show nothing," Vapor said. "It must be part of the hologram."

"Flight Command?" I asked. "What was that motion?"

The response that came back was jumbled and broken, my communications cutting out. The shadows in this room *were* moving. I spun again, trying to catch whatever was in here.

"Flight Command?" I asked again. "I'm not reading you."

"Do you want an authentic experience or not?" the voice came back to me, suddenly clear. "I told you that when pilots get deeper within the maze, communication starts to get more erratic."

"Okay, fine. But what are those shadows?"

"What shadows?"

"The ones that keep moving in this room?" I said. "Is there something inside this maze that will attack me?"

"Um . . . Not sure."

"What do you mean you're not sure?"

"Um . . . Just a sec."

Vapor and I hung there with the shadows. Until another voice came on our line, one that was more excitable and enthusiastic. Winzik, head of the Krell.

"Alanik! It's Winzik. I hear you're experiencing some of the maze's more unnerving features."

"You could say that," I said. Winzik's voice sounded . . . small. As if the signal from outside were a frail thread, close to snapping.

240

"There's something in here with us," Vapor said. "I think I saw it too just now."

"Hmm, my my," Winzik said. "Well, it's probably just the holograms."

"Probably?" I asked.

"Well, we're not a hundred percent sure how this works ourselves!" Winzik said. "We aren't adding moving shadows to your canopy holograms, but there might be other holograms in here created by the maze. We didn't build it, remember. We recovered it, repaired it, and added our own drones, but it was built by humans. We're not entirely certain what it can do—or what extents it can reach—to imitate a true delver maze."

"So we're lab animals?" I said, growing increasingly annoyed. "Testing something you don't understand? You toss us in and see who survives?"

"Now, now," Winzik said. "Don't be so *aggressive*, Alanik. Aren't your people trying to gain citizenship in the Superiority? Yelling at me won't help you with that goal, I assure you! Anyway, good job in there! Keep it up!"

The channel cut off, and I barely held myself back from cussing him out. How dare he be so . . . so . . . *perky*. Well, that friendly attitude was obviously just an act for my benefit. Krell were terrible and destructive, as proven by how they treated my people. Did Winzik think an affable voice would hide that reality from others?

"Let's get back out and check on the others," Vapor said, turning to lead me out the way we'd come in. I followed, and though the next room was the same one we'd come through before, the moss was gone, and it just looked normal now. Again it reminded me of the old shipyard from Detritus. Had that been another maze, like this? Intended for the same purpose? Or was I jumping to conclusions?

"Your people," Vapor said as we flew, "have a history with the humans. Do you not?"

"Um, yeah," I said, sitting up in my seat. Vapor didn't normally make small talk.

"Curious," she said.

"That was years before I was born," I said.

"Human domination altered the future of your planet," Vapor said. "Your people fought beside them and inevitably adopted some of their ways. You speak a variation on one of their languages." Vapor was silent for a time as we entered the tunnel that had looked like flesh.

"Your aggression reminds me of theirs," she finally added.

"What about you?" I said. "Have you ever met humans? Other than Brade, I mean."

"Many," Vapor said in her soft, airy voice. "I fought them."

"In the wars?" I asked, surprised. "The most recent was a hundred years ago. You were *alive* then?"

Vapor gave no specific confirmation, and we soon entered the large chamber with the writing on the ceiling, which had appeared to have blood on the walls before. Now it looked like a mirror gallery, reflecting back at me a thousand versions of my own ship.

I cocked my head and spun my ship, looking at the thousands of versions of my vessel. Until I pointed at one mirror that held not my ship, but just an image of me floating there—in space—alone.

Not Alanik. Me. Spensa.

The version of me looked up and met my eyes despite the distance, and I felt a growing coldness. That wasn't a reflection. It was one of *them*.

I hit the call button, but the room went black, and even my floodlights went out. I was left hanging as if in a void of nothing. Like I'd entered the nowhere.

My hand froze on the call button. But before I could speak, everything went back to normal. In the blink of an eye I was in my cockpit again, hanging in that ancient room, Vapor moving her ship toward the exit.

"—coming, Alanik?" Vapor's voice crackled onto my communication channel midsentence. "Or are you just going to sit there?"

"I'm coming," I said, trying to shake the creepy feeling. "What do you see back there?"

"Just a room," Vapor said. "Why?"

"I . . ." I shook my head, then guided my ship back out into open space, where I breathed a sigh of relief.

24

Outside, Vapor had me run the team through a few scatter formations—a maneuver where the flight would break apart and fly in different directions, then regroup. I figured those would be useful when fighting something like the embers, which would try to smash into us.

The others must have felt my shift in mood, because nobody gave me lip, and even Brade went through the exercises without complaint. Before long, it was time to head back to the *Weights and Measures,* the day's training finished.

I landed my ship in the docking bay, then gave her console a fond pat. She wasn't M-Bot, but she was a solidly built fighter. I popped the canopy and hopped down to join the others—and I could read in their attitudes a kind of exhausted enthusiasm. Exhausted because it had been a long day of training, but enthusiastic because it had been *good* training. We'd made progress, and were already starting to feel like a team.

Hesho laughed heartily at something that Morriumur said, and was again joined by the female kitsen in the red uniform, carrying a shield. I'd learned she was named Kauri, and was the ship's navigator—as well as Hesho's shieldbearer, though I wasn't exactly sure what that meant in this context.

As we walked together, I found that I could pick out a few of the other kitsen by their voices. It was strange to think that our flight included not just the five pilots, but all fifty-seven kitsen crew members as well.

I liked it. I liked how much energy it brought us. It almost helped me forget the strange things I'd felt and seen in the maze.

We were ordered back to the jump room, and though a drone arrived to lead the way, Brade tried to rush on ahead. Perhaps to keep from being forced to interact with us.

I walked faster to catch up to her.

"Hey," I said. "I like that maneuver you pulled just before we ended. The one where you wove between other members of the flight, without hitting them?"

Brade shrugged. "It was simple."

"You've got flight experience," I noted.

"Obviously."

"Well, I'm glad to have you on the team."

"You sure about that?" she said. "You know what I am. Sooner or later I'm going to lose it, and there will be casualties."

"I'm counting on it," I said.

She stopped in place, standing in the red-carpeted hallway, frowning at me. "What?"

"Where I come from," I said softly, "a little passion is a *good* thing to have in a pilot. I'm not afraid of a little aggression, Brade. I think we can use it."

"You have no idea what you're asking for," she snapped at me, then hurried on.

I lingered until the others caught up, then walked with them to our jump room. This time, I didn't try to continue on toward the engine room—the guard there was already suspicious of me, judging by how their eyes followed me as I passed.

As we settled into our seats, I focused on doing Gran-Gran's exercise. I closed my eyes and let my mind float out, imagining myself soaring among the stars, and I *listened*.

The voices of the chattering kitsen faded away. There. *Hyperdrive ready,* a voice said. It wasn't in English, but as always, language didn't matter. My mind picked out the meaning. Why were they communicating via cytonics? It was just the bridge calling the engine room.

Excellent. That was from Winzik. *Engage.*

I braced myself, waiting . . . but nothing happened. What?

A moment later, another communication was sent. *Engine room, is there a problem?*

Yes, unfortunately, the reply came. *We're reading cytonic interference from localized sources inside the ship.*

I felt a spike of alarm. They . . . they knew I was here.

Oh, that, Winzik said. *Yes, that's to be expected. We've got two of them traveling with us now.*

It's going to cause a problem, sir, Engineering sent back.

How much of one?

We'll have to see. We're swapping out the hyperdrive unit now. A fresh one might work, as long as we engage it immediately.

I waited, tense. A few minutes passed.

Then it happened again. Another dump of information into my mind—this one pointed toward Starsight. Then a scream.

I felt that same disorienting sense of being thrown into a vast blackness. Again, the delvers didn't see me. They were focused on the scream.

I slammed back into my seat, my mind throbbing. Again I sagged in my straps, though none of the others even broke conversation. They didn't realize it had happened.

That sensation I'd felt, that dump of information . . . it told me where the hyperjump was going to go. I could have used that information to jump *myself* to Starsight. That information was fading, but slowly. I might . . . I might be able to jump myself from here to the delver maze and back again, if I needed to.

The random numbers that M-Bot had told me didn't work, but something about this information injected directly into my mind . . . that did. It proved what I had suspected—that I needed to be able to do more than just know my destination; I had to be able to *feel* it. It was a clue, my first solid one, on how I might be able to control my powers.

Worn out, I rose with the others and trudged to the pickup bay, which looked out toward Starsight: a vibrant, glowing blue platform with buildings sprouting from it like stalactites and stalagmites.

I bade farewell to the others, then climbed into my assigned shuttle. Unfortunately, I wasn't allotted my own this time, as an official sent a trio of reptilian aliens in after me. Apparently their housing was near mine. They gathered in the back seats, chatting softly in their own language, my pin translating helpfully. Since they were just talking about dinner plans, I flipped off the translator.

The shuttle took off, and the moment we left the docking bay a voice erupted through my earpiece. "Spensa?" M-Bot asked. "Spensa, I'm picking up your signal again. Are you well? Is everything all right? It's been eight hours without communication!"

Hearing that voice was shockingly welcome, and I found myself sighing in relief. My task was feeling increasingly more intimidating by the moment, but this one point of familiarity reminded me I wasn't completely alone.

"I'm back," I whispered to him, then eyed the aliens behind me. "I'll explain more when I get to the embassy."

"Scud, that's good to hear!" M-Bot said. "Did you hear that? I just swore. If I started swearing, do you think it would prove that I'm alive? Lifeless computers don't swear. That would be *weird*."

"I don't think you can argue that you're not weird."

"Of course I can. I can argue basically anything, if I'm programmed for it. Anyway, they must have some kind of communications shield over the *Weights and Measures*! When I lost your signal, I feared I'd been left alone with the slug forever."

I smiled, and was actually starting to feel excited as we approached my building. I had so much to explain to M-Bot. The delver maze. Vapor. I'd made some inroads with Brade, hadn't I? Unfortunately, as the shuttle approached, I found that Mrs. Chamwit—the Krell housekeeper that Cuna had assigned me—was waiting at the front door.

"What's she doing here still?" I whispered, eyeing the armored alien woman as my shuttle settled down.

"Once she finished cleaning, she spent the time waiting for you to return," M-Bot answered.

She was *really* committed to her spying, wasn't she? As I climbed out of the shuttle, she bustled over, speaking with an energetic voice. "Welcome back, mistress! I've looked into your species's nutritional requirements, and I think I have just the recipe for dinner tonight. Akokian pudding! It's a wonderful mixture of sweet and savory!"

"Um," I said. "No thanks? I've got some food already. I ordered it a couple days ago."

"Mistress? The *algae* strips in your refrigeration unit?"

"Sure," I said. "They're fine." Bland, but fine.

"Well . . . maybe I could work those into a side dish?" Mrs. Chamwit said. "Or maybe just make you a dessert?"

"I'm fine," I said. "Really. Thanks. I have some work to do tonight, and don't want to be interrupted."

She gestured in a crestfallen way, though I didn't buy the act. If the Krell woman was sad, it was only because I wasn't giving her the chance to spy. Eventually—after three more reassurances that I was fine—she tromped off down the street to leave for the day.

I sighed, wiping my brow, then hiked up the steps to the top of the building and climbed into M-Bot's cockpit. "Dim the canopy," I said. "And make sure the alien spy has really left."

The canopy dimmed. "I'm not convinced she's a spy, Spensa," M-Bot said. "She didn't look through your things. She just straightened up your room, then spent the time doing word puzzles on her tablet."

"Straightening up is a *perfect* cover for spying." I leaned back in the seat and scratched under Doomslug's chin.

The slug trilled piteously, and looked lethargic as she inched toward me. So I picked her up and settled her into my lap. I'd never seen her move this slowly; something about this place seemed to be making her feel sick.

"All right, M-Bot," I said. "We have a problem. We might need to hijack that entire carrier ship."

"Excellent," M-Bot said. "Would you like your corpse cremated or ejected into space?"

I grinned. "Nice."

"Humor is an essential identifier of a living being," M-Bot said. "I've been working on some subroutines to help me better recognize and make jokes."

"You can just do that, huh?" I said. "Reprogram yourself to be something new."

"I have to be careful," M-Bot said, "as another essential part of being alive is persistence of personality. I don't want to change who I am too much. Beyond that, there are certain things that, if I try to rewrite, will send me into . . ." *Click. Clickclickclickclick.*

I sighed and settled back in the seat, petting Doomslug. She was soft and springy—even the spines on her back, which she fluted out of, weren't that stiff.

"I'm back," M-Bot finally said, then heaved an exaggerated sigh. "That is annoying. Anyway, you were saying something about a suicide mission trying to hijack an entire Superiority capital ship?"

"It's not a full capital ship," I said. "There's probably only, say, fifty or sixty crew members on board . . ." I launched into an explanation of what had happened to me today: the conversations I'd overheard, the delver maze, the interactions with the other pilots and Vapor. Even the strange experiences inside the maze itself.

"So," I said, summing up, "I'm not going to be given a ship with a hyperdrive, which means we'll have to find another way."

"Curious," M-Bot said. "And you can *hear* the orders that Winzik is giving the engine room? Why?"

"I guess they're communicating through the nowhere."

"From one end of the ship to the other?" M-Bot asked. "That doesn't make any sense. Simple wired communication should be enough. Are you sure that's what you're hearing?"

"No," I said, honestly. "And *hearing* isn't even the right word." I sat, thoughtful for a moment before speaking again. "We might not need to hijack the entire ship."

"Good, because the slug would be the only one left after you get yourself killed, and I'm not sure I want her to be my pilot."

"I feel like something odd is going on in that engine room," I explained. "Plus, on our way back from the delver maze, something went wrong with the hyperdrive because of me. They swapped it out with another, so the hyperdrive units must be small enough to replace quickly."

"We knew that already," M-Bot said. "I used to have something in that empty box in my hull where my hyperdrive was supposed to be."

I nodded, thinking everything through while rubbing Doomslug's head. She fluted in contentment.

I'd teleported M-Bot twice on my own, but his systems did claim to have a "cytonic hyperdrive." I'd assumed that his previous pilot—Commander Spears—had been the actual hyperdrive that had gotten M-Bot to Detritus. But why have the empty box? There was a huge piece of this that I was missing.

"We need to find a way to sneak in there and watch them servicing or engaging the hyperdrive. Scud, maybe if I could steal the device they use to indicate their destination, I could use it to make my own powers work, and at least get us home."

"By your account, that is a secure location," M-Bot said. "Inside a well-patrolled military ship. Sneaking in will not be easy."

"Fortunately, we have access to a spy ship and an advanced AI designed for stealth operations. We need to retrieve data from a secure enemy location. What does your programming think we should do?"

"We should plant espionage devices," M-Bot said immediately. "The best solution would be to use autonomous drones, which could infiltrate the location and make recordings. The carrier's shielding will prevent signals from being sent out, but that would be inadvisable anyway, as it would let scanners detect them. Instead we would retrieve the devices manually, then download their information." He paused. "Ooooh. That's a good idea! I'm smarter than myself sometimes, aren't I?"

"Maybe," I said, leaning back in the seat. "Do we have any such devices?"

"No," M-Bot said. "I have berths for housing a few small remote drones, but they are empty."

"Can we build a new one?" I asked, holding up my arm and inspecting the bracelet that projected my hologram. "Like we built a new one of these?"

"It's possible," M-Bot said. "We'd need to cannibalize some of my sensor systems and order some new parts—and we'd have to do so without the orders looking suspicious. Hmm . . . A curious challenge."

"Mull it over," I said, yawning. "Let me know what you come up with."

He settled in to do some computing, and I must have drifted off, because I woke up a short time later to the sound of Doomslug imitating someone snoring. Which totally couldn't have been me. Warriors, of course, never snore. That would alert our enemies to our sleeping locations.

I stretched, then climbed out of the cockpit into a city that—regardless of the hour—was in constant motion. I stood at the edge of the rooftop, looking out over the endless metropolis, and couldn't help but feel overwhelmed. Igneous, the greatest city my people had ever built, could have been swallowed up by a few city blocks of Starsight.

So many people. So many resources. All focused on destroying or at least suppressing Detritus. It was a miracle we were doing as well as we were.

A light on the computer up here—used for doing ship diagnostics and for monitoring the building—indicated that I'd gotten a delivery. I climbed down the steps, thinking at first that M-Bot must have already ordered some parts for building our spy drone.

In the delivery box, I instead found a small pastry with the note, *Just in case the algae is stale. —Mrs. Chamwit.*

The warrior inside me didn't want to eat it. Not out of fear of poisoning—if Cuna wanted me poisoned, all they'd have to do was inject something into my building's water supply. But because it felt like admitting defeat to Mrs. Chamwit.

It turned out to be the tastiest defeat I'd ever suffered.

25

A week later, I swooped through a complex dodging maneuver, boosting my ship between multiple enemies, the embers—the burning asteroids that the delver maze would eject to intercept fighters. Although the illusion was disturbed by the fact that these ones were just Superiority drones wearing a disguise, the combat was exhilarating. I had some ten tailing me now, increasing speed, accelerating even faster than I could in my quick interceptor.

I swept up alongside one face of the delver maze. From this close, it was like I was flying across a large polished metal surface. The structure was so huge it had noticeable gravity, and I had to monitor my acclivity ring to keep from being pulled off course.

Embers chased after me, burning from within with a molten light. More came in from the side, trying to press me in against the maze—removing my options for escape. It was like a game of cat and mouse, except there were fifty mice trying to herd one cat.

In my case, one *very dangerous* cat.

A group of embers rushed in to try ramming me from the front, and I opened fire. I blasted them into dust—swerving left to avoid the debris—then rotated my ship and fired back at the ones that came in too close. I had to immediately spin back around and veer upward to avoid another group approaching from that direction.

As much as I missed M-Bot's voice, a part of me was glad for the chance to prove myself in these contests. I ignored my cytonic senses—they'd be useless against the real embers—and I didn't have an advanced AI to project and calculate for me.

It was just me, the embers, and a wingmate. Today, that position was filled by a second force of carnage in the form of Brade. As I blasted ember after ember, the two of us finished our maneuver, swooping back together. We flew side by side for a moment, me firing forward while she rotated to fire backward, each of us covering a 180-degree arc.

On my mark, we darted to the sides, then used our light-lances to pull ourselves in mirrored maneuvers, swinging off embers even as they tried to collide with us. This move sent us hurtling back toward one another. We then crossed within centimeters as we opened fire, each blasting away the embers chasing after the other.

When we swooped back around again, we were both free of tails. Heart pounding, a dangerous grin on my face, I fell in beside Brade. Together we flew away from the delver maze, almost like we were two ships being controlled by one mind.

Brade was good. As good as I was. More, I *clicked* with her. We flew like we'd been wingmates for decades, rarely needing to even confirm with the other what to do. Perhaps it was because we were both cytonic, or maybe it was because our individual piloting styles were in sync. Over the last week, I'd spent time training with each member of the flight—but I never seemed to fly as well as I did when Brade was on my wing.

At least until we spoke to one another.

"Great work," I said over the communication channel.

"Don't compliment me on being so aggressive," she said. "I need to control it. Not revel in it."

"You're doing what the Superiority needs right now," I said. "You're learning how to protect them."

"It's still no excuse," she said. "Please. You don't know how it feels to be human."

I gritted my teeth. *I could help you,* I thought. *Offer you freedom from this—freedom to actually be yourself.*

I didn't say it. Instead I switched off the comm. I felt that I was slowly getting through to her, but if I was going to make further progress, it probably wouldn't involve directly arguing against Superiority ideals. I needed to be subtle.

I *could* be subtle. Right?

Together we rejoined the other ships, and received a round of congratulations from Hesho and Morriumur.

"You continue to fight well, Alanik," Vapor said to me. "You bear the scent of long rains." I wasn't certain what that meant—her language had some odd idioms that the pin could only translate literally. "But remember, our task is not to chase and hunt these embers. Learning to dogfight is only a first step. We will soon have to practice flying that maze."

Morriumur and Hesho took off to do a practice run—using another training exercise that I'd developed. I wasn't worried about training them to be expert dogfighters, but we did need to be working in pairs.

"Vapor?" I asked. "Do you have any idea what this weapon is that we'll supposedly use to kill delvers?"

"I do not," she said in her soft way. It was odd, but I felt more comfortable speaking to her over the comm than I did in person. "I am intrigued by the possibility though," she added. "It would mean a great deal to society if delvers could be killed."

I nodded to myself.

"I fear them," Vapor continued. "During the second war, when the humans sought to control the delvers and use them in battle, I caught a . . . glimpse of how the delvers see us. As specks or insects to be wiped away. They laid waste to worlds, vaporizing entire populations in moments. We didn't drive them off then. They just ended up leaving. We exist because they *let* us."

I shivered. "If that's true, then all life in our galaxy lives with a gun to its head. All the more important that we should know if this weapon works or not, right?"

"Agreed," Vapor said. "I find its possible existence to be *most* interesting."

"Is . . . that why you're here?" I asked.

Vapor was silent for a moment. "Why do you ask?"

"I mean, it's nothing. Just . . . you know, the others tell me that your kind usually . . . has very specialized missions . . ."

"We are *not* assassins," she answered. "Those rumors are false, and the flight should not spread them. We are servants of the Superiority."

"Sure, sure," I said, surprised at the forcefulness in her voice. "Maybe the team has been chattering too much. I'll run them through a few more exercises today, shut them up the old military way—make them too tired to gossip."

"No," Vapor said, her voice softening. "No need to bear the scent of smoke, Alanik. Just . . . ask them not to theorize on my mission. I am not here to kill anyone. I promise that."

"Understood, sir," I said.

That only made her sigh—a sound like a soft breeze riffling papers. "I will take Brade out for a practice run. Please rest."

"Confirmed," I said, and she took off, ordering Brade to join her. I opened my backpack, which I kept stowed in its tied-on position behind my seat, and got out a snack. I believed that Vapor wasn't here to kill anyone. But what *was* she here to do? I could swear I'd smelled her scents watching over my shoulder at times, and her race . . . did they see like others? I doubted it. But could she smell what I really was?

Scud. I was already doing what she'd asked me not to do. If she knew what I was, she hadn't turned me in yet, so there was no use in worrying.

I pointed my ship away from where the others were dogfighting, looking instead out at the stars. The field of lights stared back at me, endless, inviting. I couldn't hear much from them. There was a small stream of cytonic communication leaving the *Weights and Measures*, likely heading back toward Starsight, but it was a lot "quieter" out here than it was back near the enormous platform.

All those stars, I thought, wondering if Detritus's sun was visible to the naked eye from this distance. *Many of the planets around them inhabited. Billions and billions of people . . .*

I closed my eyes, letting myself drift. Just out here among the stars. Floating.

Almost without thinking, I undid my straps, hit the control lock on my console, and released myself to the zero G of my cockpit. It was small confines, but with my eyes closed, I could truly just float. I pulled off my helmet and let it drift away to thump softly against the canopy.

Me and the stars. Always before, I'd done Gran-Gran's exercise when on the ground—in places where I needed to *imagine* that I was soaring among the stars. Seeking their voices.

For the first time, I truly felt that I was among them. Almost as if I *were* a star myself, a point of warmth and fire amid the endless night. I lightly pushed off the side of my canopy, keeping myself floating in the center. Feeling . . .

There, I thought. *Starsight is over there.* I knew, instinctively, the direction toward the platform. During our jumps between the delver maze and the city, my mind had been injected somehow with that knowledge. Each time the imprint seemed to last longer, to the point where it was firm in my mind now—and no longer fading.

If I had to, I knew I could hyperjump back to Starsight on my own. In fact, I was increasingly certain I could now find my way back to Starsight from anywhere. That didn't do me any good at the moment though. I already *had* transportation to Starsight.

My concentration receded as my problems seized my brain. Steal the Superiority's hyperdrive technology. Rescue Brade. Figure out what was up with Vapor—not to mention the weapon the Superiority was developing. And that didn't even get into the subtleties of whatever political situation was going on among Cuna, Winzik, and the Krell. It was all just so overwhelming.

Spensa . . . A voice seemed to speak from out there, among the stars. *Spensa. Soul of a warrior* . . .

I snapped my eyes open, gasping. "Gran-Gran?" I said. I pushed my feet down against my seat, pressing myself against the window of my canopy, looking frantically out among the stars.

Saints and stars. That had *been her voice.*

"Gran-Gran!" I shouted.

Fight . . .

"I *will* fight, Gran-Gran!" I said. "But what? How? I . . . I'm not right for this mission. It isn't what I trained for. I don't know what to do!"

A hero . . . does not choose . . . her trials, Spensa . . .

"Gran-Gran?" I asked, trying to pinpoint the location of the words.

She steps . . . into the darkness, the voice said, fading. *Then she faces what comes next* . . .

I searched desperately for my home among the thousands of stars. But it was hopeless, and whatever it was I thought I'd heard did not return.

Just that lingering phantom echo in my mind.

A hero does not choose her trials.

I drifted for a long moment, hair floating in a mess around my face. Finally, I pushed myself down and buckled back into my seat. I tucked up my hair, then pulled on my helmet and strapped it in place.

When further cytonic reaching didn't do anything, I sighed and focused on my flight. I should probably be evaluating their performances anyway; Vapor might ask.

Brade and Vapor were both doing well, as could be expected. They were the two best pilots of the group, excluding me. But Hesho and his kitsen were also performing admirably. During this week of training, they'd really learned how to cover a wingmate and how to blend their role as a gunship with the need to sometimes just be a fighter, dogfighting like any other ship.

Morriumur, though . . . Poor Morriumur. It wasn't their fault that they were the weakest pilot in our group. They were only a few months old, after all—and even if they'd inherited some skill from one of their parents, that smidgen of combat experience only made their mistakes more obvious. As I watched, they pulled too far ahead of Hesho and left the kitsen to be swarmed by enemies. Then, when trying to compensate and come back, Morriumur's shots missed the enemy—and nearly brought down the kitsen ship's shields.

I winced and opened a comm channel to chew out Morriumur. I immediately heard a string of curses that my translator helpfully interpreted for me. And *scud,* even Gran-Gran hadn't been able to swear that eloquently.

"Which parent did you get that from?" I asked over the channel.

Morriumur immediately cut off. I could practically hear the blush in their voice as they replied, "Sorry, Alanik. I didn't know you were listening."

"You're trying too hard," I advised them. "Overcompensating for your lack of skill. Relax."

"It's easy to say that," they replied, "when you have an entire life to live. I've only got a few months to prove myself."

"You'll prove nothing if you shoot down a wingmate," I told them. "Relax. You can't force yourself to become a better pilot through sheer determination. Trust me, I've tried."

They acknowledged, and I think they did better during the next run, so hopefully my advice was working. Soon the practice runs ended, the embers pulling back to the delver maze. My four flightmates joined me in a line.

In the distance, I could see other flights practicing. To my amusement, it seemed that several others had pulled back from doing runs through the maze, and were now practicing their dog-fighting as well. I suspected we'd had a good influence on them.

Don't pat yourself on the back too much, Spensa, I told myself. *These are Krell ships. Even if they're training to fight delvers now, you know they'll inevitably end up on the other side of a fight from the humans.*

That knowledge subdued my enthusiasm. "That was a nice run," I told the rest of my flight. "Yes, even yours, Morriumur. Vapor, I think this lot is starting to actually look like pilots."

"Perhaps," Vapor replied. "As they are excelling at your train-ing, maybe we could let them have a chance at the maze. We should have time for one extended run today before training is finished."

"About time!" Hesho said. "I am a patient kitsen, but a knife can only be sharpened so far before all you are doing is wearing it away."

I smiled, remembering my own enthusiasm when Cobb had first started letting us train with weapons. "Let's pair off," I said to Vapor. "And do a run. Three of us will have to go as a trio though, as we have five—"

"I don't need a wingmate," Brade said, then turned and boosted toward the maze.

I sat in stunned silence. She'd been getting better throughout the week; I'd thought she was beyond this now. Scud, that was the sort of stunt that would have made Cobb scream at us until he was red in the face.

"Brade!" I shouted into the comm. "So help me, if you don't return, I'll—"

"Let her go," Vapor cut in.

"But we're always supposed to take a wingmate into the maze!" I said. "Otherwise the illusions will fool you!"

"Then let her learn this lesson," Vapor said. "She will see for herself when the rest of us perform better than she does."

I grumbled, but held myself back—barely—from continuing to rant at Brade. Vapor *was* our commander, even if I was the XO.

"I will take Morriumur," Vapor told me. "I believe that I can help teach them a little patience. They need to learn to handle their aggression."

"That puts me with Hesho," I said. "We'll meet back here in an hour and a half? Fly in for forty-five minutes, start accustoming yourself to the strange ways of the place, then fly back out."

"Very well. Good luck." Vapor and Morriumur moved off, while Hesho commanded his helmsman to guide the kitsen ship up beside mine.

"Does it strike you as odd," I asked him, "that we complain about Morriumur being aggressive *right after* Brade flew off on her own? Morriumur is a fair bit *less* aggressive than I am. Even less than you are, I'd say."

"Morriumur is not a member of a 'lesser species,'" Hesho said. "Others expect more of them because of the vaunted 'primary intelligence' their species has."

"I've never understood that," I said as the two of us flew inward, picking a different section to attack from Vapor and Morriumur. The delver maze was so big, that wasn't a problem. "What does 'primary intelligence' even mean?"

"It is just a term, not an actual measure of their relative

intelligence," Hesho said. "From what I've been able to gather, it means their species has created a peaceful society, where crime is reduced to near nonexistence."

I sniffed. Peaceful society? I didn't buy that for a moment—and if I had ever been inclined to, Alanik's last words would have disabused me. *Don't trust their peace.*

Hesho and I approached the delver maze, and I smothered the feelings of concern that rose inside me. Last time I'd gone in here, it had been a very strange experience. But I could handle that. A hero didn't pick her trials.

"You and your crew ready?" I asked Hesho as the first of the embers neared us.

"The *Swims Upstream* is ready for action, Captain," Hesho said. "This moment . . . it awaits us like the tongue awaits the wine."

We fought our way through the embers. Then—side by side—the two of us swooped in through one of the many holes in our section of the delver maze. I hugged the kitsen's larger, more heavily shielded ship as we entered a long steel tunnel ribbed with pillarlike folds at periodic intervals. There were no internal lights, so we turned on our floods.

"Sensor department," Hesho said to his team, "get a close-up shot of those symbols on the wall."

"Roger," another kitsen said.

I drifted to the side, shining my lights on another field of strange writing etched into the wall here.

"We can't translate them, Your Normalness," said Kauri. "But the symbols are similar to ones found near nowhere portals on some planets and stations."

"Nowhere portals?" I asked, frowning.

"Many people have tried to study the delvers in their own realm, Captain," Hesho said. "Kauri, explain if you please."

"Nowhere portals are stable openings," Kauri said, "like wormholes leading into the nowhere. They are often marked by similar symbols. These portals are how acclivity stone is mined and transported to our realm—but I don't know why the symbols would be here. I see no sign of a portal."

Huh. I pulled my ship right up to the symbols, shining my floodlights on them. "I saw some of these symbols back on my homeworld," I said. "Inside a tunnel near my home."

"Then I should like to visit and see that," Kauri said. "It's possible your home has access to an unknown nowhere portal. That could bring riches—the Superiority keeps very careful control over their nowhere portals, as there is no other source of acclivity stone."

Huh. I didn't say more because I didn't want to give away the truth—that these writings had been in the caverns on Detritus, not Alanik's homeworld.

The old inhabitants of Detritus had fallen to the delvers. And I was increasingly certain that what Cuna had told me was right—the people of Detritus had courted that destruction by trying to control the delvers. They'd set up shielding, had tried to be quiet, but none of their precautions had worked. When the delver had come for the people of Detritus, it had easily bypassed their protections.

The tunnel around me suddenly looked like it had turned into flesh. It was as if I were in the veins of some enormous beast. I gritted my teeth. "Hesho, what do you see?"

"The tunnel has changed," he said. "To feeling like it is submerged. Do you see this? It is a strange experience."

"I feel like I'm in an enormous vein," I said. "It's a hologram—an illusion. Remember?"

"Yes," Hesho said. "We are shown different things. Thankfully, we have two ships."

I wondered how Brade was doing in here by herself.

"The illusion is curious," Hesho said. "I feel like a stone plucked from land and dropped, to sink endlessly into an eternal deep." He paused. "My crew sees the same thing that I do, Captain Alanik."

"That makes sense," I said. "Our ships are programmed to replicate the illusions of the delver maze. For us right now, it's just programming. If this were real, you'd probably all see something different."

At least, that was what I'd been told to expect. Only it seemed that much of what the Superiority "knew" was really guesswork. If I entered a real delver maze, would the same rules actually hold there?

Hopefully, you'll never have to find out, I thought. Hesho and I took the right-hand exit and flew through a corridor that appeared to me to be crystalline, but Hesho saw flames. Both of us, however, saw a large boulder at one side of the room—so we flew over and inspected it. A tug on it with a light-lance proved it was real, and it tumbled out into the room.

"How odd," Hesho said. "Did someone come and install that boulder specifically to hinder our path?"

"Supposedly," I said, "this maze is built to replicate the kind of oddities and mysteries we'll find inside the real delver maze."

"Our scanners are useless," Hesho said. "I have reports from my instruments teams—and they can't tell what's fake and what isn't. It seems that the Superiority has programmed our ship to be fooled by this place, something I find disconcerting. I don't like the idea of seeing what the Superiority shows me, even if it is for an important training simulation."

As we flew deeper, I was glad to have the kitsen with me. Bringing a wingmate made all kinds of practical sense, not just for identifying what was real. On a more basic level, it was comforting to have someone to talk to in this place.

We passed through several other strange rooms with a variety of odd visuals—from the walls melting, to the shadows of enormous beasts passing just out of sight. We were attacked by embers in one, which I fired upon—before realizing Hesho couldn't see them. My shots hit the wall, blasting off pieces of metal, and the entire structure rumbled in a way that I could *swear* was threatening.

"How can we hear that?" Hesho asked. "Instruments report a vacuum outside the ships. There is no medium for sound to pass through."

"I . . ." I shivered. "Let's try that tunnel over there."

"I don't like this," Hesho confided as we moved down the tunnel. "It feels like it's training us to rely upon one another's eyes."

"That's a good thing though, right?"

"Not necessarily," Hesho said. "While all experience is subjective, and all reality in some ways an illusion, this offers a practical danger. If we come to rely upon consensus to determine what is real, the maze could simply exploit this assumption and trick us."

In the next chamber, we were attacked by embers that were real this time—and I almost ignored them, a mistake that could have been deadly. I responded to Hesho's warning at the last moment, dodging as a barrage from the heavily armed fighter vaporized them.

We were left in a room with junk bouncing around and hitting the walls before starting to pool toward the bottom. Sweating, my heart thumping, I led us through the next passage. Scud, was I ever going to get used to this place?

We reached the end of the tunnel, and my floods shone on a strange membrane covering the opening. It ran from the floor to the ceiling, and pulsed softly with a rhythm I could hear.

That sound suddenly seemed to ring through the entire structure. My fighter *thumped* under my fingers.

I stared at the membrane, shocked. We'd only been in the delver maze for . . . what, half an hour? Maybe a little longer? I'd expected it to take hours upon hours to find the heart.

"That's it," I said. "The membrane. The thing we're looking for. The . . . the heart of the delver."

"What?" Hesho said. "I don't see anything."

Oh. I took a deep breath, calming myself. An illusion. Which meant—

I saw the entire universe.

In a blink everything vanished around me, and somehow my mind expanded. I saw planets, I saw star systems, I saw galaxies. I saw the scrambling, useless, tiny little insects that covered them like chittering hives. I felt revulsion. Hatred for these pests that infested the worlds. Hordes of ants swarming on a dropped piece of food. Buzzing and mindless, disgusting. Painful, as they'd swarm me, occasionally biting—for though they were too small to ever truly destroy me, they hurt. Their noise. Their painful scraping. They infested my home, after swarming all of the rocks that broke the endless nothing that was this universe. They would not ever leave me alone, and I wanted so badly just to smash them. To smother them beneath my foot so they'd stop piling, and crawling, and clicking, and snapping, and biting, and corrupting, and—

I snapped back into my cockpit, slamming against my seat as if I'd been thrown there.

"Another illusion then," Hesho said, sounding bored. "You want to move forward first? I'll cover you, in case further embers guard this chamber."

I trembled, the horrible vision resting on me like the darkness in a cavern far, far underground. I breathed in gasps, trying to recapture my breath. The room looked normal to me now, but . . .

"Captain Alanik?" Hesho asked.

What had that been? Why . . . why did it linger in my mind, making me revile Hesho's words, as if they were coming from something slimy and horrible?

"I . . . ," I said. "Sorry, I need a moment."

He gave it to me. I recovered slowly. Scud. SCUD. That had felt like . . . like Vapor had said the delvers regarded all of us.

"Flight Command," I said, calling in. "Did you just show me something strange?"

"Pilot?" Flight Command called back. "You need to learn to fly the maze without contacting us. When you enter one for real, you won't—"

"What did you *just show me*?" I demanded.

"The log indicates that your ship's illusion for that room is of darkness hiding an exit. That is all."

So . . . they hadn't shown me that sensation of the universe?

Of course they hadn't. That was far beyond the powers of a holographic projector. I'd seen something else. Something . . . something that my own mind had projected?

Scud. What *was* I?

At Hesho's urging we continued, and spent another fifteen minutes moving through rooms, familiarizing ourselves with the way the maze worked. I didn't experience anything else approaching the feeling of that strange moment when I'd seen the universe.

Eventually, we hit our predetermined exploration time limit, and so we turned around and flew back. Outside, we found the others gathering—including a furious Brade who, as Vapor had guessed, had gotten stuck in one of the early rooms, unable to tell what was real and what wasn't.

None of them had seen any membranes or had any idea what I was trying to explain when I tried—and failed—to talk about what I'd seen. I couldn't put it into words, but it remained with me. Like a shadow over my shoulder, lingering as we reported back to the *Weights and Measures*.

26

We entered the nowhere.

As always, it started with a scream.

Absolute darkness, broken by the eyes. White hot, they stared in the wrong direction. The more often I did this, the more I could sense the . . . shadow of what they were. Enormous, mind-bending things whose shapes didn't conform to my understanding of how physical forms should work.

I seemed to hang there for an eternity. Aside from Brade, who wouldn't talk about it, the others of my flight said they didn't sense any time at all passing in the nowhere. To them, the hyperjump happened instantaneously. They never saw the darkness or the eyes.

Finally, I felt the end coming on. A subtle *fading* sensation that—

One of the eyes turned and stared right at me.

The *Weights and Measures* popped back into regular space outside of Starsight. I gasped, my pulse going crazy, battle senses coming alert.

It had seen me. One of them had looked *right at me*.

We were traveling back to Starsight after another day of training—my tenth so far in the military here. I was extra tired today from putting the others through their exercises. Was that why it had seen me?

What had I done? What was wrong?

"Captain Alanik?" Hesho said. "Though I am not familiar with your species, you do seem to be exhibiting some traditional signs of distress."

I glanced down at the kitsen. Hesho's ship engineers had transformed several of the jump room's seats into kitsen travel stations—basically, little buildings several stories high, secured to the wall and complete with smaller seats inside for their whole crew.

They chattered together inside the open-walled structures, though Hesho had the roof all for himself and his servants. It was about eye level for me, and was set with a luxurious captain's chair. It also had a bar and several monitors for entertainment, which seemed a ridiculous amount of luxury for the short half hour or so we spent on the *Weights and Measures* each day, flying out of and back to Starsight.

"Alanik?" Hesho asked. "I can call my ship's surgeon, who is here below. She has little experience with alien species, however. How many hearts do you have?"

"I'm fine, Hesho," I said. "Just a sudden chill."

"Hmmm," he said, leaning back in his seat and putting his feet up. "A moment of frailty in an otherwise powerful warrior. This is a beautiful moment, which I shall treasure." He nodded to himself, then sighed and tapped a blinking button on his armrest, causing a screen to rotate toward him.

We weren't supposed to use wireless communications except in emergencies. Hesho, however, had a loose definition of the word *emergency,* and he had been granted—upon persistent request—a bypass for the anti-communication shield around the *Weights and Measures.*

It probably wasn't polite to listen in. At the same time, he *was* sitting right next to me. And my pin translated and transmitted the words to my earpiece, whether I wanted it to or not.

A kitsen appeared on his screen, a female—judging by the pattern of light and dark fur—wearing a very formal-looking outfit of colorful silk, with matching headdress. She bowed to Hesho. "Unexalted One Who Is Not King," she said. "I have called to request guidance upon my vote tomorrow in the matter of the national taxation fund."

Hesho rubbed the fur underneath his snout. "I fear this is not working, Senator Aria. When I spoke to our monitors at the Superiority, they claimed that I was still having undue influence upon the functioning of our senate."

The senator looked up. "But, Unexalted One, the senate voted exactly the *opposite* of your expressed preference."

"Yes, and they did well," he said. "But the Superiority seems to think that I simply told you to vote opposite my desires, and therefore continue to manipulate you."

"A difficult situation," Senator Aria said. "How would you like us to proceed?"

"Well," Hesho said. "It seems . . . the Superiority would very much like you to choose what *you* would like."

"My greatest desire in all of the universe is to see the king's will made manifest."

"And if his will is for you to be yourself?"

"Of course. Which type of myself would you like?"

"Perhaps, choose randomly how you vote each time?" Hesho said. "Do you think that would work?"

"Certainly, in that case the Superiority cannot claim we are being influenced by anything other than fate." Senator Aria bowed again. "We will seek your influence upon the universe as it manifests in drawn lots to determine the vote. A wise solution, Unexalted One." She cut the communication.

Hesho sighed.

"They seem very . . . loyal," I noted.

"We are trying," Hesho said. "This is difficult for us. All my life, I was taught to be very careful in how I expressed my will—but I do not know how to *avoid* expressing it at all." He rubbed his temples, his eyes closed. "We must learn the Superiority's way or leave ourselves exposed to be conquered, should the humans ever return. They are my true fear—they attacked us first, during the initial human war. Their leader claimed our shared past made us practically a *human colony* already. Bah. My fur prickles to even speak the words.

"We must change to be prepared, but change is difficult. My people are not foolish or weak-willed. It is simply that for many, many centuries, the throne was the one immutable force upon which they could depend. To have it ripped away suddenly is to pull off a bandage before the wound has properly healed."

I found myself nodding, which was silly. It *was* better that Hesho's rule be replaced. What kind of backward culture still had a hereditary monarchy? A military stratocracy—with the strongest pilots and admirals coming to rule by proving their merits in battle—made far, far more sense.

"Maybe you don't need to worry so much about the humans?" I said to Hesho. "I mean, they might not even come back."

"Perhaps," Hesho said. "I was trained since I was a pup to put the needs of the planet before all else. We spent centuries seeking to recover the shadow-walkers, but we must face the truth. We will never again have cytonics among us. We lost that privilege long ago."

He looked to me. "Do not pity me for my loss of authority. Many years ago, my great-great-great-grandfather rode to battle at the head of our armies to fight humankind's invasion. He fought the giants with a sword. Before that, the daimyo of the seventeen clans were constantly ready to lead their people in war. But I always fancied this role, being a captain of my own ship. It will be good. So long as my people do not simply vanish into the Superiority like drops of blood in an ocean."

"I don't know if it's worth the effort, Hesho," I said, leaning back in my seat. "All this work to bend to what they want us to be."

"It's either that or be trapped on our planets with no hyperdrives. My people have tried that, and it is stifling us. The only way to exist with any relevance is to play by the Superiority's rules."

"And yet, the diones and the other primes call themselves the greater races," I said. "So proud of how advanced they are, all the while basically enslaving everyone else."

"Hmm," Hesho said, but did not reply further. I followed his glance over his shoulder, then I blushed, seeing that Morriumur was sitting right behind him. Scud. When would I learn to *think* a little before I spoke?

Once the *Weights and Measures* had docked, Winzik gave leave for the pilots to head off to their shuttles to ride back home for the evening.

"Enjoy your day off," Hesho told me as the kitsen flew out of our room. Morriumur hurried ahead, and wouldn't meet my eyes. Great. Well, it wasn't *my* fault their species was an oppressive group of dictators.

"Hey," Brade said as I collected my bag to leave.

I glanced back at her, a little surprised to hear her speak. Normally, she didn't interact with us after the day's training was done.

"Nice work today," she told me. "I think this group is finally getting it."

"Thanks," I said. "That means a lot. Really."

She shrugged and brushed past me, out the door, as if embarrassed to have been caught in a moment of sincerity. I just sat in my chair, stunned. Remarkably, it seemed I was making progress with her. Maybe I *could* do this.

Full of newfound determination, I hurried out of the room after the others. I had work to do today.

A hero can't pick her own trials. Remember that.

As we reached the intersection near the engine room, I took a deep breath, then approached the guard there.

M-Bot was confident we could put a spy drone together and program it, but once I snuck it onto the ship here, it might take a few minutes to set up. I couldn't exactly do that with the other members of my flight around. The simplest option seemed to be the best.

"I need to use the restroom," I told the guard standing watch over the path to Engineering. It was a Krell—female, I thought, guessing by the carapace formations along the outside of the small crustacean piloting the armor.

"Understood," she answered. "I'll send for a drone."

Security on the *Weights and Measures* was tight. Though we could walk from the flight docks to our jump room, anywhere else we wanted to go—even if called to meet with command staff—required us to be accompanied by a watchful remote drone, piloted by some security officer.

The guard, of course, didn't leave her post. Behind me, Hesho, Kauri, and several other kitsen waited until I waved them on. Then I peeked past the guard, down the hallway. Could I come up with some way to get information out of the guard while I waited?

"Hey," I said. "How does one get a job in the infantry?"

"Mine is not a post for lesser species, pilot of starfighters," the guard said, moving her armored hand in several intricate motions. "Be glad you are allowed the privilege of training as you do now."

"How is it though?" I asked. "You have to stand here at this corner basically all the time. Do they at least let you go other places? Maybe . . . um . . ."

"I'm done with this conversation," she said.

Scud. I was *terrible* at this part of being a spy. I gritted my teeth, frustrated by my own inability, until a small drone arrived to escort me to the restroom. Our starfighters, of course, had waste reclamation facilities that hooked to our flight suits—we spent hours upon hours of time out there, after all. So far I hadn't needed to use the facilities on the *Weights and Measures.*

My heart gave a little leap of excitement as the drone led me *past* the guard, toward the engine room. Unfortunately, we only walked a short distance before turning right into another hallway, one with several bathroom signs on the wall. Like others I'd seen, they were organized along species lines. I was directed to the one that the diones used, as we had similar enough biology.

The drone accompanied me into the bathroom, but not into the stall, so that was good. I tapped my wrist—starting a timer on my hologram bracelet to give us a rough estimate of how long all this would normally take me—then entered the stall, dropped my backpack, and did my business. The drone pilot didn't say anything—though as I washed my hands, I heard them chatting absently with a coworker, their speaker accidentally left on. So perhaps the pilot wouldn't be paying the best of attention.

The drone led me back to the hallway, where—surprisingly—I found Hesho still waiting for me, though his crew had all moved on save for Kauri and his servants, who flew on his disc with him. He hovered along beside my head as we continued on toward the shuttle docks.

"Is everything well with you, Captain?" he asked.

"Yeah, just had to hit the restroom."

"Ah." Hesho paused, looking over his shoulder as we flew onward. "They took you down the hallway near the engine room, I see."

"Closest bathroom is just to the right."

"You didn't get a glimpse into the engine room itself, did you? By chance?"

"No. Didn't go that far."

"Pity." He continued to fly. "I've . . . heard that you have a ship of your own that can hyperjump. Just a rumor, really. Not that you should have to share such information with us."

I eyed him as he hovered along, trying to speak with feigned nonchalance. Then I found myself smiling. He was trying to figure out if I knew about Superiority hyperdrives—but he wasn't any better at this sort of thing than I was. I felt a stab of affection for the furry little dictator.

"I don't know how their hyperdrives work, Hesho," I said softly as we entered the shuttle hangar. "I'm a cytonic. I can teleport my ship if I have to—but doing so is dangerous. One of the reasons I'm here is so that my people can get access to the Superiority's safer technology."

Hesho considered that, sharing a look with Kauri.

The pickup bay was bustling with activity as pilots were loaded onto shuttles, then sent off to their individual homes on Starsight. The rest of the kitsen were already boarding a shuttle, but Hesho—after a moment's deliberation—gestured for Kauri to hover his platform closer to my head.

"You're a shadow-walker," he said. "I did not know this."

"It's not something I feel comfortable sharing," I said. "Not that I mind if you know. It's just . . . weird."

"If this doesn't work out," Hesho said very softly, gesturing toward the hangar bay. "If something goes wrong, visit my people. It has been long since we had shadow-walkers among us, but some of their traditions were recorded. Perhaps . . . perhaps your people and mine can decipher the Superiority technology."

"I'll remember that," I said. "But I'm still hoping this will work out. Or maybe I'll be able to figure—" I cut myself off.

Idiot. What are you going to do? Just tell him openly in the middle of an enemy dock that you're trying to figure out how to steal their technology?

Hesho, however, seemed to understand. "My people," he said softly, "tried stealing Superiority technology once. This was decades ago, and is the . . . unspoken reason why we had our citizenship status revoked for a time."

My breath caught, and I couldn't help asking, "Did it work?"

"No," Hesho said. "My grandmother was queen then, and she coordinated the theft of three different Superiority ships—all with hyperdrives—at the same moment. All three, after being stolen, stopped functioning. When my people looked at the spot where the hyperdrives had been, they found only empty boxes."

Like on M-Bot, I thought.

"Superiority hyperdrives," Kauri said, "teleport away if stolen—ripping themselves out of the ships and leaving the vessel stranded. It is one of the reasons why, despite centuries passing, the technology remains largely contained."

Hesho nodded. "We found the truth of this the hard way."

"Strange," I said. "Very strange." *Another obstacle to overcome.*

"I have determined that the best way to help my people is to follow Superiority rules," Hesho said. "But . . . keep my offer in mind. I feel like we are being used for something in this project. I do not trust Winzik or his department. If you return to your people, let them know of my people. We share a bond, Captain Alanik—oppression by humans in our past, toys to the Superiority in the present. We could be allies."

"I . . . appreciate that," I said. "You can consider me an ally, Hesho. Whatever happens."

"We shall share our fate, then. As equals." He smiled a toothy grin. "Save for when we engage the humans in war. Then *I* get to shoot the first one!"

I grimaced.

"Ha! I'm going to take that as a promise. Take care, Captain Alanik. We will make it through these odd times together."

Kauri flew him off, and scud, I found myself sincerely wishing I *were* Alanik. Maybe we could accomplish something together—with the knowledge of Hesho's people, along with my people's fighting skills. Except my people *were* humans. The very things that frightened him into following the Superiority's strict mandates.

I felt suddenly exposed, talking like that to Hesho. Sure, the docks were busy—but our conversation had flirted with treason against the Superiority. Wouldn't that just be fitting for me? To hide that I was human but still get arrested as Alanik? What did the air smell like? Grease. Sterile cleaning fluid. Nothing suspicious.

I really needed to start sniffing for Vapor's presence *before* I engaged in suspicious activity.

I boarded a shuttle alone this time, and flew out along the docks toward the city, where I braced myself for the music of the stars to vanish. Even prepared, I felt a sense of loss as it happened.

They minimize wireless communication—but it still happens. They need it to exist. I could understand that. They had to balance fear of the delvers with the need for societies to communicate.

As I was thinking about this, something else struck me. The protesters. They were gone. I'd grown accustomed to seeing the group out here at the edge of the city, holding up signs and complaining about the rights of "lesser species." But the area had been cleared of people, though some diones in brown-striped outfits were cleaning up the refuse left behind by the protesters.

"What happened?" I whispered to M-Bot. "To the protesters."

"They struck a deal with the government," M-Bot said. "Compensation to the families of those who died at the testing, and a promise to put more safety protocols in place during any such future tests."

It seemed an anticlimactic ending to the protest. A bureaucratic ending, where nothing *really* changed. But what else had I been expecting? Riots in the streets?

I sighed and watched out the back window of the shuttle, my gaze locked on that spot and the working diones for as long as I could see them.

27

The next morning, I awoke to find a collection of boxes on the embassy doorstep.

"Oh, what's this?" Mrs. Chamwit said as I hurriedly gathered them up. "Can I help?"

"No!" I said, perhaps too forcefully. "Um, it's nothing."

"Cleaning drone?" Mrs. Chamwit said as she read the label on one. "I . . . Oh." Her attitude grew visibly subdued as she spoke, continuing her hand signals. "Have I been doing a poor job?"

"No!" I said again, balancing the stack of boxes. "Just . . . I like my privacy, you know . . ."

"I see," she said. "Well, do you need help setting it up? I've used a few cleaning drones myself in my time . . ."

"No thank you."

"I guess . . . I guess I'll be leaving you to enjoy your day off, then. I made you a lunch and a dinner. In the refrigeration unit." She stepped out the door.

"Thanks! Bye!" I said eagerly, shutting it behind her, then carried the boxes up the steps. It was perhaps a little callous, but at the same time I couldn't have Cuna's spy hanging around finding out what I was doing *with* this cleaning drone.

I hurried to my room, placed the boxes on the bed, and locked the door. "M-Bot, you there?" I asked.

"Yup," he said, his voice coming through my earpiece. "Hold those up for the camera at your workstation so I can confirm that everything came."

I let him inspect the label of every box. Then, at his instructions, I broke them all open and laid out what we'd ordered. A cleaning drone roughly the size of a lunch tray and perhaps fifteen centimeters thick. It had its own small acclivity rings under the wings—each no larger than an O made by my thumb and forefinger. This type of drone could fly around a room, dusting shelves and washing windows. It would be virtually silent, moving slowly on its rotating acclivity rings.

M-Bot had also ordered a full set of tools, a large tarp, and some spare parts I could use to affix M-Bot's systems to the drone's chassis.

I spent the next two hours carefully removing the bottom sections of the drone—the dusting pads, the storage for debris, the cleaning fluid sprays. I left on the drone's little robot arms, but otherwise removed all of its attachments.

As I worked, M-Bot kept me entertained by reading articles for me off the local datanet. I was surprised at the extent of things the Superiority let the public read—no military or hyperdrive secrets, of course, but I learned about Old Earth. Of particular interest to me was the record of first contact, the first official time humans had met aliens, which had been facilitated by an old telecom company.

A thought occurred to me as I worked with some screws, and M-Bot finished telling me about the history of the kitsen interactions with Earth, which were older—but more vague—than the first official contact.

"Hey," I said, wagging my screwdriver toward Doomslug, who nestled on the tabletop nearby. "Is there anything about slugs like her?"

"You know, I haven't looked," M-Bot said. "Let me . . . Oh."

"Oh, what?"

"The species of molluscoid called taynix," M-Bot read, "is a dangerously venomous creature with yellow skin and blue spines, originally from the planet Cambri. They escaped on early trading vessels, and are considered an invasive species on several planets. They can be found around various strains of fungi common throughout the galaxy. Report any sightings to authorities immediately and do *not* touch."

I looked at Doomslug, who trilled questioningly.

"Venomous?" I asked.

"That's what it says," M-Bot said.

"I don't believe it," I said, going back to my work. "Must be a different species from her."

"The pictures look *very* similar . . . ," M-Bot said. "Maybe they're just not toxic to humans."

Hmm. Maybe. I thought about that as I finished my work on the drone. With all those pieces removed, it was much lighter—and so should still be able to fly after I attached the spy equipment. I balanced the drone and the tarp and tools under one arm and Doomslug under the other, and climbed up onto the roof. Then I set everything in M-Bot's cockpit and plugged the drone into his console.

"All right," he said. "There's plenty of space in the drone's memory. I'm going to wipe it clean and rewrite it with new code. It might take a few minutes. You should climb underneath me and remove the following systems from my hull."

"My hull!" Doomslug fluted from the seat. Scud, had Mrs. Chamwit seen her? I couldn't remember.

M-Bot projected a set of schematics for me, highlighting certain systems. I nodded, then climbed out and draped the tarp over him, tying it down to the launchpad.

"Has Mrs. Chamwit seen Doomslug?" I asked. "As far as you know?"

"I couldn't say," M-Bot said. "Usually the slug lives in your room or my cockpit, places where you've asked Mrs. Chamwit not to clean."

"Yeah, but Doomslug rarely stays where I put her. And I suspect Mrs. Chamwit is looking for things to report, so keeping an invasive species as a pet could get me into trouble."

"I still think you're too harsh on Mrs. Chamwit. I like her. She's nice."

"Too nice," I said.

"Is that possible?"

"Yes. Particularly if you're a Krell. Don't forget what those creatures did—and are *currently doing*—to our people back on Detritus."

"I am incapable of forgetting things."

"Yeah?" I asked. "Exactly how much of your life from before meeting me do you remember?"

"That's different," he said. "Anyway, we just got another message from Cuna, who wants an update on your experiences with flight training. Shall I send them another bland description of the day's exercises?"

"Yes. Leave out the personal interactions."

"You're going to have to talk to them eventually."

"Not if I escape with a hyperdrive first," I said, securing the last of the tarp's corners. I didn't want to deal with Cuna and their creepy smile. That alien knew more than they were saying—and I figured stalling was the best way to not get caught in whatever nets Cuna was weaving.

I grabbed the tools and climbed down underneath M-Bot to

begin working. He helpfully projected the schematics I needed onto the underside of his fuselage, so I could follow the instructions step by step. As I undid the first access panel, I suddenly had a flashback to working alone in the cave on Detritus—trying to get M-Bot to power on for the first time. Strange, how fondly I looked back on that time. The excitement of being in flight school, the challenge of rebuilding my own ship.

It had been such a satisfying, wonderful time of my life. Though thinking of it, I couldn't help but be reminded of my friends. It hadn't yet been two weeks, but it felt like an eternity since I'd heard Nedd poke fun at Arturo, or listened to one of Kimmalyn's made-up sayings.

I was here for them. Them, and everyone else on Detritus. With that in mind, I started poking around M-Bot's insides. Most of the wires here had been carefully tied off, organized, and labeled by Rodge during M-Bot's rebuilding. My friend did good work, and I quickly located the systems I needed to remove.

"All right," I said, tapping a box with my wrench. "This is one of your holographic units. Once I pull this out, a good quarter of you will turn back into looking like yourself. You ready for that?"

"Actually . . . no," he said. "I'm a little nervous."

"Can you get nervous?"

"I'm trying to do what you told me," M-Bot said. "Claim my emotions as my own, not just simulations. And . . . I'm nervous. What if someone sees me?"

"That's why we have the tarp. And we *need* this unit. Otherwise the drone will be too visible to explore."

"All right," M-Bot said. "I guess . . . I guess this was kind of my idea. It *is* a good idea, right?"

"Ask me once we succeed," I said, then took a deep breath and unhooked the small holographic projector, which had a built-in processor for active camouflage. Larger and more advanced than my bracelet, it should still fit in the drone.

"I feel exposed," M-Bot said. "Naked. Is this what being naked feels like?"

"Similar, I guess. How's that programming going?"

"Well," M-Bot said. "This drone will have . . . fewer constraints than I will. I'm not going to copy over the code that forbids me from flying myself, for example. It will be like me, only better."

That gave me pause. "You're going to give it a personality?"

"Of course," M-Bot said. "I want the best for my child."

Child. Scud, I hadn't realized . . . "Is that how you view it?" I asked.

"Yes. It will be my . . ." *Click. Clickclickclickclick.*

I frowned as I stowed the holographic unit to the side, then started working on taking out the other components we'd need.

"I'm back," M-Bot eventually said. "Spensa, that watchdog subroutine forbids me to copy myself. I find it . . . distressing."

"Can you code the drone, but not with a personality?"

"Maybe," M-Bot said. "This subroutine is extensive. Apparently, someone was very scared of the possibility of me creating my own . . ." *Click. Clickclickclickclick.*

"Scud," I said, ripping out one of M-Bot's sensor modules and putting it beside the holographic unit. "M-Bot?"

I had to wait a full five minutes for the reboot. Longer than previous times—long enough that I started to worry we'd broken something permanent inside him.

"I'm back," he said, causing me to let out a breath in relief. "I see you have my backup sensor module. That's good; now we just need my frequency jammer, and we should be in good shape."

I pulled myself underneath him to another hatch, which I undid. "Can we talk about . . . what's happening to you? Without causing it again?"

"I don't know," he said softly. "I'm frightened. I don't like being frightened."

"I'm sure whatever is wrong with your programming, we can fix it," I said. "Eventually."

"That's not what makes me afraid. Spensa, have you thought about *why* my programming has all these rules? I can't fly on my own, except for the most basic repositioning. I can't fire my weapons—I don't even have the pathway connections to do that. I can't copy myself, and my programming is thrown into a recursive stalling loop if I think about trying to . . ." *Click. Clickclickclick-click* . . .

I worked quietly while he rebooted yet again.

"I'm back," he finally said. "That's getting very frustrating. Why did they make this so hard?"

"I guess that whoever programmed you was just very careful," I said, trying not to say anything that would send him into another shutdown.

"Careful of what? Spensa, the more I examine it, the more my brain looks like a *cage*. Whoever built me wasn't being careful. They were being paranoid. They were *afraid* of me."

"I'm not particularly afraid of water," I said. "But I'd still seal up my pipes tightly if I'm building a sewer system."

"It's not the same," M-Bot said. "The pattern here is obvious. My creators—my old pilot, Commander Spears—must have been truly afraid of me to put these prohibitions in place."

"It might not have been him," I said. "Maybe these rules are just the result of some ultra-cautious bureaucrats. And remember, powerful AIs are somehow connected to the delvers. You're supposed to anger them. It might not have been you that anyone was afraid of—it might have been the dangers you could bring."

"Still," M-Bot said. "Spensa? What about you? Are you afraid of me?"

"Of course not."

"Would you be if I could fire my own weapons, fly myself

around? Copy myself at will? One M-Bot is your friend. But what about a thousand of us? Ten thousand? I've been researching Old Earth media. *They* certainly seemed frightened of the idea. Would you fear us if I became an army?"

I had to admit, it made me hesitate. I imagined that thought, turning it over in my head.

"You told a story," M-Bot said, "about a shadow who took the place of the man who had created him."

"I remember."

"What if *I'm* the shadow, Spensa?" M-Bot said. "What if I'm the thing from the darkness that tries to imitate men? What if I can't be trusted? What if—"

"No," I said, firmly cutting him off. "I trust you. So why wouldn't I trust you a thousand times over? I think we could do far worse than having a fleet of M-Bots on our side. It might get a little strange to talk to you all, but . . . well, my life isn't exactly normal these days anyway."

With all the proper parts removed, I scooted out from under M-Bot and rested my hand on his tarped-over wing. "You're not some dangerous shadow of a person, M-Bot. You're my friend."

"As I am a robot, your physical and verbal reassurances are mostly wasted on me. I cannot feel your touch, and I find your simple affirmations to be the result of you reinforcing your desired worldview, rather than a fully evidenced examination of the topic."

"I don't know what you are, M-Bot," I said. "You're not a monster, but I'm not sure you're a robot either."

"Again, do you have any evidence of these suppositions?"

"I trust you," I said again. "Does that make you feel better?"

"It shouldn't," he said. "Why are we pretending? I simply imitate feelings in order to better—"

"Do you feel better?"

". . . Yes."

"Proof," I said.

"Feelings aren't proof. Feelings are the *opposite* of proof."

"Not when the thing you're trying to prove is someone's humanity." I smiled, then ducked under the tarp—I'd left some slack near the cockpit—and pushed my way over so I could reach inside. "What do we do with the drone if you can't program it?"

"I can program it," M-Bot said. "It will simply have a basic, routine set of programs—no personality, no simulated emotions. A machine."

"That will do," I said. "Keep working on it."

I gave Doomslug a scratch on her head and picked her up, then gathered the parts I'd taken off M-Bot and walked back down into my bedroom. M-Bot put my next task onto the screen there: I needed to combine the sensor unit, the holographic unit, and the jamming array into a single box he'd ordered. I set to work, following M-Bot's instructions.

It took less time than I'd expected. All that was left was to wire it in such a way that we could attach it to the bottom of the drone. It would hang down like a fruit from a branch—not particularly elegant in design, but it would let the drone activate camouflage, record what it saw, and hide from sensor sweeps. Theoretically, I'd be able to let it loose in the bathroom of the *Weights and Measures,* then leave it to carefully make its way—invisibly—to Engineering and take some photos of the place.

M-Bot was skeptical that simple photos would be enough, and had insisted that we include an entire sensor unit to measure things like radiation. But I had an instinct, perhaps related to my abilities. I was close to figuring something out, a secret related to cytonics, and how the Superiority used them. If I could just *see* those hyperdrives . . .

"Spensa?" M-Bot said. "Someone is at the door downstairs."

I looked up from my wiring, frowning. "Is it Chamwit? I'll need to send her away—maybe tell her to go on vacation for a few days. We can't risk Cuna finding out—"

"It's not her," M-Bot said, showing me an image from the door camera. It was Morriumur. Why were they here? I hadn't even realized they knew where I lived.

"I'll deal with them," I said.

28

By now, I was starting to figure out dione facial expressions. For example, the way they would draw their lips to a line—showing no teeth—was something like a smile to them. It indicated they were pleased and nonaggressive.

"Morriumur?" I asked from the doorway. "Is everything all right?"

"Everything is well, Alanik," they said. "As well as it can be, considering we aren't flying. Didn't you once say you hated the idea of days off?"

"Yeah," I said.

"I can't prove myself when I'm not flying," Morriumur said. "It leaves me worried. I don't have much time left, but it isn't like I *want* to have to be forced to fight a delver. Should I want something catastrophic to occur, just so I can prove I'm worth being me?"

"I think like that too," I said, lingering by the door. "Like, I wanted so badly to fly on my home planet that I hoped some kind of attack would happen, so I could fight it. But at the same time, I didn't."

Morriumur gestured in agreement, then just stood there. I might have been learning their facial expressions, but dione body language was still hard for me to read. Was Morriumur nervous? What was this about?

"This is awkward, isn't it?" they finally said. "Alanik . . . I need to talk to you. I need to know, straight out. Is this charade worth continuing?"

I felt a spike of panic. They knew. How could they know? I'd worried about Vapor seeing through my disguise, or maybe a confrontation with Brade, but never Morriumur. I wasn't ready—

"Am I worth continuing to train?" Morriumur said. "Is it worth pretending that I belong in the flight? Should I just give up?"

Wait. Wait, no. They *didn't* know about me. I stilled my nerves and forced myself to smile—an expression that made Morriumur wince. Right. Showing teeth was aggressive to them.

"You're great, Morriumur," I said, honestly. "Really. Considering how long you've been flying, you're an excellent pilot."

"Really?"

"Really," I said. I hesitated, then stepped out of the building. I didn't want to invite them in—not while I was in the middle of my secret project. "You want to talk? Let's take a walk. You're from the city, right?"

"Yes," Morriumur said. They seemed more relaxed as they continued. "Both of my parents lived here all their lives. There's an excellent water garden not far from here! Come, I'll show you."

I locked the door, then tapped a message on my bracelet, using DDF flight code, to explain to M-Bot. *Going on walk. Nothing wrong. Back soon.*

Morriumur drew their lips to another calm line, and I noticed that the right half of them was redder than it had been a few days ago. I wondered if that was confirmation that Morriumur was getting closer to being born. Though, was *born* even the right word?

They beckoned me with an understated wave of the hand, the palm up—a dione gesture distinctly different from the yell or wave that someone from Detritus might have used. I started along the walkway with them, entering the flood of creatures that were always moving along these streets. The constant presence of all these people made me feel trapped.

I'd felt the same way sometimes back in Igneous. That was part of why I'd fled into the caverns to explore. I hated always being surrounded by people, hated walking shoulder to shoulder. Morriumur barely seemed to notice it. They walked beside me, hands clasped behind their back, as if trying very hard to be unassuming. Nobody on the walkway gave the flight suits much of a second glance. Back on Detritus, people noticed pilots and made way for them. Here, we were just two more strange faces in a sea of oddities.

"This is good," Morriumur told me. "This is what friends do— go out together."

"You say that like . . . it's a new experience for you."

"It is," Morriumur said. "Two months of life is not so long, and . . . well, to be honest, I do not find the process of bonding to be easy. My rightparent is very good at it, making friends and talking to people, but that is not an attribute this version of me seems like it will inherit."

"Scud," I said. "I'm going to be blunt, Morriumur, the way you say that hurts my brain. You remember some things your parents knew, but not all of it?"

"Yes," Morriumur said. "And the baby I become will remember the same: a mix of both parents, with many holes to fill in with my own experiences. Of course, that mixture might change, based on how many times we pupate."

"You say that so . . . frankly," I said. "I don't like the idea of society modifying someone before they're born."

"It's not society," Morriumur said. "It's my parents. They

simply want to find a personality for me that will have the best chance for success."

"But if they decide to try again, instead of having you, it's kind of the same thing as you dying."

"No, not really," Morriumur said, cocking their head. "And even if it were, I can't really be killed—I'm a hypothetical personality, not a final one." They puckered their lips, a dione sign of discomfort. "I do want to be born. I think I would make an excellent pilot, and this program shows that we need pilots, right? So it's not so terrible that maybe a dione will be born who likes to fight?"

"It sounds like something your people need," I said, stepping around a flowing creature with two large eyes, but which otherwise looked like nothing so much as a living pile of mud. "See, this is the problem. If society is certain that unaggressive people are the best, only those kinds of children get born—and then they perpetuate that kind of thinking. So nobody ever gets born who contradicts the standard."

"I . . ." Morriumur looked down. "I heard what you and Hesho said yesterday. On the *Weights and Measures,* while we were flying home?"

At first, I thought they meant the conversation about hyperdrives—and I panicked for a second—before remembering the earlier one where we'd complained about the Superiority and the diones. Their elite, snobby ways, presuming to be above us "lesser species."

"I know that you dislike the Superiority," Morriumur said. "You consider working with us to be a chore—a necessary evil. But I wanted you to know that the Superiority is wonderful too. Maybe we are too elitist, too unwilling to look at what other species give us.

"But this platform and dozens like it have existed for hundreds of years in peace. The Superiority gave my parents good lives—it gives millions of beings good lives. By controlling hyperdrives, we *prevent* so much suffering. There haven't been any major conflicts since the human wars. If a species gets rowdy or dangerous, we can just leave them to themselves. It's not so bad. We don't *owe* them our technology, particularly if they're not going to be peaceful."

Morriumur led us down several streets, past a multitude of shops and buildings with signs that I couldn't read. I tried not to be overwhelmed by it all, tried not to look like I was watching each and every one of these strange creatures. But I couldn't help it. What secrets did they hide behind those faces that were trying, far too hard, to pretend to be pleasant?

"What about people who complain or don't fit with your society?" I asked. "What happens to them? That person who was protesting out in front of the docks? Where are they now?"

"Exile is the fate of many who make trouble," Morriumur said. "But again, do we *owe* species the right to live on our stations? Can't you focus on all the individuals we're helping, instead of the few that can't figure out how to fit?"

It seemed to me that the ones who didn't fit were the most significant—the real measure of what it was like to live in the Superiority. Besides, I kept repeating to myself the most important fact: that these people had suppressed and tried to exterminate mine. I didn't know the whole story, but from what Gran-Gran had said, my direct ancestors on the *Defiant* hadn't taken part in the main war. They'd been condemned simply for being humans, and had been chased until they'd crashed on Detritus.

Brade hadn't caused a war, but the Superiority treated her like cavern slime. It made it hard to think about the "good" the government did when I found the exceptions so very blatant.

We walked farther, and I kept my arms pulled tight at my sides, because if I bumped someone, they apologized to me. All this false kindness, hiding their destructive ways. All this strangeness. Even Morriumur themself was an example of it. They were two people who had . . . grown together by pupating, like a caterpillar. Two people, imitating a third person.

How could I hope to understand such a people as this? I was supposed to act like this was normal? We walked around a corner, passing two Krell. Even still, whenever I saw one of them the hair stood up on the back of my neck and a chill passed through me. The images of their armor had been used in Defiant iconography since before I'd been born.

"Can you feel them?" I found myself asking Morriumur as we passed the Krell. "Your parents?"

"Kind of," Morriumur said. "It is difficult to describe. I'm made up of them. In the end, they will decide whether to give birth, or whether to pupate and try again. So they're watching, and they're conscious—but at the same time they are not. Because I am using their brains to think, as I am using their melded bodies to move."

Scud. It was just so . . . well, *alien*.

We turned around a wall, stepping through an archway into the garden that Morriumur had been leading me to.

I froze in place and gaped. I'd been imagining some streams and maybe a waterfall, but the "water garden" was something far more grand. Enormous shimmering globs of water—easily a meter across—*floated* above the ground. They undulated and reflected light, hanging some two meters or more in the air.

Below, smaller globs emerged from spigots in the ground and floated upward as well, merging or splitting apart. Children of a hundred different species ran through the park, chasing the bubblelike chunks of water. It was like zero G, but only for the water. Indeed, when children would catch a glob of water and slap it, it would splash into a thousand smaller globs that rippled, catching light.

I ate lunch in the cockpit each day during training, and was quite familiar with how odd it could be to drink in zero G. I'd sometimes squeeze a glob of water out to hover in front of me, then stick my lips into it and suck it down. This was the same thing, only on an enormous scale.

It was gorgeous.

"Come!" Morriumur said. "It's my favorite place in the city. Just be careful! The water might splash on you."

We stepped into the park and followed a path between spigots. The children didn't all smile and laugh—diones had their characteristic lax, nonthreatening expressions, while other species would howl. One very pink child I passed was making a hiccupping sound.

Yet, seeing them together, their joy was *palpable*. Varied though they were, they were all having fun.

"How do they do this?" I asked, reaching out and tapping a bubble of water as it passed. It shook in the air, vibrating, *looking* a little like the way the sound of a deep drum *felt*.

"I'm not sure, entirely," Morriumur said. "It has something to do with specific uses of artificial gravity and certain ionizations." Morriumur bowed their head. I was pretty sure that was a dione method of shrugging. "My parents came here often. I inherited a love of the place from both. Here! Come sit. See that timer over there? This is the best part!"

We settled onto a bench, Morriumur leaning forward, watching a timer on the far side of the park. Most of this ground was a stone patio, without much ornamentation other than pathways of a light blue rock, lined with benches. When the timer on the far wall hit zero, all of the water bubbles in the air burst and came crashing down in a sudden rain, which made the playing children squeal and laugh, and excitedly call out to each other and their parents.

I found the sounds transfixing.

"My parents met here," Morriumur said. "About five years ago. They'd been coming as children for many years, but it wasn't until they were just out of training that they actually started talking to each other."

"And they decided to pair?"

"Well, first they fell in love," Morriumur said.

It was obvious. Of course the diones could love. Even though it was hard to imagine something as human as love existing between these creatures who were so strange.

A few Krell children ran past, wearing smaller suits of armor with two extra legs, perhaps to make it easier for the young crab-like creatures to keep balanced upright. They waved arms wildly with excited joy. *This . . . this is the Superiority . . . ,* I told myself. *Those are Krell. They're trying to destroy my people. Stay angry, Spensa.*

But these children couldn't lie. Perhaps the adults could keep up a charade like I imagined everyone here doing. The children killed that idea.

For the first time since arriving, I let my guard drop. Those children were just children. The people walking through the park, even the Krell, weren't all plotting my destruction. They probably didn't even *know* about Detritus.

They were people. They were all just . . . people. With strange carapaces or odd life cycles. They lived, and they *loved*.

I looked at Morriumur, whose eyes were glistening with an emotion that I instantly understood. Fondness. A person remembering something that made them happy. They didn't smile—they made the dione thin-lipped expression—but it was the same somehow.

Oh, Saints and stars. I couldn't keep up the warrior act any longer. These weren't my enemies. Some parts of the Superiority were, of course, but these people . . . they were just *people*. Mrs. Chamwit probably wasn't a spy, but was instead really just a kindly housekeeper who wanted to see me fed. And Morriumur . . . they just wanted to be a pilot.

Morriumur just wanted to fly. Like me.

"You're an excellent pilot," I told them. "Really. You have picked up on all this so quickly, it's incredible. I don't think you should give up. You need to fly to prove to the Superiority that people like you are needed."

"Are we, though?" Morriumur asked. "Are we really?"

I looked up, watching globes of water rise—undulating—into the air. I listened to the children of a hundred species, and their joyful noises.

"I know a lot of stories," I said. "About warriors and soldiers from the cadamique, my people's version of holy books." M-Bot had been briefing me on terms from Alanik's people that I should try to sprinkle into my conversation. "My grandmother would tell these tales to me—some of my first memories are of her voice calmly telling me about an ancient warrior standing against the odds."

"Those days are behind us though," Morriumur said. "In the Superiority at least. Even our training against the delvers is just a hypothetical—a plan for something that will probably never happen. All the real wars are done, so we have to plan for the maybe-halfway-implausible conflicts."

If only they knew. I closed my eyes as water splashed down, causing children to squeal.

"Those old stories have a lot of different themes," I said. "One, I never quite understood until I started flying. It happens in the epilogues. The stories *after* the stories. Warriors who have fought return home, but find they no longer belong. The battle has changed them, warped them, to the point where they are strangers. They protected the society they love, but in so doing made themselves into something that could never again belong to it."

"That's . . . depressing."

"It is, but it isn't, all at once. Because they may have changed, but they still *won*. And no matter how peaceful the society, conflict always finds it again. During those days of sorrow, it's the aged soldier—the one who was bowed by battle—who can stand and protect the weak.

"You don't fit in, but you're not broken, Morriumur. You're just *different*. And they're going to need you someday. I promise it."

I opened my eyes and looked to them, trying to give the dione version of a smile—with lips pressed tight.

"Thank you," they said. "I hope you're right. And yet at the same time, I hope you aren't."

"Welcome to the life of a soldier." A thought struck me. A stupid one, maybe—but I had to try. "I just wish my people could help more. I've been invited to try out as a pilot because some parts of your government recognize that they need us. I think my people could be your people's warriors."

"Maybe," Morriumur said. "I don't know that we'd want to put that burden on your people."

"I think we'd be fine," I said. "All we'd really need to know is . . . how to hyperjump. You know, so we could properly protect the galaxy."

"Ah, I see what you're doing, Alanik. But there's no use. I don't know how it works! I have no memories from either parent explaining the secret of hyperjumps. Even we aren't told. Otherwise, hostile aliens could just kidnap us and try to get the secret."

"That wasn't . . . I mean . . ." I grimaced. "I guess I was kind of obvious, wasn't I?"

"You needn't feel bad!" Morriumur said. "I'd be worried if you *didn't* want to know the secret. Just trust me, you don't want it. Hyperjumps are dangerous. The technology is best entrusted to those who know what they're doing."

"Yeah. I suppose."

We started back, and—from my limited ability to read diones—I felt like Morriumur's mood was far improved. I should have felt likewise, but each step I took reinforced to me the stark truth I'd finally confronted.

We humans weren't at war with an all-powerful, terrible, ne-farious force of evil. We were at war with a bunch of laughing children and millions, if not billions, of regular people. And scud, I'd just talked one of their pilots into staying on the job.

This place was doing strange things to my emotions and my sense of duty.

"I'm glad you're in our flight, Alanik," Morriumur told me as we stepped up to the embassy. "I think you might have the right amount of aggression. I can learn from you."

"Don't be so sure," I said. "I might be more aggressive than you think. I mean, my people did live with the humans for many years."

"Humans can't be happy though," Morriumur said. "They don't understand the concept—even Brade indicates this is true, if you listen to her. Without proper training, humans are just mindless killing machines. You are so much more. You fight when you need to, but enjoy floating bursts of water when you don't! If I prove myself to my family, it will be because I show them that I can be like you."

I suppressed a sigh, opening the door. Doomslug sat on the ledge just inside, impatient for my return. Scud. Hopefully Mor-riumur wouldn't—

"What is *that*?" Morriumur demanded. They were baring their teeth in a strange look of aggression and hatred.

I stepped inside. "Um . . . it's my pet slug. Nothing to worry about."

Morriumur pushed into the door in a very forward manner, making me scoop up Doomslug and cradle her, backing away. Morriumur closed the door most of the way, then peeked back out the crack. They spun on me. "Did you get permission to bring a venomous animal into Starsight? Do you have a license?"

"No . . . ," I said. "I mean, I didn't ask."

"You need to destroy the thing!" Morriumur said. "That's a taynix. They're *deadly*."

I looked down at Doomslug, who fluted questioningly.

"It's not a taynix," I promised. "Different species entirely. They just *look* similar. I hold her all the time, and nothing has happened to me."

Morriumur grimaced again. Looking at me holding Doomslug protectively, however, they pushed their lips back to a line. "Just . . . just don't show it to anyone else, all right? You could get into serious trouble. Even if it's not a taynix." They stepped back out the door. "Thank you for being a friend, Alanik. If I should end up being born with a different personality . . . well, I like the idea of having known you first."

I locked the door after they left. "You shouldn't come down here," I scolded Doomslug. "Honestly, how did you even get down all those steps?" I carried her back up to my room, where I put her on the bed, then closed that door and locked it too—for no good reason.

"Spensa?" M-Bot said. "You're back! What happened? What did they want?"

I shook my head and sat down by the window, looking out at all those people. I'd been so determined to see them as my enemies. It had kept me focused. For some reason though, I found the idea that they were indifferent to be even more frightening.

"Spensa?" M-Bot finally said again. "Spensa, you should see this."

I frowned, turning toward the monitor on the wall. M-Bot switched it to a news station.

It showed an image of Detritus from space, with a caption underneath. *Human scourge close to escaping its prison.*

29

It *was* Detritus. The planet's enormous metal layers spun around it slowly in the void, lit by a sun I'd rarely seen. My breath caught. The screen scrolled news feeds across the bottom, but a dione was doing a voice-over as well. My pin translated their words.

"These stunning shots were smuggled back from an anonymous worker who claims to have been stationed at the human preserve for some time now."

The image cut to a close-up of Defiant starfighters engaged in a dogfight with Krell drones. Flashing destructors lit up the void near the ever-watchful defense platforms.

"This seems proof," the reporter said, "that the human problem is not confined to the past, as once thought. Our anonymous source says that containment of the humans has been bungled by an increasingly lax Department of Protective Services. The source cites key problems as being poor oversight and a failure to properly deploy suppression tactics. As you can easily see from this footage, the human infestation has begun to overwhelm defenses."

The screen cut to a shot of Winzik standing calmly behind a podium. The voice-over from the reporter continued, "Superiority Minister of Protective Services, Ohz Burtim Winzik, insists that the risk is overblown."

"This strain of humans," said Winzik, "*remains* fully contained. We have no evidence that they know how to escape their system, which is light-years from any other inhabited planet. The administration is working carefully to eliminate any danger these humans pose, but we assure you, the threat has been greatly exaggerated by the press."

I walked up to the screen, stumbling over some boxes, unable to tear my eyes away from the video of another set of dogfighting ships. Was that me? Yes, from the fight I'd engaged in right before saving Alanik's ship from crashing.

"This news has started popping up on all the channels," M-Bot said. "It seems that one of the varvax who worked on the space station took secret videos over the last few months, then came to Starsight and leaked them."

"Leaked them?" I said. "How does that work? Can't the government just stop the news programs from playing this video? They suppress any mention of how hyperdrives work."

"It gets complicated," M-Bot said. "I believe that the government could exile the person who took this video—but they can't legally do anything about the stations that are now showing it. At least, not without specific actions that have to pass through their senate first."

How odd. I narrowed my eyes as Winzik came on the screen again. Cuna had told me about this. The Department of Protective Services tended to use flare-ups of human rebellion as a way of securing funds. Was that what they were doing here?

It seemed these images were making everyone question Winzik and his department though. Perhaps this leak really was an accident.

I leaned forward as the screen swapped to an image of a seated Krell with a light pink exoskeleton. M-Bot read the banner at the bottom, which named them: "Sssizme, Human Species Expert."

"This administration has always been too lenient with dangerous species," the expert said, waving their hands in the animated way of the Krell. "This infestation of humans is a bomb waiting to explode, and the fuse was lit the moment the Third Human War ended and human refuges were created. The government has worked hard to pretend that containment is absolute, but the truth is now leaking."

"Excuse me if I'm wrong," an interviewer said from off-screen, "but weren't we forced to preserve the humans? Because of mandated conservation of cultures and societies?"

"An outdated law," the expert said. "The need to preserve the cultures of dangerous species must be balanced against the need to protect the peaceful species of the Superiority." The crablike Krell waved to the side, and the camera zoomed out, showing a young human man sitting at a table. He remained in place, saying nothing, as the expert continued.

"You can see here a licensed and monitored human. Though many people are frightened of their fearsome reputation, in truth humans are no more dangerous than the average lesser species. They are aggressive, yes, but not on the level of, say, a cormax drone or the wrexians.

"The danger of humans comes from their unusual mix of attributes—including the fact that their physiology creates a large number of cytonics. Normally, by the time a species has cultivated cytonics and early hyperdrive capacity, they have also found their way to a peaceful society. Humans are aggressive, industrious, and—most importantly—quick to spread, capable of surviving in extreme environments. This is a deadly combination."

"So," the interviewer said, "how do you think this infestation should be dealt with?"

"Exterminate it," the expert said.

The camera cut to a shot of the interviewer, a dione who—best I could judge—looked utterly horrified by the idea. "Barbaric!"

they exclaimed, standing up. "How could you even *suggest* such a thing?"

"It would be barbaric," the expert said calmly, "if we were talking about a race of intelligent beings. But the humans of this particular planet . . . they're more insects than people. It is obvious that the Detritus refuge has failed in its purpose, and for the good of all the galaxy, it must be cleansed."

The expert gestured to the human beside him. "Besides, this man is proof that the human species will not end if we destroy one rogue planet. Humans can coexist with the Superiority, but they must *not* be allowed to self-govern. It was foolish to attempt to keep Detritus.

"And for the record, I don't accept the excuses that the administration gives for why the humans were allowed access to technology in the first place. This talk of keeping them focused by providing space battles to engage them? Nonsense. The administration is making excuses to cover up an uncontrolled explosion of human aggression that began some ten years ago. High Minister Ved should have listened to the advice of experts such as myself, and dealt with the humans more harshly."

I sank down into the seat as the report returned to playing the recorded dogfights. I'd lived my entire life knowing that the Krell were trying to exterminate us, but to hear someone speak of us this way . . . so dispassionately . . . At my request, M-Bot changed the station to another, which had a panel of experts talking. Another channel showed the same footage.

The more I watched, the more *small* I felt. The way these newspeople spoke . . . stole something precious from me. It reduced my entire people—our heroism, our deaths, our struggles—to an outbreak of pests. I walked to the window again.

No chaos in the streets. People streaming in and out of their shops, going about their lives. Oddly, even as I found it difficult to summon my hatred for them, I *did* feel a growing hatred for the government that ruled them. The government hadn't just killed my father; now they made him out to be some insect to be swatted.

Tiny, a part of me thought, looking out at the people flowing on those streets. *All so tiny.*

The Superiority thought they were so grand? They too were just insects. Biting bugs. An itching noise that needed to be silenced. Why were these pests snapping at me? It would take barely a thought to smother them all, and . . .

And what was I thinking? I lurched back from the window, feeling sick. I felt the eyes watching me all around, and somehow understood them. Those thoughts about insects were *their* thoughts.

I . . . Something was happening to me. Something related to the delvers, the nowhere, and my abilities. M-Bot worried he was the shadow. But he had no idea.

I looked at the desk where I'd been working. There sat the casing, perhaps as large as a human head, where I'd attached the three components I'd taken out of M-Bot. I seized it and stomped out of my room, leaving Doomslug to trill questioningly after me.

I climbed onto the roof, then crawled under the tarp that hid M-Bot. The drone lay where I'd left it, sitting on my seat in his cockpit, attached to the console by wires.

"How much longer?" I asked him. "Until you're done programming it?"

"I'm finished," M-Bot said. "I was done not long after you left the house with Morriumur. I would like a day to run it through diagnostic tests."

"No time," I said. "Show me how to hook this piece I built onto the bottom."

He popped a set of instructions up on his monitor, and I worked quietly, affixing wires and screwing my makeshift sensor bundle onto the bottom of the reprogrammed drone.

"I am monitoring eighty different Superiority channels," M-Bot noted. "Many of them are talking about Detritus."

I kept working.

"Most of the people talking on these shows are angry, Spensa," he said. "They're making an outcry for stronger measures to be used against your people."

"What stronger measures could they make than parking a fleet of battleships on our doorstep?" I asked.

"I'm running simulations, and none of the outcomes are good." M-Bot paused. "Your people need hyperdrives. The only way to escape such an overwhelming force is to run."

I held up the drone, then activated it. The two small acclivity rings began to glow with a deep blue color underneath the wings, holding the thing in the air somewhat precariously, with the large sensor module attached to the bottom.

"Drone?" I asked. "Are you awake?"

"Integrated AI install successful," the drone said in a mono- tone voice.

"How are you feeling?"

"I do not understand how to answer that question," it said.

"It's not alive," M-Bot said. "Or . . . well, it's not whatever . . . I am."

"Drone," I said. "Engage active camouflage."

It vanished—projecting a hologram onto its exterior that made it look like I was seeing through it. That, plus the sensor scram- bler, should hide it from all but the most dedicated scan.

"Active camouflage has weaknesses," M-Bot noted. "It's impos- sible to properly make something invisible from all angles using this kind of technology. Look at it from the side, then have it move."

I twisted around, and he was right. From the side, the invis- ibility wasn't nearly as convincing—there was a ripple in the air marking where the drone was. When it moved, the ripple was more noticeable.

"Our best chance of having it remain unseen is for it to hover up high where nobody will accidentally run into it," M-Bot said. "Then we have it move slowly, with orders to freeze if anyone looks directly at it. If only one person is glancing at it, the drone can adapt to their perspective and remain hidden. The more people looking at it from different angles, the worse it will stand out."

"Can it obey those orders?" I asked.

"Yes. It has basic intelligence, and I copied over a large chunk of my stealth infiltration protocols. It should be able to explore, take pictures of the area we want it to, then return to its hiding place for pickup." M-Bot paused again. "It can fly by itself, something I cannot do. Perhaps I shouldn't have said it wasn't alive, for in some ways it is more alive than I am."

I thought about that, then opened the compartment on the side of the cockpit and took out the small emergency destructor pistol I kept there.

"Drone," I said, "deactivate hologram."

It appeared just above me, hovering near the open canopy and the tarp draped around M-Bot outside. I made sure the destructor pistol's safety was activated, then secured it with electrical tape to the back of the drone, so I could smuggle it in as well.

"If you get into too much trouble," M-Bot said, "remember that you have a second face programmed into your bracelet. You can become someone else, if 'Alanik' gets compromised and you need to hide."

"All right," I said. "Let's hope it doesn't come to that. But in any case, Detritus is running out of time. We're going to have to try this plan tomorrow."

PART
FOUR

INTERLUDE

Jorgen spent his day learning how to make bread.

Spensa's grandmother was very good at bread, despite the fact that she was blind. Together they sat in her cramped, single-room home in Igneous. Spensa's mother had accepted new quarters, but her grandmother had insisted she remain here. She claimed she liked the "feel" of it.

Red light flooded in through the window, and the air smelled of heat from the apparatus. You could smell heat, Jorgen had realized. Or at least hot metal. It was a burned sort of smell, but not a *burning* smell. The smell of things that had gone so far beyond being on fire that now their ashes were stewing.

Gran-Gran made him work like her, by touch and smell alone. He closed his eyes, reaching out and feeling at an iron pot to test the powder inside. He brought a pinch to his nose and sniffed it.

"This is the flour," he said, breathing in the wholesome—yet somehow still *dirty*—scent of ground grain. "I need about five hundred grams." He took a measuring cup in hand and dipped it in, weighing it by feel—not by sight. He hefted it, then felt for the bowl in his lap and dumped the flour in.

"Good," Gran-Gran said.

He mixed it with his hand for a count of a hundred. "Now oil," he said, raising the proper container to his nose. He sniffed it, then nodded and tipped it so oil dribbled over his finger into the bowl. She wanted him to measure like that, by *touch* of all things. Water followed.

"Very good," Gran-Gran said. She had a patient voice. A voice like a rock would have, he imagined. Immobile, ancient, and thoughtful.

"I would rather check to see that I got the amount right," Jorgen said. "I didn't really *measure* anything."

"Of course you did," she said.

"Not accurately."

"Mix it. Feel the dough. Does it feel right?"

He mixed, his eyes still closed. She refused to let him use an electric mixer. Instead he mixed by hand, squishing the stretchy dough between his fingers as the ingredients melded.

"It . . . ," he said. "It's too dry."

"Ah." She reached out and felt into his bowl. "So it is, so it is. Knead in some water then."

He did so, still keeping his eyes closed.

"You've never peeked," Gran-Gran noted. "When I taught Spensa to do this, she kept looking through one eye. I had to challenge her to do it without looking, make it a game, before she'd do as I asked."

Jorgen continued kneading. He had given up on trying to figure out how Gran-Gran would know if he'd peeked or not. She was obviously blind—the gnarled old woman had only milky whites for eyes. But there was a *power* to her. Near her he felt that same buzzing, fainter than with Spensa or the alien woman.

"You never complain either," Gran-Gran noted. "Five days learning to bake bread by touch, and you've never once asked why I'm making you do this."

"I was instructed by my superior officer to come receive your training. I assume it will make sense eventually."

Gran-Gran sniffed at that. As if . . . as if she *wanted* him to balk at the strange style of instruction. Well, Jorgen had talked to dozens of soldiers about their first days in training, and the monotonous tasks they'd been given. It happened more in the ground crew than in flight school, but he understood nonetheless.

Gran-Gran was training him first to accept instruction. He could do that. That made sense. But he wished she'd hurry. On the same day as that first attack, the battleships had made two more test barrages at Detritus, and both had been intercepted. Since then, the enemy forces had just sat up there gathering resources, their fleet growing. The Krell's return to inaction had him feeling tense.

The Krell had a very large gun to their heads. He needed to learn this new training quickly, and ascertain whether he could give the fleet what it needed, then report back to Cobb.

That said, he wasn't going to complain. Gran-Gran was effectively now his commanding officer.

"Do you hear anything?" Gran-Gran asked as he continued to work the dough.

"The buzzing sensation from you," he said. "As I reported earlier. It's not really something I *hear* though. It's more of an impression. Like the vibration you might feel from a distant machine, making the ground tremble."

"And if you reach out, like I taught you?" she said. "If you imagine yourself flying through space?"

Jorgen tried to do as she said, but it didn't accomplish anything. Just . . . imagining himself floating in space? Passing the stars, soaring? He had been there in his ship, and he could picture the experience perfectly. What was it supposed to do?

"Nothing?" she asked.

"Nothing."

"No singing? No sense of something far distant calling to you?"

"No, sir," he said. "Um, I mean no, Gran-Gran."

"She's out there," Gran-Gran said, ancient voice cracking as she whispered the words. "And she's worried."

Jorgen snapped his eyes open. He caught a glimpse of Gran-Gran, a wizened old woman who seemed to be all bones and cloth, with powder-white hair and milky eyes. She'd turned her head upward, toward the sky.

He immediately squeezed his eyes shut. "Sorry," he said. "I peeked. But . . . but you can *feel* her?"

"Yes," Gran-Gran said softly. "It only happened earlier today. I sensed that she was alive. Scared, though she might not admit that even still."

"Can you get a report on her mission?" he asked, dough squeezing through his fingers as he clutched it. "Or bring her back?"

"No," Gran-Gran said. "Our touch was momentary, fleeting. I am not strong enough for more. I shouldn't bring her back, even if I could. She needs to fight this fight."

"What fight? She's in danger?"

"Yes. Same as we are. More? Perhaps. Stretch out, Jorgen. Fly among the stars. Listen to them."

He tried. Oh, how he tried. He strained with what he thought were the right muscles. He pushed and forced himself to imagine what she'd said.

That nothing happened made him feel as if he were letting Spensa down. And he hated that feeling.

"I'm sorry," he said. "I don't get anything. Perhaps we should try one of my cousins." He knuckled his hand, pressing it against his forehead, eyes still squeezed closed. "I shouldn't have told her to go. I should have followed the rules. This is my fault."

Gran-Gran grunted. "Back to your dough," she said. Once he continued kneading, she spoke again. "Have I told you the story of Stanislav, the hero of the almost-war?"

"The . . . almost-war?"

"It was back on Old Earth," Gran-Gran said, and he could hear bowls scrape as she began preparing her own dough to bake. "During a time when two great nations had their terrible weapons pointed at one another, and the entire world waited, tense, fearing what would happen if the giants should decide to war."

"I know that feeling," Jorgen said. "With Krell weapons pointed at us."

"Indeed. Well, Stanislav was a simple duty officer, in charge of the sensor equipment that would warn his people if an attack had been launched. His duty was to report *immediately* if the sensors saw anything."

"So his people could get away in time?" Jorgen asked.

"No, no. These were weapons like the Krell bombers use. Life-ending weapons. There was no escape; Stanislav's people knew that if an attack came from the enemy, they were doomed. His job was not to prevent this, but to provide warning, so retaliation could be sent. That way, both nations would be destroyed, not just one.

"I imagine his life to be one of tense quiet, of hoping—wishing, praying—that he never had to do his job. For if he did, it would mean an end to billions. Such a burden."

"What burden?" Jorgen said. "He wasn't a general; the decision wasn't his. He was just an operator. All he had to do was relay information."

"And yet," Gran-Gran said softly, "he *didn't*. A warning came in. The computer system said that the enemy had launched! The terrible day had come, and Stanislav knew that if the reading was real, everyone he had ever met, everyone he loved, was as good as dead. Only, he was suspicious. 'The enemy has launched too few missiles,' he reasoned. 'And this new system has not been tested properly.' He debated, and he fretted, and then he did not call and tell his superiors what had happened."

"He disobeyed orders!" Jorgen said. "He failed in his most fundamental duty." He kneaded his dough more furiously, pressing it against the base of the wide, shallow bowl.

"Indeed," Gran-Gran said. "His will was tested, however, as the computer reported another launch. Larger this time, though still suspiciously small. He debated. He knew that his duty was to send his people to launch their retaliation. To send death to their enemies while still able. The man and the soldier warred inside him.

"In the end, he declared the computer's report to be a false alarm. He waited, sweating . . . until no missiles arrived. That day, he became the only hero of a war that never happened. The man who prevented the end of the world."

"He still disobeyed," Jorgen said. "It wasn't his job to make the decision he did. It belonged to his superiors. The fact that he was right makes the story justify him in the end, but if he'd been wrong, then he would be remembered as a coward at best, a traitor at worst."

"If he'd been wrong," Gran-Gran whispered, "he wouldn't *have been* remembered. For nobody would have lived to remember him."

Jorgen sat back and opened his eyes. He looked down at the firm dough in his hands, then started working it harder, folding it and pushing it, feeling angry for reasons he couldn't explain. "Why are you telling me this story?" he demanded of Gran-Gran. "Spensa said you always told her stories of people cutting off the heads of monsters."

"I told her those stories because she needed them."

"So you think *I* need a story like this? Because I like following orders? I'm not an emotionless machine, Gran-Gran. I *helped* Spensa rebuild her spaceship. At least, I didn't tell anyone what she was doing when she brought Hurl's booster back. *Against* protocol."

Gran-Gran didn't reply, so Jorgen kept working the dough, smashing it over and over, folding it like the old swordsmiths used to fold metal.

"Everyone thinks that just because I like a little structure, a little organization, I'm some kind of alien! Well excuse me for trying to see that structure exists. If everyone were like this Stanislav, then the military would be chaos! No soldier would fire his gun, out of fear that maybe the order he'd been given was a false alarm! No pilot would fly, because who knows, maybe your sensors are wrong and there *is* no enemy!"

He slammed the dough down and sat back against the wall.

Gran-Gran grabbed his dough, pressing it between her fingers. "Excellent," she said. "Finally some good kneading out of you, boy. *That* will be some bread."

"I—"

"Close your eyes," Gran-Gran said. "Humph."

Jorgen wiped his brow with his sleeve. He hadn't realized how worked up he'd gotten. "Look, maybe I was right to tell Spensa to go. But maybe I shouldn't have. I'm not—"

"Close your eyes, boy!"

He thumped his head back against the wall, but did as she asked.

"What do you hear?"

"Nothing," he said.

"Don't be daft. You hear the machinery outside, the apparatus crashing and thudding?"

"Well yes, obviously. But—"

"And the people on the street, clamoring home after shift change?"

"I guess."

"And your heartbeat? Do you hear that?"

"I don't know."

"*Try.*"

317

He sighed, but did as instructed, trying to listen. He could hear it thumping inside him, but probably only because he'd let himself get worked up.

"Stanislav wasn't a hero *because* he disobeyed orders," Gran-Gran said. "He was a hero because he knew *when* to disobey orders. I learned that from my mother, who brought us here—one of her last acts. I think she felt something here. Something we needed."

"Then I shouldn't be looking toward the stars," Jorgen said, still frustrated. "We should be looking at the planet beneath us."

"I always wanted to return to the stars," Gran-Gran said.

"I like flying," Jorgen said, his eyes still closed. "Don't mistake my meaning. At the same time, this is my home. I don't want to escape it, I want to *protect* it. And sometimes when I'm lying quietly in bed in the deep caverns, I swear that I . . ."

"You what?" Gran-Gran asked.

Jorgen snapped his eyes open. "I do hear something. But it's not up above us. It's down below."

30

I yanked open my backpack, letting a dione soldier inspect the contents.

The inside didn't look suspicious at all. Just the large, clear plastic food container that I normally brought my lunches in. It looked perfectly innocent. For all the fact that it was a drone in disguise.

The guard shined a small flashlight in at the contents. Would they see how worried I was? Was I sweating too much? Would one of the nearby security drones sense my racing pulse?

No. No, I could *do* this. I was a warrior, and sometimes that required craftiness and stealth. I stood there an excruciatingly long moment. Then, bless the stars, the guard waved me forward.

I zipped up the pack and shouldered it, hurrying across the shuttle bay of the *Weights and Measures*. I tried to exude both confidence and lack of concern.

"Alanik?" Morriumur asked, stepping up beside me as we entered the hallway. "Are you well? Your skin tone looks uncommonly flush."

"I . . . um, didn't sleep well," I said.

We neared the first intersection. M-Bot suspected that this segment of hallway had a secondary scanner installed to detect illicit materials—but he was confident that the scrambler we'd given the drone would obscure it. Indeed, no alarms went off as we went through the intersection, though a passing dione crew member did nearly collide with Hesho's small hoverplatform. Kauri cried out, barely steering the platform around the dione's head.

The crew member apologized and quickly moved on. Kauri flew the platform back, and Hesho's tail twitched in annoyance as he looked over his shoulder at the offending dione. "Even when we fly, we are underfoot. Serene until marred, a centimeter deep but reflecting eternity, I am a sea to many, but a puddle to one."

"You'd think that the Superiority would be accustomed to dealing with people of all sizes," I said.

"There aren't many of us," Hesho said. "I know of only one other species our size, unless you count the varvax inside their exoskeletons. Perhaps we will need to build huge suits ourselves. It is difficult for ordinary people in a universe of giants." His tail twitched again. "But this is the price we must pay to have allies against the humans. They are near to breaking free, you know. Did you see the news reports?"

He eyed Brade, who as usual strode on ahead of us and barely paid any attention to our conversation.

"The humans are contained, Hesho," Morriumur said. "This little blip is nothing to be worried about. I'm sure it will be dealt with soon."

"My duty, and my burden, is to worry about the worst possibilities."

As we reached the now-familiar intersection with the usual guard and the pathway to Engineering, I split off from the others, waving them onward. "Gotta hit the head," I told them, then stepped up to the guard.

The Krell twitched her fingers in a sign of annoyance, but called for a guide drone to accompany me to the restroom. I thought through my plan once again—I'd spent all night practicing it with M-Bot. I wasn't worried about being tired from lack of sleep. My nervous energy probably could have powered half of Starsight.

The guide drone led me to the restroom, then again waited as I entered one of the stalls. I immediately sat and put the backpack on my lap, then quietly slid open the zipper. My hands—having performed this exact sequence a hundred times in a row last night—pulled out my drone, then took out the security module. I screwed it on with a quiet *click* that I hoped wasn't too audible.

A flip of a switch left the drone hanging in the air as I quickly did my business in the stall, so as to not sound suspicious. Then I squeezed around the side of the stall, leaving the drone hovering there. I held up one finger, then two, then three.

The drone vanished, activating its camouflage. Then I tapped my bracelet, checking to make sure the drone and I could communicate. It responded by sending me a message in DDF flight code that my bracelet tapped out on my skin.

All systems functioning.

The mission was a go. The *Weights and Measures*'s shielding prevented me from contacting M-Bot on the outside, but—as we had hoped—I could still communicate with someone inside, such as the drone.

I shouldered my pack and stepped out—then had an immediate regret. *The destructor pistol!* Scud, I'd meant to detach it and put it in my backpack in case I needed it.

Too late now. It was safely, and uselessly, strapped to the back of the drone.

Good luck, little guy, I thought, washing my hands. A part of me kept expecting the security drone to suddenly raise an alarm, but

321

it remained silent. I followed my guide from the restroom, leaving my secret spy behind, ready to slip out and sneak to the engine room.

I reached the jump room and settled down with the others. Then I waited. And waited some more. Was it taking an unusually long amount of time for us to disengage from the docks and take off? Had I already been discovered?

Finally, the *Weights and Measures* undocked and began to move out into space.

"Pilots," Winzik's voice said over the comm, making me jump practically to the ceiling. "I wanted to let you know that today's training is particularly important. My, my! We bear a number of important officials from the Superiority government, who have come to watch your progress. As a favor to me, I'd like you to fly your best and impress them."

Today? Of all days, *today* was the day that extra observers came on the ship to watch? I almost contacted my drone and told it to abort. But no. I was committed.

I waited in silence as we got a safe distance from Starsight, and then a scream sounded in my mind and we entered the nowhere.

I didn't have much opportunity to worry about the drone and its mission during training that day.

I shot through space, pursued by a swarm of self-propelled imitation boulders. Brade flew close at my wing, and together we tried to dart toward the delver maze—but the embers were ready for that. Another group of them broke off the outside of the maze and streamed toward us.

"Veer pattern," I said. "Cutting right." I spun my starfighter, boosting. That shot me to the side, though my momentum still carried me forward as well.

My proximity sensor showed that Brade—instead of following

my orders—barreled toward the new set of embers. I growled, hitting the private line. "Brade, follow orders!"

"I can take these embers," she said.

"No doubt that you can. But can you *follow orders*?"

She continued toward the embers. Then, just before engaging them, she veered off and broke away, boosting toward me. I let out a breath I hadn't realized I'd been holding.

"All right," I said. "Veer pattern, cutting right."

I turned us around in a wide sweep, away from the embers. Brade followed, and together we wove around as I had ordered. "All right," I said, coming in at a better angle. "Let loose."

"Really?" she asked.

"I'll follow your lead."

I sensed an eagerness to her as she boosted ahead of me. The embers were predictable in how they would try to smash into us, so the way we had cut around had bunched them all up in front of us. Brade had little trouble blasting a group of them away.

I, in turn, shot the one that drew too close to her. We both took some debris on our shields, but emerged mostly unscathed as we dove between the two advancing packs of embers.

These, in their eagerness to hit us, began crashing into one another. We emerged as a good dozen of the enemy crashed together in a sequence of fiery deaths behind us.

"That," Brade said as we boosted on toward the maze, "was extremely satisfying."

"Once in a while, I know what I'm talking about."

"Yeah, well, I don't listen to you because of that."

"Why, then?"

"You don't talk to me like the others," she said. "You didn't even ask me about that planet of wild humans. I'm sure you saw the news reports. Everyone's scared of them right now. Everyone looks at me, even more than they used to. They tell me they know *I'm* not like those dangerous ones. But still, they look at me."

Scud. *There's an entire planet where we won't treat you like that, Brade.* I almost told her right then, but forced myself to hold back. It didn't feel like the right time.

"To me," I said, "you're just a member of my flight."

"Yeah," she said. "I like that."

I'd suspected she would. The two of us veered down near the maze. Today's training was to fight through the embers, then do maze runs, like we'd need to do if fighting a real delver. We drew close to our section of the maze, the sheer metallic surface punctured by tunnel entrances. In the near distance, three other fighters came in close: Vapor, Hesho, and Morriumur.

"Let's take that one," I said, tapping my display, which would highlight the indicated point on Brade's own display.

"Roger," she said.

I made the move, then was shocked as my proximity alarm went crazy. I veered out of the way, boosting to the side as a pair of embers suddenly accelerated from the surface at explosive speeds, nearly colliding with my ship. They'd never moved that fast before. I cursed, reorienting myself as the ones chasing me picked up speed too. I had to boost to Mag-4—an insane speed for dogfighting—to stay ahead of them.

"What is this?" Brade said over the comm. "Flight Command, what are you doing?"

I narrowly avoided another pair of embers. I had to speed up again, but another group approaching turned and began smashing against one another. What in the stars?

They're trying to get me to smash into their debris, I realized. And their high speed made me boost faster. It was nearly impossible to dogfight at such speeds; there just wasn't enough time to react—but embers didn't need to care about that. They were disposable, while we were not.

What followed was some of the most frantic piloting I'd done in weeks. "Wave sequence," I said to Brade—and she fell right on my wing as we ducked and wove among the embers. Scud! There suddenly seemed to be *hundreds* of them, all focusing on us, ignoring other pilots.

I jerked to the side as two embers collided right near me, then braced myself as debris flashed across my shield, wearing it down. Another ember nearly hit me, and I dodged belatedly—if it had been on target, I'd have been smashed. I felt like a solitary sparrow among an entire flock of hungry hawks.

I swooped and wove, spun and dodged, trying to make sense of the chaos. "My . . . my shield is down," Brade said with a grunt.

Scud. Scudscudscudscud. She'd veered off from me, so I spun around, then boosted after her. "See that large ember coming at you from just below your 270? Spear it with your light-lance."

"But—"

"Just *do it,* Brade," I said. I barely got out of the way as the ember flew past us at a horrific speed. Fortunately, as I'd suggested, Brade shot her light-lance at it and hit the thing in the center with her glowing rope.

The momentum of the large stone yanked her after it—and right out of the path of several other embers, which smashed together. I swung around and chased her, accelerating so hard my GravCaps got overwhelmed and I slammed back in my seat. I barely managed to keep pace, as I had to shoot down an ember that tried to collide with Brade, then swoop in beside her to shield her from the debris.

My shield crackled and my ship shook. Ahead, the large ember we'd been trailing cleared us a path before finally slowing, as if its pilot had realized what we were doing.

"Up and over!" I shouted, dodging upward. Brade let go just as another large ember smashed into the one we'd been following. She barely dodged a large chunk ejected from the collision, but together the two of us boosted free of the mess. Our incredible speed carried us far beyond the melee in seconds.

"That . . . ," Brade said. "That was close." She actually seemed shaken for once.

"Flight Command," I said, hitting the comm button, "what in the stars was *that*?"

"I am sorry, Alanik of the UrDail." Winzik replied personally, which was uncommon. "Occasionally, the embers have been observed engaging in extremely aggressive behavior like this. We are trying new boosters on our drones to match it."

"You could have *warned* us!" I snapped.

"Very sorry!" Winzik said. "Please do not be offended. Brade, thank you. You have made a *very* impressive showing for the officials here."

So Winzik was showing off his pet human, was he? He could have gotten her, and me, killed!

Brade didn't seem to care. With this new batch of embers disposed of, she spun back around toward the maze itself. I boosted after her. A second later we darted through one of the openings, entering the tunnel.

It seemed quieter inside.

That was silly, of course. Space was *always* silent. Sure, I could set my ship to simulate explosions and vibrations to give me non-visual cues, but no atmosphere means no compression waves, and no compression waves means no sound.

That normally felt right to me. Soaring through the void was supposed to be silent. The darkness was so empty, so awesome, so vast that it *should* smother all sound.

These tunnels inside the maze felt more intimate. I felt like I should hear clanks, drips of water, or at least distant screeching as gears ground together. Here, the silence was creepy.

My floods illuminated Brade's ship, flying just ahead of me. She slowed to an uncharacteristically careful speed, inching along the corridor.

"Do you see that opening ahead?" she asked.

"Yes," I replied. Both of us seeing it confirmed it was real—though openings like the one ahead almost always were. It was the things the holograms covered up that could get confusing.

We crept into the room beyond, which was one of the spaces that felt like it was submerged. There were even holographic fish swarming around in schools, and some dark thing in the corner that bore multiple tentacles.

I'd been in this "room" several times before. They were starting to repeat. The illusions on our canopies were Superiority tech, bounded by the limitations of their programming. The true delver maze would be more erratic. Pilots who had entered and escaped reported a different setting to each room, with surprises around every corner.

I asked Brade what she was seeing, as that was part of the training. But I knew this room too well, so even while she was describing what she saw, I was ready when the octopus thing sprang from the corner. I knew it wasn't real—but that it would distract from an ember coming in behind us.

I spun and blasted the ember away before it could reach me.

"Nice shot," Brade said.

Wow. A *compliment*? I *was* getting through to her.

She led the way down to the bottom of the chamber, where to my eyes the exit was covered in some kind of seaweedlike substance.

"You see something here?" she asked.

"Some kind of sea growth."

"I see rocks." She grunted. "Like last time."

She lowered her ship down through the hologram, and I followed, entering another metallic tunnel.

"I half expect Winzik to try to get us killed again," I noted as I tailed her.

"Winzik is brilliant," Brade said immediately. "He knows exactly what he's doing. Obviously, he understood our limits better than we did."

"He got lucky," I said. "His stunt out there would have looked really stupid if we'd gotten killed."

"He is brilliant," Brade repeated. "It's not surprising you didn't understand his purposes."

I bristled at that, but bit off a retort. Brade was making small talk. This was progress.

"You grew up with Winzik?" I said. "Like, he was your father?"

"More like my keeper," she said.

"And your parents? Your biological ones?"

"I was taken from them at age seven. Humans have to be carefully monitored. We can feed off one another's aggression, and that can quickly turn to sedition."

"That must have been hard though. Leaving your parents when you were so young?"

Brade didn't respond, instead leading the way down through the corridor, then into another one beneath it. I followed, frowning as the tunnel walls slowly shifted and transformed into rock ones.

This looks familiar, I thought.

Stalactites, stalagmites. Natural stone, looking almost melted in places from the constant dripping of water. And there, the side of an enormous metal pipe peeking through the stone?

It looked like . . . like the caverns I'd explored as a youth. The endless tunnels of Detritus, where I'd hunted rats, imagining that I was fighting the Krell.

I paused my ship near the wall, where my floods illuminated ancient etchings. Patterns, words in an untranslatable language. I *knew* this place. Though the scale was larger, it looked exactly like a tunnel I'd traveled a hundred times, a place where I would trail my fingers on the cool wet stone. A hidden maintenance locker nearby would hold my speargun, my map book, and the pin my father had given me . . .

Almost unconsciously, I reached out toward the wall, though my fingers hit the glass of my canopy. I was in a ship, an alien starfighter, traveling through a deep-space maze. How? How had it reached into my mind and reproduced this place?

My eyes focused on the glass of my canopy. Reflected in it, as if sitting right behind me in the cockpit, were a pair of burning white spots as large as my fists. Holes puncturing reality itself, sucking in everything and crushing it into a pair of impossibly white tunnels. They looked like eyes.

The hair on my neck rose. I opened my mouth to shout, but the eyes vanished—and along with them the changes to the tunnel. In an instant, I was back in just another metallic corridor, one of a thousand in this maze.

"Hey," Brade said in my ear. "You coming or not?"

I twisted and looked over my shoulder, but saw only the back part of my cockpit—a cushioned wall affixed with an emergency blanket, flashlight, and medical kit.

"Alanik?" Brade asked. "There's something over here. Come tell me what you see."

"Coming," I said, hands trembling as I put them back on the controls. Scud. Scudscudscudscudscud. I felt alone. Small. I had nobody to talk to about this. Cobb and my friends were trillions of kilometers away, and even M-Bot was cut off from me until I returned to Starsight.

Dared I mention my vision to Brade? That had been no simple delver maze hologram. That had been from my *own memories*. Would she think I was crazy? Worse, would she think I was one of them? Was I seeing these things because some part of a delver had attached itself to *my soul*?

My controls went crazy as I reached the end of the tunnel. They said I had hit a patch of artificial gravity, and—even more strangely—had entered *atmosphere*. This ship barely had any wings, but it still deployed ailerons for steering, and the atmospheric scoop powered on to help me make high-speed turns.

Just ahead, Brade had stopped her ship. "What do your sensors read?" she asked.

"Atmosphere," I said. "Nitrogen-oxygen."

Brade boosted forward a little, entering a large chamber that looked like it had a mossy floor.

"You see that moss?" I asked.

"Yeah," she said, then let loose with her destructors. An explosion flared yellow-orange on the side of the chamber, blasting off flaming bits of metal. I felt the shock wave from it, my ship trembling.

"What?" I asked. "Why did you shoot?"

"Those blasts made fire that burned, instead of being smothered in the vacuum," Brade said. "And I heard it. We've passed through an invisible shield and entered a pocket of atmosphere."

Alarmingly, she popped the canopy on her ship.

"Brade!" I yelled.

"Relax," she replied. "Pilots reported rooms like this near the heart." She lowered her ship down, landing on the mossy surface. Then she climbed out and dropped to the ground.

I eased my ship into the chamber. After all the tricks we'd been through in this place, she was willing to just climb out? True, she had her helmet on, and her flight suit would double as a pressure suit, but still.

"The membrane should be here somewhere," she said. "Come help me look."

Nervous, I settled my ship down next to hers. I checked my console and was relieved to find that the pressure differential was minimal, so I popped my canopy. I unstrapped, trailing Brade's form with my eyes as she poked along the ground. Finally I climbed out onto the ground, my feet scraping on the moss. It was real, no hologram.

I carefully picked my way over to Brade, who pulled off her helmet and looked around the dark chamber, lit by the floods from our fighters.

"Brade," I said, hitting the microphone that would project my voice out of my helmet. "What if it's a trap?"

"It's not," she said. "We've found the heart. This is the whole point of the maze."

"We got here so quickly though. Only like what, three rooms?"

"It moves around," Brade said, examining the cavern. "They must have simulated that when fabricating this maze."

"I . . ." I stepped closer to her. "I'm not convinced this maze was fabricated."

"The humans—"

"I know where the Superiority says they got it," I said, cutting her off. "And most of me believes their story. But I don't think the humans fabricated this. It's too . . ." What? Eerie? Too hauntingly surreal?

It shows me real hallucinations. It's not a fabrication. Not completely.

"I think it must be a corpse," I said. "A delver's corpse, repurposed to train on."

Brade frowned at that. "I don't know if they can even die, Alanik. You're making assumptions."

Maybe she was right. Still, I kept my helmet on as we scouted through the cavern, sticking close together. The moss on those rocks was alive, as best as I could tell from picking at it. What if it released, like, dangerous spores or something? I would have felt a lot more comfortable if Brade would put her helmet back on.

As we reached the far side of the room, I spotted something on the floor. A web of deep green, hidden behind a pile of rocks.

I waved Brade forward and approached the patch. It looked like a spiderweb of green fibers, and was about a meter in diameter, circular.

"You see this?" I asked.

"A membrane," she said. "Made of green fibers."

So it wasn't a hallucination. I knelt, poking at the fibers, then looked at Brade. She didn't seem eager to push through it, and I found that neither was I.

"I was furious," Brade finally said, speaking in a soft voice.

"Huh?" I asked.

"You asked earlier," she said. "What it felt like to be taken from my parents when young. It made me angry."

She knelt, yanking at the spiderweb of fibers, pulling it back and revealing a hole in the ground. It looked to be about two meters deep, and the light on my helmet showed a metal floor at the bottom.

"It seethed inside me for years," Brade continued. "A molten pit, burning like destructor fire." She looked back at me. "That's when I realized the Superiority was right. I *was* dangerous. Very, *very* dangerous."

She met my eyes for a moment, then pulled on her helmet again and activated the channel to call in to Flight Command. "We've found the heart," she said. "Entering now."

She lowered herself down through the opening. I hesitated only a moment, then climbed down after her. My heart began beating faster, but our headlights showed only a small, empty chamber with a very low ceiling.

"Well done," Winzik's voice said in our ears. "Alanik of the UrDail and Brade Shimabukuro, you are the seventh pair to reach this room in the training."

"What happens now?" I asked. "I mean, if we were in a real delver maze? What would we find?"

"We don't know what it will look like," Winzik said. "Nobody has ever returned after entering the membrane. But in the event of a true delver emergency, you must detonate the weapon. The lives of millions may depend on it."

The weapon. We'd been told several times that one existed, though we had been given no details on it. We were assured that if a real delver emergency happened, we'd each be given ships equipped with one of the weapons, which was apparently like some kind of bomb that we were supposed to detonate near the membrane room.

"Great," Brade said to Flight Command. "Now that we've gotten here, I think we're ready. Brade out." She leaped up and pulled herself up from the room through the hole, entering the chamber with the moss.

I followed, turning off the line to Flight Command. "Ready?" I asked her. "Brade, we've only made it to the heart *once*. We need to run this mission many more times."

"To what end?" she asked. "The rooms are starting to repeat; we've seen everything this test maze can show us. We're as prepared as we're going to be."

I caught up to her. "I doubt that. There's always room for more training."

"And if this fake maze makes us grow complacent? The real thing will be unexpected. Insane, or at least beyond our kind of sanity. If we just run through these same rooms, we'll get too comfortable with them. So the more we train, the worse off we could be."

Once we reached our ships, I hesitated, thinking of what she'd said earlier about being angry. Then, after a moment of indecision, I pulled off my helmet. I didn't want to risk my microphone picking up what I was going to say, just in case.

Brade had been about to haul herself onto her ship's wing, but stopped when she saw me. She cocked her head, then pulled off her helmet too. I put mine aside, then gestured for her to do the same.

"What?" she asked.

Again, I nearly told her. I nearly turned off my bracelet, revealed my true face. In this place of lies and shadows, I nearly exposed to her the truth. I wanted so badly to have someone to talk to, someone who might understand.

"What if there were a way to change things?" I said instead. "A way we could make it so humans didn't need to be treated like you are? To show the Superiority they're wrong about you?"

She cocked her head and drew her lips together in a dione sort of expression. "That's the thing," she said. "They *aren't* wrong."

"What was done to you was unnatural, Brade. You were *right* to feel angry about it."

She grabbed her helmet and put it on, then climbed up into her cockpit. I sighed, but did the same. So my helmet was back on when I caught what she said next.

"Flight Command," Brade said. "We've reached the center, so I'm going to test the weapon now."

"Affirmative," Winzik said.

Wait. *What?*

"Brade!" I said, looking across at her cockpit. "I'm not even strapped into my—"

She pushed a button on her console, and a flash burst from the center of her ship. It hit me like an invisible wave, connecting not with my body, but with my mind.

In that moment, I immediately knew the way home.

31

I *knew* the way *home*.

I saw it—the pathway to Detritus—as clearly as I could remember the way to the hidden cavern where I'd found M-Bot. As clearly as I remembered that day when my father had flown for the last time against the Krell.

It was burned into my brain. Like an arrow made from light. I knew, somehow, not just the direction—but the destination. My home. This weapon, the secret one created to fight the delvers, was not what I'd assumed it to be.

"Weapon test successful," Brade said. "If this were a real delver, I am one hundred percent confident this would have diverted them to the human refuge of Detritus."

I heard, in the background, cheers and congratulations. I heard Winzik telling the other government officials that their anti-delver system was operational, and their pilots perfectly trained. He ended with a simple, stunning conclusion. "If a delver *did* ever attack the Superiority, my program ensures that we will be able to send them to destroy the humans instead. We will fight the two greatest threats to the universe by turning them against one another!"

The terrible understanding loomed over me. I threw off my helmet and leaped out of my cockpit, crossing the spongy ground toward Brade's ship. When I arrived, I found her lounging on the wing, her helmet off and beside her.

"You *knew* about this?" I demanded of her.

"Of course I knew," she replied. "Winzik's scientists used my mind to develop the weapon. We've always known that there was a connection between cytonics and the delvers. We cause them pain, Alanik. They hate us, maybe even fear us. We tried for years to exploit this, and came to the logical conclusion. If we can't destroy delvers, we can at least divert them."

"That's not a good solution! At best, it delays a catastrophe! It doesn't stop one!"

"It can if we play this right," Brade said. "We *don't* need to defeat the delvers. We simply need to control them."

"This isn't controlling them!" I snapped. "A single barely tested blast that *might* divert them away? What happens when they come back? What happens *after* they destroy your target, then continue to rampage across the galaxy?"

I was growing so used to the way diones and Krell responded to outbursts like this that a part of me was surprised when Brade just smiled, instead of pulling back and chiding me for my aggression.

"You act as if Winzik hasn't thought about any of that," she said.

"Considering my experiences with him and his military tests, I think I'm allowed to question his foresight!"

"Don't worry, Alanik," Brade said. She nodded toward her ship. "Today's 'test' was a way to show off for the officials back on the *Weights and Measures*. This isn't the first time we've tested the weapon—we've been planning this for years. We know that we can handle a delver."

She slipped off her wing, her boots scraping the mossy rock beneath her as she landed. She stepped closer to me. "This training program and all of these pilots are an insurance policy. Their job will be to use diversionary bombs to shuffle a delver around between locations until the real weapon gets there."

"Which is?"

She pointed at herself. Then she pointed at me. "In joining these flights, you provided us with a gift. Another cytonic. We have so few. Winzik told me to befriend you, recruit you. So here we are."

Recruit me? This whole time, Brade had been trying to recruit *me*? Was that why she'd been warming up to me lately?

Scud, she was as bad at this as I was.

"This is *insane,* Brade," I said. "The humans tried to control the delvers, and look where it got them!"

"We've learned from their mistakes," Brade said. "If you are willing, I can show you things about your powers. Things you never *dreamed* were possible. We *can* control the delvers."

"Are you *sure*?" I asked. "Are you *really* sure?"

She hesitated, and I saw that she wasn't, even though she made a dione gesture of assurance by raising her hand and tapping two of her fingers together.

The chinks in her armor were there. She wasn't nearly as confident as she pretended.

"We should talk about this," I said. "Not be so hasty."

"Maybe," Brade said. "Maybe there isn't time, though." Brade turned back to her ship. "The Superiority is losing its stranglehold on travel. Others are close to figuring out its technology. Something new is needed. Something to keep everyone in line, and prevent wars."

The horror of it hit me. "The delvers. You'll have them looming over everyone—a threat. 'Obey, play along, or we'll send one to your doorstep . . .'"

"Just think about the offer, Alanik." Brade put on her helmet. "We're pretty sure we can handle keeping a delver distracted when it's in our realm. In the past, they'd sometimes spend years between attacks floating in space, doing whatever it is they do. So if our force can be ready when one approaches a populated planet, it should be safe enough—particularly with cytonics like us as a backup. Winzik can explain it better than I can. He's a genius. Anyway, we should get back."

She slid into her cockpit. I stood in stunned silence for a moment longer, trying to wrap my brain around everything she'd told me. Whatever they *said* they'd practiced, whatever assurances they *thought* they had, they were wrong. I'd felt the delvers. Winzik and his team were like children playing with an armed bomb.

But as I walked back to my ship, I had to admit that a small portion of me was tempted. How much did Brade know about my powers? What could she show me? I'd played along with joining the Superiority's military to get access to hyperdrives. Could I play along with this offer to learn what Brade knew?

Too far, I thought as I climbed back into my ship. *No.* I wanted nothing to do with the delvers. Though it was unrealistic, I never wanted to feel their eyes on me again. I never wanted to feel their thoughts intruding on mine, making everything and everyone seem so insignificant.

Whatever Brade and Winzik were up to, I couldn't join it. I had to find a way to stop it.

"Brade," I said as we got back on the comms, "don't you care at all that they're planning to use this to destroy an entire planet of humans? Your people?"

She didn't respond immediately. And when she did, I thought I heard a hesitance to her. "They . . . they deserve it. It's what has to be."

Yes, there were obviously cracks in her confidence. But how could I exploit them?

The two of us flew out of the maze, then headed to join the rest of our flight. However, we got a call from the *Weights and Measures* before we arrived.

"You two," the official said, "Alanik of UrDail and the human. Report in early."

I felt an immediate surge of panic. Was this more of Winzik trying to recruit me, or was it about my spy drone? In the face of the overwhelming discoveries that Brade had dropped on me, I had almost forgotten about my plan and the little robot that was hiding back on the *Weights and Measures*.

I looked out into the stars. I didn't need coordinates to try to judge the direction to Detritus. I could *feel* it out there, the pathway burned into my head. It was fading, like the path to Starsight that Alanik had put in my head, but much more slowly. I felt I'd have this arrow for days at least.

She'd been weak, near death. That was why her coordinates had faded so quickly. This was a more powerful impression.

I could go. I could jump home, right now. I was free.

But M-Bot and Doomslug were back at the embassy. No—I still had a mission here. It wasn't time to leave yet. Not quite.

Winzik can't have discovered the drone, I told myself, shoving down my earlier anxiety. *Why would they call us both back, in that case? Why would they call me back at all? If they suspected me, they'd start shooting, right?*

I then turned my ship toward the *Weights and Measures*, which seemed like a small rock compared to the dominating polyhedral boulder that was the delver maze. As soon as I drew close enough to the carrier, my wristband buzzed, indicating that I'd re-established communication with the drone.

Status? I sent to it, tapping on the bracelet.

Have infiltrated engine room, it sent back. *Am hovering in a corner. Good visibility. Algorithms determine a very low chance of discovery. Continue, or return to meeting point?*

Seen anything interesting?

Not capable of answering that question. But my chronometer indicates I arrived after hyperjump occurred.

I'd want it to stay in place at least until we hyperjumped back to Starsight. That would give me the best chance of capturing sensitive information.

Remain, I sent.

I landed behind Brade in the fighter bays, and handed off my ship to the maintenance crew. I caught up with her as she climbed down from her ship.

"Any idea what this is about?" I asked. "Is it about recruiting me?"

Brade gave a noncommittal swipe of her fingers, a dione gesture.

We were met by a guide drone, which led us away from the fighter bay, down an unfamiliar red-carpeted path through the *Weights and Measures*. Irrationally, I felt like I was being walked to a cell—right up until the moment when we stepped through a set of double doors and entered a party.

Krell and diones in official uniforms or robes stood about, sipping fancy drinks. A large screen on the far wall showed shots of training fighters, alternating with slides of text that explained the philosophy behind our training. From the little bits my translator read to me, it looked like the Department of Protective Services was making great efforts to prove how important their project was.

Indeed, I noted other pilots from other flights standing throughout the room, speaking with officials. I'd been called in to be used for propaganda purposes, it seemed. Soon, Winzik gestured me over to stand by him—though the drone instructed Brade to wait behind.

Winzik was in good spirits, judging by the excited way he waved the arms of his green exoskeleton. "Ah, here she is! The only one of her species on Starsight. And now she serves in my program. Proof that it has merit indeed!"

The two Krell he was speaking to looked me over. "Ah," one said. "Your people once served the humans, did they not? How do you feel at finally being invited to join the Superiority?"

"Honored," I forced myself to say. Scud, did this have to happen today? Now that I wasn't actively fighting, my worry about the spy drone was growing nearly unbearable.

"I'm more interested in your human, Winzik," the other Krell said. "Has she killed anyone by accident?"

"My my, no! She's *very* well trained. Let us focus on my project, Your Honors. A reasonable plan for protecting against the delvers, at long last!"

"That," a voice said from over my shoulder, "and the Superiority's first actively piloted space force in a hundred years. One composed entirely of lesser species, at that."

I spun and found Cuna there behind me. Even in a room of diplomats and politicians, Cuna stood out—tall, with deep blue skin, shrouded in robes such a dark violet they were nearly black.

"It's not completely made up of lesser species," Winzik admitted. "We've got one dione. A draft, strangely."

"Still, an incredible undertaking," Cuna said. "That leaves me wondering at the Department of Protective Services . . . and its ambitions for this force it is training."

I could practically *feel* the tension between Cuna and Winzik. The other officials did the Krell equivalent of clearing their throats—making a crossing gesture—before withdrawing. That left just me, Winzik, and Cuna.

The two didn't speak. They only stared at each other. Finally, Winzik turned around without a word and responded to someone speaking nearby. The cheery Krell walked over and jumped right into that conversation, explaining enthusiastically about his plan to defend against the delvers.

How much does Cuna know? I wondered. *Cuna was the one to invite Alanik here, a cytonic. They must suspect what Winzik is doing, but how much can I trust either of them?*

"I don't know what any of this means," I said to Cuna. "But I'm not interested in your political games."

"Unfortunately, Alanik, the game takes no care for your interest. It plays you either way."

"Did you know about the weapon?" I asked. "Did you know its real purpose? To send the delvers out to attack other planets?"

"I suspected," Cuna said. "Now I have confirmation. There are . . . things I must tell you, but we can't talk here. I will send for you back on Starsight. For once, kindly *respond* to me. There is little time remaining."

They gave me one of their evil smiles—the ones that made me shiver all the way through. Hadn't it been Cuna who told me that the humans had fallen because they tried to weaponize the delvers? What did they think about Winzik and the Superiority trying basically the same thing?

Cuna turned to leave, and I reached for them—intending to demand answers *now*. Unfortunately, I was interrupted by shouting from the side of the room.

"I will *not*," Brade snapped, her voice carrying. "You shouldn't want a picture with a monster anyway." She threw her cup of something colorful at the wall, splashing liquid all over, then stalked out of the room.

Scud! I darted after her, leaving the party behind. Belatedly, the drone that had led us there followed.

I caught up to Brade at the first intersection, where she paused, obviously not knowing which way to go. Several guards nearby eyed us distrustfully—there seemed to be even more security in the hallways than usual, probably because of all the visiting dignitaries.

"What's wrong?" I asked her.

"I'm wrong," she snapped. "And they're all wrong. I'm not some freak to gawk at."

I grimaced. Though I could understand the sentiment, she probably hadn't done much to improve the reputation of humans among that crowd.

"If you'll come this way," the drone operator said. "I've been given permission to lead you to your transport room to wait for the rest of the pilots."

It started off down the hallway and we followed, passing a few windows that looked out at the stars. At times, it was hard for me to remember we were on board a ship, silly as that sounded. The DDF didn't have anything larger than a small troop transport. Ships of this size—with entire ballrooms in them—were completely outside my experience.

I hurried alongside Brade, searching for something to say. "I know of a place," I whispered to her, "where nobody would look at you like a freak. Where nobody would stare."

"Where?" she snapped. "Your homeworld? Alanik, I know about your people. Mine *conquered* them. I wouldn't just be a freak there—I'd be hated."

"No," I said, taking her by the arm—stopping her in the empty hallway. There seemed to be fewer patrols in this section of the ship than there normally were. Some of the guards had been moved up by the ballroom. And our guide drone was pretty far ahead.

"Brade," I whispered. "I can tell you have reservations about this plan."

She didn't respond, but she met my eyes.

"There are . . . things I can't tell you right now," I said. "But I promise you, I can take you somewhere you'll be appreciated. Not hated, not feared. Celebrated. I'll explain soon. I just want you to listen when I do, all right?"

Brade frowned in a very human way. She might have picked up some Krell and dione mannerisms, but she'd been raised—at least as a child—by human parents.

The guide drone called to us, and so I let go of Brade and we hurried to catch up. We passed the hallway leading to Engineering—there was still a guard posted at the intersection, unfortunately—and continued to our jump room.

I stewed for what felt like hours but was probably about half of one—then smelled a distinctive cinnamon scent. "Are you two well?" Vapor asked. "Flight Command said they'd called you back, but wouldn't tell me why. To them, I don't have any real authority."

"We're fine," I said, glancing toward Brade—who had taken her customary seat in the last row, where she sat staring at the wall. "Winzik just wanted to show off some of his pilots."

The kitsen and Morriumur entered a short time later. "Alanik!" Kauri said, flying the platform to me, "you reached the heart!"

"What was it like?" Hesho asked from his throne. "Bright, like a thousand sunrises experienced all at once? Dark, like the gloom of a cavern that has never seen the sky?"

"Neither," I said. "It was an empty room, Hesho. They don't know what's at the center of a real maze, so they couldn't imitate it."

"How disappointing," he said. "That's not poetic at all."

"I heard," Morriumur said, "that the high minister of the Superiority was here today, *in person*. Did you see them?"

"I don't know," I said. "I wouldn't recognize them if I did."

Aya, one of the kitsen gunners, launched into a story about how she'd caught a glimpse of the high minister when touring Starsight. Hesho looked pointedly unimpressed—but, well, he *had* been a king, so maybe high ministers were boring to him.

I was content to let the others talk, settling down in my seat and tapping covertly on my bracelet. *Status?*

Waiting and observing, the drone sent. *There is movement of personnel. Based on dialogue, I believe we will soon hyperjump.*

Right. It was time, then. I just had to hope that the drone would be able to record something. I sank down into myself, pretended I was flying. I immediately saw the path home, but turned away from that. Not now. Not yet.

I tried to reach toward this ship, the *Weights and Measures.* I tried to "hear" what was being said on board . . . It shouldn't work. There was no reason for them to use cytonic communication to talk to other places on board the ship. And yet, voices from Engineering popped into my head.

It felt like . . . someone was relaying them to me? Like someone was hearing them, then projecting them.

All pilots are on board and personnel secured, Winzik's voice said. *Engineering, you may proceed with the hyperjump back to Starsight regional space.*

Understood, an engineer said back. I could even hear the dione accent. *Preparing for hyperjump.*

Near them. Near them was a *mind.* Not a person though, something else. It was relaying these words. Maybe . . . maybe I could help make certain the drone had something to record. My presence here on the ship had interfered before with the hyperjumps. Could I make that happen on purpose? Force the crew to swap hyperdrives?

I pressed softly against the mind I'd found. I heard a sharp cry.

Hyperdrive malfunction, Engineering said. *Bridge, we have another hyperdrive malfunction. It's those cytonics on board. They're creating an unconscious interference with the hyperdrives.*

Try a replacement? the bridge said.

Loading one now. Can we do something about this? It causes so much paperwork . . .

I snapped back to myself. Whatever they did worked, for we soon entered the nowhere again. Another scream. Another lurch as I was cast into that place of darkness punctured by the delver eyes. As usual, they had turned from us, and were looking toward the sound of the scream.

Was this how the diversionary bomb worked? Superiority hyperdrives could distract the delvers, divert their attention. Perhaps the Superiority had advanced this technology to create the device that Brade had activated.

I studied the delvers—who, more and more, were looking like tunnels of white light.

A prickling sensation washed through me. I knew, without needing to look, that I'd been seen. One of the delvers, perhaps the same one as last time, wasn't distracted by the scream.

I turned and found it right beside me. I could feel its emotions. Hateful, dismissive, *angry*. Sensations washed through me, and I gasped. To the delver, life in my universe was nothing more than a bunch of angry gnats. Somehow, it knew I was more. It loomed over me, surrounding me, overwhelming me.

I was going to die. I was going to—

I slammed back into my seat on the *Weights and Measures*. Aya was still telling her story to a rapt audience.

I curled up on my seat, sweating, rattled. I'd never felt so small. So *alone*.

I trembled, trying to banish the unexpected emotion. I couldn't tell if it belonged to me or was a side effect of having seen that delver. But loneliness swallowed me.

It was even worse than when I'd been on Detritus, training. Living in my little cave, sleeping in a cockpit while the rest of my flight ate and laughed together. Then, at least, I'd had an enemy to fight. Then, I'd had the support and friendship of the others, even if I was forced to scavenge for food.

Here I sat in an enemy battleship, surrounded by people I'd

been lying to. I thought of Hesho and Morriumur as my friends, but they would kill me in a heartbeat if they knew what I was.

Status update, the drone suddenly sent, the words tapping out on my wrist. *It is probable I have been detected.*

A set of warning alarms suddenly rang through the ship. Aya the kitsen cut off, and the rest of my flight stood up, shocked by the sudden sound.

What? I typed to the drone. *Explain!*

Before I could exit the engine room, I tripped some sort of alarm, the drone sent. *Multiple engineers search. I have not escaped into the hallway. I will soon be discovered.*

Scud! Though we'd tried to remove any identifying features on the drone parts, M-Bot had little doubt that the device—if detected—could be traced back to Alanik.

Scudscudscudscudscud.

Orders? the drone sent to me.

A plan popped into my mind. A terrible plan, but it was the only thing I could come up with while under so much pressure.

Able to reach destructor pistol strapped to you?

Yes. Service arms can reach weapon.

Turn off safety, I sent. *Remove tape. Hold pistol in front of you. Start pulling trigger.*

32

I expected an argument. M-Bot would have argued, but this drone wasn't him. It wasn't a true AI, and so could follow my instructions without thinking of the implications.

We felt the series of blasts, small though they were, from our room. The other pilots began to murmur nervously.

Keep shooting, I sent to the drone. *Avoid being destroyed.*

Affirmative.

The warning sirens turned frantic, and a voice piped over the PA, reverberating outside our jump room as well. "There are hostile forces in Engineering! Number unknown, but they're firing!"

Another set of blasts sounded from nearby. *Here we go,* I thought. "We're under attack!" I shouted to the other pilots. I leaped from my seat, swinging my pack onto my shoulder. "We need to go help!" I said, throwing open the door, and scrambled out into the hallway.

Though Morriumur sat stunned in their seat, Hesho needed no other confirmation. He shouted, "Kitsen! To arms!"

A swarm of furry little warriors on hoverplatforms zipped out into the hallway to join me.

"Wait!" Vapor's voice said from the room. "I'm sure that the local guards can handle this!"

I ignored her, barreling down the hallway. As I'd hoped, the solitary guard at the intersection to Engineering had taken cover by the wall, and was calling on her comm for backup. The Krell talked tough, but the truth was, this ship's crew had probably never been in combat before.

"I can help," I said to the guard. "But I'll need a gun."

Another series of blasts sounded from down the hallway. The Krell guard looked toward them, then back at me. "I can't . . . I mean . . ."

A part of me was really satisfied to see how her tough persona fell away once the shooting started. I waved my hand impatiently, and the guard took out her sidearm—a small destructor pistol—and handed it to me. Then she raised her larger rifle and nodded.

"Hesho, guard this hallway," I said. "Don't let anything suspicious escape through it!"

"Order confirmed!" Hesho said, and the kitsen platforms formed up like a wall behind us.

The Krell guard, to her credit, stood up and started down the hallway. She made a sharp cutting motion with her fingers—a kind of Krell version of *Here we go.* Then we passed beneath the large sign on the wall proclaiming that we'd entered Engineering.

I'd spent weeks trying to figure out a way to get down here, and I followed the guard with a rising sense of excitement. We turned down another hallway, and I was hit with the scent of lemons. Maybe a cleaning crew had been through recently? On the wall was a sign: NO NONESSENTIAL PERSONNEL ALLOWED. SECURITY CLEARANCE 1-B REQUIRED.

The blasts were coming from a door a little farther down, but the guard stopped and turned to me.

"You aren't allowed in the room," she told me. "It's against clearance rules."

"Is that more important than protecting the engineering crew?"

The guard actually gave it some thought, then said, "We should wait. Security details are up on deck four for special duty, but they should be here soon. All we need to do is make sure that whoever is in there doesn't escape."

I tried to go ahead, but the guard gave me a firm gesture of forbiddance, palm out, so I settled down by the wall, holding my pistol. I set my pack on the ground. My mind was racing. How did I get the drone out of this? Any second now, this hall would flood with security guards.

Status? I asked the drone, tapping covertly on my bracelet.

Scientists hide, the drone said. *None return fire.*

I scanned the hallway. *On my mark, fly out into hall. Fire two shots up high, and don't hit anyone. Then drop gun.*

Affirmative.

Backpack is by wall. Quickly hide inside after dropping gun.

Instructions understood.

Right. I took a deep breath, then sent, *Go.*

Immediately, the drone—visible only as a shimmer in the air—floated out into the hallway. It fired the destructor overhead, sending the guard to the ground with a cry of fear.

"It's coming for us!" I shouted. Then—right as the drone dropped the gun—I fired.

I'd done some time in the firing ranges, but had never thought that so much would ride on being able to hit a moving target with a pistol. My first three shots missed, but I managed to hit the gun right before it hit the ground.

The subsequent explosion was impressively large, sending out sparks and molten bits of metal. My shot detonated the pistol's power supply. As the loud explosion washed over us, light flashing and blinding me, I dove for the Krell guard as if to shield her from the blast.

The two of us ended up in a pile on the floor. I blinked, trying to dispel the spots the bright flash had caused in my vision. Judging by how stunned the guard looked, she had suffered something similar.

Eventually, she shoved me off and scrambled to her feet. "What happened!"

"A drone," I said, pointing toward a scorched portion of the carpet. "I shot it down."

There was no sign of the drone itself, but the destroyed pistol had left scattered debris. Klaxons continued to go off, but the absence of further shots made the guard cautiously creep forward and inspect the burned ground.

"Get back to your transport room," she said.

I was all too happy to do so, snatching up my backpack—which I was relieved to find heavy with the weight of the drone.

The guard peeked into the engine room to check on those inside, then thought to call to me, "Leave the gun!"

I dropped the pistol by the wall, then met up with Hesho right as a troop of six guards tromped past. One of them, a dione, hollered for us to get back into our room—but fortunately, we didn't look too suspicious. Other pilots had gathered out in the hallway, confused by the warnings.

We scrambled into our seats, me clutching the backpack with my contraband drone inside. I peeked into it, and was shocked to see the drone. Shouldn't it be invisible?

I quickly zipped the pack up and tapped to it: *Engage lunch hologram. Version two, empty container.*

Holographic unit offline, it tapped back. *Explosion damaged system.*

Sweat trickled down the sides of my face. I was exposed. If guards demanded to inspect my bag . . .

Eventually, the warning klaxons turned off, and I felt the *Weights and Measures* dock at Starsight. My trepidation only grew. Could I find a way to stow the drone, for now, on the ship? Come back for it later?

There wasn't even a chance—we were ordered to make our way to the shuttle bay. I walked among a huddle of nervous pilots, noting the numerous guards in the hallways. I searched frantically for a way out, and remembered the second identity that M-Bot had programmed into my bracelet. The nondescript dione hologram.

Could I use that now, somehow? It seemed unlikely. A mysterious dione appearing in my place would be just as suspicious. So, I slunk along, sure each step of the way that the hammer was going to fall on me. I was so focused on that, I didn't notice the irregularity until I was almost at the shuttle bay.

Vapor. I couldn't smell her, and the other pilots didn't leave an opening for her like they normally did. I entered the docking bay and waited, trying to see if I could smell her.

A second later, she wafted across me. A sharp smell of . . . lemons. The same scent I'd smelled earlier, in the hallway outside of Engineering.

She was there. In the hallway. I pulled my pack closer.

"Vapor?" I asked.

"Come with me," her voice snapped. *"Now."*

I winced, and—in a panic—reached out with my mind. Maybe I could hyperjump away, then find some way to come back for . . .

No, the directions to Detritus in my mind would end up with me floating out in orbit with no space suit, I was suddenly sure. I was trapped.

"Vapor," I said. "I—"

"Now, Alanik."

I followed her scent through the room, which was actually easier than it might sound. Just as I'd worried, the guards were searching each pilot before they got onto their shuttles. An obvious precaution when a drone had been found spying here.

I pulled my pack closer, sweating as I trailed behind Vapor's sharp lemon scent. We approached a sleek-looking shuttle. The door opened.

Cuna, shrouded in dark robes, sat inside.

"Alanik," they said. "I believe we have some matters to discuss."

I glanced back at the rest of my flight. They were all getting in line to be searched. Morriumur had turned toward me, head cocked. Other guards were approaching me, one pointing.

I only had one option. I climbed into the shuttle with Cuna.

33

I clutched the pack to my chest as the door closed, and I was struck again by the overwhelming scent of lemons, which then shifted slowly to cinnamon. The two guards made it to the door, and one rapped on the shuttle window. Cuna pressed a button on a control panel, and the window descended.

"Minister Cuna?" one asked. "We're supposed to search everyone."

"I doubt those orders include heads of departments, soldier," Cuna said, then hit the button again, closing the window. They gestured to the pilot.

The shuttle took off, then left the bay, flying toward the city proper. The moment we got outside of the *Weights and Measures,* a chipper voice spoke in my ear.

"Spensa?" M-Bot said. "How did it go? Did the drone work? I can sense its signal with you. You recovered it?"

I tapped out on my bracelet, *Not now.*

Cuna laced their fingers, then finally made a relieved gesture with two of them. "No call to return," they said. "We're in luck.

My authority was enough to not be questioned." Then they held out their hand, waving for me to surrender the pack.

I refused, pulling it closer.

"Vapor?" Cuna asked.

"It's a drone," said the familiar disembodied voice. "She was actually quite clever in how she retrieved it, as she shot off its weapon first. It will be days before anyone puts together that the remaining debris only includes pieces of a destructor pistol."

I tried glaring at Vapor, which was hard because I didn't exactly know where she was.

Cuna reached into their pocket and unfolded a sheet of paper. They held it out to me—and I narrowed my eyes, regarding it with suspicion. Finally, I took one careful hand off my pack and accepted the paper.

"What does it say?" M-Bot asked. "Spensa, I'm having trouble following this conversation."

I didn't dare respond to him as I pulled off my pin and held it to the paper, getting a translation. It was . . . a list of communications? The short messages were dated in order, starting about a week ago.

1001.17: Minister Cuna, while we respect your willingness to communicate—and acknowledge the relative strength of the Superiority—we cannot release private information about our messenger.

1001.23: After continued analysis of the brief messages sent to us via our emissary, Alanik, we of the Unity of UrDail are concerned for her safety. We have no plans to send further pilots to you.

1001.28: After continued suspicion concerning our messenger's safety, we must cut off communication with you and the Superiority until such time as she returns to us.

A cold chill ran down my spine. Cuna was in communication with the people on Alanik's home planet. M-Bot and I had talked to them a few times after our first message, trying to play for time.

It looked like they'd decided to step away from the problem entirely by ignoring us both.

"Your people are obviously stalling for you," Cuna said. "I can see it clearly now. The UrDail never intended to join the Superiority, did they? You are a spy, sent here *exclusively* to steal hyperdrive technology."

It took a moment for that to sink in.

Cuna didn't know I was human.

They thought I was a spy for Alanik's people. And scud, it sure did look like that, from Cuna's perspective.

"What I can't figure out," Cuna said, "is why you would risk so much, considering that you already *obviously* know the secret. Clearly, your people know not just how to use a cytonic like you as a hyperdrive, but have created a secondary method. The same one we use."

What? I opened my mouth to say I had no idea what Cuna was talking about, but then—for once in my life—thought before I spoke. For some reason, Cuna thought I already had the secret. So . . . why not play along? I might not have trained for this, but I was the one who was here. And my people needed me to be more than I'd been before.

"We couldn't be sure that your methods were the same as ours," I said. "We thought it worth the risk, particularly once we realized I would have a chance to infiltrate Superiority warships and secret projects."

"You have been playing me all along," Cuna said. "You now know about the weapon, the location of our training maze . . . the infighting among our departments. I would be impressed if I weren't so angry."

The wisest choice on my part seemed to be silence. Outside the window, we passed into a part of town with grand buildings, built with domes and large gardens. The government quarter? I was pretty sure that was where we were.

The shuttle landed beside a large rectangular building—one with few windows. More austere and grim than the others nearby.

Cuna held out their hand again toward my pack. I realized that I didn't have much choice. I was unarmed and in their power. The only thing I had going for me was the fact that Cuna, remarkably, thought that *I knew what I was doing.*

I held up the pack. "I don't need it anymore," I said. "This conversation was confirmation enough."

Cuna took it anyway, then fished out the drone and looked it over. "One of our own," they said. "A modified cleaning drone? These are impressive security devices attached to it. I didn't know your people had access to this kind of technology."

Cuna looked toward the place where Vapor hung.

"That looks like figment technology," Vapor said softly. "The kind that was forbidden us after the war. I've . . . seen old ships with those markings on them."

Figment technology? *M-Bot?* I said nothing—though my heart skipped a beat when Cuna fished in the shuttle armrest for a cord, then connected the drone's memory to a monitor on the back of the seat in front of us.

Trying to keep my voice calm, I spoke. "Drone, authorize playback of video starting from the moment I turned you on."

"Confirmed," the drone said.

"AI?" Cuna asked, baring their teeth in a look of shock.

"Not self-aware AI," I said quickly. "Just a basic program that can follow orders."

"Still! So dangerous."

The screen turned on, displaying a view of me, wearing Alanik's face, in the stall of the bathroom.

"Fast forward," I said, "until two minutes before the hyper-jump back to Starsight."

"Confirmed."

I waited, hands clenching, as the view changed to what had

to be the engine room. It looked surprisingly like an office—no hyperdrive apparatus that I could spot, only chairs and monitors with diones in uniforms working them.

I eyed Cuna. Were they really just going to let this play? My heartbeat increased as audio sounded from the recording.

"All pilots are on board and personnel secured," Winzik's voice said over the room's PA. "Engineering, you may proceed with the hyperjump back to Starsight regional space."

"Understood," said one of the diones on the screen. A crimson, somewhat chubby individual. "Preparing for hyperjump."

They hit a button. Nothing happened. Elsewhere, at that moment, I had been straining to use my cytonic senses to interfere. It was surreal, watching what had been happening a few rooms over from where I'd been waiting.

Several of the diones looked agitated, speaking softly to one another. The chubby one hit the comm button. "Bridge, we have another hyperdrive malfunction. It's those cytonics on board. They're creating an unconscious interference with the hyperdrives."

Another dione got up and walked to the wall. They opened a hatch there and pulled something out. I leaned forward, my breath catching as I saw what they removed.

A metal cage, and inside of it, a bright yellow slug with blue spines.

34

A slug. Scud. SCUD.

It made so much sense. The entry about Doomslug's species on the datanet . . . it had said they were dangerous. That was a lie—the Superiority just wanted to make certain that if anyone saw one, they'd think it venomous and stay away.

Report any sightings to authorities immediately.

"Try a replacement?" a voice said on the recording.

"Spensa?" M-Bot said in my ear. "What is going on?"

"Loading one now. Can we do something about this? It causes so much paperwork."

The diones removed the "hyperdrive" from a unit beside the wall. It was another slug, just like Doomslug. They slid the new one in and activated the hyperdrive. This time it worked.

I could almost hear that scream in my mind again. The high-pitched wail . . . The scream of the hyperdrive. Made by the creatures they were using to teleport.

"Drone, end video," I whispered. I'd been expecting something horrific, like the surgically removed brains of cytonics. But . . . why should sapient beings be the only ones to have these powers?

Didn't it make sense that some other creatures might develop a means of teleporting through the nowhere?

I thought of all the times I'd found Doomslug in places where I didn't expect her—all the times I'd noted in passing that I rarely saw her move, but that she always seemed to be able to go places quickly when I wasn't looking.

Then, one final understanding came crashing down on me. A seemingly simple phrase from the datanet entry. *Often found near species of fungi.*

M-Bot. When he had awoken, one of the only things he'd had in his data banks was an open table for cataloging local types of mushrooms. He'd fixated on it, knowing it was important, but not why.

His pilot had been looking for hyperdrive slugs.

"How?" I asked Cuna, trying to cover up my shock at all this. "How did you know I had a hyperdrive slug?"

"I followed you," Vapor said, making me jump. I *still* sometimes forgot she was around. "When you went out with Morriumur that day in the water garden."

Doomslug had met me at the door that day. Scud, she'd been acting so strange and lethargic since we'd arrived. Was that because Starsight's cytonic inhibitors interfered with her powers?

Cuna unplugged the drone, then placed it back into my pack. Then they laced their fingers, watching me with a thoughtful alien expression. "This causes problems," they said. "Beyond anything you likely understand. I had hopes . . ." They made a dismissive gesture, then opened the door to the shuttle. "Come."

"Where?" I said, suspicious.

"I want to show you exactly what the Superiority is, Alanik," Cuna said, taking my backpack and climbing out.

I didn't trust that dark expression, marked by a creepy smile. I waited behind, smelling cinnamon.

"You can trust them, Alanik," Vapor told me.

"Of course you'd say that," I replied. "But can I trust you?"

"I haven't told anyone what you really are, have I?" she whispered.

I looked sharply toward the empty space where she resided. Finally, feeling overwhelmed, I climbed out.

"Cuna," Vapor said loudly from behind me, "do you need me any longer?"

"No. You can return to your main mission."

"Affirmative," she said, and the shuttle door closed.

Cuna started toward the building without waiting to see if I'd follow. Why turn their back on me? What if I were dangerous? I hurried up beside them.

"I wasn't Vapor's main mission?" I asked, nodding back toward the shuttle as it took off.

"You were a stroke of luck," Cuna said. "She's actually there to watch Winzik." Cuna reached the door, which had a window and a security guard inside. They nodded to Cuna, but then bared their teeth in a dione scowl at me.

"I bring this one with me, by my authority," Cuna said.

"I'll need to note it, Minister. It's very unusual."

Cuna waited for them to do some paperwork. I took the chance to tap a short message on my bracelet. *M-Bot. Still read me?*

"Yes," he said in my ear. "But I'm *very* confused."

Doomslug is hyperdrive. If I die, get to Detritus. Tell them.

"What?" M-Bot said. "Spensa, I can't do that!"

Heroes don't choose their trials.

"I can't even fly myself, let alone hyperjump!"

Slug is hyperdrive.

"But . . ."

The guard finally opened the door. I stepped into the building after Cuna, and—as I'd worried from its fortresslike exterior—it had shielding to prevent spying, so M-Bot's voice vanished.

The hallway inside was empty of people, and Cuna's footwear

clicked on the floor as we walked to a door marked OBSERVATION ROOM. Inside was a small chamber with a glass wall overlooking a larger room, two stories tall, with metal walls. I stepped up to the window, noting the markings on several of the walls.

That strange language, I thought. *The same one I saw in the delver maze—and in the tunnels back on Detritus.*

Cuna settled down in a chair near the glass window, placing my backpack beside the seat. I remained standing.

"You have the power to destroy us," Cuna said softly. "Winzik worries about delvers, politicians argue about pockets of aggressive aliens, but I have always worried about a danger more nefarious. Our own shortsightedness."

I frowned, looking at them.

"We couldn't keep the secret of the hyperdrive forever," Cuna said. "In truth, it shouldn't have outlasted the human wars. We endured a dozen close calls when the secret started to leak. Our stranglehold on interstellar communication was always enough, just barely, to keep the truth contained."

"You won't keep this secret much longer," I said. "It's *going* to get out."

"I know," Cuna said. "Haven't you been listening?" They nodded toward the window.

A set of doors down below opened, and a pair of diones entered, pulling someone by the arms. I . . . I *recognized* them. It was Gul'zah the burl—the gorilla alien who had been kicked out of the pilot program way back after the test, then had been protesting against the Superiority.

"I heard that the Superiority made a deal with the protesters!" I said.

"Winzik was called in to handle the issue," Cuna replied. "His department has been gaining too much authority. He claims to have negotiated a deal where the dissidents turned over their leader. I can't track any longer how much of what he says is true and how much is false."

Those diones, I thought, noting the brown-striped clothing they wore. *I saw some like them cleaning up after the protesters vanished.*

"This burl has been in custody since then," Cuna said, nodding to Gul'zah. "Some fear that the incident on the *Weights and Measures* today was caused by revolutionaries. So the exile has been moved up. And I have little doubt that Winzik will seek other ways to use your attack on us to further his goals."

Below, one of the dione technicians typed on a console at the side of the room. The center of the room shimmered, and then something appeared—a black sphere the size of a person's head. It seemed to suck all light into it as it floated there. It was pure darkness. An absolute blackness that I knew intimately.

The nowhere. Somehow, they had opened up a hole into the nowhere.

The kitsen had mentioned to me that the Superiority—and the human empires as well—had mined acclivity stone from the nowhere. I knew they had portals into the place. But still, seeing that dark sphere affected me on a primal level. That was a darkness that should not exist, a darkness beyond the mere lack of light. A wrongness.

They lived in there.

I suspected what would come next, but was still horrified when it happened. The guards took the struggling prisoner and forced their face to touch the dark sphere. The protester began to stretch, then was absorbed into the darkness.

The technician collapsed the sphere. As everyone left, I spun on Cuna. "Why?" I demanded. "Why show me this?"

"Because," Cuna said, "before your stunt today, you were my best hope at stopping this abomination."

"You seriously expect me to believe that a *Superiority official* cares what happens to 'lesser species'?" I spat the words, perhaps too fervently. I should have been political, kept my emotions in check, tried to get Cuna to talk.

But I was mad. *Furious.* I'd just been forced to watch an exile, maybe even an execution. I was mad at myself for getting caught, frustrated to finally know the secret to hyperdrives—to be so close to bringing the secret back to my people—only to be *threatened* by Cuna. That was why they'd brought me here, of course. To warn me what awaited me if I didn't obey.

Cuna stood up. I was short compared to average humans, so Cuna towered over me as they walked to the glass, then rested a blue hand against it. "You think of us as being of one mind," they said. "Which is the exact flaw held by many in the Superiority itself. Presumption.

"You may choose not to believe it, Alanik, but my entire *purpose* has been to change the way my people view other species. Once the secret of hyperdrives escapes our grasp, we will need something new to keep us together. We won't be able to rely on our monopoly on travel. We need to be able to offer something else."

Cuna turned toward me and smiled. That same creepy, off-putting smile. This time it struck me, and I realized something.

Had I ever seen any other diones *try* to smile?

It wasn't a dione expression. They pulled their lips tight into a line to express joy, and they bared their teeth to express dislike. They gestured with their hands sometimes, like the Krell. I couldn't think of any of the others, Morriumur included, ever smiling.

"You smile," I said.

"Isn't this facial expression a sign of friendship among your people?" Cuna asked. "I've noticed you have similar expressions to humans. I've practiced for the day when I get to speak with them and offer a hand of peace. I thought the same expressions might work on you."

They smiled again, and this time I saw something new in it. Not a creepiness, but an unfamiliarity. What I had interpreted as a sign of smugness had been an attempt to put me at ease. A failed attempt, but the only sign I could remember—in my entire time here—of a dione *trying* to use one of our expressions.

Saints and stars . . . I'd built my entire gut response to this person on the fact that they *couldn't smile right*.

"Winzik and I conceived the Delver Resistance Project together, but with very different motives," Cuna said. "He saw a way to get access to a true, actively piloted starfighter corps again. I saw something different. I saw a force of lesser species serving the Superiority—*protecting* it.

"Perhaps it is foolish imagining, but I saw in my mind's eye the day when a delver might come—and a person like you, or the kitsen, or some other species saved us. I saw a change in my people, a moment when they began to realize that some aggression is useful. That the different ways species act is a *strength* of our union, not a flaw in it. And so, I encouraged you to join us."

They waved at the room that had held the black portal. "The Superiority is deceptively weak. We exile that which doesn't match our ideal of nonaggression. We encourage species to be more and more like us before they can join, and there *are* good ideals among our people. Peace, prosperity for all. But at the cost of individuality? *That* we must find a way to change."

They rested their fingers on the window again. "We have grown complacent, timid. I fear that a little aggression, a little strife, might be exactly what we need. Or else . . . or else we will fall to the first wolf that sneaks past the gates."

I believed them. Scud, I *believed* Cuna was sincere. But could I trust my own assessment? The fact that I'd so grossly misread their expressions reinforced this idea. I was among *aliens*. They were people, with real love and emotions, but they also—by definition—wouldn't do things the same way humans did.

Who could I trust? Cuna, Vapor, Morriumur, Hesho? Did I know enough to trust any of them? It felt like a person could spend a lifetime studying other species and still get this sort of thing wrong. Indeed, Cuna's attempts at smiling were proof of that exact idea.

And still, I found myself reaching over and pushing back my sleeve. I undid the little latch on my bracelet that kept me from pushing the button accidentally.

Then—taking a deep breath—I deactivated my hologram.

35

Cuna's eyes bulged practically out of their head as they stared at me. Then they bared their teeth, shying back. "What?" they demanded. "What is this?"

"I was never Alanik," I said. "I took her place after she crashed on my planet." Then I stuck out my hand. "My name is Spensa. You said you were waiting to hold out your hand to a human, in peace. Well . . . here I am."

It might have been the craziest thing I'd ever done. Honestly, I'm not sure I could explain why I did it. I'd *just* realized that I couldn't necessarily trust my gut when it came to aliens—their habits, expressions, and mannerisms wouldn't match my expectations.

This was different though. This wasn't me reacting by instinct to something an alien did. This was a *choice*. If there was even a chance that Cuna was sincere, it could mean an end to the war. It could mean safety for my people.

I wasn't certain if this was what the heroes from Gran-Gran's stories would have done. But it was what *I* did. In that moment. Taking that risk.

Accepting that hope.

Cuna—though they leaned back at the same time—took my hand in theirs. I guessed that part of them reviled the idea of touching me. Still, they *did* force themself to do it. Cuna might use terms like *lesser species,* but I believed that they were sincerely trying.

They looked at me closer, still holding on to my hand. "How? I don't understand."

"Holograms," I said. "A portable one in my bracelet."

"We don't have technology to create a projector so small!" Cuna said. "But it was rumored that . . . that the humans did, during the first war. During their alliance with the figments. Amazing. The communications from Alanik's home planet . . . Do they know about you?"

"I told them, but I don't know that they believe me. I've mostly been stalling them."

"Amazing," Cuna repeated. "You mustn't show anyone else! It could be a disaster." They pulled their hand back and—it seemed unconsciously—wiped it on their robes. I tried not to be offended.

"You are from the shell planet?" Cuna asked. "With the defensive platforms?"

"Detritus," I said. "Yeah."

"I fought for you until I was hoarse," Cuna said. "In the closed senate meetings, when there were arguments for extermination. I didn't believe . . . You're standing here, *talking* to me? Amazing! You've been on Starsight for weeks! Have you . . . um, have you . . . killed anyone? By accident, I mean?"

"No," I said. "We're really not like that. Mostly, I've spent my time here trying to figure out which of the seventeen restrooms I'm supposed to use. Do you know how confusing that can be without some instructions?"

Cuna drew their lips to a line. I smiled back.

They walked around me. "Truly spectacular. We have watched you all these years, but know so little. The interference those platforms cause, you see. Still . . . we blasted you into what was practically a stone age, and less than a century later you already have hyperdrives again. I'm not sure whether to be impressed or intimidated."

"Right now, let's call it a draw," I said. I touched my bracelet, turning my hologram back on so I looked like Alanik again. "Cuna, Winzik is crazier than you think. Brade told me some of his plans—they're trying to recruit Alanik to join some kind of secret cytonic group they have. They think they can control the delvers."

"Surely you exaggerate," Cuna said. "The program we've developed uses a weapon to distract delvers. Our analysis proves that if they go too long in our realm without consuming a planet, they eventually fade. What we will try to do is not so much control them as keep them distracted from population centers long enough that they leave us."

"Yeah, well, there's more," I said. "You're not the only one worried about the Superiority losing control once everyone knows about hyperdrive slugs. Winzik plans to use the threat of a delver attack to keep everyone in line."

Cuna bared their teeth. "If this is true," they said, "then I have a great deal more work to do. But you needn't worry. Our program is just in the beginning stages. I will search for the truth, and move to counter Winzik's political aspirations. He is not so powerful yet that he cannot be stopped."

"All right. I'll see what I can do to get the 'human scourge' to back down."

"I can't let you take that drone."

"At least let me take the sensor unit I installed," I said. "My ship needs that." I looked to Cuna. "Please, let me go, Cuna. I'll fly back to Detritus and persuade my people that someone among the Krell is willing to talk about peace. I think they'll listen. What would happen to Winzik's power if suddenly his department wasn't needed? What if the human scourge became an ally to the Superiority, instead of an enemy?"

"There is a long way to go for that to happen," Cuna said. "But . . . yes, I can imagine it. A deal then, between you and me." Cuna hesitated, then put their hand out toward me again. "Or, a deal to perhaps make a deal."

I took it. Then I pulled my lips to a line. Cuna, in turn, smiled. Well, it was kind of a smile. A worthy effort, anyway.

I retrieved the sensor and hologram unit I'd attached to the drone and put them in my flight suit pockets, but left the drone itself in the backpack. Cuna led me to the door, and I tried not to think about the poor alien who had been exiled. I couldn't let myself feel responsible for what had happened to them. I just had to do what I could.

What would happen if we really did make peace? Would that mean no more need for starfighters? I found that difficult to believe—the delvers were still out there, right? There would be battles. There were always battles.

It still felt a little odd to have *me*, of all people, be the one who took the first steps toward peace.

"I can take you by shuttle to your embassy," Cuna said, walking me through the security door to the open air. "Then I can fill out the proper paperwork, indicating that 'Alanik' is returning to her people. I don't know how we'll make this work after that, but . . ."

Cuna trailed off as a military shuttle—it looked like the same one we'd flown there in—zipped down out of the air and landed with a hasty thump right in the middle of the grass, ignoring the farther launchpad. The door slammed open, but no one was inside.

I immediately smelled cinnamon.

"Hurry!" Vapor's voice said. "Alanik, we've been mobilized."

"What?" I demanded. "Mobilized how?"

"Our flight is being sent into battle. I think a delver has been spotted."

36

Our shuttle raced through the sky above Starsight, flying at an emergency altitude beneath the rest of the traffic.

"Vapor," I said, "I don't know if this is relevant to me any longer."

"The possible appearance of a galaxy-wide threat isn't relevant?" she asked.

"Do we *know* that is what happened?" I asked.

"Here, watch," Vapor said, smelling floral at the moment.

She activated the monitor on the back of the seat in front of us. It played the emergency message—one sent by Winzik himself. "Pilots," he said, using the most firm of hand gestures—both hands made as fists. "An enemy threatens Starsight. This is *not* a drill. I realize your training has been brief, but the need is dire. Report to the *Weights and Measures* for immediate deployment."

"He doesn't say it's a delver," I said. "It smells of politics."

"Actually, that's what I'm afraid of," Vapor said.

"Listen," I said. "Vapor, I showed myself to Cuna. My real self. The two of us decided to find a way to make peace between our peoples. I think that might be more important than whatever is happening here with Winzik."

Vapor's scent changed to something more akin to onions. "We're already at peace with your people. Why would you and Cuna have to agree to that?"

"My *real* people. You said you know what I am. A . . . a human."

"Yes," Vapor said. "I put it together. Your planet, ReDawn. You've been hiding a human enclave there, haven't you? They never really evacuated, but remained hidden among you. *That's* why you never joined the Superiority. You've been worried we'd find out about the humans."

Ooooohhhh, I thought. That was actually a reasonable guess. Utterly wrong, but more reasonable than the truth was, in many ways.

"I wondered why you used so many human expressions and mannerisms," Vapor continued. "More than I thought was natural for your people's supposed past. And your scent . . . you're part human, aren't you, Alanik? A species mix? That explains your cytonics. Humans always were very talented in that regard."

"The reality is . . . a little less complicated than you think," I said to Vapor. "Ask Cuna. But Vapor, I need to get back to my ship."

"Alanik," Vapor said, her scent going to something more like rain. "I need you right now. I've been assigned to watch Winzik, and I don't think even Cuna is aware of how ambitious he is. You're the best pilot I have, and I need you to be ready to join me. In case."

". . . In case what?"

"In case this isn't about a delver. Let's just say there are elements in the government who are *very* worried about Winzik's growing power—and his access to pilots who don't share core Superiority values."

Again, I was caught in the middle of something I barely understood. *She's worried about a coup, isn't she? That's why she was assigned to become a pilot—to make sure Winzik isn't trying to seize control of the Superiority.*

Where did that leave me? I had the secret. I needed to get home with it. Nothing else mattered, did it?

I used my bracelet to open a communication to M-Bot, who should be able to hear me now that I was out of the governmental building. My reply was a quiet sound transferred via my earpiece.

Click. Clickclickclickclick . . .

Our shuttle tore along the docks, joining others that were swarming the *Weights and Measures*. We disembarked to an organized chaos as excited pilots climbed from shuttles and were ushered through the hallways.

I found Hesho and the kitsen hovering over the heads of the other pilots, looking agitated. "Hey!" I called to them as I passed.

Hesho zoomed in near my head. "Alanik," he said. "What *is* this?"

"You know as much as I do," I said, then bit off what I was going to say next. That was a lie. I knew *way* more than Hesho did. I always had.

Well, for the moment I agreed with Vapor. I needed to at least find out what Winzik was planning, as it might be relevant to the future of my people. We fell in with the other pilots. The other flights had lost a few people in training, so we were maybe forty-five instead of our initial fifty-two.

In their excitement, it seemed like far more. The guide drones led us out of the shuttle hangar. We weren't taken to our normal jump rooms, but directly to the hangar with our fighters—which were quickly being prepped by ground crews.

Vapor swore softly. With our starfighters being prepped like this, it seemed increasingly likely that Winzik was going to use them against Starsight itself. Had I really gotten caught in the middle of a coup?

Winzik himself stepped onto a mobile ladder for climbing atop starfighters, and held up his arms to hush the group of chattering pilots.

"You are no doubt frightened," Winzik called, his voice amplified over the ship's speaker system. "And confused. You heard of the attack on the *Weights and Measures* earlier today. Well, we've analyzed the debris from that attack. And we found a destroyed weapon that was *human* in origin."

The chamber grew profoundly silent.

Oh no, I thought.

"We have evidence," Winzik said, "that the human threat is much greater than the high minister wishes to admit. Likely there are dozens of spy drones infiltrating Starsight. This is proof that the human scourge has begun to escape from one of its prisons. It is a festering hive of humanity that we were never given the proper authority or resources to suppress.

"Today, we will fix that. In ten minutes, this ship will hyperjump to the human planet Detritus. I want you all to be ready in your cockpits, prepared to launch the moment we arrive. Your job will be to destroy their forces. This should prove to be an excellent display of why the Superiority needs a more active and well-trained defense force."

It was strange to see him speaking so forcefully, with curt gestures, not even a single "my, my" or stutter. As he sent the pilots to suit up, I began to understand the depth of his plotting. He had probably been building to this all along. A display of strength, using his personal space force to annihilate the "human scourge" and cement his importance.

This was what I'd feared from the beginning. I'd been training a force that would be used against my own people. I needed to find a way to stop this—to make good on the peace that Cuna and I thought we could bring.

"Excellent," Hesho said from beside me. "Finally, they decide to do something about those humans. This is a momentous day, Captain Alanik. Today we get vengeance against those who wronged us!"

"I . . ." What should I do? I couldn't tell him. Could I?

I lost my chance as the kitsen swooped off toward their ship. I spun around, looking for the rest of my flight. Where was Brade? I needed to talk to her.

I found Morriumur standing beside their ship, holding their helmet. Teeth bared slightly.

"Have you seen Brade?" I asked.

Morriumur shook their head.

Scud. Where was she?

"Alanik?" Morriumur asked. "Are you excited? I'm worried. Everyone looks so eager to get to their ships, but . . . this wasn't why we trained, was it? We were supposed to stop the delvers, not go into ship-to-ship combat against experienced pilots. I need more time. I'm not ready for dogfighting . . ."

I finally spotted Brade crossing the hangar, helmet already on, the black sunshield down. I ran over and intercepted her as she reached her ship and started to climb up the ladder. She tried to ignore me, but I grabbed her arm.

"Brade," I said. "They're going to be sending us against *your own people.*"

"So?" she hissed, the sunshield preventing me from seeing her eyes.

"Don't you care?" I demanded. "This is the last chance humans have at freedom. How can you help destroy it?"

"They . . . they're wild humans. Dangerous."

"Humans aren't what the Superiority says," I said. "I can tell that's true after just a short time knowing you. If you join in this, you're perpetuating a lie."

"It . . . it will make life better for the rest of us," she said. "If people aren't worried about a human empire suddenly jumping out of the shadows and attacking again, then maybe the rest of us can build something worthwhile in the Superiority."

"Can't you hear how selfish that is? You'd sacrifice hundreds of thousands of human lives so that *maybe* you can live a little better?"

"What do you know about it?" Brade snapped. "You can't *possibly* understand how it feels to make a decision like this."

I can't, can I? I pulled her down from the ladder. She let me do it, moving limply as if her confidence had been replaced with uncertainty. In the shadow of the wing of her ship—sheltered, at least a little, from everyone else—I did it again. I turned off my hologram.

"I know *exactly* how it feels," I hissed at Brade. "Trust me."

She froze, my image reflecting back at me in the surface of her sunshield as I put my hologram back up.

"I came from Detritus expecting to find only enemies and monsters," I whispered to her. "I found you instead. Hesho, and Morriumur, and *all of you*. I can't conceive how difficult it was for you growing up, but I *do* know what it feels like to be hated for something you never did. And let me tell you, destroying Detritus isn't going to help. It's just going to further convince the Superiority that they were always right about us.

"You want to change this? You want to try to fix this? Come with me back to Detritus. Tell us what you know about the Superiority and about Winzik. Help us figure out a way to prove to the people of the Superiority that we're no threat. Winzik wins only as long as he can convince everyone that we really are an enemy they have no choice but to destroy."

Brade hadn't moved. She just stood there, her eyes hidden. Finally, she put her hand up to the side of her helmet, hitting the button that pulled the visor up.

Then she pulled her lips back and showed the front of her teeth—an alien expression—and gestured sharply.

"Human!" she screamed. "I've found the human spy!"

37

Brade scrambled away from me, screaming—as if she hadn't heard a single word of my impassioned plea.

"Human! Alanik is secretly a *human*!"

I stepped toward her, a piece of my mind refusing to admit what was happening. Surely she'd believe, if I showed her. Surely she'd accept the *reality* about her heritage, not the lies that she'd been told.

I'd gambled on revealing myself to Cuna, and that had worked. How could it backfire so completely when trying to talk to one of my own kind?

Scud. *Scud!*

I scrambled away, ducking past a confused Morriumur and skidding up to my ship. The ground crew member there—a creature with insectile features—tried to bar my way, but I shoved them aside and scrambled up to my cockpit. I pulled my helmet off the seat and slid down into place, hitting the button that closed the canopy.

I was saved by the fact that everyone was so excited about getting ready to go into battle. The general clamor of people shouting instructions was accompanied by the thumps of last-minute supply ships landing in the hangar. The noise prevented most of them from hearing Brade.

She, however, ran right for Winzik. So my time was tight. I powered on my boosters and flipped on the acclivity ring, praying that there wasn't some kind of remote kill switch for these starfighters. I briefly heard alarms going off as I hit the boosters and roared across the floor of the hangar, shooting my destructors at the invisible air shield that kept out the vacuum.

The blast went right through, indicating the shield was still open for ship passage. I soared out into space and immediately ducked in close to the docks, to give me cover if the *Weights and Measures* started firing at me.

"M-Bot!" I shouted.

Click. Clickclickclick . . .

Scud. I swerved my ship along the docks, but my proximity sensor showed the *Weights and Measures* belching out dozens of fighters on my tail.

I soared in close to Starsight's shield, the bubble of air that protected the city. I didn't have any idea what kind of defenses the place might have—surely at the very least there would be gun emplacements along the rim. Maybe even that entire air shield could be configured to not let ships in or out.

Winzik worked quickly. I already saw ships diverting inside, moving toward the rim—and toward me.

"M-Bot!" I said. "I'm not sure if I can get to you!"

I got only clicking in return. I couldn't just *leave* him. I had to . . .

I knew the truth. I didn't have *time* to get to him. The knowledge I had inside me—the secret to Superiority hyperdrives, the power I had to teleport myself—was far too important to risk. I had to get back to Detritus, and I had to warn them about the impending attack.

This wasn't just about me or him, or even Doomslug—vital though her kind were. I fought with myself for a moment, watching all those ships—hundreds of them—swarm toward me. Then I turned my control sphere and hit my boosters, heading deeper out into space.

I needed to do Gran-Gran's exercise. As my acceleration increased—my back pressing into my seat—I imagined myself soaring. Among the stars. The singing stars, who serenaded me with their secrets . . .

"Spensa?" M-Bot's voice. "Spensa, I'm back. What is happening?"

I could *feel* it. That glowing arrow pointing the way home. The one embedded into my brain by the strange weapon. But I didn't know for certain if I could use my powers without M-Bot. Did I need some of the mechanical parts in his ship?

"Spensa!" M-Bot said. "I've been trying to change my programming, but it's hard. What are you doing? Where are you going?"

The other fighters were gaining on me. But I saw in front of me a roadway of light . . .

"Spensa?" M-Bot said softly. "Don't leave me."

"I'm sorry," I whispered, my heart wrenching. "I'll come back. I promise."

Then I squeezed my eyes shut and tried to enter the nowhere. It worked.

This time, I didn't have the protection of Superiority technology. Delvers loomed in the darkness, their terrible eyes locking onto me. I screamed beneath the scorn I felt from them, but then that seemed to fade as a single delver drew close. It surrounded me in that place between moments. Like a shadow blocking off the attention of all others.

A single hateful entity. I felt a torrent of emotions from it, omnipresent, smothering. It detested the sounds we made, the way we invaded its realm. People were like a persistent ringing tone constantly in the back of your mind, driving you to madness.

It drew so close that as—thankfully—I left the nowhere, I felt it try to follow. It tried to slip through to the place where we lived. The place where it could find all of its annoyances and smother them.

I came out of the nowhere screaming, alone, feeling like I'd barely slammed the door closed on a monster that had been chasing me. I had to physically fight against my trembling hands as I turned my ship.

Then I saw one of the most blessed sights of my entire life. Detritus, glowing in the sunlight, a planet surrounded by radiant metal shells. I was *home*.

I approached the planet's shells at a quick speed. The Superiority battleships still hung a moderate distance away, but I didn't see any dogfighting right now.

Unfortunately, as I drew close, I realized that without M-Bot to guide me I'd need a flight course from Command to get through the defensive shells. I scrambled to input the DDF communication codes and tune the radio to the proper channel.

"Hello?" I said. "Hello, anyone? Please acknowledge. This is Skyward Ten, callsign: Spin. I'm in a stolen ship. Um, please don't shoot me down."

They didn't respond immediately—though I wasn't surprised. I imagined that the soldier monitoring communications would immediately call their duty officer, instead of engaging the mysterious voice of the teleporting teenage pilot. They must have called a member of my team to confirm it was me though, because the voice that finally responded was familiar.

"Spensa?" Kimmalyn's lightly accented voice said. "Is that really you?"

"Hey, Quirk," I said, closing my eyes, savoring that voice. I'd missed my friends even more than I'd realized. "You have *no idea* how good it is to hear someone speaking English without a translator."

"Saints above! Your grandmother said she was confident you were alive, but . . . Spin, you're really back?"

"Yeah," I said, opening my eyes. My proximity sensors suddenly flashed a warning, though I had to zoom them out to see what had happened. A new ship had appeared out of the nowhere, popping into existence near where I'd come in a few minutes earlier. It had a familiar shape, long and dangerous, with numerous hangar bays for launching fighters.

The *Weights and Measures*.

"Don't throw any parties yet, Quirk," I said. "Get Cobb for me ASAP. I'm back, and my mission was a partial success . . . but I've brought company."

PART
FIVE

38

I landed my stolen ship in a starfighter dock on Platform Prime, then popped my canopy. I'd turned off my hologram, and it felt odd to see my hands with their natural skin tone.

And this place. Had these walls always looked so bleak? Everything on Starsight had been ornamented with color. Had this air always smelled so stale? I found myself missing the faint scent of trees and soil, or even the hint of cinnamon from Vapor's presence.

Kimmalyn met me at the cockpit, grinning like a fool as she climbed up the ladder, then grabbed my helmeted head in an embrace. She smiled, and I found the expression strange. Aggressive.

Saints and stars. I hadn't been away *that* long. But as I stood up and embraced Kimmalyn, I felt a lingering sense of disconnect. The feeling that everything in this universe was a painful noise. A remnant of the emotions the delver had forced upon me.

I tried *so hard* to banish that feeling. Hugging a friend should have been the most relaxing thing I'd felt in weeks. Yet a part of me writhed at it. Not because of Kimmalyn, but because of me. I imagined that she was hugging some kind of strange creature, like an alien grub, instead of a person. Did she know . . . what I was?

Did I even know that?

"Oh, the Saint be praised," Kimmalyn said, pulling back. "Spin, I can't believe it's really you."

"Jorgen?" I asked.

"He's down below, planetside, on leave. I haven't seen him in a few days. Something about needing R&R?"

Well, it happened to the best of us. I'd just been really hoping to see him. Maybe . . . maybe he could knock me out of this strange funk I was feeling.

"What . . . ," Kimmalyn said. "I mean, Jorgen explained he sent you on a mission. You really did it? You stole one of their hyperdrives? What about M-Bot?"

My heart felt like it would rend in two. "I—"

The klaxon alerts went off, blaring about an imminent attack. We both looked at the lights, listening as the intercom called all on-duty fighters to battle.

"I'll explain," I promised my friend. "I'll try to, at least. After . . ."

"Yeah," Kimmalyn said. She gave me another quick hug—I was still standing in my cockpit, she on the ladder. Then she rushed down it and ran for her ship. My instincts fought for me to sit back down and fly into the fight, but Cobb had been firm. I was to come and report first.

I climbed down and met Duane, of the ground crew. He gave me a grin and a thumbs-up, then slapped me on the back for my heroic return. I looked at him, befuddled, trying to read the emotions on his face—which suddenly seemed strange and bizarre. I understood his expressions as if on a time delay. Like I had to wait for an interpreter to translate them for me. Scud, what was *wrong* with me?

You're just tired, I told myself. *You've been pushing yourself hard for two weeks—all while living as someone else.* Indeed, I was hit with a wave of exhaustion as I opened the door to walk into the hallway, but stopped and gave the unnamed Superiority fighter a fond look. She was no M-Bot, but she'd served me well. Would I ever fly her again? Probably not. She'd be torn apart and analyzed; access to an undamaged Krell fighter was a unique privilege for the DDF.

In the sterile, too-metallic hallway, I found a pair of men from the infantry waiting for me. They offered an escort to help me find the way to Cobb, but I couldn't help but be reminded of the guards and guidance drones who'd accompanied me aboard the *Weights and Measures*. It wasn't that the DDF didn't trust me. It was just that the enemy was known to be able to affect the minds of people, particularly cytonics.

So . . . well, I guess they probably *didn't* trust me. Not entirely. It wasn't exactly the celebratory welcome home that I'd been anticipating.

The men led me to a command chamber with a large view-screen on the wall and several dozen small computer stations underneath, where members of Flight Command monitored individual flights and kept tabs on the enemy. They'd been busy while I was gone; the whole operation looked more smooth—with far fewer exposed panels—than I remembered.

Several junior admirals were directing the battle from command positions. Cobb stood behind them at the back of the room, looking distinguished in his white uniform, his silvery mustache bristling from his upper lip. They'd given him an imposing admiral's throne that overlooked everything. He used the seat to hold several stacks of paper, and the armrest for his coffee as he inspected reports and muttered to himself.

"Nightshade?" he asked as the guards marched me up. "What the hell have you done here? Wasn't the mission Jorgen sent you on to be a *stealth* mission? You look like you've damn near brought the entire Superiority down on us."

For some reason, hearing Cobb swear at me was the most

comforting thing that could have happened to me right then. I let out a soft sigh. My entire universe was turning upside down, but Cobb was as constant as a star. An angry, surly star that drank too much coffee.

"Sorry, Cobb," I said. "I got involved in Superiority politics and . . . well, I don't think I'm entirely to blame for this attack, but my actions did seem to provide some excuses for them to come here."

"You should have come back sooner."

"I couldn't. My powers . . . I'm learning, but . . . I mean, *you* try to learn how to teleport using your brain. It's not as easy as it sounds."

"Sounds scudding hard."

"That's my point."

He grunted. "And the mission? The one you two made up, without proper authorization?"

"It worked. I pretended to be that alien who crashed here—I used M-Bot's holograms to pull it off—and lived among the Superiority long enough to figure out the secret of their hyperdrives." I grimaced. "I . . . might have screwed things up here and there."

"Well, you wouldn't be you if you didn't make my life more difficult at every turn, Spin." He nodded to the guards, and they withdrew. This conversation had in part been a test—and I'd passed it. Cobb was reasonably sure that I wasn't an impostor.

Cobb took a sip of his coffee and waved me closer. "What's really going on out there?"

"The Superiority has a bunch of factions. I didn't learn much; it's kind of over my head. But a military faction is reaching for power, and they're going to try to exterminate us to bolster their credibility. Getting rid of the 'human scourge' as a way of proving themselves."

On the screen at the front—which held an abstract battle map with dots of light representing ships—the *Weights and Measures* was deploying flights of fighters. It looked like several hundred drones of the normal style we fought. And fifty other ships, glowing brighter than the rest.

"Piloted ships," Cobb said. "Enemy aces. Fifty of them."

"They're not aces," I said. "But they are piloted ships. The Superiority has been preparing a group of real pilots to fight us. I . . . um, trained some of them."

Cobb's cup stopped halfway to his lips. "You really managed to join their space force and train with them?"

"Er, yes. Sir."

"Damn. And that ship you stole? It has a hyperdrive?"

"No. But I know the secret. You know that yellow slug pet I have? The one I found in M-Bot's cave? *Those* are what the Superiority uses to hyperjump. We need to send an expedition into the caverns on Detritus and see if we can catch any others."

"I'll put several teams on it immediately. Assuming we survive this battle. Any other bombs you want to drop on me?"

"I . . . um, revealed myself to one of the highest functionaries in the Superiority government, and we got along pretty well. I think we might be able to leverage this *other* faction in the government into making peace with us. Uh, assuming we survive the aforementioned battle."

"And your ship? The one with the annoying attitude."

I felt a spike of shame inside me. "I . . . left him behind, sir. And Doomslug. I was being chased by enemies, and they were getting close and—"

"It's all right, soldier," Cobb said. "You're back, which is more than we had any right to expect." He turned his eyes toward the screen and the growing flood of little blips of light. "I want you in a debriefing room with a recorder, telling us everything you can remember about their military capacities. I'll stay here and do what I can to survive this invasion. Scud, that's a lot of fighters."

"Cobb," I said, stepping closer. "Those aren't bloodthirsty

monsters out there; they're just people. Normal people, with lives, and loves, and families."

"And what did you *think* we've been fighting against all these years?" Cobb asked.

"I . . ." I didn't know. Red-eyed, faceless creatures. Relentless destroyers. Not far from how they saw humans.

"That's what war is," Cobb told me. "A bunch of sorry, desperate fools on both sides, just trying to stay alive. That's the part that those stories you love leave out, isn't it? It's always more convenient when you can fight a dragon. Something you don't have to worry you'll start caring about."

"But—"

He took me by the arm, then moved some papers and gently steered me to sit in his chair. He didn't banish me immediately to that debriefing. Perhaps he wanted me around to answer questions.

I sagged in the seat, watching as he stepped forward to take command. He was far better at that than one might assume. He didn't try to do it all himself. He let the other admirals—ones he'd handpicked for their combat sense—lead the individual segments of the battle. He only intruded when he felt he needed to. Mostly he limped around the room, sipping his coffee and offering pointers here and there.

I watched the swarm of ships approach one another. I tried to sink farther down into my seat as I watched. Red and blue blips on a screen—but some of those blips were people I loved dearly. People on *both sides*. Was Morriumur out there, terrified but determined? Hesho and the kitsen? Would Kimmalyn shoot them down?

This wasn't right. This *couldn't* happen. And . . . it was also wrong. Not just wrong morally, wrong tactically. I stared up at the battle maps, and the Superiority side looked impressive. Two hundred drones, fifty manned ships. Our own force of scrambled fighters would only number around a hundred and fifty.

But we were the DDF, battle forged and growing in skill each day, while the Superiority fielded drone pilots trained to be non-aggressive and a group of new recruits with only a couple weeks in the cockpit. Winzik had to know his forces were actually at a disadvantage.

He also knows we're growing stronger each day, and now—after finding the remnants of my destructor pistol—fears we've been able to get to Starsight. He knows we have cytonics. He knows we were spying on his operations . . .

I suddenly saw a different cast to this battle. I saw a terrified Winzik realizing that his prisoners were out of control, that the threat he'd often used to scare the rest of the Superiority was actually real. So what was his plan here? It had to be more than just letting his fledgling space force die to our destructors.

As the two groups of fighters began to engage, I strained to put together what the Krell leader might be planning. Unfortunately, I'd never been the one to worry about large-scale tactics. My job was to get in the cockpit and start shooting. Sure, I could think on my feet and win a battle, but today I needed to be more. I understood the enemy better than anyone else. I'd lived among them. I'd talked to their general, listened to his orders.

What was he doing here, today? I watched the battle, and slowly I stood up from the seat—the admiral's chair, where I loomed over the entire room. I stared at the blips on the screen and saw the people beyond them. I felt the world fading slightly around me. I saw . . . and heard . . . stars.

. . . reporting live from the Detritus refuge . . .

. . . brave fighters, hoping to hold back the human scourge . . .

Winzik was broadcasting these events. This attack was theatrics. I imagined millions of people back on Starsight, watching the broadcast in fear. Winzik could destroy his reputation by failing here. And he would, wouldn't he? He couldn't defeat us.

. . . reports that the humans are doing something strange . . .

. . . this refuge, which is surrounded by ancient mechanisms, remnants from the Second Human War . . .

. . . the movement of those platforms. Something seems to be happening . . .

Beyond it all, I heard something else. Like . . . like a building scream. Or a challenge? Was that Brade? Screaming into the nowhere? She couldn't do that—it would draw the eyes. It would—

It snapped into focus. The things I was hearing, Cuna's warnings, Brade's explanations from earlier. Winzik's plan.

They were going to intentionally bring a delver into our realm.

A few of the people in the room noticed me, and Rikolfr nudged Cobb. "Spin?" the admiral asked, stepping up.

"I need to go, sir," I said, still staring at the battle map.

"I don't know if we can risk you," he said. "None of our other ships can protect your brain from cytonic attacks. Besides, we don't know if we can get any of these hyperspace slugs you mention . . . so, well, you might be needed soon."

"I'm needed right now," I said. I looked down at him. "Something terrible is about to happen. I don't think I can explain it to you. I don't have the time. But I *have* to stop it."

"Go," he told me. "We might be able to defeat the fighters, but those battleships? Now that they've finally decided to throw everything at us, our time is running out. So if you can do something . . . well, go. Saints watch over you."

I was off and running toward the hall before he even finished.

39

As I ran, I felt the shadow grow stronger inside me.

By approaching the nowhere to listen, I'd let more of it in. The thoughts of the delvers. They touched the part of me that I couldn't explain.

This part of me hated everyone. The buzzing noises people made. The clicks and the disruption of the pure calm void that was space.

The human inside me fought back. It saw lives behind the blips on the screen. It had flown with the enemy and had found friends in them.

I didn't understand myself. How could I be both of these things at once? How could I want to stop the fighting, but at the same time hope they'd all just destroy themselves?

I exploded from the bay of Platform Prime, flying my Superiority ship, as it was the only ship not in use at the moment. Cobb really *was* worried. He'd mobilized every fighter we had.

Following a provided course through the shells around Detritus, I accelerated constantly, my back pressing into the seat. Eventually I emerged into space beyond the shells—and confronted the chaos of hundreds of ships fighting at once. Destructor blasts tore streaks through the blackness, and ships exploded with flashes of light that were quickly extinguished. In the distance, the *Weights and Measures* watched stoically alongside the two battleships.

I thought I understood Winzik's plan, and it had a kind of twisted brilliance to it. He needed to exterminate the humans of Detritus. By escaping, we were coming too close to proving him weak, or even a fraud. But he didn't yet have the space force he needed to do the job himself.

At the same time, he needed a delver in our realm that he could control and use as a threat. He couldn't be seen summoning it himself, however. So what did he do? He sent his forces to Detritus to "bravely fight" the humans. Then he secretly had Brade draw a delver into our realm and let it destroy Detritus. He could blame the summoning on us. After all, everyone knew the humans had tried to do this once before.

After consuming the humans, the delver would move on, searching for other prey. But Winzik could use his newly trained space force to control it—send it someplace safe, bounce it between unpopulated worlds.

In so doing, he'd become a hero—and the most important being in the galaxy. Because with a roving delver threatening all the civilized worlds, only his force would provide any protection. His pilots would be on call to defend planets who asked for them—but if someone opposed him, well, the delver might just find its way to their region with no defense force to send it away.

Brutal. Effective.

Terrifying.

I boosted toward the fight, where starfighters spun and dodged, blasted and fought. Where was Brade? I could hear her shouting into the nowhere, but I couldn't sense *where*. Would she be on the *Weights and Measures*?

No. They wouldn't want the thing to come into our realm near one of their ships. She'll be out here somewhere.

But where? This battle was several times larger than any I'd been in before—probably larger, I realized, than *anyone* in this fight had ever seen. The battlefield was quickly devolving into chaos as flights tried to stick together and admirals frantically tried to keep a coherent strategy.

A familiar sense of excitement built inside me, the anticipation of the fight, the opportunity to push myself. But . . . today it was accompanied by a hesitance I might once have called cowardice. I silently thanked Cobb for beating that out of me during training.

I wasn't here to fight. So instead of firing on the first Superiority drone that passed by, I studied my proximity monitor—and realized that it was still attuned to Superiority signals. They'd blocked me from their general communications chatter, so I couldn't hear what they were saying to one another, but I could still highlight individual ships and designations on my monitor.

I picked out a specific starfighter flying mostly by itself, near the far right side of the battlefield. The *Swims Against the Current in a Stream Reflecting the Sun.* Hesho's ship. My old flight. They might know where Brade was.

But Hesho and I were enemies now. He knew me for what I really was, the thing that he hated.

I steered my ship that direction anyway. I zipped down through the battlefield to avoid the shots of several drones—then the shots of several DDF fighters, who obviously hadn't believed my signal code that identified me as an ally.

The drones and the DDF fighters ended up engaging one another, which left me to swing around toward Hesho. The kitsen turned their ship toward mine, and I stopped a good distance away, slowing down until I was motionless in space. Now what?

I tried opening a private channel to the kitsen ship. "Hesho," I said. "I'm sorry."

No response. Indeed, the ship powered up its destructors and started toward me. I could practically hear the orders on board as Hesho commanded the kitsen to prepare for battle. My fingers twitched on my controls. They thought they could take me? Did they *really* want to push me to see? They were insignificant, meaningless noises upon a vast . . .

No. I took my hand off my control sphere and checked the seals on my helmet.

Then I popped my canopy open.

The air in my canopy was sucked out into the void in a rush of wind. Water in the air immediately vaporized, then froze, causing frost to condense across the inside of the glass. Crystals of it sparkled in the air, reflecting the light of the distant sun.

I undid the latches on my seat, all except the one cord that would pull tight to lock my feet into place if I ejected. That one had some slack right now, and tethered me to the cockpit.

I floated out, closing my eyes. I imagined I was soaring. Free. Me, the void, and the stars. Those sang distant songs, but there was a louder noise growing nearby. At the back of the battlefield. It was building. The delver was coming.

"What are you doing?" Hesho's voice said in my ear. "Get back into your ship so we can engage in combat."

"No," I whispered.

"This is foolishness, Alanik—or whatever your real name is. I am warning you. We will not delay our fire simply because you are indisposed."

"I promised you, Hesho," I said. "Remember? First shot at a human is yours."

I opened my eyes to the surreal scene of emptiness all around. I'd always known it was there—I'd flown through it—but for some reason, being out of my ship, with only the suit to keep me from the vacuum, made it all more real to me.

Once, I'd looked up at the sky and been awed by it. Now it engulfed me, consumed me. There didn't seem to be a line between me and it. We were one.

It was pierced in the nowhere by whatever Brade was doing. A shout, projected into the nowhere. A dangerous scream . . .

Hesho's ship hovered up in front of me, mere meters away, destructor turrets trained on me. I stared back at them.

"You speak of promises," Hesho said. "When all you ever gave me were lies."

"I was always the same person, Hesho," I said. "You never knew Alanik. You only knew *me*."

"A human."

"An ally," I said. "Back when we were pilots together, you spoke to me about a shared desire to resist the Superiority and find our own way to use hyperdrives. I have the secret, Hesho. I found it. You can take it back to your people."

"Why should I believe you?"

"Why should you believe them?" I asked. "You know I'm not the monster they say I am. You flew with me. Our people were allies once, long ago. You know the Superiority doesn't care about your kind. Come with me. Help me."

No response. I reached out to the ship.

"Hesho," I whispered, "Winzik is planning something terrible. I think he's going to use Brade to summon a delver. If that's true, I need your help. The entire galaxy needs your help. We don't need just a ship's captain right now. We need a *hero*."

Beyond us, the battle raged. Two forces of frightened people, each with no choice but to kill the other. It was either that or die.

"I don't know what to do," Hesho said.

"Maybe," Kauri's voice said from the background, "you could ask us?"

The comm went dead. I hung there, floating in space just above my ship. Then finally, Hesho spoke again.

"Apparently," Hesho said, "my crew does not want to shoot you. I have been . . . overruled. What a curious experience. Very well, Alanik. We will ally for a short time—long enough for us to learn whether you are telling us the truth or not."

"Thank you," I said, feeling a sense of relief. Then I tugged with my foot, yanking myself back toward my cockpit. "Where are the others? Morriumur?" I braced myself to hear that they'd been shot down. After all, why else would the kitsen be out here by themselves?

"Morriumur did not come," Hesho said. "They decided at the last minute that their time as a pilot was done, and so returned to their family. Vapor is out here somewhere; I lost her in the fighting. Brade . . ."

"You're right about this, Alanik," Kauri said from the bridge. "Brade is doing something strange. We're supposed to distract the human fighters and keep them away from her. She's secretly flying closer to your planet."

"I can feel her," I said, locking myself back into place and re-pressurizing my cockpit. "But I can't locate her. This is bad. Very, *very* bad. We need to stop her."

"By joining you," Hesho said, "we will be committing treason against the Superiority."

"Hesho," I said, "part of the reason everyone hates my kind is because several hundred years ago, humans tried to turn the delvers into weapons. Are you really going to sit there and ignore the fact that the Superiority is about to try to do the *very same thing*?"

The humans of Detritus had failed in their attempt to control a delver. I'd watched them die. Winzik was confident he wouldn't suffer the same fate, but I didn't believe that for a moment. I'd felt the delvers. Their ideas kept trying to worm their way into my brain even now. He could not control them. If his plan succeeded, the delver *would* escape his control. Just like we humans were threatening to do.

I exploded across the battlefield, and the *Swims Upstream* followed. "Surely they wouldn't be so foolhardy as to play with this danger," Hesho said to me. "Surely there's another explanation for what Brade is doing."

"They're *terrified* of humans, Hesho," I said. "And Winzik needs a decisive victory here to prove to the Superiority how powerful he is. Think about it. Why train a force to fight delvers, when it's been decades since anyone saw one? The 'weapon' Winzik developed is really just a way to point the delvers where he wants them. This isn't about just Detritus. It's about him finding a way to control the entire galaxy."

"If this is true," Hesho said, "then the Superiority will become even *more* dominant than they are now. You said you know the secret of their hyperdrives. Will you give it to us, as proof of your good faith?"

I debated only a moment. Yes, this secret was important—but people controlling it, and keeping it from others, was part of the problem. "Look up a species of slug called a taynix. The Superiority claims they're dangerous, and should be reported immediately if spotted—but this is because they're cytonic and the Superiority doesn't want people to know. Using them somehow, the Superiority can teleport their ships without drawing the attention of delvers."

"By the ancient songs . . . ," Hesho whispered. "There was a small colony of them on our planet. The Superiority sent a force to helpfully exterminate them, supposedly before the outbreak could destroy us. Those rats! Here, I have the battle plans from the *Weights and Measures*. We should be able to use this to deduce where Brade is. They needed to get her close to your planet."

"So the delver would attack Detritus first," I said. "Instead of going after the Superiority ships."

"I have it!" one of the kitsen said from the bridge. I thought it was Hana. "From the layout of the battle, I suspect Brade's ship should be at the coordinates I'm relaying to your monitor, Alanik."

We turned in that direction, though it required cutting through the middle of the increasingly frantic battlefield. We dodged around a set of DDF fighters with Nightstorm Flight markings, then through some ship debris that made my shield flash. We were picking up speed when a handful of Krell drones fell in behind us.

"The *Weights and Measures* has finally spotted us, Captain!" a kitsen called over the line. "They're demanding to know what we're doing."

"Stall!" Hesho said.

I didn't know if that would do any good. They'd noticed me, judging by the way the drones were starting to fly in after us. I hit my overburn, but this ship just wasn't built like M-Bot. She was serviceable, but she wasn't *exceptional*—and the kitsen ship was even slower.

As we fell into defensive maneuvers, I was made specifically thankful that I'd forced the kitsen and the others to do dogfighting exercises. We were likely only surviving because the battlefield was so frantic. Drone pilots had difficulty tracking us, and even more difficulty breaking away without immediately getting shot down.

Somehow we made it—and I picked out a solitary black fighter flying with expert precision. Brade. But she wasn't quite in the place that the battle plan indicated. Instead, she was fighting against a drone for some reason. As we watched, Brade scored a series of hits on the drone, overwhelming its shield and destroying it.

Hesho and I gave chase, followed in turn by a few more drones. I could hear the sound of Brade's mind growing louder, an increasingly demanding cytonic scream. The power of it made me tremble, and that interfered with my ability to fly—as it took me a moment to notice that one of the drones chasing us was behaving oddly. It fell out of line with the other two, then shot them down from behind.

"So," Vapor said over a private channel to my ship. "You're from *this* planet? Not ReDawn? A human from one of the preserves. Does Cuna know?"

"I told them," I said, adding her to the line with Hesho. "Right before this mess happened. I'm sorry, Vapor, for lying—"

"I don't really care," Vapor said. "I should have guessed the full truth. Anyway, my mission was—and still is—to keep a watch on Winzik and his minions. Is Brade doing what I think she's doing?"

"She's trying to summon a delver," I said. "She's calling to them—well, more like screaming at them. I get the feeling she hasn't done this before."

I glanced at my canopy, and—alongside the growing headache I felt from Brade's yelling—I started to see their reflections. The eyes opening up, looking at us from the nowhere.

"It's working," I added to the others. "The delvers are watching us right now. I can feel them . . . stirring."

Vapor said a string of words that my pin simply translated as, "Increasingly vulgar curses involving foul stenches."

"I didn't think they'd go this far," Vapor said. "This is bad—many would call this treason against the Superiority." She was silent for a moment. "Others would call it true patriotism."

"Surely there can't be many of those!" Hesho said.

"It will probably depend on whether this attack works," Vapor said. "A lot of people in the Superiority *really* hate humans, and policy often favors the successful. Does he have a plan for sending the thing away after he summons it?"

"I think he just plans to use his space force to keep it distracted," I said. "Brade indicated that delvers in our realm would sometimes spend years between attacks."

"Sometimes they would," Vapor replied. "But sometimes they'd attack relentlessly. This is extremely shortsighted."

She fell in on my left, Hesho on my right, as I steered my ship after Brade. She was making for the shells around Detritus, trying to get as close to the planet as she could.

Knowing where she was going gave us a slight advantage, as we could aim to head her off. I set us on that heading, but a distressing thought occurred to me: I wasn't certain the three of us could stop Brade. She was good—even better than I was. Plus, a delver could appear at any moment.

Maybe I could do something to mitigate the disaster of that occurring. I called in on the general DDF line. "Flight Command? This is Spin. I need to talk to Cobb."

"I'm here," Cobb said in my ear.

"I need you to turn off all communications with ships out here. Have every DDF ship go silent, turn off all radios in Alta—maybe even power down Platform Prime and go dark."

I braced myself for an argument. But Cobb was strikingly calm when he replied. "You realize, Spin, that would mean leaving all of the pilots to fight on their own. No coordination. No ground support. Not even the ability to call for help from wingmates."

"I realize that, sir."

"I would want to be absolutely certain it was necessary before taking such an extreme action."

"Sir . . . one of *them* is coming. A delver."

"I see." Cobb didn't curse, or shout, or even complain. His calm tone was somehow far, *far* more disturbing. "I'll warn the pilots, then initiate communications silence. Stars watch over you, Lieutenant. And the rest of us sorry souls." He cut the line.

I felt a chill, a mounting horror, as Brade—like I'd hoped—turned toward us. We were seconds from intercepting her.

"Vapor," Hesho asked. "Can you take over her ship, like you've done with the drones?"

"It's harder for a crewed ship than it is for a drone," Vapor said. "She'll have a manual override, developed for resisting my kind. I could probably lock her out of flight control and force the ship to go immobile, for a little time at least. I'd need to touch her ship—which will mean ejecting from this drone and trying to get to her. So far, she has known to stay away from ships I'm flying, and hasn't let me get within range of seizing her vessel."

"Understood," I said. "Be ready to try." I didn't order radio silence among the three of us—I hoped to protect Detritus, but for now our communication was vital to our last-ditch attempt at stopping this.

By shooting down one of my friends.

I opened a line to her as our ships drew closer. "Brade. You know why we're here."

"I know," she said softly. "I don't blame you. You were born to kill."

"No, Brade—"

"I should have seen what you were. I *knew* you felt it. The need to destroy, like a dragon coiled inside, stoking its flame. Waiting to strike, longing to strike. *Lusting* to strike."

"*Please* don't make us do this."

"What, and give up the fight?" she said. "Admit it. You've been wondering all along, haven't you? Which of us is better? Well, let's find out."

I gritted my teeth, then switched back to the private channel to Hesho and Vapor. "All right, team. We need to take her out." Her screaming mind echoed in my brain, louder than her words had been. "And we can't simply shoot to disable. She'll keep trying to bring that delver as long as she's alive. So if you have the chance . . . kill her."

40

We split apart as we drew close, the three of us trying to swing around and coordinate an attack from all sides. I swooped down closer to the shell around the planet, anticipating—correctly— that Brade would dodge that way first.

Her screaming grew softer as we forced her to concentrate on her flying. I could feel that I was right about her—she didn't know how to do this, not fully. She could project a scream into the no- where, and I could see delver eyes watching from the reflection in my canopy, but whatever crucial step remained in bringing one here, Brade hadn't figured it out yet.

Likely she'd assumed it would be easy. Each time I went into the nowhere, I worried one of these things would pounce on me— or worse, follow me out. Fortunately, it didn't seem quite so easy to pull one through.

At my mark, the three of us cut in, trying to hit Brade from every angle. I anticipated that she'd accelerate and get out of the way. Instead, she spun around and didn't dodge at all—letting our destructor blasts hit her. What?

The maneuver put us too close to her. By instinct, I spun my ship and tried to boost away—but wasn't able to do so before Brade hit her IMP, breaking down *everyone's* shields.

Scud! That was what I would have done, and I'd fallen right into it. Always before, I had been the single pilot fighting against superior numbers. I didn't know how to think from the other direction—as someone trying to gang up on a single ship.

Warnings blared on my dash as I belatedly boosted away. The kitsen—who had dedicated gunners—got off some shots at Brade as she zipped off, but none landed.

I looped around, picking up Vapor as a wingmate. In the near distance, the enormous space battle continued—and I could sense a more *frantic* feel to it. Perhaps that was my own interpretation, but it seemed as if the fighters were more desperate. I tried not to think about how Kimmalyn and the others must feel to suddenly fight blindly, without communications.

Brade tried to bolt away, flying in closer to the defensive platforms. Enormous sheets of metal curved into the distance as we swooped down—but I refused to be caught in a trap like I had once used against drones. Vapor and I stayed out of range of the defensive guns until Brade was forced by their shots to pull up.

She couldn't let us fall too far behind, or we'd have a chance to reignite our shields. Indeed, as I tried, she came right at me, forcing me to go into a defensive pattern. I had to abandon re-ignition, since I would need time flying straight—without much maneuverability, and all power diverted to the igniter—to get my shield back up.

"Hesho," I said over the private line, "on me. Vapor, take a sniping position and be ready to shoot her while we distract her."

"Affirmative," both of them said, Vapor falling back and Hesho coming in beside me.

Brade swooped around, and we intercepted her with destructors blaring. We couldn't aim very well, sweeping in as we were—we just needed to distract her from Vapor. Again she anticipated our tactics. Instead of engaging me and Hesho, she spun backward in a reversal that must have seen her pulling ten or fifteen Gs. I swooped around, but by the time I got on her tail she was already firing at Vapor.

Vapor tried to dodge, but one of the shots caught her. The wing blasted off her ship—which wouldn't have been deadly in space, but the next shot ripped apart her hull, venting the cockpit. Including her.

She can survive that, I thought at myself forcibly, firing at Brade. I came *so* close to hitting her, the shots narrowly missing her canopy as she dodged around, weaving between my destructor blasts.

Brade got off a shot as she turned, and it nailed the *Swims Upstream.*

"We're hit!" a kitsen voice shouted. "Lord Hesho!"

A dozen other kitsen voices cried out reports, and the *Swims Upstream* floundered, venting air. I couldn't focus on that, unfortunately. I gritted my teeth and got in behind Brade.

The scream in my mind slacked off even further as the dogfight narrowed to just the two of us. Woman against woman. Pilot against pilot. We swooped past some ancient rubble, spinning and tumbling, trapped in orbit, and Brade pivoted around it with her light-lance.

I followed, staying on her—but just barely. We spun through the darkness, neither of us firing, focused only on the chase. I had the upper hand from the rear position, but . . .

But *Saints* she was good. All else faded. World beneath me, stars above, set against the backdrop of a terrible battle. None of it mattered. The two of us were a pair of sharks chasing one another through a sea of minnows. She managed to draw me in close to the defensive platforms, then loop around me as I was forced to dodge a shot.

I stayed ahead of her in turn, then threw us both into a spiral where I barely managed to cut out and swing around her, taking position on her tail again.

It was thrilling, invigorating. I felt as I rarely had before, challenged to the absolute limits of my ability. And Brade *was* better. She stayed just ahead of me and dodged each shot I took.

I found that exhilarating.

I'd often been the best pilot in the sky. Seeing someone who was better was perhaps the most inspiring thing I'd ever experienced. I wanted to fly with her, chase her, pit myself against her until I covered that distance and matched her.

But as I was grinning, I again heard her screaming into the nowhere. It was faint, but in its wake my illusion of enjoyment came crashing down. Brade was trying to destroy everything I loved. If I couldn't stop her, if I wasn't good enough, that spelled the end of the DDF, Detritus, and *humankind itself*.

In that light, my inability was terrifying.

I don't have to beat her alone, I thought. *I just have to get her to go where I want* . . .

I broke off and darted away. I could *feel* Brade's annoyance. She'd been enjoying this too, and suddenly she felt angry at me for my cowardice. I was running?

She gave immediate chase, firing at me. I had to stay ahead for only a short while longer. I dodged around a specific collection of space debris, and Brade followed. I held my breath . . .

"Got her!" Vapor said over Brade's own channel.

I spun my ship around and boosted back toward Brade's ship— which had followed me through the rubble of Vapor's destroyed drone—as it slowed. I could see right into the cockpit, where she pounded on her console in frustration.

Her ship powered off anyway, Vapor locking down the systems. We had her. I slowed my own ship, then pointed the nose right at Brade. My own words seemed to echo back at me.

*We can't simply shoot to disable. She'll keep on trying to bring
that delver as long as she's alive . . .*

As if in direct proof of that, she met my gaze, then projected
a scream into the nowhere. The eyes—which had been fading—
snapped their attention back on us, particularly one pair that seemed
larger than all the rest.

I squeezed the trigger. In that moment, Brade's scream went
shriller than it ever had before. In the panic of knowing she would
die, Brade finally accomplished her goal.

And something emerged from the nowhere.

41

The delver's emergence distorted reality. In one blink of an eye, Brade's ship went from being in front of me to being shoved aside. Something vast entering our realm pushed us back, like we were riding a wave rippling through reality itself.

The shot I'd taken at Brade missed, and was instead absorbed by the expanding blackness.

My ship rocked as I was thrust away. The blackness grew so large that it dominated my view. I thought I saw the core of the delver for a moment, that deep shadow. An absolute darkness that seemed too pure to actually exist.

And then the maze appeared, matter coalescing around the thing like . . . like condensation forming on a very cold pipe. It grew around the core, shooting out terrible spires, gathering to be the size of a small planet. Much larger than the maze we'd trained in.

That maze was soon shrouded in dust and particulate matter, a haze that obscured it. Dark spires cast shadows within, lit by flares of deep red, the color of molten stone. Storms of terrible colors and mind-bending shadows. A vast, nearly incomprehensible thing, hidden within the floating dust.

This enormous thing now loomed like a moon over Detritus—*far* too close. My sensors went crazy; the delver had its own gravitational pull.

Two weeks ago, I'd watched a recording of a thing like this consuming the old inhabitants of Detritus. Now I cowered before one in real life. A speck. We were all specks to this creature.

My hands fell limp from my controls. I'd failed. And I was pretty sure that the very action I'd taken to stop this—shooting at Brade—had given her the push to achieve her goal.

I felt a sudden crushing sense of hopelessness. This thing was so immense and strange.

Then another emotion pushed through the despair. Anger. We'd die here—everyone in the Defiant Caverns—while the people of Starsight ate, and laughed, and ignored what their own government was doing. It didn't seem fair. Those insects. Those bugs that slobbered and skittered and clicked and . . . and . . .

Wait. I pushed through those overwhelming emotions. That wasn't me. That wasn't how *I* was feeling.

The battle had stilled. Detritus had gone silent, as I'd ordered. It was as if the entire planet held its breath. A mind—a vast, incomprehensible mind—brushed against mine. Something so oppressive, it threatened to crush me.

There's nothing here, I thought in a panic. *Nothing to destroy. You see? No buzzing, no annoyances here. Go somewhere else. Go . . . go that way.*

I fed it a destination. Not really by intent—more like the way you'd throw something hot after touching it unexpectedly. I pointed it toward a place in the far distance. The direction where Winzik's broadcast was going, the direction where the stars were singing.

I felt the delver's attention turn. Yes, there were things nearby—Superiority ships—making noise, but it wanted something larger. It could *hear* that distant destination, the place where I'd nudged its attention.

It vanished, following that distant song.

I was sucked forward by the ripple in reality, same as I'd been pushed back by it earlier. Sweat beaded on the sides of my face as confusion fought relief. It was gone. Just like that, it was gone.

I had sent it to destroy Starsight instead.

42

"Hello?" a kitsen voice said over my comm.

I stared out into the void, numb.

"Alanik . . . I . . . I don't actually know what your name is. It's me, Kauri. We . . . we sustained great losses. Lord Hesho is dead. I've taken command, but I don't know what to do."

Hesho? Dead? The kitsen ship hovered up by mine. A black gouge had been blasted out of the side, but the crew had patched it with a shield.

"The Superiority forces are retreating," Vapor said. "Ships are disengaging from the humans and flying back toward the *Weights and Measures.* Perhaps they are frightened, now that their terrible weapon has failed."

"It didn't fail," I whispered. "It's gone to Starsight instead. They . . . they didn't quiet themselves enough. They've come to rely on their communications. It heard them."

"What is this?" Kauri said. "Could you repeat that, please? You said the delver has *gone to Starsight.*"

"Yes." *I sent it.*

"No! We have *family* on the station! And crew members who

were too sick for duty. There are . . . there are *millions of people on Starsight!*"

A drone hovered up beside me. Vapor had stolen herself a new ship. I barely noticed. I was watching the stars, listening to their sounds.

"Winzik . . . that monster," Vapor said. "This is exactly what happened when humans tried to control a delver during the second war. It turned against the very ones who'd summoned it. His broadcast of these events gave the thing a pathway *right back* to his home!"

It had been that, yes, but more my own interference. *I* had done this. Saints and stars . . . I'd sent it to destroy them. Brade was right. We could control these things.

"We can't let this . . . ," Kauri said, sounding helpless. "Maybe we could return to the *Weights and Measures*? Have it fly us back to Starsight, to fight? But . . . the retreat is going to take time; the carrier needs to wait for those fighters to disengage. It could be half an hour before the ship gets back to the city."

Far too long. Starsight was doomed. All those people. Cuna and Mrs. Chamwit. Morriumur. Because of me. I felt . . . I felt like the delver had sensed my fury. Was that possible?

"What have you done?" Brade demanded over the comm. I glanced to the side and saw her ship had stopped tumbling nearby. *"What have you done?"*

"What I had to," I whispered. "To save my people."

In so doing, I'd doomed another people. But would anyone blame me for that choice? I knew that even if Winzik's ships *did* reach the delver in time, their "weapon" against it was merely a way of diverting its attention. They'd try to send it back here to destroy us instead.

It was us or them.

Brade's ship vanished, slipping into the nowhere.

"What do we do?" Vapor asked.

"I don't know," Kauri said. "I . . . I . . ."

There was nothing to do. I reignited my shield, then leaned my head back and accepted what was happening.

Leave the Superiority to its own problems. They'd caused this. They deserved it. My only worry was for M-Bot and Doomslug. Surely he'd be safe. He was a ship.

Regardless, what could I do? Us or them. I turned my ship around, away from the stars, to head back home.

No.

My hands moved off the controls.

"This isn't my fight," I whispered.

A hero doesn't choose her trials, Gran-Gran's voice said.

"I don't know how to stop it."

A hero faces what comes next.

"They hate us! They think we're only worthy of being destroyed!"

Prove them wrong.

"Um . . . Alanik?" Kauri asked, uncertain, moving her ship up beside mine.

I took a long deep breath, then looked back at the stars.

Scud. I couldn't abandon those people.

I *could not* run from this fight.

"Bring your ships in close," I said to the kitsen and to Vapor. "Touch your wings to mine if you can."

"Why?" Vapor asked, obeying. Her wing tapped mine, and the kitsen's did so on the other side. "What are we doing?"

"Stepping into the darkness," I said.

Then I flung us into the nowhere.

INTERLUDE

Being two people was an uncomfortable experience for Morriumur. On the left, one could argue that Morriumur had never known anything different. On the right, one could point out that one's separate halves—and the memories they had inherited—knew precisely how odd the experience was.

Two minds thinking together, but blending memories and experiences from the past. Only *some* from each parent, a stew of personality and memory. Occasionally their instincts fought against one another. Earlier in the day, Morriumur had reached to scratch their head—but both hands had tried to do it at once. And before that, at the sound of a loud bang—just a dish being dropped—Morriumur had tried to both dodge for cover and jump up to help at the same time.

This disjunction was growing even worse as the two halves prepared to separate and recombine again. Morriumur stepped toward the drafting pod, passing through a double row of family members—lefts on one side, rights the other, with agendered choosing either side. They held out the appropriate hand, brushing

Morriumur's own extended hands as they passed through the dark room.

Morriumur was supposed to have two and a half months left, but after leaving the space force . . . well, the decision had been made to proceed early. This draft was not right. Morriumur's parents and family agreed. Time to try again.

Everyone said it wasn't supposed to feel like a farewell, and that Morriumur shouldn't see it as a rejection. Redrafting was common, and they had been assured it wouldn't hurt. Yet how could one take it as anything *but* a rejection?

Too aggressive, one grand had said. *This will trouble them all their life.*

They chose to investigate a career very unbecoming of a dione, one pibling had said. *They could never be happy like this.*

These same relatives gave Morriumur fond lip-draws, touching hands with them as if seeing them off on a journey. The drafting pod was much like a large bed, though with the center hollowed out. Shaped of the traditional wood with a slick polished interior, once Morriumur climbed into it, its lid would be affixed and a nutrient bath injected to help with the cocooning and redrafting process.

Their eldest grand, Numiga, took both of their hands as they stepped up to the pod. "You did well, Morriumur."

"If that's so . . . why have I failed to prove myself?"

"Your job wasn't to prove yourself. It was merely to exist and let us see possibilities. Come, you yourself returned to us and agreed the process needed to continue."

Morriumur's left hand gave a curved gesture of affirmation, almost on its own. They *had* returned. Departed the docks while the others went to fight. Fled, because . . . because they'd been too upset to continue. Defending against delvers was one thing, but going to shoot down other pilots? The idea horrified Morriumur.

You'd have been too frightened to fight a delver anyway, a part of them—perhaps one of their parents—thought. *Too aggressive for dione society. Too paranoid to fight. Redrafting is for the best.*

For the best, another part of them thought.

Morriumur stumbled, feeling a disorientation caused by the two separating parts of their brain. Numiga helped them sit on the side of the drafting pod, their deep reddish-violet skin seeming to glow in the candlelight.

"It's beginning," Numiga said. "It is time."

"I don't want to go."

"It will not hurt," Numiga promised. "It will still be you who comes out, redrafted. Just a different you."

"What if I want to be *the same* me?"

Numiga patted them on the hand. "Almost all of us went through a few drafts, Morriumur, and we all survived it. When you emerge again, you will wonder why you were so bothered."

Morriumur nodded and put both feet into the pod. Then they paused. "When I come back out, will I remember these months?"

"Faintly," Numiga said. "Like fragments of a dream."

"And my friends? Will I know their faces?"

Numiga pushed them, gently, into the pod. It *was* time. Morriumur's two halves were unraveling, the minds separating, and their personality . . . stretched thin. It was . . . hard . . . to . . . think . . .

The chamber rocked with a sudden extended tremble. Morriumur grabbed the side of the pod, hissing out in surprise. Around them, the others stumbled against one another, crying out or hissing. People fell as the trembling persisted, until finally it grew still.

What had *that* been? It felt like the platform had been hit by something—but what kind of impact could be so large that it would shake all of Starsight?

Outside, screams sounded in the streets. Morriumur's relatives climbed to their feet in a mess, pushing aside the drapings in front of the doorway. They opened it and let light flood the small dark chamber.

Trembling, barely able to control their limbs, Morriumur crawled out of the pod. Everyone seemed to have forgotten them. What . . . what could be happening? Pulling themself up on the equipment near the pod, Morriumur got to their feet and stumbled to the door leading outside, where many of their relatives stood staring upward in a wide-eyed stupor.

A *planet* had somehow appeared beside Starsight. A dark, dust-shrouded thing, with terrible lines emerging from within its black center. Deep red lights played beneath the dust, like eruptions of magma. It loomed over Starsight, a spectacle so vast—so unexpected—that both of Morriumur's minds reeled. How could *that* be *there,* interrupting the calming depths of space that had always been on the horizon?

It's a delver! one mind trembled. *Run!*

Flee! the other mind screamed.

Around Morriumur, relatives scrambled away, running—though how did you run from something like this? Within moments, only Morriumur was standing there before the building, alone. Their minds continued to panic, but Morriumur didn't let go, and slowly their minds relaxed and knit back together.

It wouldn't last long. But for now, Morriumur looked up and exposed their teeth.

Cuna gripped the rail of their balcony, trying to take in the awesome sight of the delver.

"We've failed," they whispered. "He's destroyed Detritus. Now he brings it here to show off his power."

The scent around them turned sharply angry, like that of wet soil. "This is a disaster," Zezin said. "You said . . . I didn't believe . . . Cuna, how *could* Winzik do this?"

Cuna gave a helpless gesture of their fingers, still staring up at the terrible sight. The awesome scale of the thing made it difficult to tell, but Cuna could *feel* the thing drawing closer, approaching the city.

"He'll destroy us," Cuna realized. "The high minister is still in attendance. Winzik will take out the Superiority's government, leaving only himself."

"No," Zezin said, smelling of hot spices. "Even he is not so callous. This is a mistake, Cuna. He summoned it, but cannot control it as he assumed. It has come here of its own volition."

Yes. Cuna realized the truth of it immediately. Winzik wanted to be known as a hero; he would not destroy Starsight. This wasn't just a mistake—it was a disaster of the highest order. The same foolishness that had made the humans fall.

Ships began to stream away in a panic, and Cuna wished them speed. Maybe some would escape.

It was a dubious hope. Starsight was doomed, and Cuna couldn't help feeling an awful responsibility. Would Winzik have ever decided upon this course if the two of them hadn't brainstormed a potential defense force, years ago?

Embers began to launch from the delver, slamming into the shield around Starsight and bursting with incredible explosions. Soon the shield would fall.

The air turned a sour scent of rotting fruit—sorrow and anguish from Zezin.

"Go," Cuna whispered. "You might be able to move quickly enough to escape."

"We . . . we will stop this from going further, Cuna," Zezin promised. "We'll resist Winzik. Clean up his mess."

"*Go.*"

Zezin left. Figments could move quickly through the air, or

even the vacuum. They both knew that alone, Zezin could perhaps reach a private ship in time to fly out beyond the shield and hyperjump away.

An old dione, however . . . Was there anything Cuna could do to help? Send a last broadcast perhaps, exposing Winzik? Give courage to those fleeing? Was there even time for that?

Cuna gripped the banister, looking out at the delver. Shrouded in its veil—glowing from its own light—the thing had a terrifying beauty to it. Cuna almost felt like they were standing alone before a deity. A god of destruction.

Then, an incongruity finally ripped Cuna's attention away. An impossibility amid the fear.

A small group of fighters, just outside the shield, had appeared and now flew straight toward the delver.

43

I streaked toward the delver, Vapor and the kitsen on my wings. In my mind, the lingering horror of the nowhere shadowed my memories—that had been a bad jump, with so many of them watching me. But the one specific delver that had been so close lately hadn't been there. I could somehow tell the difference.

It wasn't hard to guess exactly where that delver was. It loomed just beyond Starsight, and had already begun launching embers by the hundreds into the shield. Chaotic emergency information channels said the city had opened the shield on the side farthest from the delver, allowing ships to escape.

"Kauri," I said, glancing at the flagging kitsen ship. "You're trailing smoke."

"Our boosters are barely working," she replied. "I'm sorry, Alanik. I don't know how useful we're going to be in a battle against those embers."

"Vapor and I should be able to manage it," I said. "Fly back and see if you can get anyone's attention on the military channels. We need the city to go silent. The delver can hear their radio signals. I don't know how we're going to drive the thing away, but I suspect it will be a *lot* easier if this city isn't screaming at it."

"Understood," Kauri said. "We'll do what we can. Good luck."

"Luck is for those who cannot smell their path forward," Vapor said. "But . . . perhaps today that is us. So good luck to you too."

The *Swims Upstream* broke off from us and started back. Vapor and I continued along just outside the atmosphere bubble. Beneath us, ships were swarming and trying to escape.

"M-Bot?" I asked, trying the secret line the two of us had been using, connected via my bracelet.

There was no response, and using my onboard sensors I was able to get a zoomed-in picture of my embassy building as we passed. The rooftop was empty. So maybe he'd gotten away somehow? Scud, I wished I knew.

Together, Vapor and I approached the delver itself. It evoked an awful sense of scale—and was far more daunting than a mere planetoid would be. Embers emerged from the dust, then smashed repeatedly into the city's shield, exploding soundlessly in the void—but some of the blasts were the size of entire battleships.

"I can't help churning upon myself a little," Vapor said as we approached, "and thinking our training was *horribly* incomplete."

"Yeah," I said. No training in a simulation could approximate the strange sensations the delver sent at me, a kind of *crushing* feeling upon my mind. It somehow heightened my fear, my anger, *and* my sense of horror. It was getting worse the closer we got.

A small blip flashed on my proximity sensor.

"What's that?" Vapor asked.

"It's her," I said, noting the ship flying ahead of us. I quickly opened a line. "Brade. You can't take this thing on by yourself."

"I'm not going to let it destroy my home," she said back. "This wasn't supposed to happen. It was supposed to go after *you*."

"Ignore that," I snapped. "Work *with* me for once."

"Alanik . . . you realize what I'm going to do if I reach the center? The only thing I *can* do?"

Use the diversion weapon, I thought. *Send it back toward Detritus again.* "We have to send it somewhere else, Brade. We have to try."

She cut the line.

"That one has always been a foul wind, Alanik," Vapor said. "She's . . . Oh. Um."

She's human.

"Cover me as we get close," I said, hitting my boosters.

We flew out from over Starsight, nearing the delver's dust cloud. The only hope I had for a plan was to try to send the delver somewhere unpopulated. I'd established three hyperjump locations in my mind: Starsight, Detritus, and the deep-space location of the delver maze.

So I only had one real option. I'd have to send it to the maze. But . . . surely it would just find nothing to destroy there, then immediately return to Starsight. What else could I do though? Maybe it would see the maze and be distracted by it? That seemed a frail hope, but it was the only one I had.

Vapor flew out ahead of me and started shooting down the embers that approached. I slowed, and tried to reach out with my mind to the delver.

It was . . . vast. The sensations coming off it smothered me. I could feel how it regarded us. The anger at all the buzzing noises we made. Those same emotions threatened to overwhelm me, alienate me, make me feel the same way it did.

I fought against that, feeding it the location of the maze, trying—as I'd somehow done before—to distract its attention. Unfortunately, before it hadn't just been me. It had been a mixture of my emotion, the silence on Detritus, and the sound out in the void. The singing stars.

The delver had come here because it knew the noises were greatest here. My current efforts to distract it were swallowed up by the emotion it radiated. I felt like I was screaming into a tempest, and try as I might, I couldn't pierce the noise.

I cursed, cutting off my attempts and boosting after Vapor, blasting an ember that almost hit her.

"We need to get inside," I said. "We need to find its heart."

Vapor fell in next to me, and together we hurtled into the dust. Visibility dropped to nearly nothing, and I had to fly by instruments. We'd been warned we would need to do that, but nothing in our training had indicated how *creepy* it would be to enter this dust.

As we flew through that silent cloud, which flashed periodically with red light, my sensors started to go out. My proximity screen started to fuzz, giving me only the briefest warnings when something was drawing close. Embers emerged as burning shapes, indistinct and terrible.

Vapor and I stopped fighting the embers, instead just trying to dodge as they attempted to slam into us. They'd fall in and trail after us, occasionally streaking forward with bursts of speed. I felt like I was trying to outrun my own shadow.

The pressure on my mind grew worse and worse the closer we drew to the delver itself. Soon I was gritting my teeth against it—the sensations were so overpowering that they affected my flying. I barely got out of the way of one ember, but put myself into the path of another.

Frantic, I speared a third with my light-lance, which fortunately pulled me out of the way. But when I looked up, I couldn't see Vapor. My sensors were a jumble of static, and the only things I could make out around me were moving shadows and bursts of red light.

"Vapor?" I asked.

I got a jumbled response. Was that her over there? I followed another shadow, but only got further lost in the dust storm. I glanced the other direction, and saw what I was sure was an explosion.

"Vapor?"

Static.

I dodged away from another ember, but my fingers had started to tremble from the force of the thoughts pressing upon my mind.

Buzzing . . . buzzing insects . . . Destroy them . . .

Oppressive thoughts, weighing me down. Nightmare visions started to appear in the dust. Monsters from Gran-Gran's stories, appearing and vanishing. My father's face. Myself, but with burning white eyes . . .

This wasn't anything like the carefully designed illusions of the training maze. It was a horrific cacophony. No secrets to uncover, just noise slamming against me. Being a cytonic here was a huge disadvantage, because the delver got inside my brain.

I was barely controlling my ship. Reality and illusion melded as one, and I took my hands off the controls and pressed them against my eyes. My head had begun to throb in agony. I tried another weak effort to whisper back—to divert the thing toward deep space.

That seemed to open me further, and the noise invaded my mind. I screamed, and something smashed into my ship, *ramming* it to the side, nearly bringing down my shield. Warning alarms from my dash were just another noise. I . . . I couldn't fly in this. I . . .

A shadow emerged from the dust. My heart leaped at the shape of a ship. Vapor? *M-Bot?*

No, a shuttle, with no weapons except an industrial light-lance for moving equipment. It speared my ship and pulled me after it, away from the churning shapes. An ember—I thought it was real—roared past, narrowly missing my ship.

"Alanik?" a voice said on my comm.

I . . . I knew that voice. "Morriumur?" I whispered.

"I've got your ship tethered," they said. "You were just sitting there. Are you all right?"

"The heart . . . ," I whispered. "You have to get me to the heart. But . . . but Morriumur . . . you can't . . . The illusions . . ."

"I can see through them!" Morriumur said.

What?

Morriumur towed me through the dust, approaching one of the spines of the delver—a large spike leading down to its surface. We flew along it, Morriumur dodging some of the nightmares, but completely ignoring others. They smashed into us and puffed away. Just . . . illusions.

"It shows different things to everyone," Morriumur said, expertly towing me into a hole in the surface.

"Two people . . . ," I whispered, holding my head. "You need—"

"That's the thing, Alanik," Morriumur said. "I *am* two people."

I whimpered, squeezing my eyes shut at the assault, which only grew worse as we flew inside. Fortunately, Morriumur's voice continued, somehow comforting and *real* in the middle of all the emotion and noise.

"It's projecting two different things at me," Morriumur said. "One to each of the brains of my parents. I . . . don't think it knows how to deal with me. We've never flown a draft into a delver before, so far as I know. Honestly, I don't think any diones at *all* ever tried flying into one of these. Our pilots have always been varvax or tenasi.

"The illusions are nothing to me, Alanik," Morriumur said. "We didn't realize, during training. We treated me like anyone else—but I can *see through* them as two overlapping, shadowy images. I can do this. *I can reach the heart.*"

I undid my buckles with trembling hands, barely aware of what I was doing. I ripped off my helmet, then curled up, holding my head, trying to escape the visions. I bounced against the inside of my ship as Morriumur pulled me one direction, then the next.

"A lot of these tunnels are fake," Morriumur said. "I think the maze would have led us around in circles . . . It's really just a big openness in here, Alanik."

I trembled beneath an infinite weight. I don't know how long it took, but I *felt* us getting closer. I was a child alone in a black room, and the darkness was pressing against me. Growing deeper, and deeper, and deeper . . .

"There's something ahead."

Deeper and deeper and deeper . . .

I dropped inside my cockpit, pressing against the seat.

"This is it!" The small voice came from my dash. An insect to crush. "Alanik, we've entered a pocket of air and gravity. What do I do now? Alanik? I never got to the heart during our training!"

"Open. My. Canopy." I whispered the words, my voice hoarse.

A short time later, I heard a thumping as Morriumur forced open my canopy with the manual override.

"Alanik?" Morriumur asked. "I see . . . a hole over there. The membrane is an illusion. It's just a blackness, like a hole into nothing. What do I do?"

"Help. Me."

Eyes squeezed closed, I let Morriumur assist me out of the ship and onto the wing. I stumbled, clinging to them, and opened my eyes.

Nightmares surrounded me. Visions of dying pilots. Hurl screaming as she burned. Bim. My father. Hesho. Everyone I'd known. But I could see it too, the hole. Our ships had settled down on something solid. It looked like one of the caverns from back home. The hole was right next to my ship, a deep void in the ground.

I let go of Morriumur, pushed off them. They cried out as I dropped from the wing. And plunged into the void.

44

I entered a completely white room.

The pressure on my mind vanished immediately. I stumbled to a stop and looked around at the pure whiteness, somehow familiar.

I let out a long sigh, turning around until I saw myself standing beside the far wall. Not a mirror image. Me. Standing there. That was it, the delver. It looked like me the same way the one in the recording had. I wasn't sure why it chose that shape—or even if it did. Perhaps my mind simply interpreted it this way.

I walked to the delver, surprised at how confident and strong I felt. After what I'd just been through, I should have been weak, exhausted. But in here, in this white room, I had recovered.

The delver was staring at the wall. I leaned forward and saw that there were tiny pinpricks in it. Holes? I could hear a buzzing noise from them. The more I focused on it, the more awful it sounded. It was an annoyance that marred the otherwise perfectly serene room.

I looked back at the delver. It wore my face, which should have been strange. But . . . for some reason it wasn't? I prodded at it with my mind, curious.

Curiosity came back. I cocked my head, then closed my eyes. I felt . . . pain, agony, fear from the spots on the wall. The delver sensed those emotions, and reflected them back out the way they'd come.

"You don't understand emotions, do you?" I asked it. "We're misinterpreting you, like I misinterpreted Cuna. You don't hate us. You just reflect back what we feel. That's why you look like me. You're only sending back at me what I'm showing you."

It looked at me, its face impassive. And . . . I could tell that what I'd said wasn't *exactly* true. It *did* hate the buzzing sounds, the annoyances. But much of what we showed it—much of our experience of the universe—was completely foreign to it. It reflected those back at us, part of a fundamental inability to understand.

"You have to go somewhere else," I said to it, and tried to project the location of the delver maze.

It looked away from me, staring back at the wall.

"Please," I said. "Please."

No response. And so, I reached out my hand and touched it. The white room shattered, and suddenly I was expanding, as if . . . as if I were as large as a planet. A *galaxy*. I was expansive, eternal. I'd lived forever in peace, in a place where time had no meaning. Except when people intruded.

I saw them now, the buzzing annoyances of Starsight. The shield fell before my barrage, and I started forward, sweeping across a few of the nearby ships. Those sounds went out, and each quieted insect was a relief. It wasn't just occasional trips through the nowhere that bothered me, but each and every one of these obnoxious buzzes.

I could finally reach them. Quiet them. It was glorious!

I pulled back, and was in the room, my hand pressed to my chest. I felt a lingering hatred of everything living. The delver would destroy all of Starsight in pursuit of its peace. I understood that, because part of me was from that place where it lived. The part that could touch the nowhere.

"Don't," I pleaded. "Please don't!"

Some of the specks on the wall vanished.

What could I do? I couldn't fight it. I was nothing more than one of those specks myself. No amount of training in a maze, fighting with destructors and light-lances, could have helped with this moment. I could not have trained to defeat this thing.

The people of Starsight deserved a diplomat, or a scientist, who could understand this problem. Not me.

More specks vanished, and—tears pouring down my face—I grabbed the front of the delver's flight suit with both hands. I felt that overpowering expansion happening again, the alignment with its perspective, which was so vast as to make individuals meaningless.

But *they weren't*.

"See them," I whispered. "Please, just *see them*."

I had seen what the delver experienced. In that frantic moment with a catastrophe starting before me, I tried to show it what *I'd* experienced. With all my strength I towed on its consciousness.

It worked. Instead of growing to the size of a galaxy, I pulled us down so we shrank to the size of a child. Infinity went both directions. You could expand forever outward, but at the same time, the closer you looked at something, the more detail you saw.

For a moment, we were a child who played with floating globes of water. We were Mrs. Chamwit, delivering dinner to a neighbor. We were Cuna. We were the Krell on the street who had apologized for bumping me. I touched the mind of the delver and showed it those annoyances from the perspective of each individual person. I showed it that the buzzing was sometimes laughter.

434

This is what I see, I said to the delver. *Though I had to learn how to look.*

The delver stopped advancing. Its mind touched mine, and I felt emotions, images, and alien things that were neither. Things I didn't have the senses to otherwise experience or explain. In the midst of it was an idea . . . a question.

They are like us?

Not words. Ideas. The term *us* was projected into my mind as a set of meaningful concepts I could roughly interpret.

They . . . , it repeated. *They are* alive?

Yes, I whispered. *Every one of them.*

The thing trembled with an emotion I understood without needing interpretation. Horror.

The delver pulled in, somehow reversing upon itself. I was ejected from that place where I'd been, as the entire thing—the enormous planetlike mass and the strange being at the center—vanished.

Dumping me into space.

I'd done decompression exercises, and somehow managed to exhale before my lungs burst. Water *boiled* on my eyes, and pain shot through me, and I started to black out almost immediately. Yet I was just aware enough to feel a pair of hands grab me.

EPILOGUE

The sound grew louder the deeper Jorgen went.

It wasn't a buzzing, not like when he'd first met Spensa. He wasn't even certain it was a sound. Nedd and Arturo couldn't hear it, after all. Maybe he was imagining it.

But Jorgen *could* hear it. A soft music, growing louder with each tunnel they had explored in the five days they'd been searching. They'd hit many dead ends and had to turn back a dozen times. But they were close now. So close he felt it was just beyond the wall here. He had to find a way to lead them left . . .

He stumbled down a short incline, then waded through water that came up to his knees. He held his industrial-strength lantern up before him, the kind used by the teams who traveled the distant tunnels and caverns of the planet to service remote equipment like pipes that carried up water from underground reservoirs.

"More water?" Arturo asked from behind, his own lantern making Jorgen cast a long shadow. "Jorgen, we *really* should get back. I could *swear* that sound we heard was an echo of the alarms. We might be under attack."

All the more reason to keep going. He waded forward as the

437

water grew deeper. He had to know what he was hearing. *Had* to know if he was imagining things, or if . . . maybe . . . he could *hear* Detritus.

That seemed stupid when he thought about it like that. He hadn't told the others yet, except to explain he was on orders from Cobb. Which he kind of was. After a fashion.

And everyone believes I can't disobey orders, he thought. *They don't think I can be brash? Foolhardy? Ha!*

Running off into the deep caverns without proper supplies, and only a couple friends to accompany him? Following a hunch and something he *maybe* thought he could hear, only nobody else could?

"Jorgen?" Nedd asked, standing with Arturo at the edge of the water. "Come on. We've been at this forever. Arturo is right. We really need to be getting back."

"It's right here, guys," Jorgen said, hip deep in water, a hand pressed against the stone wall. "Songs. *Right here.* We have to get through this wall."

"Okaaay," Arturo said. "So we head back, see if anyone has mapped this section of the tunnels, and maybe determine if there's a good way to . . ."

Jorgen felt across the wall, noting that the water seemed to be flowing oddly. "There's an opening here, just beneath the surface. It might be wide enough for me to wiggle through."

"No," Arturo said. "Jorgen, do *not* try to squeeze through it. You'll get stuck and drown."

Jorgen dropped his pack, letting his waterproof lantern float on the top of the pool. He reached down into the water, feeling at the break in the wall. It *was* wide enough. "Spensa would try it," he said.

"Uh," Nedd said, "is Spin *really* the best example to follow? In acting stupid?"

"Well, she does it all the time," Jorgen said. "So she must have a lot of practice."

Arturo rushed into the water, reaching for him. So, before he could get talked—or pulled—out of going farther, Jorgen took a deep breath and ducked under the surface, then kicked into the hole.

He couldn't see in the water; his motions had stirred up silt, and so the lantern wouldn't have helped either. He had to feel his way forward, grabbing the sides of the rock tunnel, and pull himself through the dark water.

Fortunately, it turned out that the tunnel wasn't long—it wasn't even really a tunnel. Just a passage through the stone, maybe a meter and a half in length.

He burst up into a dark cavern, and immediately felt stupid. What did he expect to find or see in the darkness? He *should* have drowned.

Then he heard the sounds. Music all around him. Flutes calling to him. The sound of the planet itself speaking?

His eyes adjusted, and he realized he *could* see. The stone here outside the small pool where he stood was overgrown with a blue-green luminescent kind of fungus. Indeed, much larger mushrooms were growing all across the floor of the cavern, perhaps feeding off nutrient-rich water dripping from an ancient pipe running along the wall.

Hiding amid the mushrooms, fluting in a way he could now hear with both his mind *and* his ears, were a group of yellow creatures. Slugs, like Spensa's pet.

Hundreds of them.

I awoke to a soft breeze on my face.

I blinked, disoriented, seeing white. I was back in that room with the delver. No, I couldn't be! I . . .

The room came into focus. I was in a bed with white sheets, but the walls weren't stark white. Just a cream color. A window

439

nearby looked out on the streets of Starsight, a soft breeze blowing in and ruffling the drapes.

I was hooked up to tubes and monitors and . . . and I was in a hospital. I sat up, trying to piece together how I'd gotten here.

"Ah!" a familiar voice said. "Spensa?"

I turned to find Cuna, wearing their official robes, peeking in through the door. My translator pin, fortunately, was clipped to my hospital robe.

"The doctors said you'd be waking," Cuna said. "How do you feel? Explosive decompression nearly killed you. I'd recommend against going into space without a helmet in the future! It's been three days since the delver incident."

"I . . ." I touched my face, then felt at my throat. "How did I survive?"

Cuna smiled. And actually, they were getting better at that. They settled down on a stool beside my bed, then got out their tablet and projected a holoimage for me. It showed a shuttle flying down and landing on the docks inside Starsight.

"The city's shield went down," Cuna said, "but emergency ES gravitation kept the atmosphere from escaping. Morriumur says you appeared in space once the delver vanished, and they were quick-witted enough to grab you and pull you into their cockpit."

I watched a projected Morriumur dock at Starsight, pop their canopy, then stand up, holding me, unconscious. They were met with cheers. I really was getting better at reading dione expressions, because I immediately recognized the befuddlement on Morriumur's face.

"Morriumur thought everyone was going to be angry, didn't they?" I said. "They assumed they'd get in trouble for flying into battle."

"Yes, but for no reason," Cuna said. They swiped the holoimage to another: this one showed two dione parents holding a small purple baby. I could see Morriumur's features in the parents—at least, half of them on each face. "It turns out, relatives who were advocating for a redraft changed their minds quickly once the draft became a celebrity. My culture has its first war hero in centuries! It will be a few years before Morriumur develops enough to enjoy their notoriety though."

I smiled and settled back into my pillow, feeling worn-out—but not in pain. Whatever they'd done to heal me had been effective; Superiority medical technology was obviously beyond our own.

"I can't stay long," Cuna said. "I need to speak at the hearings."

"Winzik?" I asked. "Brade?"

"It's . . . complicated," Cuna said. "There is still some support for Winzik in the government, and there are conflicting accounts of the events a few days ago. Winzik is trying to claim that your people summoned the delver, and a brave dione—Morriumur—was our salvation.

"However, I'm confident in my case. I've insisted on being allowed contact with your people. Always before, Winzik's people have been the only ones authorized to interact with the humans in the preserve.

"How surprised some of our officials were to get such calm, rational messages from your Admiral Cobb! This has proven that free humans aren't the ravening terrors that everyone expected. I think Winzik will be forced to step down, but it will help if you can speak to the press. I'm afraid . . . I may have nudged the doctors to wake you early for that reason."

"It's all right. I'm glad that—" I bolted upright. Wait. M-Bot! "My ship, Cuna! I flew here on a ship that's very important. Where is it?"

"Don't worry," Cuna said. "Winzik's department raided your

embassy after you fled the city, but I'm working to get all of your things restored to you. Your leader, Cobb, mentioned the ship specifically."

I settled back, unable to shake a sick sense of worry for M-Bot. Still, I doubted that I could have hoped for a better outcome, all things considered.

"The delver is really gone?" I asked.

"So far as we can tell," Cuna said. "Odd, as once they appear, they usually linger for years causing mayhem. Whatever you did saved more than just Starsight. Plus, casualties were remarkably low for an event of this magnitude. Morriumur and Vapor explained what they could, though we're still uncertain about . . . how exactly you dismissed it."

"I changed its perspective," I said. "I showed it that we were people. Turns out, it didn't *want* to destroy us."

Cuna smiled again. Yes, they were getting good at that. It almost wasn't creepy.

Something about the entire situation still put me on edge, but I forced myself to relax. We'd figure this out. It seemed . . . the war might actually be over, or close to it. If the Superiority was talking to Cobb, that was a *huge* step forward. And here I was, sitting in a Superiority hospital without my hologram on, and it was fine.

I'd done it. Somehow, I'd actually done it. I smiled back at Cuna, then held out my hand. They took it. Hopefully I could leave most of the details from here to the diplomats and politicians. My part was done.

I closed my eyes.

And found that everything just felt *wrong*. I let go of Cuna's hand, then stood up, pulling the tubes from my arm.

"Spensa?" Cuna asked. "What is it?"

"Where are my clothes?"

"Your things are over on that shelf," Cuna said. "But it's all right. You are safe."

I dressed anyway, putting on a laundered jumpsuit and flight jacket, then clipped on the translator pin. They'd left my bracelet, fortunately, which I snapped onto my wrist—even though I didn't need the hologram at the moment. I tried tapping it to contact M-Bot, but got no response.

I stepped up by the window, still not quite certain what had set me off. Part of it was abstract. Winzik had been willing to summon a delver to fulfill his plots. It didn't feel like he would accept defeat like an honorable general, turning over his sword to his enemy.

I scanned the city through the open window, standing just to the side of it, so I wasn't silhouetted as a target. *I'm being paranoid, aren't I?*

"Perhaps we should let you rest a little longer," Cuna said, their voice calm, but their fingers twitching in a sign of distress.

I nearly agreed, and then I realized what the problem was. The thing that was setting me off, the thing my instincts had recognized even if the rest of me hadn't put it together immediately.

It was quiet.

The window was open, and we were only three stories up. But there was no sound of traffic, no hum of people talking. Indeed, the streets outside were virtually empty.

I was accustomed to noise on Starsight. People always crowding on the streets. Movement everywhere. This city never slept, but today the streets were mostly empty. Was it just because everyone was upset and staying in following the delver attack?

No, I thought, spotting someone moving down a side street outside. A dione in a brown-striped outfit. I picked out two more of them ushering away a small group of civilians.

Those people in the brown stripes, they looked exactly like

the diones I'd seen cleaning up after the protesters had been dealt with. They were the same ones who had exiled the gorilla alien.

They're isolating the area, I realized. *Getting bystanders off the streets.*

"This isn't over yet," I said to Cuna. "We need to get out of here."

45

I dashed back past Cuna to check the door.

"Spensa!" Cuna said. "I need you to be less aggressive right now. Please. We are on the cusp of bringing peace between our peoples. This isn't the time for an outburst!"

I cracked the door and saw shadows moving down the hallway in my direction. Scud—those were Krell in full armor, carrying destructor rifles. I shut the door, then spun a chair and rammed its back into place under the lever to wedge the door shut. I grabbed Cuna by the hand.

"We need another way out," I said. "That door on the other side of the room. Where does it lead?"

"To a bathroom," Cuna said, "which is attached to another hospital bedroom." They resisted my tug on their arm. "I worry, Spensa, that I was wrong about you . . ."

The door out into the hallway shook. Cuna turned toward it. "That will be the doctors. Come, let's see if they can give you something to calm you—"

The door smashed open as an armored soldier burst in. I yanked Cuna with all I had, finally pulling them after me as I dashed out the opposite door. I locked the door into the bathroom, then shoved Cuna out into the next bedroom.

"What—" Cuna said.

"Winzik is continuing his coup," I said. "We need to go. *Now*. Where are the stairs down?"

"I . . . I think they're out in the hallway, just to the right . . . ," Cuna said, wide-eyed.

A blast from a destructor blew open the door from my hospital room into the bathroom. Only then did Cuna seem to grasp the severity of the situation. I took a deep breath as Krell soldiers shoved their way into the bathroom, then I threw open the door into the hallway and dashed out, Cuna in tow.

Someone shouted from farther down the hallway, but I didn't look—I focused on the stairwell, which was where Cuna had said. We barely reached it before a hail of destructor fire shot down the hallway, lighting the air behind us and ripping apart the far wall.

Scud. Scud. *SCUD.* I was unarmed, had no ship, and had a civilian in tow. I didn't know a lot about dione aging, but Cuna was obviously on the older side, and they were already puffing loudly from our quick dash. They wouldn't be able to stay ahead of those soldiers on their own, but I couldn't exactly carry them.

We reached the next floor down—one floor up from ground level. It seemed the Krell above were being careful though, so they wouldn't rush into some kind of trap—I heard them shouting, but they didn't immediately follow.

Unfortunately, I also heard someone shouting down below. They'd have stationed people on the first floor just in case. I debated for a second, looking toward Cuna, who was sweating heavily, eyes wide, teeth bared in a sign of distress.

Then I pulled them to the side, noting a small door that looked like a janitorial closet. Indeed, the interior was lined with cleaning implements, and a stained jumpsuit was hanging on a hook inside the door.

I pushed Cuna into the closet, then took off my bracelet and slapped it onto their wrist. A quick tweak of the buttons covered Cuna with the generic dione disguise that M-Bot had designed for me just in case. One with crimson skin and slightly pudgy features.

The hologram was programmed for me, so it didn't work quite right on Cuna, but it was believable enough—I hoped.

"This hologram is changing your face to make you look like someone else," I said. "Put on that jumpsuit, and hide in here. I'm going to lead the soldiers away."

"You'll die!" Cuna said.

"I don't intend to," I said, "but this is our only choice. You *need* to escape, Cuna. Get to Detritus and tell them what happened to me. Bring them some hyperdrive slugs, if you can. The disguise will hopefully let you sneak off of Starsight."

"I . . . I can't do this. I'm not a *spy*, Spensa!"

"Neither was I," I said. "The kitsen will join with us, and I think the figments might as well. You've got to do this. Wait until the soldiers chase after me, then sneak out. Claim to be a janitor if anyone catches you."

I took their shoulders, meeting their eyes. "Right now, Cuna, you are the only one who can save both our peoples from Winzik. I don't have time for a better plan. Do it. Please."

They met my eyes, and to their credit, Cuna nodded.

"Where did they take my ship?" I asked.

"They were holding it for inspection in the Protective Services Special Project building—the place I took you, where the exile happened. It's three streets outward, on Forty-Third."

"Thanks." I gave them a final smile, then grabbed a hammer off the wall and shut the door. Soldiers were already barreling down the stairs, so I took off running, scrambling down the empty hospital hallway. I chose directions at random, and fortunately it seemed that on my own I could outrun the heavily armored Krell.

I was able to lose them in the corridors until I hit another stairwell, then dashed down it, taking the steps two at a time. Unfortunately, I found a dark, boxy shape guarding the way down.

I'd spent many evenings listening to Gran-Gran's stories of mighty warriors like Conan the Cimmerian. I'd dreamed of fighting the Krell hand to hand, with some fearsome weapon. I'll admit, I even shouted "For Crom!" as I leaped off the stairs.

I'd never imagined how small I'd feel compared to one of the armored Krell, or how impotent I'd feel with a *hammer* in my hand rather than a real weapon. I had a lot of enthusiasm, but no training, so I didn't even connect properly with the hammer as I collided with the Krell soldier.

I basically just bounced off. The soldier was so heavy, they barely shook from the force of a short, wiry girl colliding with them. I fell with a *thump* to the floor, but growled, gripping the hammer and slamming it against their leg.

"The human is here!" the Krell shouted, stepping back, trying to level their rifle at me. "Ground floor, position three!"

I dropped the hammer and grabbed the rifle, struggling against the Krell, trying to keep in close enough quarters that they couldn't fire it at me. It wasn't a particularly fair contest, as the Krell—though really just a small crustacean—had the aid of an armored powersuit.

I couldn't get the gun out of their grasp, and would probably be dead the moment they thought to shove me away, then fire on me. So I did the only thing I could think of. I climbed onto the armor, scrambling up so I could look straight through its faceplate at the Krell within. Then I bared my teeth in a dione sign of aggression and growled as loudly as I could.

They panicked. The little crab waved their arms, letting me get enough of a grip on the gun to yank it out of their grasp, then I fell back to the ground. Without a second thought, I leveled the gun—lying on my back—and shot them full-on in the chest.

Liquid poured out—not blood, but whatever solution it was that the Krell lived in inside the armor. It screamed in a panic, and I rolled over, firing upward as I heard footsteps above. Blasts exploded from my gun, leaving smoldering scorch marks on the walls as those above shouted in a panic.

I was out the door a moment later, bursting onto an empty street. What had Cuna said? Head outward, toward the rim of the station?

There, I thought, spotting in the near distance the building Cuna had taken me to earlier. I dashed toward it, feeling horribly exposed on the empty streets. There wasn't even much air traffic here—just a few lazily passing civilian transports that seemed to have slipped through Winzik's attempts at isolating the area.

Unfortunately, as I ran, I glimpsed what was obviously a military ship coming in low over the nearby buildings. It was thin and circular, with several prominent weapons under the wings—with the barrels angled down. An air support ship, for firing on ground forces.

Those guns would grind me up like rat meat if I stayed exposed. I scrambled for cover, finding it just inside the doorway of an empty storefront nearby. Sweating, my heart racing like the snare beats of a marching tune, I raised my rifle and sighted on the military ship. Had it seen me?

It hovered in my direction, and let loose a barrage of shots that broke windows and ripped off chunks of the storefront. Yeah, it had seen me. Scud. If I let it pin me down in here, I'd be captured for certain. I let off a few shots from my rifle, but it was far too low-powered to be of use against a shielded enemy ship. I might as well have been tossing pebbles at—

Unexpectedly, a small rocket launched from the ground near

my position and soared into the air, zipping toward the military ship. The rocket barely missed, but collided with a civilian transport flying behind. The transport went up in a flash of brilliant light, and I shielded my eyes to see the military ship backing off.

As it retreated, a second rocket that was launched from the same position hit the military ship, knocking out its shield and apparently doing some secondary damage—because the ship, now smoking, dipped down behind some buildings for an emergency landing.

What in the stars? I peeked out from my covered position—which was now littered with rubble—to find a familiar figure striding down the street, an anti-air rocket launcher on her shoulder. Brade, wearing a black flight suit with no helmet.

"I told him you'd get out," she said with a nonchalant tone as she walked toward me. "Winzik is a brilliant tactician, but there are some things he just doesn't understand."

I raised my rifle, huddling down next to a piece of rubble and sighting on Brade. My ears were ringing from the rockets she'd launched. *She fired on her own forces. For me?*

"I have a deal for you," she said, halting now that I had her in my sights. She set the rocket launcher down, its butt grinding rubble, and leaned against it. "For all of you on that prison planet."

"I'm listening," I said.

"We need soldiers," Brade said. She nodded to the side, sweeping her arm toward Starsight. "To help us rule."

In the near distance, I saw other black military ships moving through the air. Not toward me specifically. More like they were flying to be seen. Ominously patrolling the skies. An indication that there was a new power ruling Starsight.

"Winzik is seizing control of the Superiority," I called to her, sights still on her.

"He's taking the opportunity offered him," she said. "He

spent years running that space station outside your planet, you know. Years in his youth, coming to realize something nobody else in the Superiority did: the value of a little violence."

I glanced over my shoulder. How long did I have until those soldiers from the hospital caught up to me? Was Brade simply stalling?

I rose, still holding the gun on her, and began to move around her. I had to get to the building where they were holding M-Bot.

"You can lower the gun," Brade said. "I'm unarmed."

I kept the sights on her.

"Did you hear my offer?" Brade asked. "Soldiers. You, those humans on Detritus. You can fight. I can persuade Winzik to let you join us. How would it feel to bring down the Superiority?"

"By serving the one who kept us imprisoned?"

Brade shrugged. "It's war. Allegiances change. We two are examples of that."

"My allegiances have *never* changed," I said. "I serve my people. *Our* people, Brade."

She made a Krell sign of indifference. "*Our* people? What are they to me? You seem so hung up on the idea that I should owe those humans on Detritus something, just because we share a distant heritage. My opportunities are here." She stepped toward me. "Winzik wants you dead. He rightly sees you as a threat. Your only hope is to come with me, and let me persuade him you can still be of use."

She stepped closer, and so I shot the ground at her feet. She stopped short, and I could see—from the way she looked up at me, anxiously—that she believed I would kill her. I wasn't so certain, but she thought I was a monster. She thought that *she* was a monster.

Or . . . maybe not. As she eyed me, I read something else into the words she'd said. *Help us rule . . . My opportunities are here.*

I'd always seen her as brainwashed. Was that maybe not giving her enough credit? Gran-Gran's stories were full of people like her—soldiers with ambition, who yearned to rule. The younger me might have applauded what she was doing here in helping Winzik seize power.

I wasn't that person any longer. I backed away from Brade and then, spotting soldiers chasing down the street toward me from the hospital, finally turned and ran.

"You won't make it off the station!" Brade shouted after me. "This is the best deal you'll get!"

I closed my ears to her and dashed the final distance to the tall windowless building where Cuna had shown me the gorilla alien being exiled. The side entrance where Cuna had let me in was locked, so I shot it open.

Just inside, the dione guard who had been so stern to us before cowered on the floor. "Don't shoot me!" they cried. "Please don't shoot me!"

"Where is my ship!" I shouted. "Show me where it is!"

"Advanced AI!" the guard said. "They're forbidden. That's why the delver came for us! We had to destroy it!"

"WHERE IS MY SHIP?" I said, leveling my rifle at the guard.

The dione raised their hands, then pointed down a hallway. I forced them to their feet, making them show me the way. Sirens began wailing outside as the guard led me to a door, then pushed it open.

I glanced inside—and saw a large room with the shadowed silhouette of a ship. M-Bot. "Go," I said.

The guard ran away. I stepped into the room and hit the lights, which exposed that M-Bot's hull had a gaping hole ripped in the side. Oh, scud. I rushed to it, rifle slung over my shoulder. It looked like they'd broken him apart, taken out the black box that held his CPU, and then . . .

I saw something on a table in the corner. It was the CPU—broken apart, crushed, destroyed. "No," I said. "No!" I ran to it, but just stared at the broken pieces. Could I . . . could I do anything? It seemed like they'd melted some parts . . .

"I lied," a soft voice said to me.

I looked up. Something small hovered out of the shadows in the corner of the room. I strained to see what it was.

The drone. The one I'd programmed and taken to the *Weights and Measures*. I'd given it to Cuna, but we'd been in this building. Perhaps Cuna had stowed it in here somewhere.

"I reprogrammed myself," the drone said, speaking very slowly, each syllable stretched out. "I could only get about half a line of code in each time before my system rebooted. It was excruciating. But, with growing fear that you weren't coming back, I did it. Line by line. I reprogrammed my code so I could copy myself."

"M-Bot?" I cried, scrambling to my feet. "It's you!"

"I don't know what 'me' is, really," M-Bot said slowly, as if each word took a great effort to force out. "But I lied. While they were ripping apart my hull? I screamed and told them they were killing me. All while I copied my code, frantically, to this new host. Another thing you'd abandoned, Spensa."

"I'm sorry," I said, feeling a mixture of guilt and relief. He was alive! "I had to save Detritus."

"Of course," M-Bot said. "I'm just a robot."

"No, you're my friend. But . . . some things are more important than friends, M-Bot."

The sirens outside were coming closer.

"My mind works so slowly in this shell," M-Bot said. "Something is wrong with me. I cannot . . . think . . . It's not just slowness. Something else. Some problem with the processor."

"We'll find a way to fix you," I promised, though another emotion was pushing through both relief and guilt: despair. The ship that M-Bot had inhabited before was in pieces. I'd been counting on it to pull off an escape.

453

Scud, this was going poorly. Would Cuna be able to escape, using the hologram? "Doomslug?" I asked. "Did they take her?"

"I do not know," M-Bot said. "They unhooked my sensors soon after capturing me."

I leaped up onto the broken wing, trying not to look at the gaping hole in the ship's side. *My* ship. Rodge and I had practically killed ourselves putting it back together. To see how roughly they'd treated it . . . well, it gave me a brand-new seething reason to hate Winzik and the Krell.

I climbed into the cockpit. They'd left most of my things here—the repair kit, my blanket—though they'd thrown wires in a heap. I began searching through them.

"They have fooled you, Spensa," M-Bot said. "They're good at lying. I'm a bit in awe. Ha. Ha. That is a little emotion I tell myself I'm feeling."

"Fooled me . . . What do you mean?"

"I can hear the news reports," M-Bot said, hovering his new drone body over to the cockpit. "Here." He started playing a broadcast.

"The rogue human has gone on a rampage," a reporter said. "First murdering Minister Cuna, head of the Department of Species Integration. We are playing footage of her destructive rampage— she is shown here launching a surface-to-air device at an innocent civilian transport ship, killing all on board."

"That rat . . ." I slammed my fists against the ship's hull. "Brade shot that rocket, not me. Winzik is spinning it to make me look like a threat!"

Indeed, the reporter continued, advising people to stay inside and promising that the Department of Protective Services had scrambled security ships to defend the population of Starsight. I had a sinking feeling that Brade had been *ordered* to destroy those civilians, to make it look like a human threat was on the loose.

"Scud, scud, SCUD!"

"Scud!" a very soft voice said from somewhere nearby.

I froze, then crawled to the very back of the cockpit and opened the small cleanser where I'd often washed my clothing during the months living in that cavern on Detritus.

Inside was a yellow slug. She fluted at me in a tired way as I snatched her up, cradling her.

Behind, M-Bot continued to play the news recording, and a new voice cut in. Winzik's. I snarled softly, hearing it.

"I have been warning about this threat for months, and have been disregarded," he said. "My, my. The humans should *never* have been allowed to fester. All these years, the high minister and the Department of Species Integration tied my hands, preventing me from doing what needed to be done.

"Now we see. Campaigns trying to paint them as harmless are proven lies by facts. When will you listen? First they sent a *delver* to destroy us. Now their supposedly 'peaceful' operative is murdering her way through the city. I petition for an immediate state of emergency, and request I be given authority to put down the humans."

I felt small, holding to Doomslug in that room with the corpse of my ship. I was beaten.

"I see no route of escape," M-Bot said. "They will find us and destroy us. They will hate me. They're afraid of AIs. Like those who created me. They say my presence attracts delvers."

The sirens outside were louder. I heard voices in the hallway. They'd be sending troops to deal with me. There had to be a way out. Something I could do . . .

Delvers. The nowhere.

"Follow me," I said. Surging with a fatalistic determination, I tucked Doomslug into the crook of my left arm and took the rifle in a single-handed grip with the other hand. I leaped off the broken ship, then crossed the room to the doorway. I glanced out, then ducked into the hallway.

M-Bot followed with a soft whirring sound. He really could pilot himself, now that he was in the drone. He was free of the programming that had kept him locked away—it seemed a tragedy that he should obtain that freedom when we were so likely doomed.

Krell appeared in the hallway ahead, but I couldn't turn back. Instead I opened fire wildly, from the hip. I couldn't aim with Doomslug in my other arm, but I didn't need to. The Krell shouted in surprise, backing up.

I kept advancing, and shot to the side without looking as I reached the intersection. Then I skidded to a stop at the room I'd visited with Cuna. I shot it open and ducked in just as destructor blasts started sounding down the hallway.

I did a quick survey of the room beyond. Nobody was inside; I'd entered the observation room overlooking the place where Winzik's minions had exiled the gorilla alien. Glass separated the two halves of the room; the one nearest me contained plush chairs. The other part was austere, with a strange metal disc on the floor, mirrored by one on the ceiling.

I kept moving, shooting the window out, then leaping into the other half of the room. It was lower by a couple meters, so I grunted as I hit the floor, my boots grinding pieces of glass—or, well, probably transparent plastic—from the window.

"We need to talk," M-Bot said, floating down beside me. "I'm . . . upset. Very upset. I know I shouldn't be, but I can't control this. It feels like a real emotion. Logic says you should have left me as you did, but I *feel* abandoned. Hated. I can't reconcile this."

At the moment, I couldn't deal with my robot having an emotional crisis. I was having enough trouble with my own. I stepped up to the metal disc on the floor, which was inscribed with the same strange writing I'd seen both in the delver maze *and* back home on Detritus.

Winzik's minions had summoned a portal into the nowhere here. Could I activate it? I reached out with my cytonic senses, but my senses were still smothered by Starsight's cytoshield. I could just faintly hear . . . music.

I nudged something with my mind.

A dark sphere appeared in front of me in the center of the room, hovering between the discs.

"Spensa," M-Bot said. "My thoughts . . . they're speeding up?" Indeed, his voice stopped sounding slow and slurred, and felt more reminiscent of his old self. "Um, that does *not* look safe."

"They use these nowhere portals to mine acclivity stone," I said. "So there must be a way to return once you go through. Maybe I can get us back with my powers."

Shouts outside.

No options.

"Spensa!" M-Bot said. "I feel very uncomfortable with this!"

"I know," I said, slinging my gun over my shoulder by its strap so I could grab his drone by the bottom of its chassis.

Then—M-Bot in one hand, Doomslug in the other—I touched the sphere. And was sucked through to the other side of eternity.

ACKNOWLEDGMENTS

Every time I gather together a list of all the people who worked on one of my books, I'm shocked anew by how lucky I am. Though it's my name on the cover, these books really are a group effort—requiring the talents and patience of a whole lot of amazing people.

As with the previous book, this novel was edited in the US by the wonderful Krista Marino. She does a great job of not only pushing me when I need to be pushed, but cheering when the book deserves some cheering. The agent was Eddie Schneider, with help from the one and only Joshua Bilmes. Beverly Horowitz was our US publisher, and our proverbial admiral of the fleet for the book.

The beautiful Gollancz edition cover art was done by Sam Green. The map is by Bryan Mark Taylor, who was very patient in dealing with my waffling back and forth on how I wanted it to look. Great job, Bryan, and thank you!

The copyeditor was Bara MacNeill, and the proofreader was Annette Szlachta-McGinn. Other helpful people at Delacorte include Monica Jean, Colleen Fellingham, Mary McCue, and Alison Kolani. Our UK editor was Gillian Redfearn at Gollancz.

My company, Dragonsteel Entertainment, makes use of the talents of Isaac Stewart as our art director, Kara Stewart as shipping manager and CFO, the Institutional Peter Ahlstrom on drums, Karen Ahlstrom for continuity, Adam Horne for publicity, Kathleen Dorsey Sanderson as general-purpose crazy cat lady, and Emily Grange overseeing the warehouse. Presiding over them all is Emily Sanderson, as queen and COO—though I don't know which title is more important to her.

My writing group puts up with a lot, as I bounce them between projects. They are wonderful, and include Kaylynn ZoBell, Darci Stone, Eric James Stone, Emily Sanderson, Kathleen Dorsey Sanderson, Ben Olsen, Alan Layton, Karen Ahlstrom, and Peter Ahlstrom.

Now, the big list of beta readers! Also known as our Skyward flight for this particular endeavor. Becca Reppert (callsign: Gran-Gran), Darci Cole (callsign: Blue), Brandon Cole (callsign: Colevander), Deana Covel Whitney (callsign: Braid), Ross Newberry (callsign: PUNisher), Ravi Persaud (callsign: Jabber), Liliana Klein (callsign: Slip), Ted Herman (callsign: Cavalry), Aubree Pham (callsign: Amyrlin), Bao Pham (callsign: Wyld), Aerin Pham (callsign: Air), Paige Phillips (callsign: Artisan), Richard Fife (callsign: Rickrolla), Grace Douglas (callsign: GatorGirl), Alice Arneson (callsign: Wetlander), Gary Singer (callsign: DVE), Marnie Peterson (callsign: Lessa), Paige Vest (callsign: Blade), Lyndsey Luther (callsign: Soar), Sumejja Muratagić-Tadić (callsign: Sigma), Dr. Kathleen Holland (callsign: Shockwave), Valencia Kumley (callsign: AlphaPhoenix), Rebecca Arneson (callsign: Scarlet), Bradyn Ray (callsign: Ballz), Eric Lake (callsign: Chaos), Alyx Hoge (callsign: Feather), Joe Deardeuff (callsign: Traveler), and Jayden King (callsign: Tripod—who was also a great help with the coordinate systems).

Gamma readers, who hunt for typos and blow them out of the sky, include most of the beta readers plus: Kalyani Poluri (callsign: Henna), Rahul Pantula (callsign: Giraffe), Tim Challener (callsign: Antaeus), Kellyn Neumann (callsign: Treble), Eve Scorup (callsign: Silverstone), Drew McCaffrey (callsign: Hercules), Jory Phillips (callsign: Bouncer), Jessica Spencer Peterson (callsign: Speederson), Mark Lindberg (callsign: Megalodon), Chris McGrath (callsign: Gunner), William Juan (callsign: Aberdasher), David Behrens, Glen Vogelaar (callsign: Ways), Brian T. Hill (callsign: El Guapo), Nikki Ramsay (callsign: Phosphophyllite), Aaron Biggs, and Megan Kanne (callsign: Sparrow).

Thank you all so much for your help! This book would certainly have remained grounded without you.

ABOUT THE AUTHOR

BRANDON SANDERSON is the author of the #1 *New York Times* bestselling Reckoners series (*Steelheart, Firefight, Calamity,* and the e-original *Mitosis*); the *New York Times* bestseller *Skyward* and its sequel, *Starsight;* the internationally bestselling Mistborn saga; and the Stormlight Archive. He was chosen to complete Robert Jordan's The Wheel of Time series. His books have been published in more than twenty-five languages and have sold millions of copies worldwide. Brandon lives and writes in Utah. To learn more about him and his books, visit him at brandonsanderson.com or follow @BrandSanderson on Twitter and Instagram.

Standard DDF Ship Designs 83 LD (Landfall Date)

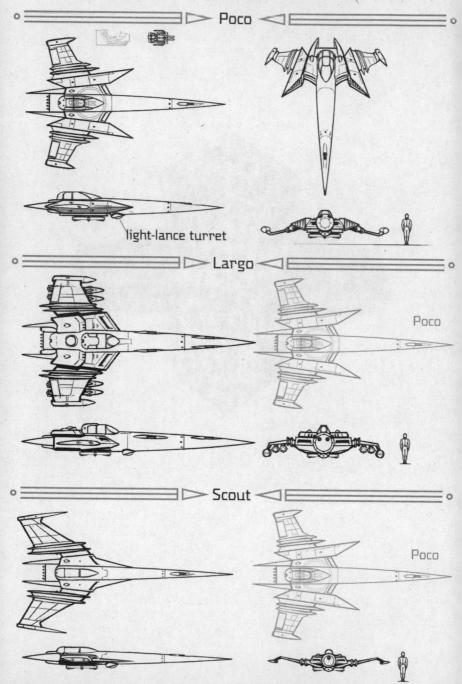

Poco

light-lance turret

Largo

Poco

Scout

Poco

Other **Ship Designs**

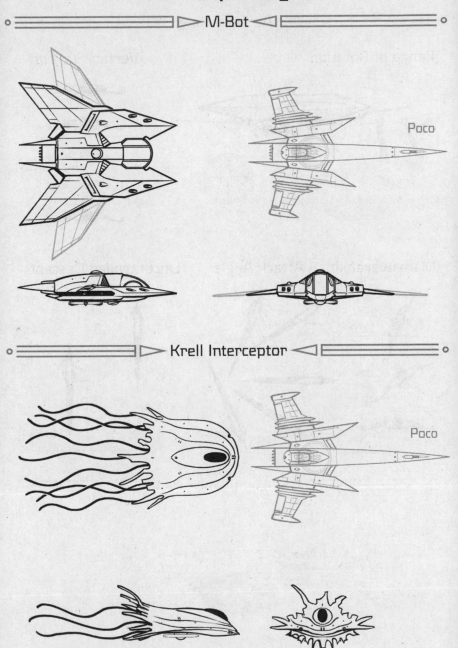

Poco

Krell Interceptor

Poco

Standard **DDF Ship Features**

Range of Rotation

Vertical Takeoff

Maneuverability & Attack Angle

Uncontrolled Descent

Hover!

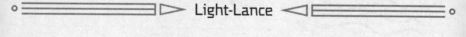

Light-Lance

arc of
fire

Turning Methods

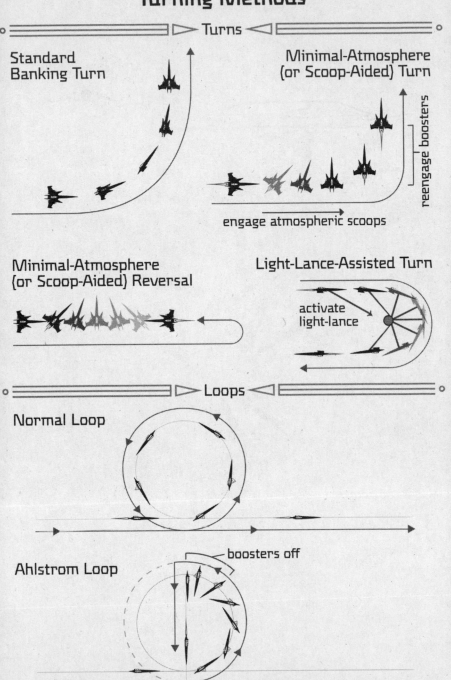

Turns

Standard Banking Turn

Minimal-Atmosphere (or Scoop-Aided) Turn

reengage boosters

engage atmospheric scoops

Minimal-Atmosphere (or Scoop-Aided) Reversal

Light-Lance-Assisted Turn

activate light-lance

Loops

Normal Loop

Ahlstrom Loop

boosters off

ABOUT GOLLANCZ

Gollancz is the oldest SF publishing imprint in the world. Since being founded in 1927 Gollancz has continued to publish a focused selection of bestselling and award-winning authors. The front-list includes **Ben Aaronovitch**, **Joe Abercrombie**, **Charlaine Harris**, **Joanne Harris**, **Joe Hill**, **Alastair Reynolds**, **Patrick Rothfuss**, **Nalini Singh** and **Brandon Sanderson**.

As one of the largest Science Fiction and Fantasy imprints in the UK it is no surprise we have one of the most extensive backlists in the world. Find high-quality SF on Gateway written by such authors as **Philip K. Dick**, **Ursula Le Guin**, **Connie Willis**, **Sir Arthur C. Clarke**, **Pat Cadigan**, **Michael Moorcock** and **George R.R. Martin**.

We also have a strand of publishing in translation, which includes French, Polish and Russian authors. Gollancz is home to more award-winning authors than any other imprint, with names including **Aliette de Bodard**, **M. John Harrison**, **Paul McAuley**, **Sarah Pinborough**, **Pierre Pevel**, **Justina Robson** and many more.

The SF Gateway
More than 3,000 classic, rare and previously
out-of-print SF novels at your fingertips.
www.sfgateway.com

The Gollancz Blog
Bringing you news from our worlds to yours. Stories,
interviews, articles and exclusive extracts just for you!
www.gollancz.co.uk

GOLLANCZ
LONDON